ON SUGAR
Hill

Ane Mulligan

HERITAGE BEACON

FICTION

Heritage Beacon Fiction is an imprint of LPCBooks
a division of Iron Stream Media
100 Missionary Ridge, Birmingham, AL 35242
ShopLPC.com

Cover design by Hannah Linder Designs

This is a work of fiction. Names, characters, and incidents are all products of the author's imagination or are used for fictional purposes. Any mentioned brand names, places, and trademarks remain the property of their respective owners, bear no association with the author or the publisher, and are used for fictional purposes only.

Library of Congress Control Number: 2021934352

All Scripture quotations, unless otherwise indicated, are taken from the Holy Bible, King James Version.

ISBN-13: 978-1-64526-299-2
Ebook ISBN: 978-1-64526-300-5

Praise for *On Sugar Hill*

Just like today, the struggle of life is very real for Cora, a heroine you'll cheer for and love. This heartwarming story of family and faith is a sure-to-please gem. This is one for your keeper shelf.

~**Michelle Griep**
Christy Award-winning author of *Once Upon a Dickens Christmas*

Mulligan's grasp of vaudeville and the theater is on full display in this engaging tale of mystery and romance. She's a true master in the Depression-era niche.

~**Elizabeth Ludwig**
USA Today bestselling author

A vaudeville star, a dash of romance, a long-kept secret, and Mulligan's trademark Southern charm makes *On Sugar Hill* a tale that is sure to delight readers and leave them begging for more. I was swept back into a different era with this heartwarming story of loss, healing, and restoration.

~**Tara Johnson**
Author of *Engraved on the Heart,*
Where Dandelions Bloom, and *All Through the Night*

What a delightful book! With fun, quirky characters, *On Sugar Hill* tells the story of a Southern woman doing what she must to survive the Great Depression without losing her sense of self or sense of adventure. Enjoy!

~ **Gayle Roper**
Award-winning author, *Sea Change, Hide and Seek*

I loved it, especially the historical detail. Mulligan really captured that time period with the stock market crash and the terminal vaudeville diagnosis. The pull of home for a small-town girl and the attraction of NYC rings true.

~**Marty Snowden**
Reader

DEDICATION

To Gail Mundy
You have encouraged me for so many years.
Your expertise as a discerning reader makes you the perfect
beta reader for me.
Thank you for all the "catches" made over the years.

ACKNOWLEDGMENTS

NO WRITER PENS A BOOK alone. There are critique partners, brainstorming pals, and research contributors. I belong to the American Christian Fictions Writers (ACFW), which has close to 3,000 members. Whenever I need an expert in any field, I can find one there. They answer questions or contribute anecdotes. I'm indebted to my writing friends! Many thanks to Kassy Paris, whose anecdote about twins came from her years of teaching.

To my extraordinary critique partners and best friends, Michelle Griep and Elizabeth Ludwig: I'm indebted to you for holding my feet to the fire and always having my back. I wouldn't want to take this journey without you.

Denise Weimer, you're a superstar editor. Thank you for your direction and making me sound better. I adore working with you!

Special thanks to Lynn A. Bowman, curator of the Museum of Buford, for his time and patience in sharing his rich knowledge of the area's history. Your help was invaluable to the writing of this book.

A huge thank you goes to my good friend, Sharon Qualls, and her twin sister, Karen Icenhour, for sharing their twin stories with me. Though not a large part of the book, they added so much flavor to this story. Thank you, Sharon and Karen.

My heartfelt gratitude belongs to Tracy Lynn Roberts for sharing her stories about her great-uncle, Rocky Venable. I first "met" Rocky when my community theatre troupe hosted a cemetery tour in Sugar Hill at the request of the Historical Preservation Society. He was one of the people we highlighted. He was a real character, and the actor, John Zimmermann, who portrayed him brought Rocky to life. I knew I had to include him. Thank you, Tracy!

A large and loud thank you goes out to all my readers. Without you, all is for naught!

Above all, I thank the Author of my life. He whispers to my heart, and my heart whispers back in stories. I never imagined a more fulfilling life than this.

Chapter 1

RUMORS SOAR IN THE WINGS of the Palace Theatre here in New York and everywhere else with a vaudeville stage. Normally, I don't give credence to hearsay, but I have high stakes in this one. My career.

Vaudeville is dying.

With one finger, I draw back the curtain a quarter inch and peek out at the audience. This stage is my favorite spot in the whole world, where makeup can turn even a plain Jane like me into a beautiful woman. Here, I'm Dixie Lynn, adored by audiences, a success, a star—not Cora Fitzgerald, a disappointment.

In the first row, Madam Dressler, my vocal coach, watches all my performances and takes notes. Aware of the rumors, she says to leave what's left of vaudeville behind and break into Broadway revues, I must perfect my singing voice. "Hard vork for expandink your vocal strength and range. Dat ees your tee-ket," she tells me every week. I'd rather be an ingénue—a leading lady. But Madam Dressler says I don't possess the required beauty, so I need my voice.

As if I didn't already know that.

Nobody's certain from whence my other talent originated. The peculiar one. I don't think it's really a talent, just an ability, but as a four-year-old, I could make my dolls talk. By the time I was six, I could throw my voice across a room. I figured if I weren't a beauty, at least I could be entertaining. I can't begin to tell you how much fun that was. Mama and Aunt Clara thought it was funny when I'd frighten the servants and the senator half out of their wits. The senator had a different opinion.

With one more peek through the curtain at the full house, I signal *ready* to the stage manager and step into place in the center of the stage. I settle my ventriloquist dummy, Sugar, on the high, round table beside me and smooth her dress. The annunciator bearing my name slides into its window at stage right.

The curtain rises.

A familiar thrill shivers through me. This is vaudeville's big time—the Keith-Albee Circuit. I throw a sparkling smile to the audience, whom I can no longer see for the bright footlights. As always, I cross my fingers inside my dummy's head. I guess I am as superstitious as my kin back on Sugar Hill.

"Sugar, Beau Wyatt is late. Do you happen to know anything about that?"

She shakes her head and denies any knowledge of his whereabouts. I know, of course. The stagehands have my other dummy beneath the table. I stick my foot under the edge of the cloth cover to make certain.

While I pretend to look for him, my hand inside Sugar guides her head to follow my every move. I proceed through the "dialogue" with her, and with the audience's first burst of laughter, my heart stops pounding in my ears. Here, on the circuit, I'm a star. They think I'm wonderful. Ahh, the magic of theatre, where one can be whom one is not.

After Sugar confesses she locked Beau Wyatt in his dressing room, she "sings" the first verse of her solo. I practice singing every single day and have perfected it, so my lips never move at all. Not the teensiest bit. Madam says it is amazing.

When it's time for the second verse, Beau Wyatt sings from underneath the table, and the audience gasps.

Theatre managers who preview my act swear I have another person hiding and demand I start over without the cloth. Most have never heard a ventriloquist throw their voice before—let alone one who's female. My future is pretty much made … unless the rumors are true. My stomach tightens.

Thankfully, the audience's applause drowns out that horrid thought.

I exit after an encore and three extra bows. In the wings, Mr. Keith greets me, enveloping my hand between his meaty fingers.

"They love you, my dear. Let's discuss your contract, then you have a dinner date with David Divine."

My brain has trouble wrapping around these two contradictions. One frightens me and the other thrills. I choose the second one.

"David Divine?" My heart flutters just thinking about him. He's Broadway's hottest actor. But me having dinner with him? I don't think I'll be able to eat. "I don't understand."

"His agent called my office. He wants to meet you. But first,"—Mr. Keith puts his hand on my elbow, guiding me backstage—"you have a phone call. Take it at the stage manager's desk, then come to my office."

I walk in a daze. Who would be calling me here? My agent is traveling in Paris, so it can't be him. With David Divine swimming in my head, I approach the stage manager. He drops the receiver into my hand, and I wrap my fingers around it but find him watching me. I turn my back until the stage door clicks shut.

"Hello?"

"Cora? Oh, sugar, I hate to have to be the one to tell you this, but … well, I suppose the best way is to just come out with it. Are you sitting down, child?"

"Miss Hattie, is that you?" My childhood best friend's mama. Why would she be calling me? "Is Glenice Jo all right?" I'd heard about her husband dying during their honeymoon. Such a tragedy.

"Yes, darlin', she's fine. It's not her I'm calling about. Cora, it's your father. The senator's dead, sugar, and your mama needs you to come home."

Various emotions swirl around me, but deep sorrow is not one of them. For that alone, I mourn.

My jaw tightens, and I squeeze the words through gritted teeth. "What happened?"

"I'm sorry to say, he hung himself in the front parlor. He used a ladder to put the rope over a beam and … oh, you don't need details now."

He's always hated that room, ever since my mama—or Fitzie, as everyone including me calls her—redecorated it and removed his prized moose head. "I can't say I'm surprised. That he chose to do it there, I mean. It was pay-back for the moose."

"Oh, Cora, I'm so sorry. But she needs you. Can you come?"

Though she can't see me, I nod. "Of course, I will. Thank you for calling me, Miss Hattie. Tell her I should arrive in Buford—uh, hang on." From the stage manager's desk, I dig out a train schedule. He always keeps one for some actor or another who's always having to catch a train to somewhere. "It looks as though I can be there tomorrow evening around dusk."

"I'll have the preacher pick you up."

After saying goodbye, I find Mr. Keith and explain the situation. His frown isn't too pronounced, which gives me hope.

"My condolences on your father, Cora. This stock market crash has affected so many." He folds his hands over the contract. "I'll hold this for your return." At least, he wants me back. That's a good sign. I hope. "Will you have dinner with David before you leave?"

Though it rings of disrespect, there has never been any love lost between the senator and me. He hardly knew I was alive, except when he wanted a whipping boy.

"Yes, I will."

Mr. Keith cocks his head to one side as if considering. Then his mustache dances on a smile. "Wonderful. I'll have my driver take you. Give me your key. While you're at dinner, my driver will fetch your bags. When you're done, he will drop you at the station."

Women should never allow themselves to fantasize about men. Sure as sunrise, when they do, they'll be in for a disappointment. And David Divine is a big one. I only remain at the table because of the excellent steak in front of me. I cut off a bite and savor it while he tells yet another boring story about himself.

When I finish eating, I look for a break—any break. Does this man ever breathe? How can I wedge a word in sideways between his? They're stacked one on top of the other.

I finally interrupt him. "My, my, you've led a fascinating life, David. But I must excuse myself. I have a train to catch." I rise, picking up my clutch purse and gloves. "Thank you for dinner." Not waiting for his response, I skedaddle past a waiter bearing a dessert tray. Ooh, a *creme brûlée* would be heaven. I keep moving, though. It's not worth another five minutes with that egotist.

At the station, I call Fitzie to reassure her I am on my way. "There's only one train leaving, and it's in the wee hours of the morning, so I'll be home tomorrow, late afternoon."

A new, childlike quality in her voice makes me fear our relationship has somehow flipped, and I am now caring for her. But perhaps with a little luck, when I get home, I'll find her capable of living as a widow and able to manage her affairs. Yes. I'll concentrate on that.

I find my seat on the train, and after a fitful sleep, I watch the scenery slide past the window, mostly farmland. Small houses. Nothing like the house I'm going home to. My father, a state senator, cultivated the impression he was larger than life. One of the reasons he was always after more money. There was never enough. Money buys power.

"It's the people's perspective of you that counts, Cora," he'd say on the rare occasion he spoke to me, usually in criticism. I never measured up to his ideal of beauty—or anything else, for that matter. Trying to count on my fingers the number of times I'd see him in any given month, my memory fails after my middle finger.

How does one mourn someone they barely knew?

Finally, at four-forty-seven, the train pulls into Buford. I'm back home in Georgia for the first time in six-and-a-half years. I settle my cloche on my head—my favorite one with the three feathers on the right side—and gather my pocketbook and coat. Evenings are cold as November arrives—not as frigid as New York, but chilly, to say the least.

The first thing I notice when I descend the steps is the acrid odor in the air. *The tannery.* I'd forgotten that particular smell. Like the Low Country has pluff mud, Buford has the tannery. Residents become used to it since most everyone works at the tannery. But in the years I've been gone, I forgot. I wrinkle my nose and breathe through my mouth.

Unlike New York's Penn Station, Buford's is small with a single wooden platform. A few cars rattle past me over the cobblestones paving Main Street. There's even a horse-drawn wagon tied to an old wooden rail. Compared to New York City, Buford is definitely behind the times. Way behind. Still, there's something about being home that makes me step out of my shoes and wiggle my toes, despite the chilly air. I've missed walking barefoot.

"Cora?"

I turn at my name and my heart trips. Standing before me is the crush of every girl who attended Buford High School—Boone Robertson. I can't believe he remembers me. Light-brown hair and hazel eyes, his greener than most, and a strong jawline—he's hardly changed. The left corner of his mouth raises. While the smile is a bit cheeky, his lips are oh-so-kissable. My face grows warm.

I hold out my hand. "Boone, it's been years." A tickle in the back of my throat robs my voice. I have to cough to clear it. "Pardon me. It's nice to see you. Why are you here? Meeting someone?"

His large hands engulf mine, and at his touch, a spark zips up my arm. I'd better watch myself around him. Falling in love isn't part of my plan. A romance is fine as long as my heart isn't involved. Men aren't trustworthy. I should know. The senator paved that road.

No man will ever be interested in you, Cora. Don't set your hopes high.

Barely dead twenty-four hours, and he's already haunting me. They say if you listen carefully on a moonless night, the trees on Sugar Hill whisper. Some believe it's ghosts, crying for mercy. That's why our porch ceilings are painted "haint" blue—to keep the spirits away. The senator's ghost doesn't deserve mercy.

"Yes ma'am. I'm here for you. Your aunt sent a note asking me to get you when the preacher got called away. I told her I'd be honored."

I raise an eyebrow. "Honored? My, my. The Boone I remember wasn't so gallant." I can't help teasing him. Back in high school, he never noticed me—or any other girl, for that matter. He was all jock—baseball-hero stuff.

To his credit, he blushes. "Sixteen-year-old boys are stupid. You gotta give them a little grace." He tips the porter and picks up my bags. "Is this all?"

"My trunk will arrive in a couple of days, so that's it."

I slip my shoes back on my feet and follow him to his truck. It's an old Model T pickup with wooden sides on the bed. On the door is stenciled "Robertson's Fine Furniture Makers."

I eye him curiously. "You're a carpenter? That takes some talent." Oops. "Wait." I frown at my faux pas. "That didn't come out right."

His laugh fills the evening air. "You thought all I could do was play ball, right?"

My face grows warm again. I hate the way my whole face turns red when I embarrass myself. Even my ears glow. "I—uh, I guess I'm guilty as charged."

I climb in the truck, tucking my skirt beneath my knees. He lopes to the front and cranks the engine, then joins me in the cab.

"I apprenticed with Amos Calhoun when I got out of high school. He never married, so when he passed away without any children, he left me the shop."

"That was a lucky break for you. Do you still play baseball? If I remember right, you were really good." We girls, the Dilly Club, watched every game back then. We all loved baseball, especially the players. There were five of us girls in our little club. I can't wait to see them again.

He lifts one shoulder in a shrug. "Yeah, I play with some guys on a couple of local teams."

He puts the truck in gear, and we cruise—as well as a Model T can—out of the parking lot. The town looks as though it hasn't changed yet is different at the same time. The old wooden sidewalk is still there—and still giving splinters to barefoot kids, I imagine. I count at least eight barbershops, almost more than there are people, which is new, but the post office isn't any different from the day I left. I'll bet the same *wanted* posters are still up.

We leave the shops behind and come to the Bona Allen Tannery, with its brick buildings still festooned for last night's trick-or-treaters. They always give out candy to the children. It was my favorite place to go on Halloween when I was a kid. But something's different. No, wait, it's not the tannery—The Shoe Fac—no. The *Chrome* Factory, where they make the stuff they use at the tannery. I twist in my seat to look back at it.

"Why does The Chrome Factory look newer than the other buildings?"

Boone sticks his arm out the window, signaling a turn. "Because it is. The old building burned down almost two years ago. They rebuilt it."

In my mind's eye, I can see the crowds gathering to watch the fire. That's big excitement in a small town. We pass the drugstore where, as a kid, I'd buy penny candy.

"Tell me about you, Cora. Everyone is pretty much in awe of your celebrity."

I hope he isn't teasing, but he appears sincere. I fidget on the seat. "How do you know about me? I changed my name in New York."

"Your mother made sure we all knew."

He didn't roll his eyes, but I wonder what Fitzie said. "Well, thank you, but it's not as glamorous as people might think. It took me a lot of hard work to make vaudeville's big circuit."

That's not quite the truth. Within a year of arriving in New York, I was a star and on the best circuit. But it makes me sound like a conceited diva, and I've always disliked those who think too highly of themselves.

Boone nods and signals another turn. "I remember the first time I ever heard you throw your voice. You must have been in the fourth grade. I was two years ahead of you. We were all outside, eating dinner, and some girl—can't remember her name—started taunting you. You stared at her all innocent-like, then 'something' in the tree behind her began to moan and howl like a banshee. She screamed and skedaddled, while you stood there with a big grin on your face."

Laughter bubbles up at the memory. "Alice Farnham. That was her name. She said, 'Y'all think you're so hotsy-totsy. Well, you ain't so dilly.' That was the start of our Dilly Club, which we named in her honor." I laugh, but my throat tickles again, making me cough. "Excuse me." A small alarm bell rings in my head. I need to watch this. My voice is my livelihood. "How is Glenice Jo? Do you see her? Her husband's death was such a shock."

"I think she's doing fine. She doesn't talk much about it. They were married just that one week."

I lower my gaze, clasping my hands in my lap. "Did he really fall off a mountain?"

Boone's grin seems rather irreverent. He glances at me. "He did, and he sang all the way to the bottom. It seems he partook of a mountain still he stumbled onto. Not knowing its potency, he drank until he was stinkin' drunk. At least he didn't realize what was happening. He didn't suffer or anything."

I don't know whether to laugh or cry. "Poor Glenice Jo. Can you imagine such a thing?"

He shakes his head. We turn onto the state road toward Cumming.

"It's not dirt anymore. When did they pave it?"

"Started a couple of years ago. They'll have it completed all the way from Rome to Lawrenceville by June. Changed the name again too. Now it's State Road 19."

"I wish they'd land on one that sticks. It gets confusing."

Boone laughs at that and turns into the Sugar Hill Militia District, and I'm caught up in memories. Granny Holtzclaw told me Sugar Hill got its name long before the War of Northern Aggression, when a wagon carrying a load of sugar broke a wheel and the bags fell out, spilling their contents on the hill. She says people called it "the hill where the sugar spilled," until somewhere along the line, it was shortened to Sugar Hill. I love it, with its dirt roads and farmlands.

One more turn, and we're on Level Creek Road. Half a mile down is my driveway. Home. The huge, two-story white clapboard house rises from a small knoll at the back of the property. It's a Southern gem, perfectly befitting a senator, surrounded by azaleas and rhododendrons. Two gigantic, ancient oak trees stand sentinel at the front corners of the house. There's a wide veranda on the second floor, held up with four pillars, and broad steps lead up to the front door. Given the memories that reside here, I shouldn't love it, but I do.

The truck engine shudders to a stop. Boone comes around, opens my door, and I scramble out. Before I take two steps, the front door flies open and Fitzie runs out, arms stretched wide. Adorned in pink silk lounging pajamas trimmed with lace and a matching floral chiffon robe, my mama is still the bee's knees.

"Cora, my beautiful sugar-pie!"

She reaches out, pulls me into her arms, and bursts into tears. Her grief catches me by surprise. There's never been any love lost between her and the senator, as far as I know. Had things changed after I left?

Chapter 2

"Fitzie, let's go in." I turn back to Boone. "Thank you so much for picking me up. Maybe—?" Why did I say that? He's not going to be interested in me. Not the real me.

"I'll call you." He sets my bags inside the door. "I'll wait a few days to let you get settled. See you tomorrow."

"Tomorrow?"

"Yes, the senator's funeral."

"Of course." How could I forget? And then Boone's gone. I close the door.

Fitzie crooks a finger over her shoulder and walks to the kitchen, but before I can follow her, Aunt Clara descends the stairs. Oh my. She's aged. Streaks of gray sweep back from her face as if an artist had painted them. Between her brows, two vertical furrows indicate she frowns often. More lines around her eyes and mouth, though still small, are prominent enough for me to see. I expected some change, but not this much. I'm trying to remember how old she is. Forty-eight, if I remember correctly.

When she reaches me, her eyes crinkle with her smile. She hugs me tight. After a moment, she pushes me to arm's length and looks me up and down.

"Well? Do I pass inspection?"

She grins and nods. Mama's elder sister, my Aunt Clara, is mute. Folks outside our family and circle of close friends think because she can't speak, she's deaf. She's not. But she perpetuates the rumor because she's a writer. Oh, the secrets she overhears. Many have inspired new mysteries.

I lay my handbag on a table in the foyer. New wallpaper with senatorial gold and royal blue stripes shouts from the entry walls, making

13

the foyer resemble the Georgia State House. And making my lip curl. Is it wrong to hope Fitzie removes it now that the senator is gone?

Linking arms with Aunt Clara, we head toward the kitchen. I pause before we go in. "How is Fitzie? She cried when I arrived. Happy tears over me being here … or grief? If it's genuine grief, I'm surprised, given the senator's ways."

Aunt Clara signs, "Not grief. Genuine frustration. Let her tell you."

I quirk an eyebrow in question. With a shake of her head, she pushes open the swinging door, and the aroma of Pearl's coffee wafts over me. A pot stands on one of the stove's *six* burners. That stove is new. I survey the rest of the kitchen. There's even a General Electric refrigerator. No icebox for the senator's house. He made sure this room had all the latest in appliances, just in case anyone happened to catch a peek through the door. That he somehow got the house wired for electrics proves his corruption and misuse of state funds. Only a few businesses near the tannery are tied into the hydro-electric plant.

No one but family would venture in. But servants talk among themselves, bragging on—or disparaging—their employers. He kept Pearl happy so she'd sing his praises.

The best part of our kitchen stands at the sink, her arms deep in sudsy water. Pearl helped Fitzie raise me and soothe my heart when the senator's harsh criticism bit deep.

At the squeak of the swinging door, she turns and her face splits with a smile. "Miss Cora, welcome home, child. Yo' a sight for these old eyes." She grabs a towel, wipes her hands, then embraces me.

My voice muffles in her arms. After a moment, I pull back and try again. "I've missed you. And your coffee. Nobody in New York adds chicory, or if they do, they add too much or not enough."

"Sit y'self down, and I'll pour you a cup and cut you a slice of sweet tater pie. Miss Clara?" My aunt nods and puts her thumb and forefinger about an inch apart for a small slice.

The back door opens, and Fitzie enters with a basket of freshly cut Michaelmas daisies, Beautyberry, Chinese bellflower, heather, and snakeroot from the garden. She opens a cupboard, rises up on her tiptoes, and retrieves a cut-glass vase. Watching her arrange the flowers evokes a long-forgotten memory from my childhood.

I must have been around three or four. I handed her daisies, one by one, and while she arranged them for her dinner party, she told me a story about a plain faerie named Sugar-pie, who lived in our garden. When the Michaelmas daisies bloomed, the faerie became beautiful. Just as I would. She took my face between her hands, kissing me and saying, "You're not plain, Cora. You simply haven't bloomed yet. You will, my darling."

I believed her then, but the senator's words soon erased the stamp of hers. Right now, while I'd prefer to talk about anything but him, decorum demands I ask.

Pearl sets coffee and pie in front of me. "Thank you, Pearl." I clear my throat and glance at Fitzie. "Where will the senator's funeral be?"

"At the mortuary, but"—she shakes her head—"I don't want to talk about him." Though a frown mars her classic beauty, her smooth alabaster skin makes her appear younger than she is. "What he did? Why, it's simply not done in civilized homes. I'm sure your grandmother is rolling over in her grave. She never has approved of him. Says he's new money and still acts like it."

Says? I glance at Aunt Clara. She gives an almost imperceptible shake of her head. Okay, I can wait. After taking an appreciative sip of Pearl's coffee, I dive into the pie.

"New York may have swell delicatessens, but they can't beat your pie, Pearl."

With a wide smile, she returns to her dishwashing.

"There." Fitzie finishes the flower arrangement and joins us at the table, after setting the vase in its center. "So, tell us about New York, sugar-pie. What's it like being on a stage in front of all those people? Why, I think I'd die of fright if I saw a sea of faces staring back at me. Oh, and are the stores as glamorous as they say in the newspapers?"

For the next half hour, I regale them with tales of being on stage, of the stores, and of my friends. Knowing how much they love a good ghost story, I tell them about the resident ghost at the Palace Theatre, even though it's odd to talk about ghosts so soon after the senator's demise. However, it's better than funeral talk—and not terribly far off-subject. I chuckle to myself at the irony.

"Russell Alexander was a musician. He had a musical comedy act. He was only thirty-eight when he died in 1915. From the tricks the ghost plays on the actors, we're pretty sure it's him."

Pearl shivers, Aunt Clara shakes with silent laughter, and Fitzie leans forward in her chair.

"Tell us more." She forks a bite of pie without taking her eyes off me.

"Usually, it's costumes missing. Although, once I couldn't find Beau Wyatt for over an hour. Then Mr. Keith found him in his locked office." I glance at Mama. "Fitzie, I know how much you like Abbott and Costello."

She clasps her hands to her chest. "I love those two. I listen to their radio show every week."

"Well, last month, they headlined our Philly tour. One night, Bud Abbott stuck his head out his dressing room door, yelling for someone to find his pants. The laundress swore they were *in* his dressing room. So, he hollers for Lou, accusing him of stealing them. But Lou was in a meeting with the stage manager. Bud grabbed his robe and began searching everywhere." I pause for another bite of pie—and to heighten the intrigue.

"How fun to actually work with them."

I swallow. "Well, I don't work *with* them, really."

Aunt Clara rolls her eyes at Fitzie, and to me, she rotates her hand in a get-on-with-it motion.

"Yes, do," Fitzie says. "Did they find his pants?"

"They did, but they'd been hidden in the catwalk."

"What's that?" At the sink, Pearl removes her hands from the sudsy water.

"It's how they reach the battens. Those are what they fly—or hang the backdrops on. Catwalks are narrow, steel-mesh walkways, about forty to eighty feet above the stage. Only special stage crew members are allowed up there."

Fitzie reaches for the sugar bowl. "Was it one of them?"

I shake my head. "No. They'd all gone out to dinner."

Aunt Clara's hands fly to form her question. "If they were gone, how did they find the pants?"

"While everyone searched the wings and stage, the pants floated down from the catwalk and landed on Mr. Abbott's head. We all realized it was Russell, the ghost. You should have seen Bud Abbott. He grabbed the pants and shook his fist at the catwalk. The rest of us just laughed. It was pretty funny."

"I ain't sure I'd be laughin'," Pearl says, wiping her hands on a towel. "Ghosts ain't nothin' to be messin' with."

"Aw, he's not a malevolent ghost, Pearl. All his pranks are innocent fun."

"Clara." Fitzie nudges her sister. "Do you remember the house on Cumming Highway, the one just over the river that Daddy always said was haunted?"

My aunt's mouth forms an *O*, and she nods, her eyes wide.

Fitzie puts her hand on my arm. "Clara and I had ridden our bikes to—well, I don't remember where we'd been." She turns to my aunt. "Do you remember?"

Aunt Clara nods and signs, "Aunt Mary Frances."

"Of course. Mama had sent her an applesauce cake. You had it in your basket because you didn't trust me not to fall."

Aunt Clara raises her eyebrows in acknowledgment, then they draw into a frown.

"Ah, I see you do remember." Fitzie giggles and tilts her head toward me. "It was your Aunt Clara who fell that day. And smashed Aunt Mary Frances' applesauce cake. You see, while we rode past that old house, Clara stopped and pointed. Up in a second-story window was a lady wearing a dress that was straight from the Revolutionary War days."

"Did you go inside to investigate?"

"I got off my bike and would have, but she"—Fitzie points at Aunt

Clara—"grabbed my arm and made me get back on. She couldn't get out of there fast enough. We'd just cleared the driveway when she fell over and smashed the cake."

Aunt Clara's hands move furiously. "I was trying to get around you. You were taking your sweet time, and my wheel hit a rut."

Fitzie laughs, then pushes her chair back and wanders out to the yard. Through the window in the twilight, I can see her enter the gate to the family graveyard. We are one of a few Sugar Hill families to have one. Most people inter their loved ones in the church cemetery. She caresses two of the headstones, then sits on the wrought-iron bench just inside the fenced area. Her lips begin to move.

"Who is she talking to?"

Aunt Clara nods to Pearl, who is returning dishes to a side cupboard.

"Your grandmother Drummond, Miss Cora. She askin' her to—" Pearl glances at Aunt Clara again. At her nod, Pearl continues. "Miss Fitzie askin' her mama to question the senator 'bout where he hid the money."

He hid it? "Why would he hide his money?" And how are Mama and Aunt Clara going to survive if they can't find it? I'm definitely going to have to get a job *here*.

Aunt Clara shrugs, signing, "There isn't any. He lost it in the stock market crash."

"He *lost* it? *All* of it?" I can't seem to wrap my mind around this.

My aunt nods. Even her hands show frustration in jerky movements. "That's why he hung himself. But your mother refuses to believe it."

"And you're sure he didn't hide some?" It would be a good thing if he had and somehow seems like something he'd do.

My aunt leans her head to one side and narrows her eyes. "Do you remember someplace you think he might have put some? We are in need, that's for certain. If you can remember something …"

"Did you look in his safe?"

She nods. "Found a few hundred dollars. Took it out to keep safe from Fitzie." I can see why Aunt Clara has it. In Fitzie's present state of mind, it wouldn't last. "Since you're home, I'll give it to you."

First, she tells me Fitzie is losing her marbles, and then she drops the bomb that we're flat busted broke. *Welcome home.*

Aunt Clara leaves the kitchen, and I take our dishes to the sink for Pearl. "I don't think I'm ready for tomorrow. I'm not sure I can put on a face of mourning."

Pearl knows me so well. She eyes me with her you-listen-to-me-now expression. "Draw on your actin' talent. It's God's gift to you."

Saturday, November 2, 1929
The funeral is every bit as bad and worse than I expected. For that matter, the day started off on the wrong note. Literally. At dawn, some over-zealous rooster made it his business to wake everyone. Now, every single-minded politician is in our foyer and parlor, vying for the press to take their photo with Fitzie—or even more unpleasant, with me. I can see the *Atlanta Constitution* headlines now—*Vaudeville star mourns father.*

"Miss Fitzgerald?" A droopy-jowled journalist snaps a photo, blinding me for a moment. He clutches his camera in one hand, along with a small pad of paper, and plucks a pencil from behind his ear. "What are your feelings about your father?"

What does he think they are? And wouldn't he be shocked if I tell him how I really feel? "To be honest, I'm still—" My throat closes. If I cough now, it could become tomorrow's entertainment story. A hand takes my elbow.

"Her father is dead. How do you think she feels?" Glenice Jo guides me away from the crowd. Before I can say a word of thanks, I'm surrounded by Martha Anne Vance, Trudie Gibbs, Millie Newcomb, and of course, Glenice Jo Armstrong. The Dilly Club. They form a tight circle around me, daring any rascally photographer to break through. I struggle not to cry from gratitude and love for my beautiful friends.

Glenice Jo's hair seems a lighter blonde than I remember it, but it's stylishly jelly-rolled away from her face, accentuating her sculpted nose and eyebrows. There's a maturity about her I can't put my finger on, but she's stunning. And sweet Martha Anne—she reminds me a little of that movie actress, Loretta Young, with her large, expressive eyes. Funny Trudie, whose sassiness is part of her charm. I've really missed her. Millie hasn't aged a bit. She still looks sixteen with her perfectly beautiful baby face. I'll bet she'll still be gorgeous when she's sixty.

The flurry of flashbulbs nearly blinds me. After one last photo of me surrounded by the girls, the press makes a beeline for my mother across the room. She catches my eye and rolls hers, making me smile. I must say, Fitzie is playing the part well. She gives the press and the crowd what they want—a teary-eyed, grieving widow. If I didn't know better, I'd say she's the actress in the family, not me. Later this evening, I'm sure she and a couple of her close lady friends will have cocktails and make fun of the press and the legislators.

"Cora." Trudie pulls my attention back to the Dillies. "Have you got a beau up in New York?"

"Nope. No time to meet anyone. But I'll bet you a fin you can't guess who I had dinner with just before I left." Although … I don't have the five dollars to bet.

Martha Anne's eyes sparkle with excitement. "Who?"

"David Divine." I let that settle on them for a moment.

"*The* David Divine?" Millie grasps my hand. "How did you meet him? I saw him on Broadway last year. He's absolutely dreamy." Her eyes close and she sighs. If she only knew.

"Don't swoon on us, Millie-billie." Trudie taps Millie's cheek affectionately. "I'll lay you odds, our Cora wasn't milquetoast with him."

I bite my lip to keep from laughing out loud. "His agent set it up. I'm sure for publicity purposes. He's pretty keen to look at, but you should have heard the line he tried to feed me."

I peek over Glenice Jo's shoulder to make sure nobody's trying to overhear us, then wink at Trudie. Neither of us are raving beauties. And she always understands me when it comes to men. Funny thing is, her daddy is the opposite of my father, and growing up, I wanted hers to be my daddy. Now, he's a widower. Trudie keeps house for him and works as a waitress in his hash house. She says, *why take care of another man?* The one she has is a good one, and you never know what a man's like until it's too late. Trudie is one smart cookie.

Trying to decide whether or not to let them keep their fantasies about David Divine, I fall on the side of not. I make a dramatic show of tossing my hands in the air. "I've never been so bored in my entire life." I straighten my suit jacket with a tug on its peplum. "Dinner with him was like listening to Louella Parsons. The only time he didn't talk about himself was when he gossiped about someone else. I can't imagine what he's saying about me right now."

Martha Anne gapes. "You're joking, right?"

"Don't be so sure." Glenice Jo nudges her. "More often than we like to believe, our fantasies about movie stars are way off base."

Millie's mama motions to her. The crowd is noticeably thinner. I breathe a sigh of relief. The front door stands wide open, and the reporters are out on the lawn, hoping to get a last-minute photograph. The girls gather their handbags and wraps from the coat tree. I delay Glenice Jo for a moment.

"How about I come by tomorrow? We can have a good natter."

Sorrow invades her eyes, then disappears as quickly as it came, leaving me to wonder if I truly saw it. She lifts her hand and wiggles her fingers. "I'll be waiting for you."

Chapter 3

AUNT CLARA IS ALREADY EATING when I arrive in the dining room for breakfast. Fitzie's plate has a folded piece of paper in the center of it—my aunt's stationery. I suck in my lip to block a giggle and pour coffee into a cup. For as long as I can remember, my aunt has vexed my mama with those little notes. Fitzie finds them on her pillow, in her makeup bag, on her plate. She hates to take the time to read them, preferring to sign. This morning should provide a bit of levity after yesterday's funeral.

After taking a goodly portion of Pearl's spicy scrambled eggs and cheese grits, I join my aunt. "Good mornin'."

Her eyes twinkle in delicious anticipation of her sister's response. Those two. Shaking my head, I take a bite of eggs. Oh my. I've missed Pearl's cooking. I follow it with a gulp of coffee. After a night of being kept awake by a pesky cough, I need the caffeine. I don't have a cold, so what can be causing the cough?

Fitzie saunters into the dining room. Below her quirked eyebrow, a muscle twitches beside her eye. Other than that, she gives no indication she's seen the note. She picks up her plate with a swift snatch, like a magician pulling the cloth from beneath a set of china. The note flutters to the floor. Aunt Clara frowns at Fitzie's back, then picks up the note, placing it squarely between fork and knife. She crosses her arms and sits back with a smirk.

My mama returns to the table with a hearty breakfast on her plate, which she lays atop the stationery. With a grin that Lewis Carroll would have coveted, she nods to Aunt Clara, then slowly sips her coffee. I've watched these two spar like this my entire life—and not always so quietly. Sometimes, Fitzie yells at her sister. Aunt Clara's gestures and miming grow large and expressive. Other times, my aunt will simply walk away from my mother, leaving Fitzie sputtering like a Model T engine that refuses to turn off.

Mama ignores her sister and asks, "What are your plans today, sugar?"

Yesterday took every ounce of social refinement all three of us have, so we skipped church this morning. "Since everyone will be at work tomorrow, today, I'm visiting Glenice Jo."

"I was pleased yesterday to see your friends haven't forgotten you."

"Fitzie, *you* forget. We're the Dillies. To them, I'm still plain old me." And I am ever-so-grateful for that. Secretly, I'd been a tad worried they might not feel comfortable around me now. Silly of me, really. After all, they've been witness to my peculiarity since third grade. To them, it's normal.

Fitzie reaches over and squeezes my hand. "Tell her mama 'hey' for me, and you two have a good time together."

After breakfast, I slip into a pair of cute, navy-blue sailor slacks with two rows of buttons in the front and a light-blue shirt. I bought the slacks at Bloomingdales in New York, and they're perfect for a bicycle ride to Glenice Jo's. A pair of canvas shoes, a sweater, and a sassy beret make me feel like a new gal. Filled with enough confidence to find a job—I only hope it will last, that I'll feel the same tomorrow. Maybe I'll try working part-time until I figure out how long I'll be here.

I call goodbye to Fitzie and Aunt Clara, who are lounging over coffee in the library. Their relationship tickles me. I didn't notice it much when I was young, but at times, they're as irritable with each other as a pair of broody hens, yet they're always together. I can't quite figure them out. Sibling rivalry knows no age limits, I guess.

On my way out, I grab a few sugar cubes and stuff them in my pocket. Then I wheel my bike from the garage. They say you never forget how to ride a bicycle. Although it's been over six years, I only wobble a tad bit before memory takes over. Once on my way to Glenice

Jo's, I lose myself in the scenery and count each blessing. Old oak trees. Farmland. Cows mooing softly when I pass. Old Mr. Howerton's mare, Honey, trots to the fence and whinnies. I stop to stroke her velvety nose and give her a treat.

"You didn't forget me, did you, girl?" I pull out one of the sugar cubes from my pocket. "And I didn't forget you either."

Honey gently lips the sugar cube from my hand, then blows a *thank you*, making me laugh. She tosses her head at my laughter and trots off, confident I will reward her next time she sees me. Honey's memory amazes me.

After another wobbly start, I'm peddling toward Glenice Jo's, just on the other side of Level Creek, about a mile and a half from the Howertons'. After a few minutes, I come to the creek and the worst part of the ride. The wooden bridge has no sides or guard rail. It's narrow and has chunks out of a few of the boards. I stop, debating whether to walk or ride my bike across it. I've taken a few tumbles off that bridge as a kid.

A horn blast behind me startles me. I jump and turn, but my foot lands in a hole and throws me off balance. Letting go of the bike, I flail my arms to regain equilibrium. I lose the battle and, with a screech, fall into the creek. My shoulder smacks against a rock, and my bike tumbles into the water, landing on top of me. The handlebar horn hits my cheekbone and squawks.

"Cora! Are you all right? I'm so sorry."

Boone Robertson scrambles down the bank and lifts the bicycle off me. He holds out his hand to help me up.

I grab his arm, rise, and shivering from the frigid water, assess my once-glorious outfit, now dripping wet. "Except for a twisted ankle, I think I'm fine. Well, other than my pride." The silly side of this tickles my funny bone. When Boone pulls out his handkerchief, I can't help laughing.

"I appreciate your gallantry, but that's a wee bit small to dry off with."

He pushes it toward me, his face red. "It's for your shoulder. I think it's cut because you're bleeding."

"Oh." The giggles fade, and I take stock of my wound. Realizing it's little more than a scratch, my smile returns. "Thanks."

"I don't know how you can laugh when I'm the reason you're in this mess. And"—he points to my cheek—"I think you might end up with a black eye. I'm really sorry, Cora. I didn't mean to honk. I was getting out of the truck to help you cross when my elbow hit the horn."

I manage to keep my eyes from popping open wide at another indication of this new gallantry he possesses. "I accept your apology and forgive you. It's fine, really. Believe me, I've had worse."

He pulls my bicycle and beret out of the creek. "Thanks for being so nice about this. Most people would be mad." He hands me my hat.

I wring out the beret as best I can and give my damp hair a toss. "There's no reason. It was an accident. But if you'd like someone to be mad, get ready. Here comes Glenice Jo." I grin at him.

Boone turns his head and winces. Glenice Jo storms up the road. She must have seen us. Her house is just a hundred feet or so from the creek.

She reaches the bridge, and after taking in my appearance, she glares at Boone. "What have you done to her?"

Boone's mouth opens, then closes. "It was an accident."

That doesn't seem to mollify her. She yanks open his truck door. "Take her and her bicycle to my house." Glancing at me, she rolls her eyes and adds, "Please."

At least, she's softened her voice. Boone helps me in, and Glenice Jo hops in beside me. While he loads my bike in the back, I whisper, "Be nice."

She stares at me for a moment, then her lips twitch. "You do look pretty funny. You're hair's a disaster."

The driver's door opens, and Boone climbs inside. He glances at us. Glenice Jo lets him off the hook.

"Okay, you're forgiven. And I'm sorry I pounced like I did. I'm just protective of Cora." At least, she has the grace to look embarrassed.

Boone's relief is palpable. "Everyone needs a friend like you, Glenice Jo."

∞

The hem of Glenice Jo's skirt falls nearly to my ankles. I hike it up. Miss Hattie's old middy blouse is fun and fits fine. It will do nicely while my clothes dry next to the fireplace. Since it's too chilly to have a picnic outside, Miss Hattie brings a snack to the sunroom. A Southern high tea, complete with a platter of her biscuits, a pot of jam, and a pitcher of sweet tea.

"Have fun, girls."

We sit on the wicker loveseat. "How many times has your mama said that to us over the years?"

"About a million." She pours the tea over glasses of ice, chipped from the block in their icebox. I like the different shapes in the glass better than the rectangular cubes from the senator's electric refrigerator. I've forgotten or I never noticed the ice up north. I take a sip, then spread a thick layer of homemade strawberry jam on a biscuit.

"Ambrosia," I manage around a mouthful.

Glenice Jo only mumbles around hers. Dressed in a pair of lounging pajamas, she looks relaxed yet sophisticated, and a bit more grown-up than I remember her. Could marriage have added that? Out back in the yard, the trees are losing their leaves. In the spring, their full branches will meet over the yard, forming a canopy of shade.

She taps my ankle with her foot. "Okay, now spill. Your letters have been great, but I want to hear all about your life among the Yankees." She has a wicked gleam in her eye.

"Actors and actresses aren't Northern or Southern or anything other than performers. We're a breed unto ourselves. Because we travel so much and are always in close quarters, we become a family of sorts. We talk about the theatre, the audiences, who made the funniest flub in the last show."

"So nobody teases you about being a Southern hick?"

"Not now. Maybe a few did in the beginning, but once I'd made my chops—proved myself—they stopped."

Glenice Jo chews another bite of biscuit and slowly shakes her head. "I don't know how you do it." She swallows. "Getting up in front of all those people? I'd be scared spitless."

That makes me laugh. "You're not afraid of anything."

"Of that, I am. All those people staring gives me the creeps."

"Occasionally, it *is* like that. Some audiences are really hard. They come ready to pelt you with rotten tomatoes if you're not top-notch."

Glenice Jo gapes at me, making me laugh again. "Have you ever had them do that to you?"

"No. I've been lucky." My hand hovers over the plate, and I debate whether to take another biscuit. I'd better not. It would end up on my hips. "There aren't any female ventriloquists who can *throw* their voice. Just me. And I only know one man who can. Mr. Stephens."

Her interest perks. "Oh? And who is he?"

"Old enough to be my grandfather, that's who."

"Oh. Fiddle. Well, besides your dinner with David Divine, is there anyone up there who has your heart?"

It's dicey, the dance of two old friends not quite at ease again yet. It's time to bring our friendship back to what it was. "You know me better than that. Romance is fine, as long as you keep your heart out of it." It can't be hurt that way.

She tilts her head, and her eyes turn wistful. "That makes me sad. You're missing so much."

"How can you say that after what happened to Willie?"

"We had a beautiful courtship and a glorious honeymoon. Willie was so romantic." She sighs and smiles. "If that's all I ever have, it's enough. I loved him with all my heart, Cora. And even more important, he loved me the same. I'll never have a minute of worry over that. And I have such beautiful memories." Her smile is brighter than footlights.

"But his death—"

Her grin turns saucy. "My Willie went out as he lived. We honeymooned in Gatlinburg and went to see Ramsey Cascades. And yes, it's true. He sang all the way down. He never knew what was happening. Not really. That's what the doctor said."

"Weren't you terrified?" I take a long draught of sweet tea to wash down the last of the biscuit.

"Sugar, I had no idea what was going on. I thought he was hiding on a ledge, singing me a silly song. He was like that. He loved to make me laugh. And he did."

I rattle the ice in my now-empty glass. "You're almost making me change my mind, but I had a lifetime of the senator telling me how homely I was. How disappointed he was in me. How he wished—well, if that's love, I don't want any of it. Not only was he gone all the time, but there were all the stories about him and other women. I hated that for my mama."

"Yet she never left him." Glenice Jo hands me a napkin. "You've got jam on your cheek."

"Thanks." I take the cloth and wipe it off. "People gossiped, but she'd pretend she didn't hear. She always rose above it, and I never saw her cry or get angry over anything he did." I pick up a throw pillow and cuddle it against my stomach. "I don't think she loved him. Did I ever tell you theirs was an arranged marriage?"

"Yes. But a lot of people in arranged marriages still managed to fall in love with each other."

"Did they? Or did they simply become comfortable with each other?"

Chapter 4

Sunday evening, November 3, 1929

AFTER SUPPER, AUNT CLARA SIGNS she has a headache brought on by the weather and goes to bed. With rain pelting the windows, Fitzie and I retire to the parlor. She wanders to the bookcase to choose something to read, while I fiddle with the radio dial. Finding a jazz station—we both love jazz—I turn the volume low and settle onto the davenport as strains of Louis Armstrong's "Ain't Misbehavin'" surround us.

"Mama?"

Her hand hovers over the titles in the bookcase, and she turns her head. "When you use 'Mama,' I know it's going to be an important question." She leaves the books and sits next to me, taking my hand. "Go ahead, sugar-pie."

"Before you married the senator, were you ever in love?"

Her eyes search mine, seeking the origin of my question—as if she knows a simple yes or no won't suffice. "There was a boy—" The doorbell interrupts her. She clamps her lips together. "Well, who do you suppose that could be?"

We don't have to wait to find out. My friends, the Dilly Club, traipse into the parlor. Millie is bearing a platter of—

"Oh, my stars." Anticipation sparkles in Fitzie's gaze as she rises to greet them. "Are those your mama's pralines?" Her previous annoyance at the interruption evaporates.

Millie bows with a flourish, taking care not to spill any of the treasures. "To properly welcome home our Cora."

"Well, sit down, girls. I'll have Pearl bring in sweet tea." Fitzie winks at me and plucks up a praline before leaving the room, then stops at the doorway. "Would y'all prefer Coca-Cola?"

The girls nod enthusiastically at the treat, and Fitzie departs in search of Pearl.

Trudie, her hair finger-waved with the ends in little curls around her baby face, takes my arm and leads me to the davenport. "There wasn't time to talk at the wake. We want to hear all about New York."

We sit, Trudie on my left and Millie on my right. The Dilly Club's true beauties, Glenice Jo and Martha Anne, take the two wingback chairs facing the davenport.

I clutch Millie's hand. "Right now, I don't want to talk about vaudeville or the people there. I want to hear all about all y'all. What's been happening here?"

Pearl carries in a tray of Coca-Cola bottles, frosty from the refrigerator. The girls stare at the novelty. Their homes still have iceboxes that are too small for storing superfluous items like Co-Colas.

I take the tray and set it on the sideboard. "Thank you, Pearl. We won't need you anymore tonight. Go listen to your program."

Gratitude flickers across her face. Pearl loves her radio shows.

Once we all have our drinks and are savoring the delectable pralines, Martha Anne glances at me, her cheeks growing pink. "I'll go first. I'm hopelessly in love, Cora. And you'll never guess with who." She lifts one foot and straightens the cuff on her sock.

Martha Anne will not go on until I ask. I swallow a sugary bite and brush the crumbs from my bottom lip. "Who?"

She places her fingertips coquettishly on her knees. "Ethan Simms."

I try to remember him from school. Then his image lands in my mind like a penny falling into the coin slot of a gumball machine. "Is he still as handsome as he was in high school?"

Martha Anne's infectious giggles delay her answer, then she recovers. "He is, but he's as shy as ever. He blushes like crazy when he sees me, but he won't talk to me. I don't know what to do." She slips off her Mary Janes and wiggles her toes inside her socks. She always did hate having her feet confined, even though she loves shoes.

We spent so many nights in one another's bedrooms, the five of us trying on makeup, styling each other's hair, and talking about boys. It was easier then. None of us were serious, and we had a new crush every other week.

Trudie takes another praline from the plate. "I don't know why you even bother, Martha Anne. If he's too shy to talk, what kind of husband would he be?"

"He's a romantic man—you can see it in his artistry." Martha Anne's sigh is dramatic, and we all laugh. If I remember right, her letters said he was the tooling artist at the saddlery.

She lifts her chin and forges on. "Besides, Trudie, you aren't one to give advice on romance. Why, you chase all the boys away with that caustic tongue of yours."

"Trudie has to protect herself. You know that." Glenice Jo's gaze takes in Trudie with tenderness. "Can you imagine caring for her daddy *and* a husband?"

Millie slides forward on the davenport and drops to her knees beside the coffee table, where she looks over the pralines. "Some women care for both a husband and a daddy—even brothers."

I pop the last bit of my praline into my mouth, tucking it in my cheek to melt. "But usually, they take on the parent and siblings after they've been married for a while. Poor Trudie wouldn't have time to adjust to a husband first. No,"—I share a conspiratorial wink with her—"she's better off as she is. Oscar appreciates her and dotes on her. What more could she want?"

Martha Anne clears her throat with emphasis, making Trudie blush and the rest of us laugh. We all get the inference.

Trudie gives a fake cough. "I figure, why add the work when dating is such fun?"

Back in her place on the davenport, Millie snorts in a most unladylike fashion, sending us all into a new fit of giggles. She's the daintiest of any of us. "Tell Cora who you date." She doesn't give Trudie a chance. "Nobody! She scares them all away."

Oh, how I've missed laughing with my friends.

Glenice Jo recovers first. "She has to be tough. The cafe gets its share of truck drivers and itinerants. I've seen them try to flirt with her. She's very good at fending them off. She only gets tough if they don't take a hint."

"Y'all know I am still here in the room, right?" Trudie gives us all the evil eye.

Nothing has changed except our ages. Instead of thirteen- and fourteen-year-olds, we're twenty-four and twenty-five. Women, not schoolgirls.

I set my bottle on the coffee table. "Trudie, I'm going to need to work while I'm home. Do you need any help at the cafe?"

Four pairs of eyes blink at me.

My spine stiffens. "What? How hard can it be? You ask people what they want, tell Oscar, and when he gets it made, you deliver it to them. Simple."

Glenice Jo reaches across the coffee table and pats my knee. "Cora, sugar-pie, you've never waited on anyone in your life. You've been waited *on*. You never had to work." She waves her hand at me, knowing I'm about to defend myself. She knows me better than anyone. "Don't get your feathers ruffled. I know you *work* in the theatre. But you're a star there and don't clear people's dirty plates." She laughs. "If you wrinkle your nose any harder, it'll pleat. I think we can find you a job somewhere else. Maybe the tannery needs a stenographer. Can you take shorthand?"

"I ... no. But I write fast."

Martha Anne leans forward. "Can you type?"

Embarrassed at my lack of salable skills, I throw my voice to the lamp on a side table next to Trudie. "Maybe."

As they laugh, I finish off my Co-cola. The fizz seems to soothe the tickle in my throat. "I may not have the same skills that y'all—"

Martha Anne interrupts, rescuing me once again. "Forget working right now. It's time to tell us about what you're going to do in New York when you go back. I hear vaudeville is dying. Is that true?"

My dear friend has no way of knowing her question pierces to my very core. "I'm afraid it is. That's why I've been working with a vocal coach. To move over to the Broadway revues, I—"

"What's a revue?" Glenice Jo pulls off an earring and rubs her earlobe.

"It's a variety show with a connecting theme between the acts or scenes. For instance, if the theme was love, then each act would have to connect to the theme. I'd introduce Sugar to Beau and have him flirt with her." That sounds lame to even me. "However, my plans are not to continue with ventriloquism. If I move over, it will be as a singer and actress."

There. I've said it out loud. The die is cast. I may not ever get to be an ingénue, but supporting roles are good too. One doesn't have to be gorgeous to be a supporting actress.

"That's wonderful." Millie claps her hands.

Glenice Jo nods vigorously. "I know you can sing."

"Acting's in your blood, honey," Trudie chimes in.

Martha Anne simply smiles her approval.

"But I need more vocal coaching. I'm not there yet."

"What?" Trudie reaches for another praline. "Who says?"

My sweet friends can't imagine any one of us not being the best. "My singing coach in New York. Y'all would love her. She's an absolute hoot. Madam Dressler. She's Hungarian, I think. Anyway, she's very good, and I was lucky to have her take me on." But I'm here now, not in New York. I swallow a lump that doesn't come from the pralines. "I need to keep working. Are there any vocal coaches here?"

Martha Anne scrunches up her face in concentration. "Not that I know of. I can think of a dozen piano teachers, but not singing ones."

"What about in Atlanta? Wouldn't there be someone there?" Trudie sets down her half-eaten praline, and Martha Anne snatches the remainder. "Hey! Get your own." Trudie leans across the coffee table and slaps Martha Anne's knee.

Popping the treat onto her mouth, Martha Anne laughs around it. She would never take a second one, so it's her way of getting a little more.

Are voice teachers so rare in Atlanta that none of them know one? "I guess I'll ask Fitzie about Atlanta. She'll know." I hope. If I don't keep up with it, I'll lose what I gained with Madam Dressler.

"Millie knows all about Atlanta." Glenice Jo stretches and bends her neck to the left, then right. "Millie, tell Cora about Lou."

Millie glances at me and back to Glenice Jo. "Are you sure?"

I frown. What's this is all about? "Sure about what?"

Trudie carefully brushes stray praline crumbs from her lap into her hand. "You can't tell anyone. Millie's on the lam."

My jaw drops. "*What?* The cops are after Millie?" I can't believe it. Millie-the-rule-follower? "Why would you be on the run? And why didn't you write me?"

Millie takes a breath and leans toward me. "I didn't want to put it down on paper in case anyone found it. At first, there wasn't anything excitin' to tell. But then it all changed." She grimaces.

"Whoa, girl." I hold up my hand. Millie tends to jump around in her story-telling, and I need to hear the first part first. "Start at the beginning, please."

She smooths her skirt, laughing. "Sorry. Okay, in 1924, after graduation, I went to Atlanta with some other girls from school. We all got jobs as stenographers and shared an apartment. My job was at a bank, and that's where I met Lou. Lou Formatti. He came in with a restaurant owner."

Ah, it's a romance. "Did he ask you out right away?" I can see why he would. Millie is adorable, her pale blonde hair confirming her Nordic heritage.

She shakes her head. "He waited outside for me to get off work. Then he walked me home." She sighs. "He was so romantic. Within six months, we were engaged."

"Engaged? And you didn't tell me?" I grab her hand, but her ring finger is bare. Wait. She said *was*. His name rattles in my head. Formatti. Form—recall dawns. "No way. The Atlanta *mafia* family?"

"Yeah, but she didn't know that yet." Glenice Jo frowns and tilts her head at me. "Hey, how do you know him?"

"I don't, but living in New York, you hear a lot about the mob. That's their home. Well, there and Chicago. Anyway, I met a mobster's ex-girlfriend last year. He's in prison. Boy, did I learn a lot."

As if she smelled rotten cabbage, Millie's nose wrinkles and her lip curls. "I wish I'd known. I'd have stayed away from him. But he was so handsome, Cora. And suave. He swept me off my feet."

Her eyes beg me to understand, but I've yet to meet a man who does that to me. "What's that like?"

She stares across the room, but I can tell the memories have overtaken her.

"The next time I saw him was at a party. When he came in, he stood near the doorway and looked around. But when his gaze settled on me, he stopped and stared for the longest time. I couldn't have looked away if I'd wanted to. It was like he hypnotized me."

Boone's eyes come to mind. Yeah, I understand that kind of hypnotizing.

Martha Anne bounces in her chair. "Tell Cora exactly how he swept you off your feet."

My friends all know Millie's story. Martha Anne's excitement makes me smile. She views life as exhilarating. Nothing ever seems to tarnish that.

"He crossed the room without ever breaking eye contact. When he reached me, he took my drink from me and took a sip. Then he smiled, set my glass down, took my hand, and walked me onto the dance floor. The party"—she kicks off her Mary Janes and pulls her legs up onto the davenport—"was in a penthouse apartment in downtown Atlanta. They had a band and a dance floor. You should have seen it. It was the bee's knees. Really posh. Anyway, he drew me into his arms and we danced. Then he asked me my name."

So I don't lose it, I wrap a loose thread around one of the buttons on my blouse. "Hadn't you said anything to him yet?"

"I couldn't. I was tongue-tied."

I don't remember a single man ever rendering me tongue-tied. Except the senator. "So he asks your name. When he told you his, didn't you have any questions? Ask him what he did for a living or something?"

Glenice Jo throws a small pillow at me. "You would have, Cora. But Millie isn't you. She didn't care. When he took her in his arms, she fell in love."

Trudie's eyes grow hard. "Everything he did was plotted to make her fall for him."

Oh no. Sweet Millie, taken in by a jerk? I reach for her hand. "Tell me."

Tears well in her eyes. "We went out every night for months. He bought me expensive gifts, but I wouldn't take them. Finally, he gave me a diamond and asked me to marry him."

The pain in her voice robs me of my breath. I take a sip of my drink so she doesn't see the tears that scald my own eyes. "Where is the ring?"

"The Feds took it when they arrested me."

I nearly spit my Co-cola. "What?" Millie hands me a napkin to dab my chin.

"Yeah." Her voice grows as hard as her eyes. "That's how I discovered just who Lou is ... or was. He used me for a safe front."

Something isn't adding up. I look at Glenice Jo. "You said *was* earlier too. What happened, and why did you get arrested?"

Millie hangs her head and picks at her nails.

Glenice Jo takes up her story. "Lou was hiding out in Atlanta, and he got into the local bootlegging. The Feds were already looking for him. And they found him. He was killed in a shootout."

My head spins. "Start again."

"What? You mean when she met him?" Trudie asks.

"No. Yes. Wait, no." I shake my head to clear my thoughts, then touch Millie's arm. "You weren't with him when he was shot, were you?" Horror shivers through me.

One side of her mouth rises in a sad little smile. "No. He'd dropped me off earlier. It was afterward that the Feds found me. They thought I was a safe house for him. You should've seen my apartment." She clicks her tongue. "My poor roommates. The Feds tore it apart looking for bootleg whiskey and stolen goods."

"Holy moly." I've read exposés about the mob, but this isn't in a newspaper. It's one of my best friends' life. "What happened when they came? Were you terrified?"

"I was confused first, then terrified. They reminded me of my Fifth Amendment rights and advised me I was under arrest for bootlegging. I tried to explain to them that I didn't know anything about bootlegging. But they said I was my boyfriend's accomplice."

I can't believe this. "Couldn't they tell you were duped?"

"Nope. God was watching out for me, though. When we got to the station, one of the local cops believed me. It turns out, he was part of the tail we had. He followed us on all our dates, which were staged by Lou to throw off the cops. Fortunately, the people we were with proved my innocence."

"Wow." I look around at all my friends. "And y'all say *my* life is exciting?"

"Poor Daddy." Millie's bright smile returns. "When I was first arrested, they gave me one phone call. Daddy drove up right away. Thank goodness, Officer Benoit—he's the cop who believed me—was still there. At least, I wasn't behind bars." She giggles. "You should have seen Daddy. He gave them our address and phone number and hustled me out of there fast."

My mind swims against the tide. "How can the rule-follower get into so much trouble? I'm glad you're all right, though." My curiosity gets the best of me. "Whatever happened to that ring?"

She flashes a sassy grin. "Daddy got it back from the Feds and found a buyer for it. We got less than half its worth, but we weren't the ones who bought it."

"How big was it?"

She straightens her arms, copying Martha Anne's coquettish pose. "Six carats."

Glenice Jo nudges me. "Close your mouth, Cora, or you'll catch a fly."

I snap my jaw shut. "I've seen some fancy jewelry in New York, but I don't think I've ever seen a diamond that big."

"The money Daddy got for it will see us through several years if we're careful. It was last summer—before the stock market crashed."

"So … you're on the lam because you think Lou's family will want the ring, right?"

"Yeah." Her eyes search the corners of the room, as though a mobster might be hiding behind a curtain or under a chair.

Glenice Jo flicks her wrist, waving away any concern. "We won't let anything happen to her. Besides, Sugar Hill is a tiny town. Not a real city, so we aren't on any maps."

The eager expressions worn by my friends reveal that they enjoy the drama of Millie's situation. Personally, I'd guess the Formattis have moved on. They have bigger ventures than finding a diamond—which might cost a lot in Sugar Hill, but considering the fortunes of Lou's family, it's spare change.

But I won't tell them that. Why take away their titillation? After all, nothing like this ever happens on Sugar Hill. It's even more exciting than me. And for that, I'm grateful. I don't like being the center of attention. That only throws a spotlight on my inadequacies. Onstage is another story. But that's work, not the real me.

Chapter 5

THERE'S NO TIME TO PLAY lady of leisure. I need to find a job. My savings from New York won't carry us for long, and I'd like to keep it intact for when I go back. I grab a pad and a fountain pen from the parlor table Aunt Clara uses for a novel-writing desk and head out to the veranda to consider my options. There's a chill in the morning breeze, and like soft silk, it caresses the back of my neck. I button my sweater and settle in the porch swing. It used to hang in the backyard, but we brought it out here yesterday with the help of Pearl's nephews. It's so nice not having to worry about keeping up senatorial appearances any longer.

Clearing my throat of a nagging tickle, I begin my list by jotting *tannery office help*. Even though I don't know proper shorthand, I'm sure I could operate a typewriter. After all, one simply finds the letter and pushes down the key. Anyone can do it.

Next, I write *Oscar's,* since Trudie said her daddy will hire me. Maybe. Oh, and Nelson's Rexall Drug Store on Main Street. Fitzie used to take me to their fountain counter for a treat when I was little. Both the Rexall and Oscar's are close enough to the tannery that the foremen and office workers often eat dinner at noon or supper after work. But waiting tables is not my preference.

I chew on the capped end of the pen, trying to recall the businesses close enough to ride to on my bicycle. There's Venable's General Store. It's only a mile from our house. Mr. Rocky's a nice man, except he thinks it's funny to show unsuspecting customers his gall stones which he keeps in a jar of formaldehyde on the top shelf. I shudder, but I draw a line under his name.

What else? Oh, Hosch's Five and Dime, except I've never operated a cash register. They're a little intimidating, but maybe I could simply hand the money to Miss Melvina and let her operate the machine.

My list is pathetically short. The front door opens, and Aunt Clara comes out with two cups of coffee, offering me one.

"Thank you. I could use it. I'm trying to make a list of places to apply for a job."

Her left eyebrow raises.

"Don't be skeptical. I can work. I'm quite capable."

Aunt Clara signs, "I'm sorry you have to. My royalties aren't enough to support us, and your mama can't seem to get it through her thick skull that we have no more money. It's gone." She drops her arms to her sides to signal she's through.

"Do you think maybe she's pretending?"

Aunt Clara turns a finger in circles next to her right temple.

"Oh no. Should I be alarmed?" Fitzie's mental condition doesn't seem that bad, but then again, she does talk to her mama in the graveyard.

My aunt pulls out a pad and pencil, scribbling, "Delusional, not crazy. Pearl and I watch her."

I find it funny how she sometimes prefers to write instead of sign. She once told me it's because Fitzie can't oversee what she's saying.

"More reason for me to get out there and find a job."

Her hands fly. "Why not use your father's connections? I'm sure you could get a job in the state senate or house."

The coffee turns to acid in my stomach. "There is no chance in you-know-where that I would work with a politician. They're corrupt snakes. Worse than snakes. Besides, I know nothing about politics, nor do I want to learn."

She lays a hand on my arm, a smile tugging her lips. She's trying not to laugh at me.

"Okay, what's so funny?"

She points at me.

"Why am I funny?" I set down the coffee cup. Its contents no longer warm me.

My aunt points to my list and signs, "What do you know about this kind of work?"

"I'm perfectly capable of learning. All I need is someone to give me a chance."

She contemplates me for a moment, then nods. Her head turns toward the road. Maybe because she *is* mute, my aunt has remarkable hearing. Sure enough, a moment later, a car clatters over the bridge and drives on past us—a cue for me to get moving.

Marshaling all my confidence, I rise. "I'll see y'all later, Aunt Clara. I'm going to get a job today."

As I'm rolling my bicycle out of the garage, I look up at the house. Hmm. An idea forms. Not a bad idea. It could work—if I can't get a job. Trudie always says it's smart to have a Plan B.

I pedal on down the driveway. My last sight before I enter the road is my aunt holding up crossed fingers in a show of encouragement.

Despite the whirling fans and potted red geranium on the desk, the tannery's acrid odor inside the office stings my nostrils and makes my nose twitch. A young woman with jaw-length, bobbed, red hair sits behind the desk, intent on her work. Her yellow suit joins the geranium in adding a bit of color to an otherwise drab room. She glances up as I approach. Judging by the pile of papers on her desk, she needs help. I'm encouraged.

"May I help you?"

I hope so. "Yes, please. I was told to come here for an employment application."

She opens her drawer, pulls out a pad, tears off a sheet, and hands it to me. "Need a pen?"

"Thanks, I've got one. Are there many positions open?"

She shakes her head. "Just one. Office help. Do you take dictation?"

No. "I haven't studied it formally, but I have my own system." My system is that I write fast.

"Sit over there." She points to a small table and chair. "Fill that out, and when you're done, I'll give you the shorthand and typing tests."

My stomach twists on the word *tests*. The moment I sit, I feel like I'm in third grade. My knees barely fit beneath the tabletop. I'm sure it's a desk from the old elementary school, meant to intimidate applicants. Well, it won't work on me. I attack the paperwork.

Name, address. That's easy.

Referred by? I write in *Glenice Jo Armstrong* and *Martha Anne Vance*.

Past employment? The Orpheum Vaudeville Circuit.

Position? Headliner.

I glance at the clerk, who is writing, then at the door. Maybe I can slip out while her head's down. I cough and she looks up.

"Are you finished?"

Darn cough made me miss that window of opportunity. I hand her the completed paper. A slight frown puckers her brow line, but she doesn't say anything. She hands me a pad and pencil. I hate pencils. I always break the point. I pull out my fountain pen instead.

She shrugs. "Sit over there and write down what I dictate. Let me know when you're ready."

Settled in the chair, I poise the pen over the paper. I can do this. "Ready."

"This goes to Mr. Daniel Forsythe. That's spelled with an *e*. Two-eight-one-seven-six Tenth Avenue, New Carlisle, Pennsylvania. Dear Mr. Forsythe—"

Two-eight—oops. My pen leaves an ink blob, obliterating the number. I try to recall what she just said.

"In regards to your recent inquiry for saddlery, Mr. Allen is able to fulfill your order and deliver within the time frame you have requested. There remains only the financial arrangements which—"

"Excuse me, was that one-six-seven or one-seven-six?"

She stares at me for a moment, then shakes her head. "Let's forget the dictation and try you on the typing test. Follow me, please."

From the way her face pinches, she doesn't hold out much hope for me as an associate office worker. I resist the temptation to throw my voice to the geranium, making it say, "Forget the test and hire the girl. She'll keep you entertained."

She leads me to a small room with a table, chair, and typewriter. A stack of paper and a small hourglass sit beside the typewriter. She pulls a similar hourglass from her pocket.

"You have three minutes. Type the paragraphs in this book and stop when the time runs out." She turns both timers over. After setting one on the desk, she exits with the other, shutting the door behind her.

Left alone, I take a piece of paper and stick it under the bar on the top of the typewriter. That doesn't look right. I'm pretty sure it has to go around the roller thing.

I glance at the hourglass on the desk. The sand is running too fast.

I stare at the machine for a second. Wait … I've seen someone do this—Mr. Keith's secretary at the Palace Theatre. How did she … oh, I remember. Setting the paper behind the roller, I turn it. Success. The book is open to a page, so I read the first sentence.

"The bridles you are interested in purchasing are custom-made at a cost of $4.87 each." *All right, I've got it.* The first letter is *T*. I hunt for a moment and find the key with *T* printed on it. I press it but nothing happens. I push harder. It clacks against the paper.

I did it! But it isn't a capital *T*—it's a small one. Why do the keys all have capitals on them if they don't print an uppercase letter? How do I make them uppercase? Everyone knows the first word in a sentence should be capitalized. Should I tell her the machine is defective? Hmm, maybe it's part of the test to see how much ingenuity I've got. *I'll just show them.* I pick up my pen and roll the paper up a bit and turn the little *t* into an uppercase *T*. There. I roll the paper back down.

Next, *h*. Where is—oh, there it is, just under and over from the *T* that isn't a real capital *T*. So the *H* must be a little *h*. I push it down with energy. Voila. Except it's not quite in line with the other letter. Maybe she won't notice. Now the *e*. That takes a little time.

The door opens, and in two steps, she's standing at my shoulder. "All right, let's see how you've d—" Her eyes move from the typewriter to me. "That's all you got? Have you *ever* typed before?"

I sigh, dropping my hands into the lap of my skirt. "No, I'm an actress—a ventriloquist in vaudeville. But I've got to find a job. Here."

She shakes her head. "Not *here*. You have no skills for here."

I'm far from an egocentric diva, but this has been a huge lesson in humility. Swallowing a lump in my throat the size of Main Street's cobblestones, I look up at her. "Do you have any suggestions for me?"

A slight smile changes her expression from I-can't-believe-this-rube to one of sympathy. "Try Venable's General Store. I heard they're looking for a clerk."

"Thank you." I pick up my handbag and leave with as much of my pride intact as I'm able. I have a new respect for office workers. Who knew it could be so hard? Sure, I can face an angry audience and soon have them laughing and even applauding. But I can't do anything practical.

I lean against the wall in the hallway outside the office, gathering my wits. In my head, the senator's words echo. *"You'll never amount to anything worth anyone's time."*

"Cora?" Martha Anne's soft voice draws my eyes from the floor. "Are you all right, sugar?"

What's she doing—oh, right. She works here. I blow out a sigh. "I'm a total flop as a secretary. Why I thought I could bluff my way through that"—I gesture back at the office door—"I don't know. Desperation, maybe?"

My dear friend links arms with me. "Come on. Let's grab dinner. My treat."

Chapter 6

Monday afternoon, November 4, 1929

Since Martha Anne and I forewent dessert following the famous macaroni and cheese at the City Cafe, my wounded pride demands a salving slice of Pearl's sweet potato pie. After resting my bicycle against the side of the garage, I hurry to the kitchen. Pearl and Aunt Clara stand side by side at the counter. Pearl squints at whatever it is my aunt holds before her. They look up when I open the back door.

"Pearl, do we have any sweet tater pie left?" I pull off my beret and toss it on the table, then pick up the coffeepot sitting on the stove's reservoir. Changing my mind, I set the pot down and go to the refrigerator for a bottle of cold Co-cola. It soothes the tickle in my throat the best. "What are you two looking at?"

Aunt Clara points to a magazine article about cookies. A bowl rests on the counter between them.

"Are we entertaining?" Visions of dollar bills with little flapping wings flying out the window obscure the recipe.

With a frown, Pearl hands me a plate with my pie. "Miss Fitzie is havin' that charlatan, Madam Tolvaj, in."

"Who is she? And why is she a charlatan?"

Aunt Clara signs, "Your mother heard about her from Blanche Longstreet."

"Okay. Uh, who is Blanche?"

"You don't remember the biggest gossip in town?" Pearl breaks an egg into the bowl. "You know, the telephone operator."

"Oh, right. I remember. She listens in on conversations." I also remember she got me into hot water when Martha Anne and I giggled on the phone about a midnight swim—sans swimsuits—in the Chattahoochee. I think we were about fourteen at the time. Fitzie thought it was funny and just a prank. It was the senator who raged about what it could do to his image.

Aunt Clara signs, "Fitzie listens in on the party line. That's how she heard about her."

"I get all that, but why is this Madam Tolvaj a charlatan?"

Pearl lifts her hand, the rolling pin threatening any apostates. "Dat woman claims to be a medium. Last year, when Miss Fitzie heard she was doin' one of them séances at Miz Teague's house, your mama called Miz Teague and asked to be invited. Don' want no mediums in this house. Mmm-mmm. Bad bizness." Her rolling pin returns to its dough with a resounding thump.

Something still doesn't add up. "Why is Fitzie having her over here?"

Aunt Clara signs, "To hold a séance. She refuses to believe the money is all gone."

Oh, sweet mercy. What will Pearl do to the cookies?

I shall attend Fitzie's gathering tonight to keep an eye on things. After slipping on my stockings, I slide the dress over my head. Its soft materials, silk and chiffon, are cool against my skin. I move to the full-length mirror and smile. Peacock-blue suits me. The back dips dangerously close to my waist. The handkerchief skirt ends in different-length points against my calves and ankles. While I may be rather plain, my gown is the berries. I pass my own inspection.

I'm halfway down the stairs when Pearl plunks a large, painted vase of fresh yellow, white, and apricot snapdragons, with a few stalks of goldenrod, in the center of the entry hall table. She's not happy about tonight. Not one bit.

She looks up. "Ah'm glad you're goin' to keep an eye on your mama, Miss Cora. I've said it before, this be bad bizness." Shaking her head, she returns to the kitchen.

I can't resist plucking off one of the snapdragon blooms. Martha Anne and I used to play with them when we were little, pinching them onto each other's nose. One of these little blooms was my first dummy. I'd pinch the blossom so it opened and closed with the syllables I spoke. I can still hear my friend's shrieks and giggles.

Fitzie's humming draws my gaze upward to the landing. Her eyes sparkle. In her hand is a fan with a scene painted on it. When she gets close, I realize the painting is her, wearing the same kimono jacket over the black lounging pajamas that she wears now. She steps off the last tread and spins to give me the whole effect of her outfit.

"Lovely, Fitzie. You look very glamorous."

"Yes, well, I want the senator to see what he gave up by his dastardly deed." Her infectious laughter echoes off the high ceiling. She glides to the round table and adjusts the vase. "You, my darling, look lovely. I don't know why the senator ever said you were plain. You are most decidedly not. Are the refreshments in the front parlor yet?"

Front parlor? I bite back a chuckle. We used to have a ladies' parlor and a men's smoking room. Now it's the front parlor and an empty room. I have no idea what she plans for the former smoking room. It still stinks of the senator's and his cronies' cigars, their power plays, and his duplicity.

"I don't know. I only came down a minute before you."

She links arms with me. "Then let's go see."

In the parlor, a round table sits in the center of the room, its tablecloth touching the floor. The long, narrow table that normally stands behind the davenport has been moved to the wall. An embroidered runner tops it, and dessert plates are to one side. As of yet, the cookies haven't appeared. A bottle of Madeira is surrounded by small, tulip-shaped wine glasses.

Pearl shuffles into the room with a corkscrew and proceeds to uncork the wine. She pours a tiny bit into a glass and offers it to Fitzie, who sniffs, tastes, and then nods her approval.

I fold my arms, considering her actions. "Do you know what you're doing, or are you merely copying the senator?"

Her laughter reminds me of faerie bells. She puts down the glass. "You caught me. I don't know much about it, but I would know if it's turned. This is from his 'private collection.' I take distinct pleasure in raiding it."

I'm unable to stop the laugh escaping through my nose. "Bravo, Fitzie. Pearl, what are you doing?"

She's bent over, one hand clutching the edge of the tablecloth, peering beneath it. A glower darkens her features when she straightens. "I's making sure there's no ghosts hiding under there." She drops the cloth and leaves the room. For her large size, she sure moves when she wants to.

I lift my eyebrows. "I thought she doesn't believe in ghosts."

Fitzie waves a dismissive hand. "Oh, she believes well enough to have our porch ceiling freshly painted every year before the cold sets in. But she also believes Madam Tolvaj is a fake. She isn't."

A shiver rattles my shoulders. "Does she use a crystal ball? Or cards?"

"Nothing like that. That's show business. Well, the cards aren't, but no crystal ball."

Fitzie crosses to the window. I can wait. She'll finish when she's ready. She peeks through the lace curtain, then turns around. "I saw her call up the spirit of Anna Teague's son. Mrs. Teague claims their son warned him about the stock market crash in one of the séances. Mr. Teague sold all his stock just in time. The night I was there, Mrs. Teague asked her son about a suitor for his sister."

The hairs on my neck stand up. "Doesn't it scare you, dabbling in the spirit world?"

The doorbell interrupts us. Pearl appears from the kitchen, scowling. From the hallway, Aunt Clara saunters toward the door, reading her manuscript, a pencil perched over one ear beneath a chartreuse beret. Fitzie glides into the hall, shooing them both away. "I'll get it."

"Don' know what's happenin' in this family," Pearl mutters on her way to the kitchen. The moment she disappears, Fitzie opens the door.

"Madam Tolvaj, I'm delighted to see you." Fitzie steps back, pulling the door open wide. "Please, come in."

The woman is a wonder to behold. Tall and so skinny, if she turns sideways and sticks out her tongue, she'll look like one of those new-fangled zippers I read about. Her salt-and-pepper hair is braided into two coils sitting on her ears like earmuffs, book-ending a shelf of curly bangs. There are so many colors in the skirt swirling around her ankles, I can neither begin to count them nor choose a dominant one. The design on the material is either Oriental or from some Eastern European country. It's intriguing, but I can't see it all for her wool, Scottish-plaid shawl. A turban-style hat wraps her head above the coils, with a large ruby—paste, in my estimation—residing off-center.

With a shake of her shoulders, the shawl slides down her arms, landing obediently into her hands. Its absence reveals a brilliant blue vest with sequined diamond patterns down the front. I've seen a lot of strange sights in vaudeville, but I've never seen a more colorful human being.

She holds the shawl out, and Aunt Clara takes it to the coat tree beside the door. She removes her beret and adds it to the tree. She's done writing for the evening.

Fitzie takes the woman's hand. "Please, come into the parlor, and we'll have a glass of wine before we begin. Pearl?" She tosses the name over her shoulder. "Please bring in the cookies."

Aunt Clara and I exchange glances. I don't know if she finds this amusing, but I certainly do. I follow Fitzie and Madam Tolvaj to the parlor doorway, where she stops.

Fitzie's brows dip. "Is something wrong?"

"No, no. I'm merely checking for harmonious mystique."

For *what?*

She nods at the ceiling and glides into the parlor humming, where she proceeds to examine everything within the room. Is she casing the joint or looking for something none of us can see? She stops suddenly, whirls, and like a skiff catching the wind, sails across the hardwood floor to me.

"My dear, you look lovely."

Fitzie hurries over. "Forgive me, I didn't introduce my daughter. This is Cora."

Madam Tolvaj smiles and takes my hand, lifting my arm out to the side and scrutinizing my gown. "Absolutely beautiful." She tucks my hand into the crook of her arm and leads me to the settee. I glance behind me at Aunt Clara and Fitzie, who—judging by the slight shaking of shoulders—are stifling their amusement.

Madam Tolvaj perches on the settee and pats the cushion beside her. "Tell me about the Palace Theatre. I saw you there last year, you know." She nods at Fitzie, who has settled in a wingback chair. "I had just met your mother, who told me about you. Since I was traveling to New York, I added a matinee to my agenda." She clasps her hands beneath her hawkish nose. "You were wonderful. So talented."

"Thank you." I can't think of a thing to say beyond banalities. What does one ask a medium? *How are your ghostly friends?* A snicker threatens to escape through my nose. I sniff it back and smile.

Thankfully, Pearl enters with the plate of cookies. She sets it on the table and pours Madeira into each glass, then leaves.

I rise. "Would you care for some refreshments?"

Madam Tolvaj eyes the cookies. "Is there chocolate in them?"

I cross to the table and peer at the plate. "No, they appear to be sugar cookies."

"Oh, good. Chocolate makes me belch. Why, I don't know. You may give me two. And a glass of Madeira, thank you."

After serving her, I pick up a glass of wine and rejoin her. I want to hear more about this woman, who fancies herself—at least, I hope it's just a fancy—a clairvoyant. Aunt Clara selects a glass of wine and a single cookie. Nibbling the confection, my aunt leans against the doorjamb. Fitzie holds a glass of wine, while Madam Medium chatters on about who she knows and who she's called up lately.

Suddenly, Madam Medium—I can't help but think of her that way—sets her glass on the coffee table and jumps up. She begins a strange little dance, bending and swaying around the room. Little hops from foot to foot intersperse the swaying. Fitzie is enraptured by the display, while Aunt Clara stares wide-eyed.

The medium stops mid-step. She cocks her head, listening. For what, I don't know. What I do know is that she puts on a good show.

Her bejeweled fingers beckon us near. "Come, come. The time is right. To the table. Hands flat on its top."

She herds us to the round table. My stomach is in knots now. I'm not sure I want to hear the senator speak to us, if, indeed, she's for real. My gaze moves from the medium to my mother, who leans forward in rapt concentration.

Aunt Clara nudges me, and we sit, laying our hands on the tabletop. Madam closes her eyes and hums a little tune I don't recognize. "My familiar likes this Hungarian lullaby." She hums some more, then stops. "Hermione? Are you there, dearest?"

The table bumps. I nearly scream and Aunt Clara jumps up. Fitzie shushes us. "Don't scare Hermione away."

Us? Scare a ghost? That's a good one. I'll bet tomorrow's breakfast, the madam bumped the table herself. Aunt Clara takes her seat, sucking in her lower lip, while I keep one eye on the medium.

"Dear?" Madam Tolvaj has her eyes closed and her head tilted back so far, I can see up her nose. "Will you please ask Senator Fitzgerald where he hid his money?" A frown pulls her entire face downward. "What do you mean, *no*? Surely you can ask him … oh. Are you sure?" She sighs. "Well, keep after him. Contact me when you have an answer."

She breathes out another deep sigh and opens her eyes.

"Well?" Fitzie asks, her face rosy. I lay my hand on her arm. Her muscles are taut.

"I'm sorry, my dear. Apparently, the senator isn't forthcoming with any information. Hermione thinks it's because he's so newly arrived that he doesn't trust her yet."

Fitzie smacks her hands on the table and pushes herself up. "How like him. Well, we won't allow him to rest in any form of peace until he gives up the secret. Madam Tolvaj, we shall try again next week."

While Fitzie pays Madam Medium and sees her to the door, I take Aunt Clara's arm and pull her to the back of the parlor. "I give credence to ghosts as much as the next Southerner, but I'm on Pearl's side when it comes to believing in Madam Tolvaj. I'll bet it was her knee that bumped the table. But I must say, she provides an entertaining evening. Maybe, if Fitzie will let me, I'll invite some of the girls next week."

Maybe Madam Tolvaj can tell Martha Anne if she'll win her Ethan.

Chapter 7

Wednesday, November 6, 1929

IT'S SIX-FORTY, AND THE SUN is climbing above the horizon—or would be if the skies weren't overcast. Today, my sights are set on a job with Oscar at his hash house. I step out the door to the porch, and a clap of thunder greets me. The skies open up, breaking loose a downpour. This better not be a harbinger of my day. I turn back into the house.

A bleary-eyed Fitzie shuffles into the foyer with her coffee cup balancing on its saucer.

"Late night?" I pull an umbrella from the stand by the front door.

"Uh-huh. Played bridge with the girls."

Her "girls" are all middle-aged women, but I guess since they went to school together, they'll always remain "the girls."

"Did you win?"

She glances at me and frowns. "I lost a dollar." Her gaze slides to the ceiling, and she wrinkles her nose. "I've got to find that money the senator hid."

"Why are you so sure he hid it? Aunt Clara says he lost it in the stock market."

"He did, but that wasn't all there was. I just know it." Fitzie empties her cup and heads toward the kitchen, then stops, turning back toward me. "Where are you off to? And how did your interviews go yesterday?"

I have to clear my throat before I can answer. "I was doing great, reciting all the items and prices I know they stock at Hosch's Five and Dime. Unfortunately, Melvina asked me to ring up a sale. She apparently expected me to know how to work a cash register without any training." I pick up my clutch bag. "I've given up, Fitzie. I'm on my way to beg Oscar to hire me as a waitress. He told Trudie he would if I ran out of luck, and I've surely done that." The foyer brightens with a flash of lightning. "I'm afraid I'm going to have to take the car. It's pouring."

"Oh dear." She crosses to the window and peers out. "That does look nasty. You can take it. I don't have anything planned. And I know your aunt is working on a new mystery. It's a bit of an exposé." Fitzie rolls her eyes.

I can't help laughing. "I just hope it doesn't get her into trouble. Do you suppose someone might try to sue her?"

Fitzie snorts and coffee shoots out her nose. "For what? Unless we find the senator's money, we're penniless." She wipes her chin. "Unless, of course, she sells this new book, but even then, we don't know what she'll get."

I won't depend on my aunt's book royalties. I've *got* to find something. "I have to go. Hopefully, I won't see you until late this afternoon." I raise my hand with crossed fingers.

Fitzie crosses hers in reply and, still smiling, wanders into the kitchen.

The drive to Buford is a bit precarious with the car slipping and sliding in the mud. I'm thankful for the driving lessons I got from sweet old Mr. Stephens in New York. Teaching me to drive on ice is close enough to Georgia mud. That training keeps me out of the ditches, at least.

I navigate the lower end of Main Street. Three blocks from the tannery, there are more businesses here. Old brick buildings abut wooden ones. Oscar's is an old livery stable, converted to a diner thirty-five years ago. After I park the Dodge nearby, I inhale a deep breath to calm my nerves over the coming humiliation of failing to obtain yet another job.

"Confidence, girl," I tell myself and push open the door to Oscar's diner.

The restaurant is small, with five booths and ten counter stools. The floor is a nondescript tan linoleum with red speckles—unless that's catsup. Trudie once told me the color was chosen to hide dropped bits of food until the floor could be mopped. A Coca-Cola poster hangs on one wall next to a list of that week's ice cream flavors. Oscar makes it himself, usually two flavors. This week, it's chocolate and vanilla. In the summer, he makes strawberry and peach.

He's behind the counter at the stove's grill, where he slaps a slice of ham next to some eggs. A large pot sits on one burner. Judging from the spicy aroma, it's chili, simmering for the dinner crowd at noon.

Thankfully, there are only two tables with customers. Trudie—looking perky in her black-and-white uniform and carrying a coffeepot and a handful of menus—waves and motions me to the back booth. I take a seat and peer closely at a particularly large speck on the floor by my chair leg. Sure enough, it's bacon. With the toe of my shoe, I slide it under the table and out of sight.

Trudie sets a cup of coffee in front of me, then nods toward a table to my left. Harvey and Ollie Bailey wave at her. "I'll be just a sec." She bustles away.

The Baileys smile at her when she hands them the menus. They look the same as they did when I left Sugar Hill. I used to love to go into their cabinet shop. It smelled of sawdust and beeswax. They live behind the shop, and Miss Ollie—short for Olive—always had freshly baked cookies for any children who happened to come in. The boys would get scraps of wood to whittle.

Ollie spies me and waves. A moment later, she sits down across from me. "I heard you were back home, sugar. It's wonderful to see you. Are you home for good? You'll have to stop by for a cookie."

"My plans are kind of open right now, Miss Ollie. As soon as the proverbial dust settles for Fitzie, I'd like to go back. I have—" I stop. I *had* a contract, but in theatre, you never know. A new talent comes along, and you're last week's leftovers. "But tell me how you and Mister Harvey have been."

"Fine as frog's hair, sugar. Well, except for a little more arthritis." She burps. "And dyspepsia—excuse me. Harvey's gout comes and goes. Seems to get worse around holidays. He had a kidney stone a month ago that threw him to the floor in pain." Her gaze slides to her husband. Despite her very honest comment, the love shining in her eyes is so sweet.

"Oh my. Uh, Miss Ollie, I believe Trudie isn't sure where to deliver your orange juice."

Her gaze shifts to Trudie, then zips back to me. "Ah. Thank you, dear. Well, don't forget to drop in and get that cookie." The front door opens, and Ollie waves at the newcomer. "Hello, Blanche. Come join Harvey and me. And see who's home?" She points to me, then sits with Harvey.

Blanche gives me a frank once-over, making me feel like the menu. Then she grins and joins the Baileys. Boy howdy, by noon, everyone within a ten-mile radius will know I'm home.

Trudie hands Blanche a menu, then crooks a finger at me. "Come on into the back."

I pick up my now-empty coffee cup and follow her. I've never been in the back at Oscar's. Inside the swinging door, I stop. It's smaller than I'd imagined. Our kitchen at home is larger. How do Oscar and Trudie manage?

To my left along one wall are two deep sinks in a soapstone counter. One is stacked with dirty dishes. On the other side of the room stands a long table and some shelves above it holding food supplies. There's a metal door in the back wall. I wonder if it's one of those walk-in coolers I've heard about but never seen.

Trudie gestures with a dishrag. "If you want to start right now, you can wash dishes. Our dishwasher came in drunk this morning, and Daddy fired him." She winces. "Look, I know it's about as low as you can get, but—"

It sure is. Ha. If my theatre friends could see me now. The princess of vaudeville reduced to washing dishes in a hash house. I can only hope that Walter Winchell doesn't find out about it.

"It's fine. I'm fine. I can wash dishes." I shoo her away. "Go do what you do."

"Okay. Bring the first sink-full out front when you're done. We need them."

Trudie returns to the diner, and I face a sink of cold, greasy water. Ick. I straighten my shoulders and think of what I need—soap powder, I know that much. So, where is it? I survey what's on the shelves. A box of soap flakes sits above the basins. I glance over my shoulder. No one's here to help me.

Well, if I'm going to wash dishes, at least it will be in warm water. I hope that's okay. I don't think I've ever washed a dish in my life. At home, Pearl does it. Even in New York, the owner of the boarding house does them. My hand hovers over the sinks for a moment. If I must, I must.

Cringing, I plunge in, find the plug beneath the pile of plates, and give it a yank. I quickly remove my grease-covered hand. The gray water swirls around, and after a couple of minutes, the sink is empty except for the dishes.

Now, to get some hot water. First, I replace the plug. At the end of the counter stands a small stove with a water reservoir. Another full pot of water sits on the burner. Why doesn't Oscar have an automatic gas hot water heater? It sure would make life easier for them. I find a match, turn the gas on, and light the burner.

While that pot heats, I take a smaller bucket and pull piping hot water from the reservoir, filling the sink halfway. I add soap flakes and just enough cold water so I won't get burned. The rinsing sink can remain cold.

"See?" I say to the empty room. "I'm not without common sense." I take up the rag and attack the pile in the sink. I wash, rinse, and set each one in a large dish drain.

A coughing spasm hits, nearly choking me. I grab a glass from the dish drain, fill it with cold water, and gulp it down. I've got to figure out why I keep coughing. I don't feel sick. I'll see if Fitzie has any ideas tonight.

When I'm sure I'm not going to cough again, I wash my hands. After I dry the dishes, I stack them on an empty tray and then hoist it onto my shoulder like I've seen busboys do.

Trudie looks over her shoulder when I push through the swinging door. "Oh, good, you've got some done."

While she unloads the tray, I send my gaze around the diner. Another table and a booth are occupied. Business appears to be good.

"Cora?" With a wry smile, Trudie points to a tub of dirty dishes. "Those are waiting for you."

Withholding an eye-roll, I smile, pick it up, and return to the back room. I'm beginning to see why that dishwasher drank. It's a never-ending task. I first toss the flatware into the depths of the sink, followed by the rest of the dishes. When this lot is dry, I take them out front.

Goodness, the place is hopping. Booth by booth, stool by stool, all chatter stops when the occupants see me. I smile hello to a couple of people and deposit the dishes on the shelves with their mates. Oscar nods and mouths a *thank you* as he flips a flapjack.

This routine continues throughout the morning. By noon, there isn't a place to sit in the diner. "Trudie, I had no idea you were so busy."

Oscar gives me an odd look, his lips thin and tight. I pick up yet another tub of dirty dishes. Strange, it's all coffee cups and no plates. I take them to the back and wash them. When I return to the front, Alice Farnham leans on the counter. The instant she sees me, she snickers.

"My, my, my. How the mighty have fallen."

I didn't care for her when we were in the fourth grade, and I don't think I'll change my opinion anytime soon. For some reason, she has always had it in for me. But before I can think of a reply, Trudie steps between us.

"Here's your bill, Alice. It's forty-five cents." Trudie holds out her hand for the money. "And some people aren't too proud to work. Unlike others I know."

What's that about?

"Well, I never."

"No, I'm sure you haven't." Trudie taps a finger in her open palm, a reminder to pay. Alice drops the money on the counter and leaves with her nose so high in the air, if it were still raining, she'd be in danger of drowning.

As soon as the door closes behind her, a customer named Albert walks over to me. He's got a connection to the tannery, being one of the Bona Allen relatives, but I can't remember his last name or how he fits into the family.

"Hey, Cora. I heard you were back home." He drops onto a stool. "I'd love to hear about your life in vaudeville."

"Vaudeville? Were you in vaudeville?" a curly-headed man asks.

"She sure is," Albert replies. "She's a headliner."

"Whassat?" A blonde I've never seen before drapes herself over Albert's shoulder.

A bearded man joins them at the counter, and Florence Meyer's daughter, Dottie, plops down beside him. All five stare at me.

"What do you do?" asks the bearded fellow.

Albert doesn't give me a chance. "She's a ventriloquist. She can *throw* her voice. That's making it sound like it's coming across the room instead of from her."

Blondie runs back to her friends. "Did y'all hear that? She's a movie star."

For a moment, I bask in the acknowledgment of my talent. Then Oscar turns away from the grill he was scrapping, his spatula held aloft in one hand. "Y'all finished jawin'? Either order a meal or move along."

Reality sets in. Alice is right. By what people can see, I've fallen a long way. I can only pray it's temporary.

Chapter 8

Friday morning, November 8, 1929

WHEN I ARRIVE AT THE diner, I park my bicycle behind it, next to Oscar's truck. Out front, there is a line of people waiting to get in. It's a good thing Oscar got a new dishwasher and promoted me to waitress. The place has been filled to capacity the last two days, but a lot of people only order coffee and take up space chatting.

I knock on the back door, and after a moment, Trudie unlocks it. I follow her to the front, where she opens the front door a mere inch. To the waiting crowd, she calls, "Y'all are early this morning. Give us five minutes, then we'll open." She secures the lock again. "You seem to be quite the draw."

"Is that good?" I deposit my handbag under the counter where Trudie keeps hers. When she doesn't answer, I straighten and turn around. Oscar leans against the grill, his arms crossed. He gives a tight nod of his head. The grill isn't sizzling. There's nothing on it. He usually has the bacon or ham on the hot grill by the time they open. I glance between them. "Is something wrong? Have *I* done anything wrong?"

Trudie sighs. "No, you haven't done anything wrong. Let's just hope customers order more than coffee today."

By noon, it's obvious people are only coming in to stare at me.

"Cora?" Oscar cocks his head toward the back room. I get his meaning and follow him.

"Cora, girl, you're a good worker, but I'm gonna have to let you go. People are just here to gawk at you. They don't eat anything. My customers who *do* eat can't get in." He rests a hand on my shoulder. "You understand it's not personal, right?"

My hopes fall to the floor along with my confidence, and I hear the senator mocking me. *Failed again. I knew you would.*

But Oscar's eyes plead with me to understand. I've loved Trudie's daddy since I was a little girl, so I kiss his weathered, bristly cheek.

"I get it. I'm sorry, though. It was kind of fun." I retrieve my handbag and slip out the back door.

Now what?

I climb on my bike and pedal home. Each turn of the wheels reminds me I have no marketable skills. What a pickle. There has to be some way to keep the roof over our heads and food on the table. There *has* to be.

When I walk in the front door, the foyer floor is covered with an old tarp. Blue and gold strips of torn, wet paper lay on top. Fitzie lifts a large sponge from a bucket and squeezes it, releasing excess water, then splats it against the wallpaper in the foyer, muttering the entire time about "the pretentious old windbag." She and Pearl have a good amount of the paper off one side already.

"I thought you were going to wait for me." I close the front door and remove my hat and gloves. "Give me five minutes to change, and I'll skedaddle back to help."

Fitzie glances over her shoulder, water running down her upraised arm. "Thank you, dear. Why are you home so early?"

"Let me get out of these clothes, and I'll tell you about it." Delaying the humiliation, I run upstairs to my bedroom.

A few minutes later, dressed in denim overalls, a shirt, and a bandana turban, I look like a scarecrow. Back downstairs, in the bucket Fitzie points to, is another sponge.

"Don't squeeze it too dry or it won't do its job," she warns. "And prepare to get wet." Her nose wrinkles charmingly. "Now, tell me about Oscar's."

I squeeze some of the water from the sponge and start soaking the wall. "The other day—"

"No, no." Fitzie reaches over and pulls my hand away from the wall. "Don't leave the sponge on too long, or it will loosen the plaster too. Move it around, and soon you'll feel the paper move."

"Okay." I do as she instructs, although tepid water runs down my arm. "This morning, my pride took a huge hit. Here I thought I was a great draw for Oscar." I grimace. "It turns out all those people were just coming in to stare at me."

Pearl follows my sponging with her scraper. "Mo' water up here, Miss Cora." She points above my head.

Dipping, squeezing, and sponging gets more water on me than the wall. "Anyway, none of those people ordered any food. They took up space drinking coffee, and his regular customers who normally order food couldn't get a place to sit." I drop my arms to my sides. "I got fired this morning. I don't know what we're going to do."

Fitzie dips her sponge in the water. "Don't worry, sugar-pie. Madam Tolvaj will get the senator to tell us where he hid the money." She lowers her voice to a whisper. "He always was a vindictive old goat. Never got over me relegating that moose head to the garage. But I truly hope she can trick him into telling."

Pearl's muttering hushes Fitzie, and she returns to her work on the wall.

We scrub in silence until the burning in my muscles forces me to lower my arms. "How did Aunt Clara get out of helping with this?"

"It's her day to volunteer at the hospital."

"What does she do there?"

Fitzie drops her sponge in the bucket and rubs her arms. "Believe it or not, she works in the laundry, washing bed linens."

My mind reels. "My dignified aunt washes dirty bedsheets?" I glance at Pearl. "I thought the hospital hired coloreds for laundry work."

Pearl harrumphs. "Some coloreds think they's too highborn to wash bedsheets."

"And Aunt Clara doesn't?"

Pearl nods, her face solemn. Fitzie winks. "By volunteering, my sister thinks she can earn points for heaven to make up for her stubborn ways."

Pearl pushes her scraper under the loosened paper. I move to the next panel. We work in comfortable silence and are nearing the last section of this wall when the doorbell rings, startling us.

I glance at Fitzie. "Are we expecting company?"

She picks bits of soggy wallpaper from the front of her shirt. "I certainly hope not. We're not ready to receive anyone."

Pearl opens the door, and Boone steps inside. Mortified at my appearance, I want to hide. Why does he have to come calling when I look like this?

He pulls off his cap. "Afternoon, ladies. Hey, Cora. I, uh, didn't realize I'd be interrupting your work. Can I help?"

His eyes hold a look of expectancy. Hopefulness. Why? Men don't like to do stuff like this. Do they? No, they don't. There has to be another reason. But before I can say no, Fitzie turns a sparkling smile on him.

"How wonderful." She hands him her sponge and leaves the room. I want to strangle her.

I turn a weak smile on him. "Uh, thanks, but you don't have to." I reach up to untie the knot on the bandana.

"But I do. I can't resist your charming outfit. Very fetching. I think you'll start a new fashion trend with the bandana."

At first, all I can do is gape at him. I glance down at my attire, and Boone snorts. That starts me laughing. I wrinkle my nose at him and leave the turban on, then point to the bucket.

"If you insist, get to it." I turn back to the wall.

Pearl's eyes bounce between us, her grin wide. Without a word, she lets her scraper fall onto the drop cloth and disappears down the hallway. Oh, I hope she's going to bring us sweet tea. My throat is parched.

I bend to wet my sponge again. "Why aren't you at work?"

"And miss this fashion show?"

"Seriously."

"Okay, to be honest, things are a bit slow right now." He dips his sponge and attacks a section next to mine. "So I decided to take the afternoon off instead of falling asleep at my desk."

The paper he's soaking loosens, so I pick up the scraper Pearl abandoned. I push the blade against the wall, starting at the baseboard. I continue to move upward, never raising the tool from the surface. Long kite-tails of obnoxious blue and gold stripes curl around my arm.

"You look as though you're enjoying this. Maybe there's a career here for you." Boone's open grin reveals a chipped front tooth I don't remember seeing before. It's a small chip and doesn't detract from his good looks. Actually, it's rather endearing.

I blink and turn my gaze back to the wall. "Not likely. But I despise this pretentious paper. Always have."

"Why's that?"

I shake my arm to release the trailings of paper entangling it. The end slaps against my ankle. Boone's fingers brush my arm when he tugs the strip, and a curious shiver slides down my spine.

"Uh … why's what?"

"I said, why do you hate this paper?"

"I don't like things that are done just to impress people. Everything the senator did was to impress or intimidate."

"Hmm."

What does he mean, *hmm*? I glance at him, but he's intent on squeezing his sponge and says no more. I push the scraper a little too hard and gouge the plaster. "Applesauce."

Boone smiles. "Don't worry about that. I can fix it before I leave. I've got dry plaster powder in my truck. Just mark it for me."

I tear off a small piece of butcher paper, wet it, and stick it on the wall to mark the plaster for repair.

We continue working in a comfortable silence. Which is new. Other than fellow vaudevillians—and they don't count—I've never spent enough time with any man to feel at ease. Glancing sidelong at him, I find I rather like it. I may have to rethink my stand on romance. Boone grins at me while he dips the sponge in the bucket, and my cheeks grow warm. I like his smile. It goes all the way to his eyes.

We're almost to the last section when Fitzie walks in and pushes the button in the foyer.

I blink at the brightness. "Oh, when did it get so late?"

She smirks. "Boone, would y'all like to stay for a bite of supper with us? We're not cleaning up, just 'as-you-are' soup and sandwiches."

Glancing down at little bits of wallpaper stuck to his pants, he makes a vain attempt to brush them off, then shrugs and grins. "Sure, sounds ducky."

"We can finish this after we eat." We traipse into the dining room, where the aroma of Pearl's hambone and bean soup replaces wet paper and plaster. A platter containing a pile of pimento cheese sandwiches sits in the center of the table.

After asking the blessing, Boone keeps us entertained with stories throughout supper. And I'm finding my rule about falling for a guy in jeopardy.

I don't want to admit my muscles are tight, but scraping wallpaper is far different than operating a ventriloquist's dummy. I finally resort to using a short stepladder to reach higher than my shoulder.

"Hey, Cora, come here. Look at this." Boone stops sponging the wall.

With an inward groan at moving at all, I climb down. "What's wrong?"

He drops his sponge in the bucket. "I think there's something under the paper here."

"Where?"

"Here." He points to a spot.

I stare at the general area where he's pointing, then I see it. A square, raised outline, barely visible. I'm thinking *so what* when Boone takes the scraper from me and gently peels back the wet paper to reveal a torn piece of what appears to be the senator's stationery. Despite my disdain for the man who fathered me, I find myself curious.

"My mama should see this." I call over my shoulder. "Fitzie?"

She pokes her head out of the parlor door. "You need me?"

I motion to her. "Come see this. Boone found something under the wallpaper."

She scurries over. "Oh! Maybe it tells where Alexander hid the money. I wonder why Madam Tolvaj didn't know about this."

Boone peers at her, a small frown crinkling his brow. Then, he carefully removes the stationery from the wall and hands it to her. Just as carefully, she lifts a folded corner and stares at the note. I glance at Boone and cross my fingers. A moment later, she wads up the scrap and throws it to the floor with a scowl.

"Not one mention of where he hid the money, just that stupid mine. If he thinks this is funny, he's sadly mistaken. There's no way I'll go into that hole in the ground, and I refuse to let him rest in peace until he tells me."

Boone's eyebrows shoot upwards. I give a small shake of my head to warn him. After Fitzie leaves, I chuckle. "She's a true Southerner and believes in her ghosts."

"You don't?"

"That jury's still out. I don't *dis*believe. Let's leave it at that."

I retrieve the note, smoothing it while trying not to tear the wet paper. It's not the senator's scrawled handwriting. This is more straight-up-and-down and half printed. Most of it is blurred from the moisture in the wallpaper.

"Sto—money—map hid—mine—not—safe."

The rest is blurred. What can it mean?

"Cora?"

I hand him the scrap.

The furrow between his brows deepens. "Do you think it's money from stocks?"

"I have no earthly idea."

He reads the note again. "I knew there were old gold mines around here, but I didn't know your family owned one."

"I'd heard stories but thought they were just that. Stories. He'd always been a state senator as long as I can remember."

Boone hands me the note. "Do you know where it is?"

"The mine?"

"Yeah. Why not take a look at it? Maybe that's the 'job' you can do." He nudges me with his elbow. "It's got to be better than Melvina's cash register or Oscar's greasy dishwater."

He's got a point, and it makes me chuckle. Then my laughter dies.

"You might be onto something. Although I don't know a thing about gold mining. I'll ask Fitzie where it is." Then something else dawns on me. "Uh, there's another slight problem."

"What's that?"

"I'm claustrophobic."

Chapter 9

HANDS ON HER HIPS AS she stands by the mahogany sideboard, Fitzie stares at me, aghast. "You can't be serious, Cora."

I lay my knife on my plate and fork a bite of scrambled egg. "Why not? I've failed at everything else." Out of my own mouth come the senator's words. I shove the eggs in my mouth to shush him. "There isn't much money left, you know. What if I find gold? Boone says the other mine owners are finding enough to live off."

Shaking her head, she picks up the coffeepot and pours herself a cup before sitting at the table. "You're more likely to find pneumonia. Besides, Madam Tolvaj is coming tonight. We don't need that old mine. We'll find the money here in the house. I remembered something the senator said once that might make him reveal where he hid it. And I've invited Hattie and Glenice Jo to join us."

Aunt Clara wanders into the dining room, manuscript rolled beneath one arm, and plants a kiss on my cheek.

"Good morning." I tip my head up to get a glimpse of my aunt. She nearly always has on a beret of some crazy color. It's a sign for us. When it's on, she's writing. *Do not disturb.* But this morning, there's no beret.

Fitzie pushes the cream pitcher toward Aunt Clara. The day after the senator's funeral, my aunt resurrected "the old cow jug." I've always loved it, but his lordship wouldn't have it on the table. Thank goodness, Pearl saved it from the incinerator.

Aunt Clara winks when she picks up the tiny cow and adds cream to her coffee.

When Clara sets down the creamer, Fitzie rests her chin on her hand, looking straight at her sister. "Cora thinks she's going to reopen the senator's gold mine."

Aunt Clara's eyebrows shoot up to nearly meet her hairline.

"That was my reaction too." Her disapproving gaze swings to fix on me. "I don't think it's safe, sugar-pie. Isn't there something else you can do?"

I throw my hands out. "What? I've tried every business around. Either they aren't hiring, or I don't have the skills. But it only takes hard work to mine for gold."

Right?

The entrance to the mine is claustrophobically small—less than three feet high. It's triangular and not like any gold mine entrance I've ever seen in history books. Those were tall and like a doorway, shored up with timbers. This is a hole in the ground carved out of rock, like a tiny tomb.

The mine sits in the middle of dense woods. Dry leaves and moss-covered rocks are its only neighbors. The sunlight is bright, and I have to squint as I squat outside the hole and peer into the dark, hanging onto a tree root that's dangling beside my head so I don't slip into the abyss. Just inside the opening, the ground slopes down at a forty-five-degree angle.

A shiver skims my shoulders, and my feet refuse to move. Did they make it like this to discourage people from entering? If so, it's working.

Shining the flashlight around best I can, I scan the tunnel-shaped cave, arched at the top. There are no rails for ore carts. I frown. Don't all mines have those? This doesn't look like what I expected. Not by a long shot. I have to do this, but I can't think of how. It's terrifying. My heart's about to beat itself right out of my chest.

"Are you just going to sit out here, or are you going in?" Boone's voice makes me jump and hit my head on the rock.

"Ouch." Though I see stars, a nervous giggle escapes me. What's he doing here? "You're dangerous. First, the creek." I let go of the root and rub my offended noggin. "Now this."

Poor Boone. Dressed in denim pants and a red-checkered shirt, he looks like a blushing lumberjack. "I'm so sorry, Cora. I came to help you explore—not cause another accident."

He did? His sheepish grin squeezes my heart. "I'm okay, really." His gaze won't release mine. I put my hand out to steady myself on the mine's entrance. "You really want to go in with me?"

"Sure. I've always had a hankering to explore deeper inside."

A new confidence floods me like a fresh breeze. "Then let's go. Did you bring a flashlight? I only have mine."

He waves a large one. "Want me to go first?"

"I thought you'd never ask." With a relieved grin, I scoot out of his way. "It's a little creepy in there. Do you think there are any bats inside?"

Absolutely fearless, he lowers himself, feet first, through the opening. "Sure there are, but that's a good thing. They eat bugs."

Switching on my light with one hand, I follow Boone, sliding on my backside down into the mine. At least, I can stand up straight once my feet touch the floor. I take in my surroundings, sniffing the air. Ew. Who knew damp rock could smell so bad? It's musty. Dank. And a cough rattles my throat.

I shine my light around the walls. It's all rock. Not flat, but uneven like a natural cave might be—not that I've ever been in one. The colors catch my attention. I never realized there were so many. I always think of rocks being gray, but the walls have uneven layers of black, rust, peach, and white. Some places look almost pink.

It's eerily fascinating. I shiver, but more from awe and—*Wait! Where's Boone?* My breath hitches.

"Boone? Where are you?"

His flashlight beam spears me when he appears from around a corner. "Come on. Where's your sense of adventure? Don't you want to see if you can spot where the gold is?"

I plant my feet. "I want to go slowly to make sure these walls don't collapse. I don't see any wooden supports." My throat closes over a tickle, and coughing doesn't do a lot to clear it.

"Don't need 'em. This is solid granite, and I see a lot of quartz in there too. That means gold." He wiggles his eyebrows, relaxing me and making me giggle.

Boone offers his hand. "Come on. Take my hand. I won't let you get lost."

As his fingers wrap around mine, a spark zips up my arm straight to my heart.

He's only being helpful. *After all, look at you. He can have any girl in town. Why would he want you?* The senator's voice echoes in my head. I may have to change my mind about ghosts. The man haunts me. I squint into the darkness.

"Come on, Cora." Boone pulls on my hand.

My feet still refuse to move. "How can you be so sure we won't get lost? I thought you hadn't been in here."

"I never said that. When I was about fourteen, a bunch of us came in here on a dare. If I remember right, there are only one or two forks. And you never make a U-turn, so it's easy to navigate."

He turns and shines his light all around. It lands on the ceiling— and it moves.

"Eek! What's that?" They look like daddy longlegs spiders. Giant ones.

He squeezes my hand. "They won't bother you. They're cave crickets. They don't like the light, so if they move at all, they're moving toward the darkness."

"I thought you said the bats eat bugs." I give into a shudder.

"They do. However, you haven't noticed there are only a couple of small bats in here."

I shine my light at the ceiling. He's right. Huh. My heartbeat slows a bit, but I realize I'm breathless. I look behind me and see the entrance, so we haven't come far in at all. "Are you having trouble breathing in here?"

"A little. There's no air circulation to pull in fresh oxygen."

The walls close in on me. A cough threatens, but I *have* to go on. It's up to me to keep a roof over Mama's and Aunt Clara's heads, not to mention keeping us all fed.

We move ahead, shining our lights left and right, up and down. Boone stops.

"Wait here. I want to see what's through this opening."

The moment he releases my hand, panic rushes over me like a tsunami. I glue my eyes to Boone's back. He stoops down and disappears into the darkness. I can't decide whether to hurry after him or turn and flee.

"It's okay, come on in, but crouch down. The ceiling's not as high in here."

I follow his instructions, but my heart pounds against my ribs. I glance back, but there's nothing. How can the dark be so obliterating? There's a total absence of light. I don't like this. It's like being in a grave. I take a tentative step forward.

"Cora—"

My stomach clenches. "What's wrong? Are we lost?"

"No, but look at this. A large vein of quartz. If we can get this out, we can crush it and extract any gold."

I crouch and step through the low opening, shining my light where his illuminates the wall. The rock is lighter, with rust- and dark-colored veining. I touch the quartz, then notice another place where the wall is very black. I touch it and feel ... something. I shine the light on my finger. Soot.

"Why would the rock have soot on it?"

"It's carbon, I think. I've heard miners build a fire next to the wall to crack the rock. It's said that makes for faster removal. I'm not sure about that, but we can talk to Mr. Shelley or one of the other mine owners about it."

I hate to leave today with empty hands. Feels like failing. My throat closes, and I have to cough before I can speak.

"Is there any way to take a piece of the quartz and crush it like you said?" I tug at a chunk of rock.

"You didn't bring any tools."

He blurs in front of me, and I can't speak around the lump in my throat. Letting my shoulders sag, I lower my light and turn back the way we came.

Boone's hand on my elbow stops me. He pulls me into his arms. "Cora, don't cry. You didn't know all this would entail." His hand caresses my back. "Let me help you. I'll find out what you'll need."

"Why? Why would you do that?"

He lifts my chin so he's looking in my eyes. His lips are so close, I can scarcely breathe. I've never let a man near enough to kiss me.

His thumb brushes my cheek, and a tremor like ripples from a stone cast upon the water radiates from my core. His gaze lowers to my mouth, and his thumb follows, caressing my lower lip. My mouth turns dry. Slowly, he lowers his head, and his lips touch mine ever so gently. His kiss deepens, and I'm floating on a wave of strange desire. All too soon, he pulls away while my heart thrums in my ears. I can't seem to catch my breath.

As effectively as flash fire cracks the walls of a mine, his kiss creates a fissure in the wall I'd built around my heart.

"Cora? Are you okay?"

I nod, incapable of words. It was my first kiss. Every night throughout high school, I dreamed about kissing Boone. I'm glad his light is shining down and not on the sappy smile on my face.

I duck my head. I've broken my own rule about men. A little voice inside my head whispers, *You've done it now. You'll get your heart broken. Just wait and see.*

Chapter 10

Monday evening, November 11, 1929

I STAY IN MY ROOM ALL afternoon, away from prying eyes. Fitzie has amazing insight when it comes to me. She'll spot any change. With Boone's kiss lingering on my lips and in my heart, I school my thoughts as best I can.

For this evening's séance, I slip into a gown the color of champagne with black beads starting at the apex of its high waist and fanning out down the length of the skirt. It has an art deco flair I love. After a final pat to my hair, which I've finger-waved in front and pinned its length into a chignon, I descend the stairs.

I don't really know why I bother to dress up for these events. I'm convinced Madam Tolvaj is as fake as the ruby in the turban she wore last time she was here. But at least this gives me an excuse to don one of my fancy dresses from New York.

The doorbell pulls me from my musing, and I hurry downstairs. Pearl opens it to Glenice Jo and Miss Hattie.

Once they hand over their wraps, I link arms with them both. "Come into the parlor. I want to talk to you before Fitzie comes downstairs."

Always a ready conspirator, Glenice Jo eyes me and tilts her head. "Is that why y'all asked us to come early?"

Ushering them inside, I catch a whiff of Miss Hattie's gardenia cologne, followed by Glenice Jo's Chanel No. 5—a wedding gift from her late husband and reminding me of the Christmas gifts I brought with me. I breathe in its arresting fragrance.

"I've done some investigating since Madam Tolvaj was here last.

The only puzzle is how she knew about the stock market and advised Mr. Teague to sell out." I drop onto the davenport. "I don't believe she's for real, but how does one explain that?"

Miss Hattie walks around the wingback chairs. "My mother—God rest her soul—told me in a dream the year after she left this world that I needed to get rid of a roast in my icebox. I had no earthly idea why, but I threw it out." She selects a chair and gracefully lowers herself into it, crossing her legs at the ankles and raising an eyebrow at her daughter.

Glenice Jo uncrosses her legs and crosses her ankles, mirroring her mama, who smiles her approval. "Anyway, the pig got into the garbage, ate it along with the other stuff, and nearly died."

I have to ask, "Are you sure it was the meat that made the pig sick?"

Miss Hattie leans forward. "Ohhhh, yes. The vet said it was bad. I'm just glad none of us ate it."

"And you say your mother warned you in a dream?"

"Mama believes that's how Granny's ghost talks to her." Glenice Jo smiles fondly at Miss Hattie.

They make a funny pair. Glenice Jo is widowed like her mama. I can't quite tell which side she comes down on regarding the validity of ghosts. I'm not even sure which side I come down on, although there's pretty good evidence with the Palace Theatre ghost. But I don't believe in Madam Tolvaj.

"Well, help me out tonight and keep a close watch on Madam Medium. I think her act, albeit entertaining, is just that. An act." I roll my eyes as Fitzie sails into the parlor.

She quirks an eyebrow at me before stopping in front of Hattie, air-kissing her cheek. "Hattie, darling, it's so good of you to come. And Glenice Jo, how are you, sugar?"

I leave her to exchange pleasantries with Miss Hattie. Otherwise, she'll pull me aside and ply me with questions. She's already sent another inquisitive glance. Pretending not to notice, I cross the room to check the evening's refreshments and remove the cloth from the round table Madam Medium will use. I want to be able to see those knees of hers.

Glenice Jo joins me to help fold the tablecloth. "How did it go in the mine? Did you find anything?"

Though we have been the closest of friends since we were in diapers, I'm reluctant to tell her about Boone … yet. I will when I'm ready.

I carry the tablecloth to the sideboard and open the drawer. "A couple of bats and some cave crickets." I laugh when her nose wrinkles. "I need to talk to the other mine owners to learn how they go about getting the gold out." I slide the tablecloth into the drawer. "Boone came by to help me look around. He told me the other mines use fire to crack the walls, making it easier to extract the quartz. Then they crush that to get the gold out. Wild, huh?"

She selects a peppermint from a bowl Fitzie keeps on the sideboard. "I've heard of that. Do you know what they use to light those fires?"

"No, I'm looking into it, though. I'm afraid this is a lot harder than I thought."

My dear friend barks a laugh. "I could have told you that. But I want to see you swing a pickaxe."

"Don't think I couldn't." I lift my arm and make a muscle. "I'd feel better, though, if I'd seen some evidence of gold. All I saw was granite and quartz."

"Hey, where there's—"

I finish her sentence, "Quartz, there's gold. I know." The doorbell interrupts us. "That's her ladyship, Madam Medium. We'll talk later. Remember, keep a sharp eye on her."

Fitzie ushers our entertainer into the parlor. She looks different. I peer at her. What could it—ah-ha! It's her hair. She's dyed it red. And it's cut short with tight curls all over her head. Tonight, she's wearing a pink and purple velvet suit, covered by the same Scottish-plaid shawl. Her hat is a puffy, lilac velvet beret, embellished with black feathers, and she carries a large satchel under one arm. That's new. And it looks heavy. What could she have in there?

Biting her lip to keep from laughing, Glenice Jo raises an eyebrow in my direction. Ignoring her so I don't giggle, I offer my hand to Madam.

"Good evening Madam Me—" I cough. "Tolvaj. How are you this evening?"

She clasps my hand. "Other than a bit of dyspepsia, I'm fit as a fiddle." Eyes bright with interest, she gazes at Miss Hattie and Glenice Jo. "And who might these lovely ladies be?"

As they rise, Fitzie completes the introductions. "Before we proceed, Pearl has made hummingbird cake. Come have some."

Madam Medium gapes at Fitzie, while I calculate the cost of the cake. Its ingredients are pricey. I'd better find gold fast. I've given up any hope of finding the senator's money. If anyone could have found a way to take it with them into the hereafter, it would have been him.

"What?" Fitzie chuckles. "Have you never had hummingbird cake?"

Madam Medium scowls and curls her lip. "I'm not particularly partial to fowl in my cake."

Miss Hattie intercedes before Fitzie can launch into the cake's origins. "It's called that because it's sweet enough to attract hummingbirds. It's a Southern favorite with both bananas and pineapple."

"Oh. Well, then, it sounds delightful." She sets her bag beside the davenport.

Aunt Clara joins the party, and while they enjoy their dessert, Glenice Jo pulls me back. "If she's truly psychic, wouldn't she know what's in hummingbird cake?"

"One would think so. Or at least she would have known we would serve it tonight and asked someone about it before she got here."

A few minutes later, Madam Medium places her empty plate on the coffee table beside her teacup and rubs her hands together. "That was delicious. But I'm most anxious to get started. I believe Hermione is in fine fettle tonight and will be ready to help us."

Glenice Jo nudges me, and a smirk tugs her lips. "I'll just bet she is," she whispers.

"No whispering, ladies. I'm well aware of your skepticism."

Glenice Jo exchanges glances with me. Uh-oh.

Madam waves a hand in dismissal. "Skeptics often turn out to be the best natural energy conductors. So let's be at it. Mrs. Fitzgerald, will you please lower the lights? And may I use your gramophone?"

Fitzie turns off the overhead light, leaving only a small lamp on a side table lit. "Certainly."

Madam Medium shepherds us to the table. "Lay your hands on the surface, pinkie to pinkie and thumb to thumb, making sure we all have a connection. I will complete the circle in a moment."

She removes a crystal ball from her bag and sets it on the table. So that's what makes her satchel so heavy. I have to bite my cheek to keep from laughing. Her theatrics are so predictable. Next, she pulls a record from the satchel and takes it to the gramophone. After cranking the handle, she sets the needle on the record. It's Al Jolson singing "Rock-a-Bye Your Baby With a Dixie Melody."

What a strange song for a séance. Glenice Jo and I stare at one another, perplexed.

"It's one of Hermione's favorite songs. She's always more responsive if I play music she likes." Madam Tolvaj begins her strange, swaying dance. Miss Hattie's eyes bulge, and Glenice Jo sucks in her lips.

Fitzie joins us at the table. "I hope this works," she whispers.

"Quiet!" Madam Medium twirls around the table, putting me in mind of a flamingo in a mating dance—not that I've seen one, but the way she juts her neck out makes me think perhaps she has. One thing, however, is very evident—the woman has no rhythm whatsoever.

After another circuit around the room, she abruptly stops. She turns off the gramophone, moves to the table, and takes her place between Fitzie and Miss Hattie. I had hopes she would sit by me. Now how will I know if she makes the table bump?

Madam rubs her hands over the crystal ball. "It's a bit foggy. Hermione? I sense you are here, darling. Are you? Will you speak?"

The table jumps. Glenice Jo startles and Miss Hattie gasps. Being seasoned séance attendees, Aunt Clara, Fitzie, and I remain calm. I try to see the woman's knees. I couldn't detect any movement from her.

"Wonderful. Is there anyone else with you?"

The table thumps twice. I have no idea if it's Hermione or the medium, but my money's on the one I can see. I peek through my lashes. Her head is thrown back, but I have the distinct feeling she's got one eye on us. Madam Tolvaj could do well on a vaudeville stage.

"Hermione, be a dear and ask the senator where he hid his money. His family is in great need."

There's a long pause. I'm beginning to think the woman has fallen asleep or gone off into a trance. Then her shoulders jerk.

"He said what? Oh my … yes, I see … indeed, it's a disappointment, but keep after him. In a nice way, of course … yes, you, too, darling. Thank you."

Madam Tolvaj's head swivels down, and she looks around the table. "Well, ladies, the senator continues in his stubbornness. I don't understand why. He can't use any of the money. It's of no value in the hereafter." She winks and titters, then she rises and circles the room, inspecting its perimeter. "Perhaps we can use logic and think of where he may have hidden it."

In a bold move, she grasps a corner of Grandfather Fitzgerald's portrait, raises it away from the wall, and peers beneath it.

Fitzie jumps up. "What are you looking for?"

Madam grimaces. "A hidden wall safe. Perhaps one you didn't know about."

I think … well, I don't know what to think. Yes, I do. Madam Medium is overdoing her act, and she's got Fitzie, hook, line, and necklace. I saw her eyeing that too. Fitzie heads toward the senator's study with Madam in her wake.

"Mama, no!" This is wrong. What started out as an evening's entertainment is careening out of control. What little money we have is in the office safe. Glenice Jo's face reflects the alarm I'm feeling.

In the doorway to the senator's office, Tolvaj stops suddenly and grabs Fitzie's arm. "Is there a back door?"

Frowning, Fitzie points in the direction of the kitchen.

Madam Medium flies back into the parlor, snatches up her crystal ball, and flees toward the kitchen. Suddenly, the door swings open, and Sheriff Koch barges in, followed by Pearl, who runs to the front door and opens it. What is going on? Maybe the medium really is psychic.

Tolvaj swiftly pivots and runs toward the open front door.

Boone bursts in and Tolvaj jockeys to run past him.

What's he doing here?

"Don't let her get away, Boone," the sheriff shouts. "Grab her."

Boone holds the medium by her upper arms while Sheriff Koch rushes over and secures handcuffs on her.

Fitzie wrings her hands.

Aunt Clara shakes her head.

Miss Hattie gapes.

Lips clamped shut, the medium glares at everyone.

"Thanks for the tip, Boone. We've been after this one for weeks." Sheriff Koch drags Madam Tolvaj out to his car.

I shut the door and turn to Boone. In a matter of a few quick moments, we went from conclave to calamity. "What just happened? Who is she?"

"A fake." He puts one arm around Fitzie's shoulders. "Mrs. Fitzgerald, she's preys on widows like you. She's duped a half dozen in Atlanta since she got lucky with the Teagues."

My mama begins to weep. "Oh, I'm so ashamed." She buries her head in Boone's shoulder.

"So I was right." I take a step closer to Boone. "But what do you mean, 'lucky with the Teagues'? And how do you know about her?" I gently take my mother from Boone's arms and lead her back to the parlor. "Come on, Mama. Let's sit down. You dry your tears and let Boone explain."

Aunt Clara, mindful of hospitality, hands Boone a plate of hummingbird cake as he sits in a wing chair.

"Thank you." After he takes a bite, he sets the plate on his knee. "To answer your question, your mother first mentioned Tolvaj while we were taking down the wallpaper in your foyer. That caught my attention. A few weeks ago, I was in Charlie Inman's barbershop for a haircut. The talk was about the Teagues and Widow Kline, who Tolvaj conned out of a fortune, leaving her penniless."

I hand Boone a cup of coffee. "So why didn't they arrest her then?"

Boone holds the saucer and lifts the cup for a sip. "She's a slippery thing. No one knows where she lives. Anyway, she uses people's grief to hold more séances, steadily increasing her fees. That's what she did to Widow Kline, who was too ashamed to tell anyone. When Mr. Teague sold his stock just before the market crashed, Tolvaj had already conducted one séance there. She then convinced Mrs. Teague it was the result of the séance and spread the word around town."

Fitzie dabs her eyes with a hankie. "If not through the séance, then how did Mr. Teague know to sell his stock?"

"He told Sheriff Koch he simply didn't believe the market could keep going the way it was. He'd made enough, he said, for his family to live comfortably. That's all he wanted. He's not greedy."

"If everyone adopted his attitude, the world would be a happier place. However ..." Standing behind Mama, Miss Hattie places her hand on Fitzie's shoulder and chuckles. "Tonight is one I shall not forget anytime soon. It was extremely entertaining."

As if the compliment was a cleansing balm, Fitzie rises, once again in complete control. "Thank you, darling Hattie. It was fun, wasn't it?"

Boone also comes to his feet and places his dishes on the sideboard. "It's time I be on my way." He takes Mama's hand. "Thank you, Miss Fitzie, for the cake. Cora, will you see me out?"

I suck in a breath, my heart racing at the anticipation of another kiss. I follow him to the foyer.

"I talked to Mr. Shelley and some of the other mine owners." Boone digs in his pocket and pulls out a folded piece of paper. "This contains written instructions, but he said he'd talk with you, show you how it's done."

No kiss, then. My heart slows, and I try not to show my disappointment. "That's swell. Did Mr. Shelley seem to mind that I'm a woman?"

Boone's sheepish grin gives him away. "Okay, he laughed at first but said you could come talk to him." His grin fades. "To be honest, I'm beginning to doubt this is such a good idea, Cora. It's awfully risky."

Suspicion uncoils like a serpent in my middle. "You seemed to think it was okay this morning." I watch him closely. He isn't thinking of moving in on the mine, is he? No. Boone's not like that. Is he?

Chapter 11

Monday, November 18, 1929

AFTER BOONE PAVED THE WAY for me with most of the local mine owners, I spent the next week learning about fire-setting. Everyone told me it was my only hope for getting the quartz out of the granite. Otherwise, it could take weeks with a pickaxe, gleaning nil to nothing. All day Saturday and Sunday after church, I hauled as much wood as I could to the mine, tossing it inside the first chamber.

Now, sitting in the mine's entrance, my claustrophobia paralyzes me again. Even the promise of gold doesn't entice me to slide down into this dark grave. The damp inside is bad for my voice. I always cough when I go in here.

Trudie, who has taken a rare day off to help me, nudges me in the ribs. "Well, are we going to sit here in the rain or go inside and do this?"

I slip her a sideways glance. In the drizzle, curls are popping away from her finger waves and spilling onto her forehead. "Are you sure about helping?"

Her face shines with her love of adventure. "Absolutely. I want to see it. I also want to get out of the rain. Let's get inside. Then we can make a decision about setting a fire."

She's always the practical one. I press the light switch on the new helmet Boone got for me. He says when I find gold, I can pay him back. I've never known a man like him. He's so giving. So caring. So hard to believe he's real.

"Cora, are you awake?" Trudie gives me a gentle push, her sleeve gathering mud from the mine entrance. "I'm getting soaked out here."

"Sorry." I take a deep breath and slide my fanny down into the mine. I'm barely on my feet when Trudie jumps to hers beside me.

"Wow, this is the gnat's whistle." She shines her light around the walls, stopping when its beam illuminates a baby bat hanging above us. She takes a step sideways and drops her voice to a whisper. "Is that what I think it is?"

"Yes." I laugh. "But you don't have to whisper. He never moves."

Trudie rolls her eyes. "Says you."

"It's true. The only way I know he's alive is he's in a slightly different place each day. I call him Fido, and his friend I have yet to name."

"Wait. Friend?" Her light swishes around the ceiling until it lands on the other bat. "Yikes! You named a bat? Why?"

Why, indeed? "In case I need someone to talk to while I'm down here. He'll keep me from losing my sanity, if I haven't already lost it."

With her index finger, she rubs beneath her nose. Is the air getting to her already?

"Okay, I'll bite. Why Fido? Isn't that a dog's name?"

I squat to pick up the bag of kindling I brought with me this morning. "Fido comes from fidelis and means always faithful. That bat is faithfully here each time I come."

Shaking her head, Trudie picks up the newspapers. "Well. I'll be. Ya learn something new every day." She turns her head and looks around. "So where are we going to build this fire?"

"In the next chamber. That's where Boone saw the vein of quartz. Once it gets going good, Mr. Shelly told me to leave. The heat will get too intense."

"Not too quickly, I hope." Trudie flaps her wet sweater. "I want to dry out some."

First, we twist newspaper into tight ropes and lay it amidst the kindling. While we work, my throat fills, and the effort to clear it makes it raw.

"Cora, are you having an allergy attack?"

"I don't know what it is. But every time I come into the mine, it gets worse. This had better work, or I won't have a voice left to continue my career." My pronouncement sounds husky to my own ears.

Trudie sighs. "Maybe we'll find enough gold from this fire business that you won't have to keep coming back. You're not looking to get rich, are you?"

"All I want is enough to keep Fitzie and Aunt Clara in the house and food on the table. I can help out with a little extra once I'm on Broadway."

But the frown that pinches my brow belies my words. It would be nice to find a large vein of gold. Then we could skip the quartz-crushing step. I cross my fingers and send up a silent prayer.

Trudie tucks in the last twist. "Having been a Girl Scout helps, doesn't it?"

"I guess. You were always better at all that than I was. Let's lay on the logs." We drag in all the wood from the outer chamber.

Puffing, Trudie wipes her forehead with a hankie. "This is harder than waiting on a herd of hungry truckers." She tosses a log onto the pile.

"Not that way." I move the log parallel with the wall. "They said to build the stack like a one-sided pyramid so it will go up the wall as far as we can get it and still leave room for air between them."

Lines form on Trudie's brow. "Up the wall? I've never heard of anything like that before."

"Me, either, but one of the fellas drew me a diagram." I search my pocket for the drawing. "Horsefeathers. Apparently, I left it at home." At Trudie's aghast expression, I add, "But I remember it."

I pick up a couple of split logs and lay them on top of the kindling. Then I add a third beside those. Remembering the next part is a struggle, but I lay the fourth in the valley between two logs. Going up isn't as easy as I thought. The pyramids top out. Finally, I manage to get them to support another row.

"Let's keep going this way. Leave the first valley empty, slanting the pile closer to the wall, then cross the next layer. Mr. Shelly said that will ensure the heat goes up instead of out so much."

We lay the last log about five feet up the wall and stand back. I strike a match. "Here goes."

I set the flame to the paper and strike a second match to move things along. The kindling catches pretty quick. After a while, fire licks over the logs. Maybe I really do have a chance at this. Wouldn't the senator be surprised?

It quickly becomes too smoky to breathe, and we both start to cough. The heat is more than intense, and we move out of the second chamber and back into the first one. I sure hope we didn't build that fire too big. Even Fido and his pal take flight, heading for the entrance. I don't blame them. It's so hot in here, the cave crickets are agitated and running about. Smoke now invades this chamber.

I stare at Trudie, my stomach churning. "Maybe we should—" An eerie creaking from inside the second chamber makes my skin crawl. The walls groan.

Trudie stares at me wide-eyed. "Has anyone else been in here?"

I shake my head. "I don't think so, why?"

"Well, if they did some—"

A loud crack echoes through the mine.

Then another. The earth groans.

Wide-eyed, we scramble for the entrance.

I shove Trudie up and out.

The ground shakes.

She turns and reaches for me.

Then everything goes black.

Why does my head hurt? I open my eyes. I'm laying half outside the mine in a drizzle. Trudie kneels over me, holding her sweater out to try to keep the rain off me. I start to sit up, but she holds me down.

"Don't move yet."

"What happened?"

"A rock hit you in the back of the head. I had to drag you out. You're cut and bleeding. Fortunately, the rock was small, so I think you'll be okay, but you might need stitches."

My fingers carefully explore the back of my head. It's sticky but doesn't seem to be that bad. There's a small knot. However, I need to know what happened in the mine more than I need a doctor. Smoke and dust pour out of the entrance.

"Where's my helmet?"

"It came off when the rock hit you."

So much for protection. Despite Trudie's loud protests, I rise gingerly and move to the entrance hole. "Trudie, I don't see any light from the fire."

She shoulders me aside carefully and sticks her head in. "Whoa." She pulls back, grabs her flashlight, and shines it inside. "I can't see much."

Fear of more failure outweighs claustrophobia. "I'm going back in."

"But—"

Before she can stop me, I slide inside, but I don't go very far. My foot hits my helmet and some rocks. I grab the helmet and turn on the light. Thankfully, it still works. I set it high on my head, holding it in place so it doesn't slide down onto the cut. With my other hand, I hold my shirt over my nose and mouth, then turn my head with its light toward the second chamber.

But there is no second chamber. Not anymore. Nothing but smoke seeps between a large pile of rock, blocking the chamber entrance and spilling into the first. What Mr. Shelly warned me about has happened. I've caused a cave-in, one that could have been the death of Trudie and me.

Shivering, I turn back to the opening and double over in a fit of coughing. "Help me up," I manage to call to Trudie.

Her hand appears and she pulls me out. The mine is gone. Or at least the part where any decent amount of gold might be. I grimace at my friend. "The fire-setting back-fired." I offer a wry smile at my pun, then shrug. "Well, at least I can tell Fitzie I didn't find pneumonia like she predicted."

Reality sets in. I'm not going to find anything in that mine. It's done for. "Oh, Trudie, what am I going to do?"

Her brow pinches and doubt fills her eyes. Then she squares her shoulders. "Go home and get dry. The Dillies will think of something."

The one thing I could do besides throw my voice, I've ruined. Tears blur my eyes and fall unchecked down my cheeks. My failures taunt me, and the senator's words haunt me as we tromp through the wet woods.

First, the tannery, proving I can't even type or take any form of shorthand. Then Hosch's Five and Dime, where a cash register proved my undoing. And I was nothing but a novelty at the hash house. A worthless novelty. And now the final spike in my wounded pride, the mine.

Marching beside me, Trudie throws her arm over my shoulders. "Come on, Cora. We'll come up with something."

"What does a woman who has no skills other than ventriloquism do?" For that matter, Fitzie's only skill is being a hostess, and Aunt Clara writes, but ...

Trudie smirks and gives me one of those knowing looks.

"Don't even joke about that." Suddenly, the image of Aunt Clara in a sexy negligee and garter on her thigh makes me giggle. "There is no way on earth we'd—wait!"

Plan B. I'd forgotten about it.

Trudie's eyes widen in horror. She claps a hand over her mouth. "I was joking. Just to make you smile. You wouldn't consider it. *Please* tell me you wouldn't!"

I chuckle. Despite the pounding in my head, it feels good. "No, not that. Something I forgot. Trudie, I'm living *in* a gold mine. Oh, it's rich. The senator will roll over in his grave." I stop and grasp her shoulders, turning her toward me. "The house. I'll open it up to boarders."

Her jaw slackens. Then her eyes light up, and she throws her head back, laughing. "Oh, my goodness, such a fitting end for all the senator's greedy aspirations. I love it, Cora!" Grinning ear to ear, we continue toward home. "And there's a need for it. Outside our little community, so many have lost their homes. Sure, a lot have gotten jobs at the tannery, but they don't have a place to live. Why, just the other day, I heard Martha Anne say they were looking for housing for new employees."

Housing, I can provide. My steps falter. "Trudie, do you think I can get a loan to do a little remodeling?"

"For a boarding house? I'll bet my best boots you can."

My mind whirls with plans. I'll have to move Fitzie, Aunt Clara, and myself to the attic. That means building a bedroom up there for us. And if we divide our three bedrooms into five, we can take in more boarders.

From the pit of my despair a few moments ago, hope arises.

Chapter 12

Monday, late afternoon, November 18, 1929

AFTER A BATH, I HOLD up a hand mirror and examine the back of my head in the medicine cabinet mirror. It's only about a half-inch long and not bleeding. I don't need stitches, but I should be careful with a comb. Gingerly, I twist my hair into a chignon, successfully covering the injury.

Downstairs, Fitzie and Aunt Clara are nowhere to be found. Sounds of supper preparation come from the kitchen. Pots bang. The thump of a rolling pin against the wooden worktable. Good. I want to talk with Pearl first, anyway. She's at the table, rolling out a pie crust.

"Hey. Need some help?"

"If'n you want to help,"—she points with her rolling pin—"you can clean up that broccoli." Knowing me as well as she does, she's aware that I don't have great culinary skills—or aspirations, for that matter—and eyes me suspiciously.

We work in thick silence for a few minutes.

"You gonna spill what's eatin' at you?"

I chuckle. "There's no pulling any woolies over your eyes, is there?" I push the bowl of broccoli away. "Here's the deal. I need to know if you will stay if I turn this place into a boarding house."

Her jaw drops. "I thought you was gold minin'. What happened to that?"

I spin the paring knife on the table. Pearl waits until it slows and claps her hand over it. "Don' you be tryin' to put me off."

A sigh escapes me. "I failed, Pearl. I caused a cave-in."

She pulls her hand from the knife and goes back to rolling dough.

"Nobody hurt?"

"No, not really." Pearl had been my nanny as well as our cook. She'll be all over me like a duck on a June bug if I don't tell her and she finds out later. Slowly, I pull my hair aside. "Only a little nick."

After a quick look and a tiny bit of her wonder salve, Pearl grunts and washes her hands. While she sets the crust in a pie tin, she eyes me. "So, mining's out." She pinches the edges of the crust. "A boarding house, you say?"

She isn't so much asking me as she's convincing herself. I let her chew on the idea. One never rushes Pearl.

"How many bedrooms?"

I take a bowl of eggs from the refrigerator and set it on the table next to her. "I want to take a portion of the senator's old office for a storage room, then turn the rest into a family parlor for us. The senator's old smoking parlor, which we no longer need, can be made into a bedroom for overnight guests." Maybe I can steal some square footage from the smoking room to make the front parlor larger for guests. The bedroom doesn't need to be that big if it's just for overnighters. "The second floor can be converted into five bedrooms for long-term boarders. That would give us six to rent out. Your room remains where it is."

Pearl beats an egg to brush on the crust. "Where all y'all gonna sleep?"

"The attic. There's plenty of room and won't take much to make it livable," I say, heading off any protests.

One brow arches, but after only a moment of the evil eye, she folds and nods, then pulls out a bowl of leftover pot roast from the refrigerator. "Well, if'n some of those rooms have a husband and wife, that could be as high as twelve people. You need to have a rate for singles and one for doubles. Doubles means more food and"—she juts her jaw at me—"more work."

Who knew Pearl had a head for business? While she cuts the meat into bite-size pieces, I take the peeled carrots and slice them. We work side by side for a few moments, each lost in our thoughts. When the potatoes have been diced and the gravy made, Pearl assembles the cottage pie. My mouth is watering already.

"How many of these would it take to feed that many people?"

She slides the pie into the oven. "Depends on how many are men and where they work."

"Why would where they work make a difference?" I pour us each a cup of coffee from the pot on the stove's reservoir and offer her one.

Nodding her thanks, she sips before answering. "If'n a man does hard physical labor, he's needin' more fuel and eats more." She pulls out a chair and sits. "A desk-job man don't use as much energy, so he don't eat as much. Unless he's one of them gluttons."

For a woman with only fourth-grade schooling, she's pretty smart. "While I work on the finances of getting us started, can you figure out the cost of feeding people? Then I can know what to charge."

A wide smile splits her face, revealing her gold tooth. "Yes'm, Miss Cora. I can do that."

I drain my cup, and, after setting it in the sink, I pause at the door. "I know how much the good Lord loves you, Pearl. You might say a prayer for me. I've got to convince Fitzie and Aunt Clara."

"Convince us of what?" Fitzie's voice startles me. Her expression skeptical, she has one hand on her hip, the other holding her handbag and hat. Behind her, Aunt Clara peers over her sister's shoulder, right eyebrow quirked. Dressed in afternoon frocks, they must've been visiting friends.

"I didn't hear you come in." I adopt an air of nonchalance and pick up the knife I abandoned next to the broccoli. "Have you had a nice afternoon? I expect you were out calling."

"Don't try to evade me, Cora Lee Fitzgerald. You're up to something. Convince us of what?"

Well, that didn't work. I drop the knife onto the counter. "Okay, come into the parlor and we'll talk."

I wait until they're settled, then tell them what happened in the mine.

Fitzie waves away my explanation like a pesky gnat. "Good riddance, is all I can say."

Aunt Clara raises a skeptical eyebrow and signs, "So now what?"

They received that part well, although the next could become sticky. "I've applied to every business within a reasonable distance. You know how those turned out. But I have an idea that I believe is perfect." I push back a wave of hair that threatens to droop over one eye.

Fitzie turns her hand in the air in a *get-on-with-it* motion. "And?"

I draw in a deep breath and push the words out through stiff lips. "A boarding house."

Aunt Clara signs, "A boarding house? Where?"

"Here."

I wait for them to shriek. But nothing happens. Fitzie's mouth purses, the wheels of her mind turning, and knowing my mother, she's envisioning herself as a hostess with a houseful of guests. Aunt Clara sees more secrets being overheard and gets a wicked gleam in her eye.

Thank You!

Fitzie grins. "It's a brilliant idea, sugar-pie. I love it."

Suddenly, a frown pulls down Aunt Clara's brow. She signs, "What about bedrooms? We only have one empty room."

"I know. I've got that figured out." I dig in my pocket and pull out the crude sketch I made before I came downstairs. I lay it on the coffee table and kneel on the floor while they examine it. After explaining my plan, I settle back on my heels.

Aunt Clara slowly nods. One eyebrow raises. Thankfully, it's the left, which means a simple question, not skepticism. She rubs her thumb against two fingers.

Fitzie voices Auntie's concern. "How are we going to afford this?"

"Trudie thinks I can get a loan, based on the need for housing."

Fitzie's love shines through her eyes. "I think this is a wonderful idea. One that's quite doable." She runs her fingers over her necklace. "Is Pearl all right with feeding all these guests?"

"That's why I was in the kitchen. I talked with her first. If she needs a helper once we have the boarders, we can afford to hire one."

Fitzie rises and grabs Aunt Clara's hand. "Let's go up and look at the attic. I want to envision what it will be like. Let me have that drawing, Cora."

"Y'all go ahead. I'm going to put pencil to paper. I need some figures to give the bank."

In the hallway, I pick up the telephone, tap the switch hook, and wait for the operator.

"Hello, Cora. What can I do for you?"

"Good afternoon, Miss Flo." I'm thankful it isn't Blanche. "I need to speak with—" Oh dear. I have no idea who to ask for. "Uh, I have need of a handyman. Do you know one, please?"

"Well, sugar, the best in the county is Boone Robertson."

Boone? My heart flutters and I suck in a breath. "He's not too busy in his furniture shop?" I pull out the stool from beneath the telephone shelf and sit.

"Unfortunately, no. Oh, he used to be busy enough to make a living, with all the rich folks in Atlanta buying from him. But he also did handy work around town. Then, with that stock market crumbling, and most of the rich folks losing their money, nobody's buying new. They're making do with what they have and cancelling new orders. He let the word spread that he's taking on more work as a handyman."

Is someone playing with me? Everywhere I turn, Boone's there. Not that I mind. My lips stretch into a smile, and my face warms.

"Thank you. Miss Flo. Will you connect me with him?"

"Sure, honey."

I don't have to wait long. A moment later, I hear his voice. "Robertson."

I frown, wondering why he's left off the *Fine Furniture Makers.* "Hey, Boone. I'd like your advice on something, but it needs to remain a secret for now."

An hour later, Pearl ushers Boone into the parlor. I'm ready with paper and pencil waiting on the coffee table. Fitzie and Aunt Clara are still up in the attic, examining the old trunks. Fitzie now thinks maybe the senator hid his money in one of them. At least she's occupied.

What I'm not ready for is how my heart skips a beat when I see him. He's wearing a plaid shirt of pumpkin, green, and brown, which brings out the gold flecks in his hazel eyes. Those eyes and the memory of his kiss make me warm all over. I turn and lead him over to the coffee table.

"Thanks for coming, Boone. Can I get you anything? Sweet tea? Coffee? Co-cola?"

"No, I'm fine, thanks. What kind of advice do you need?"

Now that he's here, I'm not sure how to open the conversation without admitting my defeats. Then again, my pride has already been hit pretty hard. I've fallen far from a vaudeville princess. I gesture to the side chair while I drop onto the floor between the coffee table and the davenport. Instead of taking the wingback, Boone sits, legs crossed, on the floor opposite me.

"Did you hear what happened in the mine this morning?"

He leans forward, his hands gripping the edge of the table. "No, did you find gold?"

I can't help chuckling at myself. "I have no idea why I ever thought I could be a gold miner. I did *not* find any gold, and no one ever will in that mine. I caused a cave-in." I wait for it to register.

And sure enough, his eyes widen. "But ... how ... you—" His gaze rakes over me. "You didn't get hurt, did you? What happened?"

I tell him the whole story. "I don't know what we did wrong, but the curtain has closed on that act. It's time to move on. I've been percolating an idea since I first started job-hunting. And now it's time to enact my Plan B, which is to turn this place into a boarding house." Saying it suddenly feels like slipping my arms into a custom-made cashmere coat. "You know your onions when it comes to building things. What do you think? Can I do it?"

Beneath the table, I cross my fingers.

"That's a swell idea." He grabs the pencil and paper. "Do you have any idea of how many boarders you want?" He jots down something I can't read.

I'm downright giddy with relief. "Six. I drew up a crude plan, but

…" I gesture to the ceiling. "Fitzie and Aunt Clara are in the attic with my drawing."

"And they're okay with this?"

"They think it's the cat's pajamas. Fitzie already sees herself as the grand hostess. Aunt Clara, being more practical, sees it as a means to an end, even if that includes more work for us all."

He poises the pencil on the paper, ready to make notes. "Tell me your plans."

I study him. Why is he so excited about it? Is it simply an opportunity for him to work? Shaking off my suspicions, I take another piece of paper from the coffee table drawer and redraw the layout.

"That gives us six rentable bedrooms, a family parlor, a guest parlor, and a downstairs storage room. What I need from you is an estimate of the cost. And how long it will take to do the work. I have to take numbers to the bank to get a loan. Also, would you do the work? I can swing a hammer … I think. At least, I can help saw wood or something. I don't think I can afford two men." My mouth is running wild, so I snap it closed.

His smile is warm, but I can't quite read his eyes. They're hooded. I lick my lips and glance at the fireplace. It's hot in here.

He nods and winks. "Okay, I can't be exact until I measure, which I'll go do in a minute. Here's what I think you'll need, though. And you can afford two helpers for me if I get Jimmy and George Horton."

George and Jimmy—Pearl's nephews. I hadn't thought about them.

Boone's list has lumber, lath and plaster, a radiator for heat in the attic, copper pipe to connect the rad, electrics, and several other things.

I swing my gaze from the paper to him. "What about furniture? What do you think it will cost to get that? Or do you want to make it?"

He grins. "I can't work that fast, Cora, especially if I'm building here. Use the Sears catalog. If you do, I think we can safely say you'll need five to six hundred dollars for everything and be ready for boarders."

I sink back. He makes it sound like a small amount, but with no income right now, it seems like a fortune. Will we really be able to pull this off?

Chapter 13

Thursday morning, November 21, 1929

AFTER A FINAL SIP OF coffee, I lay my napkin on my breakfast plate and rest an elbow on the chair arm. "I'm going to the bank this morning. Boone's fixing to get me firm numbers on the supplies, but his original estimate is close enough, and he said I should go."

Fitzie adds a quick splash of cream to her coffee. She's cut back on the amount, bless her. I believe my aunt and I may have finally gotten the idea across to her that we're poor. She takes a sip, grimaces, and adds two spoonsful of sugar.

Then again, maybe not.

Another sip, and this time Fitzie smiles. "Are you going to tell them the plans? I think the attic will be like a romantic hideaway for us."

Aunt Clara rolls her eyes at her sister and crosses her fingers at me.

I thank her and return my attention to Fitzie. "I hope you don't think having a boarding house is just a lark. It's going to be a lot of hard work. Remember, if I'm going to return to New York, you, Aunt Clara, and Pearl will have to do all of it yourselves."

She waves a dismissive hand at me. "We'll hire a couple of Pearl's granddaughters. One can be the maid, and the other can help in the kitchen."

I have to give her that one. Employing Pearl's granddaughters is a good idea. "You'll still have to help out some, though, Mama."

"If you go back, Clara and I will manage the house and the guests. I've always ordered the household supplies and food. We'll keep the books too." She glances at her sister. "Won't we, Clara?"

My aunt looks up from her manuscript, nods, and smiles. She won't be much help if she's in the middle of a new book. However, since the senator's demise, she contributes a good portion of her income to the household, and people are still reading. For that, I'm thankful.

I pour half a cup of coffee from the carafe on the table. "How's the new mystery coming along? And whose secrets are you exposing in this one?"

"Ours." She signs the single word, then rests her hands in her lap.

My mind reels. Has my aunt finally slipped a cog? "What do you mean?"

She hands me her title page. I read, "'The Mystery in the Guest House.' But what's the secret we're supposed to have?"

Her hands move expressively, with purpose. "I don't know what it is … yet. But I believe if I can write it the way I want to, it will bring us more boarders."

Fitzie laughs. "You are sly, sister. And brilliant." She folds her napkin and lays it on her plate. "And people think Clara's the crazy one in our family."

I suck in my lower lip and send a stern look Aunt Clara's way. "As long as those boarders don't try to break into the walls to solve the mystery."

My aunt's silent amusement reassures me. She'll make sure the secret, whatever it is, doesn't involve our walls.

Pearl carries in a fresh pot of coffee. "Miz Fitzie, don' forget Thanksgiving's coming quick. My sister's husband says he's fixing to get a wild turkey, if'n y'all want it."

Fitzie holds out her cup for Pearl to fill. "That would be wonderful. Tell him thank you. I hated the idea of settling for a chicken, but Cora"—she gives me the evil eye—"is being tight with the purse strings. Now that we have a turkey—and I know we're all thankful the senator is gone—let's celebrate. For propriety's sake, we'll keep it small. Just our usual close friends, Glenice Jo and Hattie, the Vances, and the Newcombs." She turns to me. "If Oscar closes the diner, we can include him and Trudie."

"She told me they were keeping it open for folks who don't have any family around."

Fitzie smiles. "That Oscar. He's a gruff one, but his heart is pure gold. All right, Pearl, plan for a dozen of us. Since your brother-in-law is getting the turkey, it's only right your family join us."

"Thank you, Miz Fitzie."

I'll find a way to pay for it. Pearl's joy is worth it. Beneath the table, Aunt Clara taps my ankle with her foot. She tilts her head toward the door, a reminder for me to get going.

I push my chair back and rise. "If you're sure you don't need the car for a while, I guess I'll slip on down to the bank now. Wish me luck."

Fitzie waves, and my aunt follows me to the door, where she hands me a twenty-dollar bill, signing, "For Thanksgiving dinner."

"Are you sure, Aunt Clara?"

"I contracted another series of stories to both *True Story* and *Ladies' Home Journal*," she signs, then smiles and waves me off.

With that bit of good news, I set off to the Buford bank, confident I'll get the loan.

Inside the bank lobby, Alice Farnham, wearing a fur coat and matching hat, both of which are overdone for daytime, cups a hand over her mouth and whispers into Blanche Longstreet's ear. At the same time, she points at an obviously poor woman, whose threadbare coat would give little warmth.

Alice and Blanche are the last people I want to see here. Alice is the niece of the bank president. If she and Blanche catch wind of why I'm here …

I turn to leave but stop shy of the door. I *need* to get that loan. I turn back around, smack into Alice's open stare. *Applesauce.*

"Why, it's Cora Fitzgerald." Alice puts a hand on her hip, her red lips stretched in a smile as fake as a four-dollar bill. "What are you doing here, of all places? I know for a fact that you don't have a job. And I don't think the bank has any use for a ventriloquist." Her sharp laughter echoes off the marble walls. Then her eyes narrow. "So tell me what business you could possibly have."

The half a dozen or so people in the lobby turn and stare at me. Blanche snickers.

I draw up to my full height, which is several inches above hers. "My business here is just that. Mine." I pass her by, heading toward a carpeted hallway.

Now, how can I get to the loan department without her seeing me? I cast around for a diversion. The ladies' room is near the door I need. That will do. I cross the lobby and go into the restroom. I wash my hands. A moment later, Alice enters.

Before she can start a conversation, I exit and run into Bud Pugh, the bank guard. With a quick tilt of my head toward the loan department door, I throw him a desperate, whispered plea. "Help!"

Catching on quickly, he winks and turns the door's lock, securing Alice in the restroom. I gape at him.

"You go do your business, Miss Cora. I'll take care of Miss Farnham. Soon as you're inside that door, I'll let her out."

I kiss his weathered cheek. He's an old sweetheart, that one. And a widower. "Thank you, and I hope you'll join us for Thanksgiving dinner next week."

"Thank you kindly, I surely will." He winks as I slip through the door to the loan department.

A hawkish man lifts his gaze from his paperwork, taking me in with a frown. I approach his desk. Even the checked pattern on his brown suit resembles feathers.

"How may I help you?" Icicles hang from his words.

"I'd like—" I clear my throat and try again. "I want to see the loan manager, please."

He leans to his left, cranes his neck, and peers behind me. "We'll wait until your husband gets here."

My nerves jangle, but this isn't the first time I've faced discrimination. I overcame it in New York. I won't succumb in Georgia. I straighten my spine and raise my chin a notch. "Then you'll have a long time to wait. I'm not married." I hold up my hand to stop him. "And my father," —this is one time I'll use his name—"Senator Fitzgerald, has passed away. I'm on my own and need a business loan."

As usual, eyes spark at the mention of the senator's name. He shoves the other papers aside and jumps up. A fawning smile appears.

"Forgive me, Miss Fitzgerald, I didn't recognize you. It's been years since I've seen you. Please have a seat, and I'll let Mr. Chambers know you're here."

Mm-hm.

While I wait, I pull out the paper with the build-out figures on it. I try to appear calm and relaxed, but it's hard. So much depends on this loan.

A few tense minutes later, the clerk returns. He holds open the door for a man whom I assume is Mr. Chambers. Beneath his suit jacket, the buttons on his vest strain to remain within the confines of their holes.

"Miss Fitzgerald. This way to my office, please." He leads me into a paneled room and gestures to a chair in front of a massive desk. "Have a seat."

When I'm situated, he returns to his seat of power behind the desk. "Now, how can I help you?"

"I need a loan to do some remodeling on our home. We want to open a boarding house."

"The senator's home?" His nostrils flare. "A boarding house, you say?"

I wait for him to add "preposterous," but he restrains himself.

"Mr. Chambers, my mother and aunt need an income. The senator lost everything in the market crash, so we've come up with an alternate source of revenue." I lay the paperwork on his desk and push it toward him. "Boone Robertson is going to do the work. He gave me these figures. The plans are modest and very doable. I need six hundred dollars to make the house ready to accept boarders." Even as I say it, my mind reels at the amount. A year's wages for many people.

"Why would Sugar Hill need a boarding house when there is the Merchant Hotel in Buford?"

I lean back in my seat, spearing him with a pointed stare. "Mr.

Chambers, local people won't stay in the Merchant Hotel. It's haunted. Only out-of-town visitors who don't know its history stay there. Besides, Miss Vance and Miss Armstrong, both of whom work at the tannery, tell me there is a need for housing for their workers. They don't normally reside in hotels, sir. They can't afford them. So you see, a boarding house is needed. The few that exist in Buford are filled to capacity."

He looks at the figures, then glances up at me and clears his throat. "I'm afraid I have to say no, Miss Fitzgerald."

No?

Over the pompous man's shoulder, I envision the senator shaking his head, rendering his judgment—*I could have predicted this would be a colossal failure.*

I draw a shaky breath, willing my tears not to betray me. "May I ask why?"

"For one, neither you nor your mother or aunt have any experience running a boarding house." Folding his arms, he leans back in his chair, which creaks in protest.

He may *think* he's won this round. But I've got generations of wisdom and wiles in my bones. I use my best Southern charm. "Mr. Chambers, I detect an accent. Where, if I may ask, are you from?"

He stills and his eyes narrow, very nearly disappearing in the folds of his pudgy face. "Chicago. What bearing does that have on anything?"

"Well, sir, I don't know about the North, but in the South, ladies have opened their homes to boarders in times of necessity. After the War of Northern Aggression, when their husbands died fighting, Southern ladies turned everything from antebellum mansions to small cottages into boarding houses to get by. Southern hospitality is bred in us. Of course, we know how to run a boarding house. Boarders are simply *paying* guests."

He snaps up straight. "Be that as it may, the bank is picky about loans at the moment. Precious few are being granted, and certainly none to women. Good day, Miss Fitzgerald." He rises, picks up my paperwork, and holds it out to me.

"That's your final word?"

He nods.

I take the papers with as much dignity I can muster, turn, and walk out. Outside his door, I pray Alice has already left the bank too. She's the last person I want to see. In fact, I don't want to see anyone. I'd crawl into the mine and lick my wounds if it weren't caved in. Instead, I step into the restroom to compose myself for a moment.

The only thing left for me to do is use my savings, although it will barely cover the cost of the remodel. I wanted to leave that money in the bank for when I return to New York, but even that seems impossible now. Broadway is a ghost of a dream.

I blot my eyes, and after a close examination to see if there are any traces of tears, I exit the restroom. Across the lobby, Alice Farnham stands chatting with her uncle. She spots me and sticks her nose in the air, then laughs with him. There's no way she could have known why I came here, except to find out I went into the loan department. How she did that, I don't know. I pull what dignity I have left around me. I refuse to rush as I leave, but in my mind, the senator sneers at me.

It will never work. You'll lose your money in another catastrophic failure.

Chapter 14

Monday morning, December 16, 1929

As I'VE DONE EVERY DAY for the past three-and-a-half weeks, I walk with my heart in my throat and hope fueling my strides down the long driveway where our mailbox sits next to the road. The senator had a small replica of the house built and set on a pole for our mail. Given its origin, I should think it ostentatious, but I've always thought it was cute. Folks in Buford have mailboxes stuck to the side of their houses by the front door, and their carriers walk house to house. Out here on Sugar Hill, we are too rural and spread out. Our delivery is by car or truck, whichever our carrier owns.

I don't mind the walk to the mailbox, except when it's raining. Then both the road and our drive are a mess of mud. Thankfully, today is dry but cold. I shiver and pull my jacket close to my neck, raising the collar to cover my ears.

Christmas is next week, and the mailbox is filled with greeting cards. I grab the stack and sort through it. Near the bottom is an envelope from my New York bank. My hand trembles, my breath coming in frosty puffs. I rip open the envelope and pull out the check. "Eureka!"

It's taken ages to get my money, but now the bank draft is finally here. I stick the remaining mail under my arm and stare at every penny I own in the world. Seven-hundred-fifty-nine dollars and eighty-seven cents. It will cover the construction and feed us until we get our boarders.

"You're going to be put to good use," I say, clutching the check as I run back up the drive. And hopefully, we'll make enough to pay me back so I can hightail it to Broadway.

Aunt Clara must have seen me coming, for the door opens the instant I jump up on the porch. She steps back for me to enter.

"It's here! We can start the work. I'll call Boone and let him know." I shove the rest of the mail into Aunt Clara's outstretched hands and run into the hallway, skidding to a stop.

Wanting to sound casual instead of like a little girl on Christmas morning, I take a deep breath, pick up the phone, and tap the switch hook.

"Operator. How may I direct your call?"

Uh-oh, I know that nasally voice. Blanche. If I try to tell Boone about the check in any kind of code-talk, she'll construe it to be something else. And if I say it outright, everyone within twenty miles will know before I hang up.

"I'm sorry, I find I don't have what I need to make this call. I'll try later. Thank you." I hang up before she can reply. "I'm going to the bank and then to Boone's," I call over my shoulder.

Fitzie pokes her head out of the parlor. "Is Blanche on duty today? I don't know why the telephone company keeps her on."

I grab my hat and coat from the hall tree, then the keys off the hook by the door. "I'll be back soon. I'm taking the car."

After patting my pocket to be sure the check is securely tucked inside, I plop my hat on my head and slip on my gloves. My first stop is the bank. Inside, I glance around for Alice. Good fortune shines on me. She isn't here. I don't need any more busybodies sticking their beaks into my business. I approach the counter. It's a young man, who appears to be in his twenties—around my age—blond with blue eyes behind wire spectacles. I try to put a name to him but come up blank.

"How may I help you, Miss Fitzgerald?"

He knows me, so I must know him. From high school? Maybe not. He isn't using my first name. Well, the best defense is a confident offense. I offer a bright smile.

"I'd like to open a checking account. And no, I'm not married, nor is my father alive." I push the check toward him.

The fellow grins at me. "I know that, Miss Fitzgerald."

He does? "You do?" I pause, a smile frozen on my lips. "Do I know you?"

His cheeks grow pink. "No ma'am. I'm Robert Lee. I was a couple of years behind you in school, but I've followed your career." His gesture sweeps to encompass the entire lobby. "Everyone in town has. We're proud to say Dixie Lynn is a Sugar Hill native."

Oh. I feel my cheeks grown warm, probably glowing as much as his. "Thank you." I only hope Robert's discreet about banking business.

He picks up the check and looks it over. "I'll have it set up for you in a jiffy." He pulls out a drawer and retrieves some papers.

It doesn't take as long as I expect—just a few minutes for a secretary to type out my information on some checks. Meanwhile, Robert writes the amount of my deposit in a little passbook and stamps it. Finally, he puts both the checks and the passbook in what he calls a temporary cover.

"You're ready to go, Miss Fitzgerald. Your actual checkbook will arrive in the mail in about ten days. If you need any more of these,"—he taps the temporary ones—"just come back in and we'll make some for you."

"Thank you."

The ease with which the task was accomplished makes me wonder if Fitzie didn't place a call to someone. She can convince any man to do what he wouldn't ordinarily do. A chuckle threatens to erupt, and I hurry out the doors before it does. Outside, I allow my mirth to spill over from the thought of Fitzie telephoning Alice's uncle. If she did, the poor man would still be shaking his head, wondering what just happened.

Next on my list is to give Boone the money to purchase the lumber and other supplies we need. When I enter his carpentry shop, I don't see him, but the place is a wonder. In the center of the room stands a large workbench with a low table resting on it. I run a hand over its surface. The wood is as smooth as satin.

Shelves on one wall hold different lengths of lumber, and on another is a vast array of jars containing nails and screws of varying lengths. Cans of paint and stain line a workbench at the back of the large room by a window.

I slide my hand over the coffee table again. Will our new furniture be as nice?

"Like it?" Boone approaches from a hallway at the other end of the shop.

I jump, then laugh. "You startled me." In sawdust-covered overalls, he looks rugged and manly. "Yes, it's beautiful. Who is it for?"

Boone smiles and strokes one of the legs. "It's a Christmas present for Mrs. Newcomb."

"That's some Christmas present." I'm tickled for Millie's mama. She always makes do and never complains. A new coffee table will thrill her. "Anyway, I got my money from New York and came by to give you a check. How much should I make it for?"

"Hold on. I've got the receipts here."

"Wait. What? You already bought the lumber? What if I hadn't gotten my money?"

"I put it on my account. I trust you, Cora." He grins. "Besides, even if you bailed on the project, I can always use lumber." He walks over to a desk, brushes off a small mound of sawdust, then pulls an invoice from a drawer. After he reads it, he hands it to me.

"It's a little over two hundred. But it's everything we'll need to finish the project, other than your furniture and paying the Hortons."

"And you. You can't work for free, Boone."

"Of course I can. I'm helping a good friend. Besides, I figure Pearl will feed me dinner and maybe send home some leftovers for supper. That's nifty pay."

I press my lips tight. *People will talk.* "Boone, I can't. I mean, yes, we can feed you, but you *have* to be paid."

"Fine. I'll add two percent to the final bill."

"That's not enough."

He folds his arms. "Take it or leave it."

"All right. I'll take it." I have to since I don't know what a builder's wages are. I glance up at him. He's got a little stubble missed by his razor just below his bottom lip. My eyes fixate on it.

He's just being nice to a widow woman's daughter. It has nothing to do with you.

I pull out one of the checks, fill it out, sign it, and hand it to him. "When can we begin?"

"In the morning. I'll be there at seven."

"Do we need to do anything?"

He smiles, folds the check, and slips it into his shirt pocket. "Have the attic and the senator's old office cleared. We'll start there."

Millie and I climb the stairs to the attic. "I really appreciate your help today, Millie." She looks so cute with a blue-and-white bandana twisted into a turban around her head.

"This place doesn't deserve to be called an attic. Attics are dirty and dusty." Her awed gaze takes in everything, even the corners, then she slides off the turban. "I guess I won't need this." She stuffs the bandana in her pocket.

"You know Pearl." I chuckle. "The minute we decided to actually do this, she attacked it with a bucket and mop. Dust motes skedaddle for their lives when she comes around. Can you believe even the rafters got a going over?"

"With Pearl? Yeah, I can." Still surveying the space, she plants her fists on her hips. "So, what's the plan?"

"We need to clear out everything. Boone said he and the Hortons will carry down the heavy trunks for us. But we'll box up the rest and take it to my bedroom. If needed, I can bunk in with Fitzie until this is ready for us."

Millie squats next to a pile of old toys, while I start on an old bookshelf.

"Cora, do you remember this?" She's holding Sam, my first ventriloquial figure. I fashioned him by removing the stuffing from a doll's head and stitching bigger lips on it. I was so proud of him and myself for making him. He was crude but workable, and I loved him.

I reach for it.

"I wondered what had become of this." I cradle the old doll. Then a memory of the senator berating me for "ruining" the expensive toy hits me upside the head. I stare into the far reaches of the attic. It was a gift from some politician. Only Fitzie's intervention saved me from becoming black and blue from the senator's belt. She must have hidden Sam up here.

"Cora? Your father—excuse me—the senator was a driven man. What demons chased him, we'll never know."

"Greed chased him." I set Sam aside to take back to New York with me.

As we work, we reminisce over toys and novels we uncover. Our laughter draws Fitzie and Aunt Clara upstairs.

Fitzie rubs her hands together. "We've finished the senator's office. We're here to help you."

Two hours later, the four of us have the attic all boxed up.

"We're ready for Boone to tackle this now." I shiver when a draft blows through a crack. "I hope they can make it warmer."

Fitzie points to a mountain of newspapers. "That's what those are for. To insulate up here. He'll nail the papers between the rafters and the lath before he plasters. That young man"—she eyes me—"has some innovative ideas."

And they come in a very nice package.

Aunt Clara shakes with amusement and signs, "This remodeling will have the town all atwitter, speculating for weeks."

They carry the last box down the stairs, and I turn to check for anything we might have missed. Not a single item remains except three heavy trunks and that stack of papers. This will become a lovely respite for Fitzie, Aunt Clara, and me. That thought puts a smile on my face. This idea isn't so far-fetched.

If we can pull it off.

Chapter 15

DESPITE BEING HOME FOR A little over six weeks, I still find that rooster's crow at first light foreign. Both in New York and on tour, we performed late, often not getting to bed until the early hours of the morning. To me, it's normal to sleep until ten a.m. But here, life stirs with the rooster, and Boone, George, and Jimmy Horton will be here soon. Eyes half open and plotting the fowl's demise, I slip on my robe and head to the bathroom.

On chilly mornings like this, I'm grateful the senator installed indoor plumbing. So many on Sugar Hill still have outhouses and bathe in a tin tub in the kitchen. Fitzie told me the senator added the upstairs bathroom last year, right after Swan House was built in Atlanta. *They* had a second-floor bathroom, so *he* had to have one too. And because the Bona Allen Tannery needs natural gas, it was available to anyone who wanted it. Naturally, the senator splurged—earning bragging rights with all his cronies—and added one of those automatic gas water-heaters.

After my morning ablutions, I run a comb through my finger waves and fluff the curls at the ends. Dressed in serviceable overalls, I skid into my chair in the dining room. Pearl grins and sets a plate of eggs, bacon, and cheese grits in front of me. The rising steam has the most heavenly aroma.

"Thanks, Pearl. Can I take you with me back to New York?" Her horrified expression makes me laugh.

Fitzie scowls at me. "You aren't stealing my Pearl. She's one of great value."

Pearl shoots me a *So there!* grin and retreats to her kitchen. Funny, now that the senator no longer rules the household, Pearl is more relaxed, less wary. I take a bite of cheesy grits.

My throat tickles, threatening a cough. "Fitzie, since I got home, I've had a nagging cough, but I feel fine. Do you know what could be bothering me?"

She stops eating and leans toward me, putting the back of her hand on my forehead.

"I don't have a temperature."

"Mamas like to check for sure." She smiles. "When does it seem the worse?"

"It was horrible when I was in the mine. But it isn't consistent."

Aunt Clara signs, "If you want my opinion, it's allergies."

"Me?" I look at Fitzie. "Did I have allergies as a kid?" I don't remember coughing.

She runs a finger around the edge of her coffee cup. "I believe you did. Some, anyway. I think your aunt is right. If you're not sick, it may well be allergies."

Panic rises from the pit of my stomach. "Is there any way to find out for sure?" I can't have a chronic cough. It will ruin my voice.

"Yes." Fitzie nods. "I'll make an appointment for you with the doctor. They have tests, and if you are allergic, you can get shots for it."

I shiver. I hate shots, but it will be worth it if they work.

"Are you and Boone starting on the attic this morning?" Fitzie stirs sugar into her coffee.

I swallow a mouthful of grits. "No. First, we have to get the downstairs reworked. We need at least one room ready to rent. I think he means to get it finished in about a week, give or take. Then start the attic."

Fitzie's knife clatters to her plate. "Good heavens. I don't want the house in a mess over Christmas."

Aunt Clara scowls and signs, "We don't have the luxury of not having the house in a mess. Cora is doing her best to turn this home into a livelihood for you—us."

Fitzie purses her lips, glaring at my aunt. Then after a moment, she capitulates to Aunt Clara's wisdom. "You're right. We can hold Christmas in the dining room." Her eyes brighten. "Sister, it will be like the Christmases when we were children." She tilts her head toward me. "We only had our good name, and that didn't buy much. But Clara and I didn't know we were poor. Your grandparents did everything they could to make our holiday merry. And it always was." She sets her coffee cup on its saucer. "Clara, we shall make this one extra merry."

Thank goodness, her cheerful determination derails an argument. I smile and scoop up a forkful of eggs. "What do you have in mind?"

"We'll invite Mr. Bud, Boone, the Newcombs, and the Armstrongs. Clara"—Fitzie pats my aunt's hand—"has written a short novelette for everyone as a present. That saves us a good deal, and I've no doubt it's a wonderful little mystery."

Aunt Clara's pleased smile tickles me. These two haven't been bickering as much as they usually do. I'm thinking this boarding—wrong, guesthouse—will be metamorphic for all of us. Or maybe it's the hard times making us appreciative of what we do have.

Boone's truck rumbles into the driveway. I gulp down the last of my coffee and run into the kitchen.

The backdoor creaks open. "Morning, Auntie Pearl. Miss Cora." Jimmy Horton tips his hat. His brother George stands shyly behind him. Both men are in their late twenties if I remember right. Both are dressed in overalls, ready to work.

From the counter, Pearl turns an admonishing eye on them. "You and George do a good job for Mr. Boone, now, y'hear?" She slaps eggs on slices of bread and hands one to each. "For your muscles."

Jimmy and George shove them in their mouths and go back outside with me on their heels. I shiver at the sharp chill in the air. Boone is untying ropes around a tall stack of lumber.

"All that is for us?"

Boone nods. "For the downstairs. I'll have another load tomorrow."

While he and the Horton boys make several trips carrying the wood into the house, I look around for something I can help carry. Spying a bucket of nails next to Boone's toolbox, I reach for the handle.

My arms and chest strain. Horsefeathers, it's heavy. I try the toolbox, but it's just as weighty. No wonder Boone is so muscular. An image of his arms straining against his shirt demands I park my thoughts there.

"You need help, Miss Cora?" Jimmy interrupts my musing.

Heat creeps into my cheeks at being caught daydreaming. "Uh, yes, please. What does he have in this toolbox? It's heavy."

Jimmy blinks and stares at me. "Tools."

Laughing, I shake my head, but at least it covers my embarrassment at being caught mooning over Boone's muscles. Jimmy tosses me a cheeky grin and lifts both the bucket and the toolbox. I follow him into the hallway.

All the lumber is piled in one end of the senator's old office, where the storage room will be. Boone sets up two sawhorses and lays a long board on top of them. He unrolls a blue paper on this make-shift table and consults it.

"What can I do to help?"

Boone raises his head. "Can you saw a straight line?"

"I think so."

"If you can, that will be a big help." He pulls out a long piece of wood and lays it across two sawhorses. "Take my tape measure and draw a line at two feet. Then take my saw and cut it."

That sounds easy enough. I pull the end out of the tape measure and set it on the board, but when I turn to walk to the other end, it snaps back into the measure box and pinches my finger. "Ouch."

"If you set the tip over the edge of the board, then keep the tape low against the wood, it won't slip off." He shows me what to do. "Try it now." Boone's patience is remarkable. If the senator were here, he'd call me stupid.

Successful this time, I mark a *V* at two feet, then using a straight edge, draw a line. I grab the saw he left for me and cut the board. "Hey, I did it."

Boone inspects my work and nods. "You're hired. Cut seven more just the same. Those will be the cross braces for a wall."

I squat to look at the plan he has laid out on the floor. "How can you tell what is what on this?"

He crouches next to me and points to one line. "This is the new wall that will turn this room into a storage room and your family's parlor. We can get that wall framed up today, lath it, then we'll plaster tomorrow. You can paint it on Thursday."

"I'll have to tell Fitzie we will be able to use the new family parlor for Christmas." I look back at the drawing. "How long will it take to do the bedroom and family parlor?"

Boone glances at George and Jimmy, who are already building the storage room wall. "Between us, we can have that done in two-and-a-half to three days. Your first floor will be complete by the day after Christmas. Then we'll move to the attic." He sits back on his heels. "Are you ready to help?"

"Let's get at it."

I'm anxious to see this place turned into a proper boarding— no, guesthouse. After I get the boards cut, Boone gives me another length for ten more. By the time I'm halfway through, my arms are burning. I can barely hold onto the saw.

Boone stops hammering and takes the saw from me. "We appreciate your help, Cora, but you're going to hurt in the morning. Go get in a tub of hot water and soak. It will help with the soreness. Most of the lumber is cut to length already, so we're good."

Another job failure after just ninety minutes of work? I peer up at him. "Are you firing me?"

Sarcasm and compassion argue for dominance in his facial expression. With a tender smile, compassion wins. "No, I want you back tomorrow. But for you to be in shape to help, you've got to stop for today."

That makes no sense, but my aching muscles leap for joy. "Okay. I'll call you for dinner at noon."

When I get upstairs, Pearl sees me. She sets an armload of laundry in Fitzie's room and, not saying a word, points to the bathroom. I strip off my overalls and shirt while she draws the water for me.

I lay my head back against the cool cast iron and let my limbs revel in the warmth penetrating them. Not having the strength left to push them under, my arms float effortlessly on top of the water. Faint hammering from the floor below echoes softly.

I feel better after soaking for a half hour. I slip into a day dress and hurry to help Pearl get dinner ready. When I call Boone, George, and Jimmy to come eat, I'm shocked at all they have finished. The wall is up, the lath nailed to about a quarter of it. Pearl has followed me and stands in the doorway.

Boone gestures her over and points to the plan. "New storage and a linen closet will go up to the second floor. Miss Fitzie wants them there to make it easier for changing linens on the guest floor. Then the old linen closet here"—he indicates a square—"becomes a large bathroom for guests. Miss Fitzie also instructed me to turn the old bathroom into a private one for you."

I had no idea Mama told Boone to do that, but it's an expense well worth it. Pearl does the work of three people. Her eyes grow large, then a smile splits her face. A sheen of moisture glistens in her eyes. "My Miss Fitzie … hmm-hmm-hmm." She beckons to the men. "Y'all come into the kitchen and have your dinner."

I need to go hug my mother.

Chapter 16

Christmas Day, December 25, 1929

I AWAKEN TO A WINTERY WORLD outside my window. Not snow, but ice. Every tree branch and plant sparkles from its crystal casing. Fortunately, the radio promises the temperature will rise to a brisk forty-one degrees by noon. I certainly hope so. Everyone is due by then for Christmas dinner.

Judging by the muffled pot-clanging coming from the kitchen, Pearl is up and already at it. Wait—

My gaze drifts to the neighbor's barn roofline, barely visible through the trees. Either I've become immune to it, or the rooster didn't crow this morning. Is he, perhaps, a frozen fowl? Could I be so lucky? I throw back the covers and grab my robe.

Rooster aside, Christmas excitement chases away any remaining cobwebs of sleep. I can't wait to read Aunt Clara's story. Funny, I'd never realized she was such a well-known authoress until I went to New York. It was eye-opening, to say the least. I only knew I loved her stories.

I clamber down the stairs and hurry into the kitchen. "Merry Christmas, Pearl." I give her a one-armed hug and pour myself a cup of coffee. "Is anyone else up yet?"

"Sure 'nuff. They's waitin' for you in the parlor."

"Are you at a point where you can join us?"

A broad grin splits her beautiful, round, ebony face. "Just waitin' for you, Miss Cora."

We traipse into the new family parlor, where Fitzie and Aunt Clara put the finishing touches on the Christmas tree Boone cut down for us yesterday.

I clap my hands in happy appreciation. "Merry Christmas! The tree looks lovely. You two have done a swell job." I adjust a piece of tinsel and eye the small pile of packages beneath the branches. I'm glad both Mama and Aunt Clara took my warnings about not going crazy with presents we can't afford.

I reach into my robe pocket and withdraw the gifts I brought from New York with me, setting them with the others. Pearl stands at the edge of our little gathering. I got her into the room with us, but that's as far as she'll come. The senator's legacy.

I reach for a small box wrapped in green-and-white paper. "Pearl, I bought this while I was still up north. The moment I saw it, I knew it was for you." I hold it out to her.

She nods solemnly, then pulls off the paper with care, folds it, and removes the lid. Her eyes grow round when she lifts out the tiny bottle of toilet water. She removes the stopper and takes a whiff. "Oh, my stars, it's orange blossoms. Thank you, Miss Cora. I've never had my very own scent water before."

I show her how to get a little on the end of the stopper and dab it behind each ear. After she receives a pretty apron from Fitzie and a watercolor for her room from Aunt Clara, Pearl retreats to the kitchen to work on her present for us. Every year, she surprises us with some fabulous Christmas breakfast concoction.

I give my aunt and mother small flacons of Chanel No.5. They cost more than I wish I'd spent, but when I bought them on sale at the beginning of October, none of us knew what was to come. However, seeing them tickled pink makes it worth the expense. When it's my turn, Fitzie hands me a small, flat jewelry box.

What—? I open it. Grandmother Drummond's rose amethyst necklace lays on a bed of black velvet.

I ease it out with trembling hands. "Oh, Mama, thank you! You know I've always loved this."

My grandmother wore the amethyst necklace every Sunday. After she died, I'd catch Mama sitting in her room, stroking the stones and weeping. We both missed her so very much. Fitzie's sacrifice touches me deeply.

She nods at the jewels in my hands. "May I, sugar?"

I hand her the necklace with a smile. "Yes, please."

Fitzie turns me around so I'm facing the mirror over the fireplace. She reaches over my head and fastens the clasp behind my neck. I gaze at my reflection. The necklace, resembling a circlet of Greek olive leaves with tiny diamonds for their stems, rests on my collarbone.

"It's exquisite," I say, all breathy and grateful.

Next, it's Aunt Clara's turn. She signs, "This is for both of you. Cora, you read it. The others are getting a story you've already seen."

Running my fingers over my necklace, I settle into the davenport and open the booklet.

"'The last thing I expected to find when we built out the attic was a mummified body. But there it was, between the rafters, under a layer of shiplap.'"

I stop, looking up at Aunt Clara. "This is new. You wrote it this week, didn't you?"

Her grin is cheeky.

"You realize Fitzie and I will lie awake in bed, afraid to go to sleep."

Her silent laughter makes me giggle, and Fitzie says, "Don't worry. You won't sleep either. Cora and I will make sure of it. Now, get on with the story."

Fitzie's good-natured teasing of Aunt Clara is just that. She's very proud of her sister. For the next thirty minutes, we are enthralled by her mystery—one moment, heart-pounding fear and the next, laughter. Nobody writes like my aunt.

When the story ends—with a twist neither of us see coming—we head to the dining room for breakfast. This year, Pearl's gift to us is a savory pie of cheese, egg, ham, and red pepper flakes.

With reverence, Pearl serves us each a large slice. "It's called quiche."

I take the first bite. "Oh, Pearl. It's heavenly. I've heard of this dish but never had any. I love it. Thank you. It's a wonderful Christmas present."

We eat in silence, each savoring every bite of her gift.

Finally, using the back of her fork tines, Fitzie collects every last crumb on her plate. "Divine, Pearl. Simply divine."

Aunt Clara hugs Pearl, then signs to Fitzie and me, "Let's go upstairs and plan our new bedroom layout and choose where we are going to want our beds. Cora, go get dressed and join us."

Soon, I'm appropriately attired and standing with them in the attic. "Maybe we can have Boone add three dormers on this back side." I point to the part of the roof that—if it had a dormer—would overlook the pond and woods. Many years ago, someone dug out the pond and dammed the creek long enough for it to fill. I grew up fishing and swimming there, a respite from the senator's harsh words.

Fitzie crosses her arms and studies the room. "We can have Boone and the Horton boys place each bed by a dormer. What do you think? Beneath or beside the dormers?"

"Beside," Aunt Clara signs. "We can put a nightstand beneath the window, and that way, we can still look out."

"I like that." I glance at each. "Which one do you two want?"

"I'll take the middle one." Fitzie reaches for her sister's hand. "That way, I'm next to each of you."

I'm not sure I fully comprehend the change in Fitzie, but there's a paradigm shift in their relationship. It's as though she's looking to her sister for affirmation. Aunt Clara *is* five years older, so it seems fairly natural. It's a subtle change and one I like. It makes me wish I had a sister. Then again, I've got my Dillies, and we're as close as sisters would be.

Aunt Clara signs, "I'll take the farthest and leave the one nearest the door for Cora. That way, if she's out on a date with a certain handyman,"—she winks at Fitzie—"she doesn't wake us when she comes in late."

I roll my eyes. "I'm going to move some of my clothes and things up here now, so I can spend tomorrow helping that handyman build our guest rooms. We need to get open."

I leave them laughing, as I always try to do with an audience.

I just hope they aren't my *last* audience.

∞

Friday, December 27, 1929

At the rooster's first crow, my eyes pop open. Applesauce. He survived the ice storm. Tough old thing. Is rooster soup any good? He crows again in protest. I wriggle under the quilts' warmth and let my mind search for the reason I don't feel nostalgic about losing my own room. But, of course, I know. The senator. My room was not a haven. Not really. When he was alive, he could throw the door open unannounced and give me a verbal or physical beating. He was clever, that one. He'd take his belt to me often, but never bruise me so anyone could see.

A familiar panic rises in my throat. But no! He's dead and I'm free of him.

God, please let the remodeling exorcize his presence from this house.

I throw on my clothes and hurry downstairs to breakfast. Fitzie and Aunt Clara aren't in the dining room yet. That's fine. It's a good day to start a new way of life. Save the dining room for guests. We can eat in the kitchen. I only hope I don't give Pearl apoplexy over it.

I push open the kitchen door. "G'morning, Pearl."

She stops rolling out biscuit dough. "It sure is. I'll bring your breakfast out directly, Miss Cora."

"Thanks, but I'll have my breakfast here." I sit at the table across from her.

Pearl's brow crinkles, then smooths, then crinkles again. She picks up her favorite tool and rolls it over the dough. Back and forth. Turn the dough. Work it again. Finally, she stops.

Her head tilts to one side and she grins. "You realize hisself would pitch a conniption fit, you comin' in here like this?" Ever since his death, she refers to the senator as *hisself*.

I laugh. "Absolutely. Fitzie may want to play hostess, and I don't know about Aunt Clara, but you can plan on me taking my meals here. After all, I'll be an employee of Fitzgerald House."

"You ain't servin' no guests. My granddaughter will do that."

I know not to argue with her. "But I will be helping you in here."

At her frown, I add, "Don't look so skeptical. I can wash dishes."

"You take care of the finances. Ruby and I will do the cookin' and servin'. If'n I need more help, I can train Jade." Pearl stares at the dough she's been working while we talk. With a harrumph, she tosses it in the trash.

I gape. "Why did you do that?"

"Too much workin' makes biscuits tough."

Pearl cottons onto why I don't want to eat with the guests. She won't pester me—at least not this morning.

The kitchen door opens at the same time I'm finishing my coffee. Once again, at the sight of Boone, my heart beats faster. His shirt strains to contain his muscular shoulders. The memory of leaning against them when he kissed me …

He hasn't said another word about our kiss. Nor has he tried to kiss me again.

You wonder why? Just look at you. You're not worth—

Heat rises in my cheeks. "Good morning."

I hurry out of the room before Boone can notice my discomfort. Fitzie and Aunt Clara are already in the dining room.

Fitzie raises her eyes from the folded newspaper beside her plate. "I wondered where you were. Why aren't you eating?"

My aunt, who views life as an adventure, nods, grins, and signs, "Is that handsome handyman here already?"

"Thank you," I mouth to her. I'll broach the subject of eating later. "Yes, Boone and the Hortons are here. They might even finish the downstairs work tomorrow."

After Aunt Clara and Fitzie finish eating, we set to work on outfitting the downstairs guest room. Last week, we moved the senator's desk into the guest parlor in case any guests need to write letters. This morning, the delivery men set the bed in place and put the mattresses on it, but Fitzie says she told them to leave the dresser and side tables in the hallway.

The three of us stand in the room, surveying it. Something isn't right. "I don't like the bed on this wall. It should go between the windows. Help me move it." Using my thigh, I give it a shove. It bumps across the floor a few inches. "It's not too heavy."

We wrangle the bed to the adjacent wall, centering it between the windows. Aunt Clara claps her hands and signs, "That's much better. Now, it has symmetry and balances the room."

Fitzie nudges her sister with an elbow. "Not to mention, it leaves more space for a sitting area." She taps her chin. "There's a chair in my room I'll sacrifice. I can use one from the attic." She disappears through the door.

Aunt Clara and I stare at each other, wide-eyed. "Who is that woman?" I ask.

She shakes her head, signing, "I've never known my sister to give away something she enjoys, and make no mistake, she loves that chair. I think she's realizing her late husband did *not* leave any money for her."

"You honestly think she's accepted it?"

"I do. And she's decided to make the best of it. I think she even enjoys beating the old goat by becoming proprietress of a money-maker—his pride-and-joy-turned-boarding-house." My aunt shakes with silent laughter. "I fervently hope he can see this."

"I fervently hope we can actually *do* this."

Using her finger, Aunt Clara turns my chin until I'm facing her. Then she signs, "Your mother was made to preside over a houseful of guests. That they are paying guests is a minor fact she'll overlook. I'll collect the money, and she'll play hostess. We can't fail."

My mama comes back, Jimmy following her with the overstuffed armchair. She has him set it in a corner across from the bed. "Thank you, Jimmy."

While Aunt Clara makes the bed, Fitzie and I slide the dresser into place and situate the side table next to the chair. The three of us stand back and look at the room with a visitor's eye. It's very inviting.

I throw an arm around my aunt and mother. "I think we're going to pull this off. I'll get the floor lamp I brought down from the attic. It will look nice between the chair and table."

By the time I get back, Fitzie and Aunt Clara have a beautiful blanket folded on the end of the bed, a lap robe over the back of the armchair, and a couple of books on the table.

In my mind, I tick off items on my list until I remember one that can be done now. "I'm going to finish the guesthouse sign."

Fitzie startles. "So soon?"

"It will take a week or two for the word to spread. Unless you want to let Blanche know."

Fitzie laughs. "I think not."

In the kitchen, I take the short board I cut for a sign. Boone did some fancy tooling on the edges the other day, so it's got a pretty shape. Now, what to put on it?

"Fitzie?" When she doesn't answer, I go in search of her. She's back in what was the senator's office—the "family" parlor now—pulling books from the shelves.

"What are you doing? Looking for a certain book?"

"Culling the senator's favorite books and moving them in the guest parlor. And I'll put a few of your aunt's favorite titles there, too, for the ladies."

"Good idea." I hold up the plaque, a frown puckering my lips. "What do you think I should put on it? What shall we call the house now?"

Balancing an armload of books, she turns to me and smiles. "It's obvious, sugar-pie. Call it Fitzgerald Guest House. For once, *we* will capitalize on the senator's name. It's all he left us. So let's turn it into a salable commodity." She snickers. "He'll pitch a hissy fit. I can imagine him bellowing all through the halls of wherever he is."

Loving her logic, I retreat to the kitchen. With an artist's brush, I paint the words in script, adding flourishes and a couple of flowers.

When it dries, I carry it down the driveway to the mailbox and nail it to the cross bar so it hangs beneath the house box.

Fitzgerald Guest House - Meals and Lodging.

Beneath the name, hooks hold the vacancy sign. Perfect. So inviting. I'm beginning to believe Aunt Clara. After all, what could go wrong?

Chapter 17

Monday, December 30, 1929

SUNLIGHT THROUGH THE GABLE VENTS dapples the attic where I stand with Boone, Jimmy, and George. Boone hangs a flashlight from a rafter, then lays out the plans on a table he'd set up by using two sawhorses and some boards. I peer at the blueprints. Here and there, solid lines run opposite dashed ones. I point at a spot on the plans. "Can you explain this to me?"

Boone's patience seems to be infinite. "Sure. These are the dormers you requested. Three of them to bring in more light and fresh air in good weather. Those"—he moves his hand to the side of the drawings—"are closets. Jimmy and George will start on those, while you and I frame out the dormers."

I push up my sleeves. "Okay, tell me what to do."

Boone rolls up the plans, then points to a pile of lumber and gives me a list of boards and their measurements. While he saws holes in the roof, I cut the boards to the lengths he wants. It takes me a couple of hours to get it all done.

Returning from the other end of the attic, Boone lets out a low whistle and palms another board from the pieces I have stacked. "You've done a lot. How are your arms holding out?"

I flex the stiffness from the muscles in my forearm. "They're good. They've learned it doesn't pay to get sore. And I just completed your list." Nodding toward my prized pile, I hold out a short piece of lumber. "This is the last one."

He takes the board, then glances around to see what the Hortons are doing. Busy with their work on the closets, they ignore us. Edging closer with a slanted grin, Boone leans down and kisses me, making my toes curl.

"You've been a big help today, Cora. The Hortons and I will have the attic finished by tomorrow, probably late afternoon. But you can be done for today."

"Kicking me out again, are you?" Too delighted by his doting smile and gesture of affection to be offended, I lay down the saw. "In that case, I think I'll go shopping." I throw him a sassy grin and dance down the stairs. *Take that, Senator.*

Downstairs, I pick up the phone and call Millie. "Want to go to Buford with me?"

"Does a duck waddle?" Her voice hums with mirth.

She's never too busy for an outing. "Great. Get yourself ready. I'm picking you up in thirty minutes."

Aunt Clara is at her desk. Today, the beret atop her head is emerald green. I don't bother her but go in search of Fitzie, who I find in the sewing room. Pearl is with her, and they are sorting through boxes and cupboards.

"What are you two up to?"

Fitzie, who sports a cute, knotted bandana turban, swipes the back of her wrist over her forehead. "I decided we need a morning room more than all this space for sewing. After all, whom among us sews?"

Her delightful laugh spurs a chuckle from me. It's impossible to be around Fitzie when she laughs and not join in.

She points to one of the tall windows that overlook the backyard. "We can place another writing table there for your aunt."

A frown weights my brow. "I don't know about that. I can just picture her writing in the middle of the guest parlor, eavesdropping on our guests."

Fitzie closes a box and slides it into a cabinet beneath the window seat that spans the ten-foot space. "You're probably right, but I'll put a desk here for her, anyway. She can have one in each room. You and I can employ the one here for writing letters if she chooses not to use it." She straightens and eyes me. "So, what are you up to?"

"Millie and I are going into Buford. I have that list you gave me of things we still need for the guest rooms." I pull it from my pocket and open it. "We're doing great on the budget, so I thought I'd go pick them out today. Boone doesn't need me." I stop and look around. "But do you?"

She waves me away. "No. Pearl and I have a plan. Go with Millie. The car keys are on the foyer table."

"Thanks." I kiss her goodbye. When I get to the door, I toss back over my shoulder, "You two behave, now."

Pearl's alto chuckle follows me out. Gratitude for a house filled with laughter flows over my heart like a balm, and with it, peace. Quite the change from when the senator was alive. I crank the engine and climb inside. Through the open car window, I glance up at the sky, polka-dotted with clouds.

"Thank You."

I shift into first gear and let out the clutch, much smoother than last time. Soon Millie is beside me, wearing a yellow-and-white dress with puffy sleeves. We head to Venable's.

"So what are we after?"

I glance at her, then turn my eyes back to the road. "I need your color sense in choosing accessories for the guest rooms." Millie has an artist's eye. She also paints beautiful watercolors.

She clasps her hands together. "Ooh, fun. I love decorating. What kind of things are you getting?"

"A few pillows for chairs, a vase or two, and lap robes. Boarders will bring some of their own personal knickknacks, I should imagine." I turn onto the now-paved Cumming Highway. "What we don't find at Venable's, we'll pick up at Allen's Department Store. Oh, and I want to buy some watercolors from you."

She twists sideways on the seat and looks at me. "You don't have to buy them, Cora. I'll give them to you."

I tighten my grip on the steering wheel, preparing for an argument. "No, you won't. I'll buy them. Dillies support each other, and that includes not taking advantage. You paid me when you had me entertain your family that time y'all came to New York. Remember?"

She frowns and turns to drum her fingers against the door. "You're right. I forgot about that. So thank you. When we get back, you can come in and take your pick."

"I've got twenty dollars budgeted for artwork."

"For twenty bucks, you can get a nine-by-twelve for each room."

"Thanks, Millie-billie." I turn into the parking lot. For a small-town general store, Venable's stocks a wide variety of items. I'm hopeful we can find most of what I need here.

When we enter the store, Alice Farnham occupies Mr. Rocky's attention. She has a length of cloth in her hands and is arguing over the price. I turn around to leave, but Millie blocks the door, her brows drawing down.

"Don't you turn tail on her, Cora. She's a nasty bit of skirt, but I'm here to help you."

"All right, but I hate confrontation." I had enough of that with the senator.

Millie squeezes my hand, and we peruse the display cases while we wait for Mr. Rocky to finish with Alice.

Finally, he sighs loudly and gives her five cents off the cloth. With a smug expression, she takes the package but drops it as I round the corner. A small tear appears in the wrapping.

An angry glare tightens the skin around her eyes. "Look what you made me do. I ought to make you pay for it, and I will if it's dirty."

Mr. Rocky picks up the wrapped cloth, then draws himself up and thrusts the package toward Alice. "I keep a clean floor, and Cora didn't do anything. You got your discount, now unless you want something else, Alice, I suggest you go and let me help these ladies."

Alice reluctantly takes the cloth, and Mr. Rocky crosses to me and Millie. "What can I do for you?"

Alice tosses her head but doesn't leave. Instead, she stands near the door, pretending to look over a rack of aprons. My only consolation is she doesn't like Millie—or any of the Dillies—any better than she does me.

I keep my voice low and enunciate as clearly as possible, but it's not easy to communicate since Mr. Rocky is a bit hard of hearing. "I need a few small pillows for overstuffed chairs."

"Overstuffed pairs of what?" He cups his ear and leans toward me.

I move closer to him. "Overstuffed chairs."

He rubs his chin, his tongue running around and around his teeth. I follow its course until he snaps his fingers. "Got just what you're looking for."

He goes behind the counter and draws his finger along the display cases until he finds the object of his search. He bends, slides open the case door, and withdraws three doll bed pillows.

I glance at Millie, whose lips purse in her effort not to laugh. "Uh, thank you, Mr. Rocky, but those aren't quite what I had in mind. Let's forget the pillows. What do you have in small vases?"

He points farther down the line of his display case. "A fine selection. Several—uh, eight to be exact."

"Why are you buying so many?" Now at the end of the counter, Alice stands with one hand on her hip and her package under the other arm.

I open my mouth, but Millie beats me to it. "None of your beeswax, Alice."

She shoots out her lip at Millie. "Shut up."

I don't need a public fight. Two more ladies have come into the store. "I'm buying a few things for our guest rooms, but I can't see how that is any of your business." She's never been inside our home, so she doesn't know how many bedrooms we have—or guest rooms. "Or interesting to you, for that matter."

"It's *not*." She opens her mouth again but snaps it shut.

Ha! She effectively ended her discourse without realizing it. Her face grows bright red. She turns with a huff and storms out the door.

"I swanney, she's a hot mess o' work," Mr. Rocky says, scratching the back of his head. "She musta been born on the wrong side of the bed and been gettin' up there ever since."

With Alice gone, I select six vases and a dozen antimacassars, since Brilliantine is as bad as Macassar oil for leaving grease stains on furniture.

Mr. Rocky doesn't carry the lap robes or the decorative pillows I want, so I pay for my purchases, and we leave. We quickly find the other items at Allen's Department Store and head back to Millie's.

Her collection of watercolors is impressive. "I had no idea you painted so many." I leaf through the first of five portfolios.

She hefts a sixth onto the table. "That's the last one. I've been painting forever, but it wasn't until last year that anyone ever paid any attention to them."

I hold up a landscape of Level Creek and set it in my *purchase* pile, then peer at the next one. A covey of little girls picnicking in a bucolic setting. Wait—

My mouth drops as I turn to peer at her. "Why, this is our house. When did you do this?"

"One Saturday when I lived in Atlanta. I was particularly homesick that morning and missed all y'all. I got to thinking about a picnic Fitzie and your aunt fixed for us in your backyard. We must have been about seven years old."

"I remember Martha Anne fell in the pond that day." Chuckling over the memory, I set the painting aside to buy.

"Speaking of picnics, Cora, did you ever go to any of the Bona Allen's moonlight picnics over at Passes Pond in the summer?"

I flip past two more landscapes and shrug. "Who would I have gone with? They were for married folks and courting couples."

Millie slides each painting I select into a large envelope. "I didn't think you had. Glenice Jo went to several with Willie before they got married. Martha Anne has gone to a few with various boys. Neither Trudie nor I ever went to one. But I've heard how romantic they are."

"Are they still having them?" I'd love to go to one with Boone. I stifle the desire to sigh and pick up another watercolor.

"I think so. I haven't heard otherwise."

I continue to leaf through Millie's work until I have the six needed paintings. After paying her, I leave with my treasures, but my mind is on a certain handyman and a summer moonlight picnic. Too bad this is still December.

When I arrive home, I find Fitzie and Aunt Clara in the morning room and show them my purchases. They love all but one pillow, which I set aside for exchanging.

"Cora, can you come up for a minute?" Boone's voice from the stairwell interrupts us.

"Sure. I'll be right there."

Fitzie waves me away. "Go. We'll put these away for now."

Wondering what he wants speeds my steps. At the attic entrance, I pause to survey their handiwork. Wow, they got a lot done in the last couple of hours. The dormers are framed, and George is outside roofing them while Jimmy places the window in the second one.

After showing me the dormers, Boone runs his hand over a window ledge, pulling a thread snagged on a wood splinter. "Uh, Cora," he stammers.

He's nervous. The knowledge sends ripples through my belly.

"Would you—I mean, do you have any plans for New Year's Eve?"

"Plans?" My heart pounds and my throat goes dry. "No, unless I'm painting up here."

"No painting. There's a dinner dance at the Merchant Hotel in Buford. Would you like to go with me?"

As in a date? Or as in friend? A friend who'll do in a pinch when he can't get a real date.

In case that mind-echo is right, I keep it light. "It sounds swell."

Boone cocks his head. "So … that means you'll go?"

I grin. "Sure, I'd love to go."

It's an effort to force my feet to step on each tread instead of floating down the stairs. In my bedroom, I flip through the hangers in my closet, looking for the right gown to wear. When my hand hits one holding a lavender dress with a flared skirt, it stops. I pull it out. It's perfect. The dress is sleeveless with a plunging back. It's tight to the bottom of the hips, then it flares in layers of soft fabric, ending in different-length points.

I walk over to the standing, full-length, oval mirror and hold it up in front of me. The dress is beautiful and makes my eyes appear bluer than—

A memory rears its ugly whisper. I was fifteen and there was a school dance. I told Fitzie about my crush on Boone, and the senator overheard during one of his rare times at home. As if it was yesterday, I hear him haunt me.

Don't get your hopes up. Look at you. You're nothing but a Plain Jane.

If anyone better comes along, I should be prepared for Boone to dump me.

Chapter 18

New Year's Eve, December 31, 1929

FITZIE AND AUNT CLARA FLIT around me, each one adding their personal touch to my gown and hair. Great-grandmother Drummond's amethysts grace my neck, and Aunt Clara's diamond studs sparkle from my earlobes. I run my hand over my hip and smooth the skirt, scarcely daring to believe the gorgeous woman in the mirror is me. No, not me. It's the dress. The lavender gown is stunning. I pull on purple satin, opera-length gloves that match the sequins and turn for their inspection. Fitzie nods and settles her long mink cape over my shoulders.

"There. You're beautiful." Through the shimmer of moisture in her eyes, love radiates.

I know better, but in this evening frock, I almost believe her. In vain, I try to subdue the butterflies in my stomach. The closer we get to seven o'clock, the more frenzied their Lindy Hop.

Aunt Clara hands me a beaded evening bag, and we descend the stairs. The doorbell rings before we hit the landing, and I hear Pearl welcome Boone. I pause, then continue my descent, Fitzie and Aunt Clara stumbling over themselves at my heels.

Boone comes into sight, and I catch my breath. He's wearing a tuxedo and looks movie-star handsome. David Divine has nothing on him. The butterflies move into a high-kicking Charleston.

"Hey, Boone."

At the sound of my voice, he turns. Everything stops as he stares at me. "Wow. Those are some glad rags. You're the hummingbird's wings."

I tamp a flicker of excitement. *He meant the dress, not you.* "You clean up pretty good yourself."

He glances down and runs a hand over his pants. "I only hope there's no sawdust on me."

As usual, Boone makes us all laugh. Aunt Clara circles him and shakes her head. "You're clean," she signs.

I kiss them goodnight and we leave. Parked outside in the driveway is a shiny red-and-black Dodge. I snap my gaze to Boone. "Whose—?"

"Your carriage, Princess Cora."

"Is that yours?"

He opens the door for me, then bows. "No. I borrowed it."

"That must be some friend to lend you a brand-spanking new car." I settle onto the soft leather seats with a happy sigh. Once he's in, I ask, "Whose is it?"

"Gavin Culver's."

My blood turns cold. I do my best to keep my tone light. "*Senator* Gavin Culver?"

"That's him."

How is Boone close enough to a politician that the man lends him his new car? I pull Fitzie's cape closer around me.

He flashes a grin at me. "Remember Thursday, when I knocked off early? I repaired an heirloom sideboard for the senator's wife. When I happened to mention I was taking you to the Merchant for New Year's Eve, he said I couldn't take a pretty lady out in my old truck, and he lent me this."

"How nice of him." What else will Boone have to do for him? He may have fixed that sideboard, but I know politicians. They always want more.

Through the window, the rising moon's waxing crescent peeks through the trees, but the shine is off the evening. Maybe it's for the best, except my heart doesn't want to listen.

We pull up to the three-story hotel. A covered balcony runs the length of the second story, and the third is dormered. A valet opens my door and offers his hand. Boone comes around and tosses him the keys as though he's done this before. I pull my lips into a smile, one my heart doesn't share.

When we're inside the lobby, Boone lifts Fitzie's cape from my shoulders. His warm fingers send a shiver skittering down my arms, and my traitorous heart thrills. He checks my cape and his top hat, tucking the receipts into his jacket pocket.

He holds out his elbow for me and escorts me to the dining room. Boone's a perfect gentleman—so different from most of the men I've known. Still, I'm not sure where this is going. The business with that senator has me on edge.

The *maître d'* shows us to our table, hands us the evening's menu with a flourish, then bows and leaves.

A nervous giggle threatens, but I subdue it, only allowing a slight smile. "He must have worked in New York at one time. He's a carbon copy of the maître d' at Delmonico's." I take a sip of water, then lower my gaze to the menu card. There are no choices on it. It simply states what we're having.

Boone glances around the dining room. "They're really putting on the Ritz tonight, aren't they?"

I let my gaze travel to the other diners, while more continue to spill into the room, everyone dressed to the nines. "It's pretty swell. I haven't been in here since I was a kid, maybe five years old. Fitzie brought me for lunch. I insisted I was grown up enough to go to the restroom by myself, but I got lost. In an upstairs hallway, I had the fire scared out of me when I saw a woman lingering outside one of the rooms. When she moved, her feet didn't touch the floor, and I could see through her. I was later told it was the hotel ghost."

Boone doesn't laugh like I thought he might. Before he can comment, the waiter arrives with our first course. While we eat, Boone tells me more stories, making me laugh often. I'm beginning to relax again and feel comfortable in our friendship. Maybe I overreacted to his relationship with Senator Culver. After all, he builds furniture for Atlanta's wealthy families. Of course, he'd rub shoulders with a few politicians.

That reinstates my good mood, and the dessert of Baked Alaska completes the restoration. One by one, band members enter and take their places on the raised platform. I'm ready for the music and some dancing. My toes already want to tap, even to the band's warming up exercises.

Boone lays his napkin on his empty dessert plate. "Will you excuse me for a moment? I need to make use of the men's room."

"Certainly." I turn my attention back to the band. There are—I do a quick count—twenty chairs, so it's a good-size group. I don't know the name. Maybe it's a new local group starting out.

"Well, well, look who's here. How did you ever manage to wrangle an invitation to this?"

I know that voice. Alice Farnham. Dressed in a bright-red dress cut way too low for propriety, she stands beside my table, her expression bold and haughty.

"I could ask the same of you, Alice, but I'm better bred than that."

"I'm meeting my date here. At least I have one." She stares pointedly at Boone's empty chair, then consults her gold wristwatch. "He should be here now." She turns and sweeps across the room and disappears past the maître d's podium.

Whoever her date is, it seems odd to meet here, but what do I know? Boone is taking his time. I crane my neck to see the dining room foyer.

"Excuse me, are you alone?" A mustachioed man with dark hair slicked back with pomade stands next to Boone's chair.

My fingers flutter to my mouth and then down to my lap. "Oh, you startled me. No, I'm not alone."

He raises one eyebrow. "I don't see anyone." He pulls out Boone's chair and sits. Leaning one elbow on the table, he rests his chin on his fist and stares at me.

"My date is in the restroom," I say loftily, raising my chin.

"I'm Walter Teague. You've heard of me?"

"I'm sorry, I haven't." I crane my neck to see the entrance over this man's shoulder.

"Ah, well, you should. I'm Bona Allen's nephew."

"And?"

"I know who you are." He leans forward with lovesick cow-eyes. "You're Dixie Lynn."

Where is Boone? I lean to the side to see around Walter, if that's really his name. I wish—ah, there's Boone. But what—?

Walter turns his head, sees what I do, cringes, then jumps up and leaves.

My attention isn't on him, though. It's on Boone—and Alice Farnham on his arm. What is she doing with him?

Without a glance at our table, Boone and Alice cross to the far side of the dining room. She tilts her head, looking up at him, and says something, making him laugh.

I start to rise but quickly sink back into my chair, my jaw slack. Though it's humiliating, I'm unable to take my eyes off them. Like picking at a scab, I watch Boone and Alice with their heads intimately together, as he guides her to a table where a man rises and shakes his hand. He gestures to a chair. Boone solicitously seats Alice, and leaning over her shoulder, he whispers in her ear. When she giggles, he sits beside her. Too close.

The scene before me blurs and I turn away. What am I to do? I can't stay here. The waiter approaches. His expression tells me he has seen and pities me. "May I take your dishes?"

Stand tall. Rise above this. I hold my head high, lay my napkin on the table, and nod. I rise and exit the dining room, fighting against tears. In the doorway, as I turn the corner, I catch a glimpse of their table. Boone hasn't taken his eyes from his new date.

The coat check girl thankfully remembers me since I don't have the claim ticket and hands over Fitzie's cape. I have no idea what I can do except walk home. The doorman opens the door, and I run out into the night.

Forging my way through the woods is better than remaining at the hotel. I don't know why Boone deserted me like that, but never again will I discount warning bells. He's just like the senator.

Anger and humiliation fuel my steps, while tears cool my face. I swipe at them with my knuckles. Boone hasn't declared any feelings for me, and I'm nothing more than a friend-who'll-do-in-a-pinch date. But to treat even a friend so uncharitably is unacceptable. He's not worth tears.

So why is my heart breaking?

Following a straight line through the woods from the hotel, it's only about a two-and-a-half-mile hike to home. I'm thankful there hasn't been any rain, but my shoes—dancing slippers, really—will be ruined all the same. Men aren't worth this. Silly me, thinking I'd found one who was different.

Like a specter, the senator's words dog me. *Men don't fall for girls who look like you.*

Lights flicker through the trees. My heartbeat kicks up a moment. But it's only Harvey and Ollie Bailey's house. That means I'm closer to home than I realized. It's a good thing because it's really cold, approaching freezing. My breath frosts when I exhale. I pick up my pace.

Thirty minutes later, I reach our driveway. The instant I see the lights in the windows, I break into a run. Instead of going in the front door, though, I head to the kitchen entrance. I don't want to talk to Fitzie or Aunt Clara. And it's late enough that Pearl should be in her room, too, reading or listening to her radio.

I turn the doorknob slowly and push open the door, stopping just before the hinge squeaks. Pearl isn't in the kitchen. Radio music in the front parlor rivals laughter on a comedy show from Pearl's room. Nobody will hear me sneaking up the stairs.

In my bedroom, I undress and slip under the covers. I no longer want to welcome in the New Year. I only hope it brings happier days than this past one. Under the covers, I allow my tears to flow again. My wounded heart needs their release.

On Friday, Boone will be here. He has about two weeks of work left to do. He and the Hortons will have to finish it without my help.

What will I do? I hate confrontation. How can I be civil when I want to slap him? But I can't hide forever.

∞

New Year's Day, January 1, 1930

I have no appetite for breakfast. A piece of toast and coffee are all I can manage. With a sigh, I finish relaying the events of last night to Fitzie and Aunt Clara. Reliving it is horrid. Heat climbs up my neck and into my cheeks.

Fitzie's brows draw together. "Why didn't you just ask him?"

The question baffles me. "What? Follow him and Alice over to their table like some fishwife? No, thank you. He doesn't owe me an explanation."

Aunt Clara's left eyebrow raises. She doesn't agree. Her hands move languidly. "Oh, but he does. As a gentleman."

"It would be too humiliating. As it is, Alice will probably spread it all over town."

Fitzie reaches across the table and squeezes my hand. "I do understand your reluctance." She turns her gaze to my aunt. "I can't count the times I had to raise my chin and stare down public humiliation. It's to be avoided if at all possible."

Aunt Clara's mouth pulls into a flat line. Her toast buttered, she sets down her knife. "I remember," she signs. "And your grace always stopped the wagging tongues." She shakes her head. "I'm truly surprised at Boone."

I cover my face again, but I can't block the memory of my shame. "I've never been so embarrassed and humiliated in my life." Another memory rises like a ghost from its grave. I lower my hands. "Well, I guess I was. Once. By the senator in front of his cronies."

Fitzie scowls. "That was the night he broke your second ventriloquist's puppet. The proper one I bought for you."

I shake off the memory and take a sip of coffee. "Anyway, I can't imagine what confronting Boone would solve. It's not as though we have a relationship or anything."

Aunt Clara's hands fly. "But as a friend, to go off and leave you like that? I can't understand how he thought you were to get home."

Her lips purse with outrage. "Or if you did. It's unacceptable. In fact, he's not welcome here until he apologizes and gives you a satisfactory explanation. Jimmy can finish the project. There's not that much to be done, anyway."

Her staunch support leaves me weak with gratitude. "I appreciate that, Aunt Clara. However, we contracted Boone to do the work. You know the old saying, 'Two wrongs don't make a right.' I will manage to stay out of the way." I rise and lay my napkin beside my plate. "Now, I'm going to call Glenice Jo."

Fitzie may have held her head high in the face of the senator's humiliating behavior, but I'm not married to Boone. And Alice Farnham is not one to leave things alone. She hates me and will rub my face in my disgrace all over town.

You can't compare with a beauty like Alice.

I pick up the phone, hoping Blanche isn't on duty, and tap the switch hook.

"Good morning. With whom may I connect you?"

Thank you. "Happy New Year, Florence. Give me Glenice Jo, please."

"Thank you, Cora, dear. Happy New Year to you and your family too."

A moment later, Glenice Jo answers the phone.

I lean against the wall. "Hey, I need some advice."

Glenice Jo paces from the door of her bedroom to the window to her dressing table and back, making me dizzy. If she unleashes her temper on Boone now, like she did when she thought he made me fall in the creek, she'll scorch his eyebrows. It almost makes me feel sorry for him. I've never seen her so angry.

She stops in the center of the room, arms akimbo. "Never in my life have I heard of a man being so rude, so uncaring, so ...so ..." She chops her hand through the air. "He's a brute. He ought to be horsewhipped."

Her fierce loyalty soothes my wounded pride. She's even angrier than I am. Madder than Aunt Clara.

"I have to know what he was thinking. If he wants to be—" She bites her lip and glances at me.

"Wants to be what?"

Glenice Jo shakes her head. "Never mind, it's not important. But I *have* to know what he was thinking." She resumes pacing, then plops on the bed next to me. She tilts her head and peers at me. "Alice Farnham?"

"Yeah. I mean, she's pretty but has such a nasty temperament."

Glenice Jo jumps up. "I'm going to call him and ask him. Point blank."

She bolts from the room, and I'm hot on her heels. "Glenice Jo, please, no." My poor pride can't take another beating.

I skid to a stop at their phone nook in the hallway.

She holds up a hand to stop me. "Thank you, Blanche." *Tap, tap, tap.* Glenice Jo's impatient toe-tapping matches my stomach's clenching. "Cora, we have to find out. I'll do—oh, hello, Boone. I've got a question for you. Why did you ditch Cora last night?" She jerks the earpiece away from her head.

Through it, I hear a storm of words, but they're hard to make out. Heavens to Betsy, what's it about? I move closer to Glenice Jo, but she turns her back.

"What? Hogwash."

"What?" My whisper is harsh. I step around so I'm facing her. "What did he say?"

Glenice Jo's eyes widen, then narrow. "Tell me exactly what happened. And don't you lie to me, mister, or I'll find out. And if I do, your reputation will be in shreds." She holds up her hand, signaling me to wait. I pace.

"Hold on." Glenice Jo crooks her finger at me. I stop pacing and join her. She holds the earpiece so we both can hear.

"Go ahead, Boone. Tell me what happened."

"Okay, the evening started out nice enough. After we ate, I had to use the restroom. When I came out, Alice Farnham walked toward me and said she hated to be the one to tell me, but she felt I deserved to know that Cora had invited Walter Teague to meet her here."

"*What?*"

Glenice Jo claps her hand over my mouth. "And you believed her? She's a known liar."

"What was I to think? Walter was draped over the table, all googly-eyed."

I wildly shake my head. "I didn't!" I whisper. "I'd never met him before."

Glenice Jo turns red. "What you should have done was go over to see what was actually happening. She didn't know him from Adam."

"That's not what Alice told me. She said Cora has had her eye on Walter for a long time."

Glenice Jo swings her free hand out. "Hogwash. She never even met the man. Didn't know he existed until last night. And as soon as you appeared with Alice, he left. It was a setup, plain as it can be." She tilts her head, spearing me with one of those knowing looks. "Boone, you were hornswoggled. I highly suggest you hotfoot it over to Cora's"— she shoos me toward the door—"and explain it to her. Alice took you *both* for a ride."

Glenice Jo hangs up. "Skedaddle home, Cora. He'll be over directly. And then we'll see who likes whom."

Chapter 19

New Year's Day, January 1, 1930

I GET HOME IN RECORD TIME, but twenty minutes have passed, and Boone isn't here yet. So where is he? My shoes leave faint imprints in the rug's pile as I pace the front parlor. If he left his place when he hung up, he should have been here fifteen minutes ago. Besides, even though I heard his explanation through the telephone, I'm still upset that he took up with Alice like he did—or at least believed her.

Maybe he decided not to come.

The stark truth hits me like a slap.

You're only friends. Why should you care about who he's with? Alice is so much prettier than a Plain Jane like you.

I bunch my hands and shout in response to the senator's words. "Even if that's true, friends deserve better treatment."

"They do." Boone's voice scares me witless.

Slapping my hand to my chest, I turn on him. "You frightened me."

"I'm sorry." He crosses the room and grips my shoulders. "Cora, please forgive me. For last night and for scaring you just now."

His eyes are unveiled and pleading. I can't stay mad. No. I *choose* not to. I take a breath and release it in a quiet sigh, the built-up tension flowing out with it. I lay one hand over his. "Tell me what happened and why you believed Alice."

He leads me to the davenport and doesn't release my hand, even when we sit. I turn sideways so I can see him. I want to read his eyes.

"When I came out of the restroom, Alice was walking toward me. She told me you had invited Walter Teague to meet you at the dance.

That startled me. It didn't sound like you, but Alice said if I didn't believe her, I should look. And well …" He rakes his fingers through his hair. "Cora. I saw him at *our* table." His eyes convey the hurt, and he quickly looks away. He swallows. "My pride was wounded."

I lay my palm on his cheek, coaxing his eyes back to mine. "Too bad that you didn't see me. Your pride would still be intact."

"He blocked you, so I couldn't see your face."

Silly man. I shift closer. "Think about this. A strange man makes a move on me. When I was in New York, I might have known what to do. There, I was Dixie Lynn, savvy and aloof. But here?" I drop my chin. "Here, I'm plain Cora."

Boone slips a finger beneath my chin and turns my head to face him. "Honey, you're not plain. You're beautiful." He leans toward me, and his lips find mine. My heart leaps as his kiss deepens. I'm lost. His arms tighten, and strange feelings invade my body. It's a good thing we're sitting because my knees are weak.

A groan fills Boone's throat, and he pulls back. My lips feel bereft.

"Cora." His voice is husky. "You are so much more than a mere friend."

I don't think I'm capable of words. I hope my sappy grin says I agree.

When he chuckles, I snuggle under his arm. "Why did it take you so long to get here after Glenice Jo hung up?"

A chuckle rumbles in his chest, and he plants a kiss on my temple. "I wanted to know the why of it all. After Glenice Jo said I ditched you, I was pretty angry. Not at her, but at Alice."

"Did you find out?"

"No. I went to her house but was told she was out. I'm not sure if I believed their butler or not. He looked down that long nose of his, and I knew exactly what he was thinking. I wasn't the sort to be associating with Alice." His brows pull together as he glances at me. "Maybe I'm not the sort to be associating with you?"

I swat his hand. "Don't be an old Mrs. Grundy. You know perfectly well Fitzie and Aunt Clara adore you."

He guffaws. "I'll bet not after last night."

I pull on my ear. "They were pretty miffed at you, all right. But not now. I gave them a quick explanation while I waited for you."

"I'm glad. I have high regard for them both."

"So." I blow out a long breath and lace my fingers in my lap. "What are we going to do about her?"

Boone cocks a brow. "About your mother or your aunt?"

"No, silly. About Alice."

He puzzles it out with a frown. "I'm not sure. I don't honestly think it's me she is after."

"What do you mean?" I tilt my head and look at him.

"After about fifteen minutes, she lost interest in me and turned her attention on Earl, the other man at the table." He slowly shakes his head. "So much for my pride." Brushing his hand over his thigh, he glances sidelong at me. "Anyway, I looked all over the hotel to make certain you weren't still there, then I went home." He reaches for my hand and rubs circles with his thumb.

"I'm glad to know you looked for me. But why do you think she isn't after you?" I flutter my eyelashes provocatively, making him laugh. "What? You're a pretty swell catch." I snuggle closer and inhale his manly scent. Do they make wood shavings and sawdust into men's cologne?

"I'm sure glad you think so, but I'm afraid this is about you. I think she doesn't want you to have any happiness or success. She's always been jealous of you. The way she talks about you concerns me."

I slip off my shoes and put my feet on the coffee table. "She's been like that since we were kids. I never have understood it."

"I think it's because you were popular and had close friends. She never had any, because she made herself feel big by making others feel small."

"That's sad. I wonder if there is something I can do to help her?"

His expression turns doubtful. "Some people don't want to be helped. Be careful around her. Her family is powerful, and you never know what could happen."

"That's what makes her animosity so strange. She has wealth, and her family has a place in society. The senator had social standing, but we never had their kind of wealth."

"I don't know what makes her tick, but avoid her where you can." He pulls me up with him. His arms stay around me. His eyes close, and he lowers his head. When his lips take mine, my heart zings to my toes and back. His kisses are addictive.

"I want to start all over with you, Cora. I'm head over heels about you. Now that you know it, I want to court you."

I'm being courted? How about that? I glance toward the upper corner of the room and wrinkle my nose. "So there."

Boone frowns. "What?"

"Nothing." I chuckle. "That was for the senator. And don't look at me like I've slipped a cog. Someday, I'll explain."

A smile lights his eyes. "I can't wait to hear it. But right now, I'm more interested in starting this courtship. How about I take you to a movie to make up for last night? *Broadway Scandals* is playing."

I put my arms around his neck. "You got me at Broadway. It's still my dream to play on a Broadway stage."

And as far as Alice goes, I've got the man. I have nothing to lose.

Thursday, January 2, 1930

Boone stands with his legs braced apart as he studies my roomy, bare bedroom. "It looks as though everything is out but the beds, so"—he pulls his hammer from his tool belt—"take this and start on that side wall." He demonstrates how to beat on the plaster. "You can get that down to the lath by the time we're done moving the beds."

"Okeydoke, smoky." I smile and turn to the wall but glance at him over my shoulder. His muscles strain under his shirt while he dismantles the heavy bed. A quiver courses through me, causing strange sensations in my belly. When he turns my way, I quickly swing the hammer at the wall, praying he can't see the red stain on my cheeks. I make an effort to control my racing heart, hoping if he notices, he'll think it's exertion from all my banging around that's causing my rapid breathing.

The moment they leave, I tie a bandana around my face to keep the dust out of my nose and mouth. The ferocity at which I attack my bedroom wall surprises me. But I find that with each swing of the hammer, a bitter memory splinters, and I feel a little freer. I make fast work of the wall adjoining Aunt Clara's room and cross to the one that is common to the master bedroom.

The senator's bedroom.

I slam the hammer into the plaster. A volcano of emotion erupts within.

I'm a child again. And I wail on that wall. The senator throwing open the door, his belt in his hands. Lath shatters beneath my weapon. The senator breaking my favorite dolls. Another confrontation banished. The strange look on his face as I cower in the corner. Again, the hammer falls. More memories fracture. Again and again, I raise my arm and swing. Again—

"Cora!" Boone's hand clasps my wrist, stopping me. "Ease up. You need to use some care, or you could cause damage."

I blink. I hadn't heard him come in. "Oh. I, uh, didn't think about causing any damage." Only the damage of the past. Rage spurred me on. Swallowing, I look at the wall. Three-quarters of it lies in ruin. With one hand, I pull down the bandana. It's wet. I swipe the back of my wrist over my eyes.

Boone stares at me, an unspoken question in his eyes.

"Dust," I say to explain the tears.

"Well, fortunately, whoever built this house did it in a hurry." Boone picks up a piece of plaster. "This is pretty thin."

"Typical of the senator. Don't worry about what's inside. *Appearance* is the important thing."

Boone tilts his head to one side, a flash of concern in his eyes. Then he raises an eyebrow. He obviously didn't know the senator well.

I gesture to all the mess. "What about cleaning this up?"

"When we get through the other wall, we'll chuck it all out the window."

With more tears near the surface, I need a few minutes to pull myself together. "I'll be back to help shortly. I need to speak with Pearl about dinner."

Downstairs, I go into the bathroom. I take a wet washcloth and hold it to the back of my neck. Boone's reaction to my statement about the senator troubles me. I want him to understand. To care. I stare at my reflection in the mirror. But can I tell him all of it?

You're in love with him. But why would you think he could ever love you?

"Mama? Are you asleep?" I whisper in the attic's darkness. Pearl, bless her heart, brought us up cookies and warm milk when we came to bed. Said she didn't want us having any trouble getting to sleep in our new digs. While I worked with Boone today, she helped Mama and Aunt Clara decorate the attic. I need to stop referring to it as *the attic*, but —

"I'm awake, sugar-pie. What's wrong? Can't sleep?"

Ghosts are haunting me. "Yeah." To my left, Aunt Clara snores softly. "Can I ask you a question?"

Covers rustle, her pillow plumps, and she sits up. "Fire away."

In a far corner of the attic, past Aunt Clara's bed, I see my little self—maybe five years old—huddled, sobbing my heart out and holding a headless doll, the victim of the senator's rage over my making it "talk." I break out in a cold sweat. Something unspeakable—

I rip my gaze from the memory and focus on Mama. "Why did you marry the senator?"

"Oh, Cora." Mama flips back her covers and pats the bed invitingly. "Come in with me, darlin'. There's room enough."

I slide beneath the covers of her double bed, and she snuggles me under her arm. "I wondered why you'd never asked when you were young. Then you were gone. I didn't think it mattered anymore."

It always mattered. But I was too afraid of the answer to ask. Am I ready tonight? I suck in a breath. "Tell me now."

Her fingers trouble a corner of the blanket. "From the first moment I saw Alexander Fitzgerald, he captured my heart. He was such a handsome man. I later came to understand it wasn't truly my heart he captured but my notion of romance." She draws the quilt up under her chin. "Your Granddaddy Drummond lost everything after the War of Northern Aggression. Remember the daguerreotype of his house in Dahlonega? Your great-grandaddy got rich in the gold strike. Within five years, he moved the family to Atlanta and became a railroad tycoon."

Her voice lowers to barely a whisper. I glance sidelong. Her eyes are open, so I wait.

"The Drummonds were the center of Atlanta's society. Then the Yankees came." Mama rubs her hand on my arm in a comforting, circular motion. For me ... or her?

"When Sherman burned Atlanta, my grandaddy lost the house. Confederate money was worthless. The Yankees took over the railroad, and Southern stockholders lost everything. All we had left was our breeding and good name."

Aunt Clara snorts in her sleep and rolls over. Mama chuckles softly.

I wait for Auntie to settle, then press Mama for answers. "So how did the family get by?"

"Ah, well, one thing Drummonds have is tenacity. You have it. My granddaddy got a job in a store in Roswell. Sure, it was Yankee-owned, but Granddaddy was a man of opportunity. While he worked, Granny educated my daddy, and as soon as he was old enough, he got a job in that very store. Started at the bottom and worked his way up. Eventually, Daddy opened his own mercantile. We weren't rich, but we got by."

She reaches over, picks up the glass of water on the nightstand, and takes a sip. "Daddy had aspirations for my future and made sure I had my coming out parties—no matter the sacrifice. And that's where I met Alexander, at the cotillion. He had money but no name. And he had his eye on politics as a means of getting—"

"Power." The word explodes from me. I clap my hand over my mouth and hold my breath. But Auntie doesn't stir.

Mama shushes me then goes back to stroking the edge of the quilt. "I didn't see it then. He carefully hid that side of his personality while we courted. Eventually, he won over Daddy and Mama. The best families in Atlanta attended the wedding of family and money." Bitterness puckers her voice.

"Oh, Mama." I grieve that she had to endure years of his mean-spirited selfishness. "You started to tell me a few weeks ago about a boy you once loved. Was that him or someone else?"

She sucks in a breath before releasing the blanket and smoothing it over our legs. "Someone else. A fine young man. But my parents were looking to restore the family wealth. They liked James, but they chose Alexander. The *good* part is, you were the result." She squeezes me and kisses my cheek. "The senator wanted a boy. I begged God for you to be a girl. Not to get back at him, but to save any child of mine from his manipulations. God answered my prayers."

And I paid for it. The Bible says God works all things to our good, but as of yet, I can't see it.

Mama gently grasps my jaw and turns my face to her. "I know it was a two-edged sword, sugar-pie. Believe me, I saw everything the senator did. But your aunt and I saved you from much more."

I push off the covers. "I can't begin to count the times I hid in this attic, my heart breaking because my *daddy* didn't love me, because my daddy was disappointed in me, because my daddy banished me from his sight. What could have been worse?"

Aunt Clara jumps up and turns on the light, her signing wild. "I'll tell you what could have been worse. Him touching you where he shouldn't. After he decapitated your doll when you were five, you ran away from him and hid. But he knew where to find you. I caught him pulling down—"

"Clara! No!" Mama's mouth is a slash of dread across her pale skin.

My aunt's face twists, and she dissolves into tears. I shudder as the memory becomes clear in my mind.

The three of us sit on the side of Mama's bed, weeping together. Fitzie out of gratitude for her sister stopping what the senator could have done to me. Me out of horror at the depth of his hatred for me. And my aunt for me, her beloved niece.

A whisper enters my soul and dries up my tears. Not words from the senator. But from a Heavenly Father, soft and healing.

I gave you two strong women to shelter you.

One ghost in the shadows vanishes. *Thank you.* Never having a loving earthly father has made it hard for me to learn to trust God.

"Thank you, Mama. And thank you, Aunt Clara." We sit in a huddle of arms and love for a few minutes.

Then, surprisingly—or maybe not so surprising, since the idea of my aunt subjugating the senator tickles me—a giggle bubbles up in my throat. "Whatever did you say to make him stop?"

With a wicked gleam in her eye, she signs, "I simply shook my pen at him. He turned white as a sheet, let go of you, and never touched you that way again."

Oh, how rich the irony. The power of the pen felled the mighty politician. I kiss Aunt Clara's cheek and then Mama's. It's been quite a night. But it's one I'll always remember. It hurt, reliving old memories, but now I've begun to release them.

Something else to be grateful for ... the Dillies. How many times in my past were those overnight visits at my friends' homes quickly conspired shelterings?

Chapter 20

Friday, January 3, 1930

BOONE HAMMERS A STUD INTO place, creating a new wall between the five second-floor guest rooms. I hand him the next one. "By the time we finish this project, I might be able to hire out as a female handyman or at least an assistant." I pass Boone another eight-foot-long two-by-four, then bend my arm at the elbow to flex. "I'm getting muscles."

He takes the board, sets it in place, then pulls a nail from his tool pouch. "Aside from you making George's hammer cry, 'Ouch!' this morning when it hit a nail and scaring him witless, yeah, you're a swell assistant." In three swift thumps, the nail head Boone pounds is flush with the wood.

I laugh. "I couldn't help it. It slipped out." George's scowl isn't the least bit intimidating. Still, I owe him an apology. I glance across the room where he works on the closet. "Sorry, George."

I'll also be sorry to see this end. I'm enjoying Boone's company each day. Maybe too much. I keep telling myself not to count on him ever becoming more than a friend, but my heart isn't buying it.

"Did I lose you?" Boone's hand extends toward me.

"What? Oh." I hand him another wall stud and sternly tell myself to pay attention to the work. Until it's done, we can't have any boarders.

The rooms are taking shape, and the walls for three of them are up. This is the last wall, then all five will be "framed," as Boone says. I try to remember the jargon so they won't tease me.

When the final framing nail is in, Boone glances at the blueprints again. "Next, we need to close up the door from the master bedroom to the bathroom."

My brows pull downward. "Why? How's that boarder going to access the bathroom?"

His lips curve into his cheekiest grin. "I think it would prove a tad awkward for the resident of bedroom *A* to have to go through the bathroom to enter his bedroom. What if another boarder is taking a bath?"

That *would* be awkward, and it makes me chuckle. "It's a good thing I'm not in charge of this." I gesture to the framing. "I'd have two of these rooms without doors at all. So what's after that?"

I attempt to make out the blueprints—nailed to the wall—but to me, the plans are nothing but a jumble of lines, dashes, and tiny notes.

Boone plants his finger on the drawing. "Here's where we move the bathroom wall back about three feet. That creates a short hall, and now boarder *A* can get to his bedroom. We'll extend the bathroom's length to make up for it."

I stick my head inside the bathroom door, where Jimmy is moving pipes for the plumbing. "Will that change the layout in here?"

He laughs. "Unless y'all wants the bathtub in the hallway, yes'm."

I take back my idea of being a handyman's assistant. I never would have thought any of this through. I edge closer to Boone. "How long until we have it finished?"

"Another week ought to do it, especially if you ladies help paint the rooms."

"Uh-oh." I suck in my lower lip and bite it. "I thought we'd be done by the end of this week. The furniture is due to arrive on Friday."

Boone stares at me. "Why did you think we'd be finished then?"

I see the senator before me. *If you don't answer right* ... My heart pounds in my throat. "The attic went so fast, I thought it would be the same here."

He surveys the work done on the room. The closets and walls are framed, but the framing is bare, needing its lath and plaster. "Yeah, I can see how you'd think that, but there's a lot more work here."

I messed up. Despite his patient tone and not a trace of anger, I hang my head. "I'm really sorry."

"Hey, there's no need." Boone reaches across the blueprints and squeezes my hand. "I'll make a phone call and have them take the furniture to my shop. When the rooms are ready, Jimmy and I can bring it back here." He smiles. "Easy fix." He picks up a bundle of lath. "Come on, Jimmy, George. Let's get moving."

"It's almost dinnertime. I'll go help Pearl. I'll call y'all when it's ready."

Though I busy my hands with mixing up Pearl's award-winning biscuits, all that occupies my mind is Boone's reaction—or lack of one. Why? The average man would've at least been frustrated. I'm back to thinking he's unlike any man I've ever known.

At the end of the day, he takes my arm. "Come see how the bathroom will lay out."

The fixtures haven't moved yet, but there's a cupboard with five doors in the new section. Except for being out of wood, it's like gym lockers, only nicer.

"That's for your boarders to leave their personal items, such as a razor, shaving cup, etc. I'll put a latch for them to attach a padlock. They'll have to provide the lock, of course."

He's thought of so many little things that will put us a step above others. I smile up at him. "Most boarders have to keep their items in their rooms and bring them to the bathroom. Ours will thank you every day."

Yep. Unlike any other man. What did I do to attract his notice? And can I manage to keep it?

Saturday, January 4, 1930
Boone and I work happily side by side with Jimmy and George, finishing the second floor. George sweeps up the last of the plaster mess off the hall floor. The dust makes me cough. I yank a hankie from my pocket and hold it over my nose and mouth until he finishes sweeping. I'll be glad when the shots Dr. Abernethy is giving me start to work.

Jimmy gathers up tools while Boone and I survey the work. All that's left to do in the bathroom is paint and install the cabinet locks. Then, on to finish the bedrooms.

"We—well, you and the Hortons, really—made fast work of this."

Boone leans on the broom handle. "It wasn't a hard build. I've done worse. Tomorrow, the plaster will be dry, and we can put on a base coat of paint. On Wednesday, we can do the second coat with colors and wallpaper, then on Friday, we'll move the furniture in."

I wrinkle my nose. "We'll help, but don't expect miracles."

"What do you mean?" He sets the broom against the doorjamb.

"Painting is harder than sawing boards. When I was around eight, Fitzie and I decided to paint my room. After one wall, we had sore muscles and gave up. I lived with three pink walls and one green one."

Boone laughs. "Don't worry. We'll all work together."

I bend and pick up a trowel lying on the floor and deposit it in the empty plaster bucket. "I'll let the word out on Friday morning about Fitzgerald House having six rentable rooms for guests."

"No bites on the one room yet?"

"No." I shake my head. "But Glenice Jo said someone at the tannery asked about it. He may come by soon."

Footsteps on the stairs herald Fitzie and Aunt Clara. My mother's voice wafts from below. "Is it safe for us to come up?"

Boone pulls the broom away from the door. "Sure, but the plaster is wet, so don't touch the walls."

They step into the hallway, eyes wide with lively excitement. "Show us around," Aunt Clara signs.

I open the first bedroom door, ushering them inside. After they look around, I lead them out. "All the bedrooms are the same. But the bathroom has really changed. Come look."

Fitzie's sharp intake of breath rewards our hard work. Even Jimmy grins at her delight. Then her brow dips slightly. "What are these cupboards for? They aren't big enough for linens. And why are there letters on them?"

"Those, my dear mother, are an innovative idea of Boone's. Each letter matches a bedroom, A through E. They're for our boarders to leave their shaving mugs and razors, soap, et cetera, in the bathroom and not have to carry them back and forth each morning. Boone will install a latch on each. The boarders—" I hold up my hand as her mouth opens to interrupt me. "Sorry, the *guests* will have to supply their own lock."

"How very clever and practical." Fitzie clasps her hands to her chest. "Have you picked out paint colors?"

I glance at Boone, then back at Fitzie. "Yes. We thought to do each room differently. Two will be paintedand the others wallpapered, since it's quicker and easier than painting. The first few *guests* can choose." Aunt Clara smiles at my emphasis. "I selected a soft blue and light green paint. I ordered wallpaper in stripes, a floral print, and a scenic one."

"Well done, sugar-pie." Fitzie turns back toward the stairs. "Well, y'all get cleaned up. Pearl said supper will be ready shortly. Jimmy, George, you'll both stay?"

"Yes ma'am, we'd be pleasured." Jimmy answers for both. I don't think I've ever heard George string two words together.

Aunt Clara follows my mother, then pauses at the edge of the steps and signs, "Aren't you two going to a movie?"

Boone slaps his forehead. "Applesauce, I forgot. Cora, can we make it tomorrow night instead? I've got a business meeting I forgot about."

I won't let disappointment park a cloud above my heart, so I give him a light-hearted shrug. "Tomorrow night will be fine. Anyway, we have a lot to do in the morning, and we should be fresh. Aunt Clara? We're counting on you and Fitzie to help with painting the base coat."

She nods, signs, "I'll have your mama ready," and heads downstairs.

Jimmy follows her with the buckets and the broom. George brings up the rear with a trashcan of lath scraps and dust.

I start to go downstairs, but Boone pulls me back and into his arms. "Even after a hard day of work, you smell good." He lowers his head, and his lips claim mine in a dizzifying kiss.

My mouth feels abandoned when he pulls away. I snuggle into his arms and smile. "And you smell like plaster—although, on you, it's quite pleasant."

He rests his chin on top of my head. We're a perfect fit. I can hardly believe all that has happened in the past two weeks.

"And now, we're almost ready to open."

Boone pulls back and looks down at me. "Do you always start talking in the middle of your thoughts?"

"Sorry. Bad habit." I move out of his arms and pick up a stray trowel that missed the bucket, tossing it in. "It comes from years of talking to dolls." I head to the stairs.

Behind me, Boone grunts. "I only hope I can keep up with you."

Monday, January 6, 1930

Supper feels so right with Boone once again sitting alongside Aunt Clara, Fitzie, and me. Jimmy and George are laughing in the kitchen with their Auntie Pearl. Maybe, one day, the old ways will change just like things are in the house.

I pass a bowl of potatoes to Boone. "Has anyone thought about naming the downstairs bedroom? We could nail a small brass plaque on the door."

Fitzie cuts her pork chop, gravy oozing over the knife as it sinks into the meat. "It needs to be fitting. In the White House, they have a Rose Room, but the senator's old office doesn't overlook a rose garden."

Aunt Clara sets down her fork and signs, "Not by a long shot. It overlooks the pond and the vegetable garden. Somehow, The Vegetable Room doesn't sound very inviting."

Our laughter rings throughout the dining room. How I love hearing it. Growing up, the senator didn't allow frivolity at mealtimes. Our house was a solemn one.

Boone stabs a potato, deposits it on his plate, and passes the bowl. "Why not use his name? Call it The Alexander Fitzgerald Room. It sounds senatorial."

Aunt Clara, Fitzie, and I exchange an amused glance. Only we— and a few very close lady friends—know how ironically ostentatious that is. The senator's whole life was a pretentious display and the absolute opposite of the real man. I can only hope he knows what we're doing to this house, his grand showpiece.

Fitzie lifts her water glass in a toast. "I approve." She winks at me. "Here's to the Alexander Fitzgerald Room. May it house many a traveler."

"Hear, hear," I add.

"To the senator." Boone doesn't get it. Maybe one day I can make him understand. But right now isn't the time. I smile at him and touch my glass to his.

Aunt Clara taps her cup with her fork to get our attention and then signs, "What about the other rooms? What shall we call them?"

"Boone and I thought they should simply be letters. A through E to match the bathroom cupboards."

"I think that's fine." Fitzie lays her fork and knife across her plate. "It's simple and easier to remember than a bunch of names."

Boone looks at Fitzie. "Would you like me to make the door plates?"

My gaze darts to him. "You can do that?"

"Sure. I use a tiny brass plate inside the furniture I make. It's just a matter of an engraver's tool." As he continues to explain, my thoughts turn inward. Why didn't I know he had such a skill?

There's actually a lot I don't know about Boone. His expression is so open while he talks about his work. My heart squeezes. I guess courtship is the time to get to really know someone.

Pearl brings in dessert—a chocolate cake—and coffee. The sweet reminds me of Mr. Stephens. It's his favorite, and he is my favorite ventriloquist. He always treated me like a daughter. I have fond memories of riding the train from one city to another while on tour. We usually sat together, unless one of his cronies like Edgar Bergen was on tour with us. He would keep me enthralled for hours with his stories of early vaudeville. I miss him, and if I'm honest with myself, I'm missing the footlights and applause.

"What do you think, Cora?" Fitzie interrupts my musing.

"What? I'm sorry, I was daydreaming."

"I asked your opinion on the rooms' nameplates. Do we want them a plain rectangle or with the corners cut out?"

"I don't really have a preference."

Aunt Clara's lips purse, and her hands move expressively. "I know which the senator would have chosen. The more decorative one." She grimaces.

"I'd say—"

"Decorative it is." Boone's words overlap mine. I'll let him keep his good impression of the senator for now. Besides, it will serve us well.

The doorbell rings. I glance at Fitzie, but her expression isn't one of expectation but question. Pearl's footsteps scurry to the door.

"Yes sir. Come in and please wait in the parlor. I'll have the proprietress come directly."

Sir? A man, then. I straighten, eyebrows raising in hopeful anticipation. "Our first boarder—I mean, guest."

Fitzie smiles and lays her napkin beside her plate. "It would appear so."

Pearl comes into the room and hands the man's card to Fitzie. While she reads it, Boone rises.

"I'll be going, but I'll be back in the morning to paint." He winks at me. "Bright and early."

"I'll be ready. And should I wish you luck on your business meeting?"

"What? Oh." He chuckles. "Sure."

Fitzie, Aunt Clara, and I go to the front parlor after Boone leaves. A man, standing near the mantel, turns. He appears to be in his late forties, judging by the gray at his temples. He's dressed in a nice suit and vest. His four-in-hand tie is navy and silver. It and his blue shirt bring out the startling azure of his eyes.

Fitzie smiles and extends her hand. "Mr."—she glances down at his card—"Walker, I'm Mrs. Fitzgerald, owner of Fitzgerald House." She gestures to me and my aunt. "This is my daughter, Cora, and my sister, Clara."

He bows over Fitzie's hand. "Charmed, ladies."

"Please have a seat." Fitzie moves to the davenport, and Mr. Walker follows. "Tell us about yourself, Mr. Walker."

"Harold, please. I've just been hired by the tannery, and a Miss Vance gave me your address. I hope you still have a room available?"

"Yes, we do. Where are you from, Harold? I detect an accent that isn't Southern."

Fitzie sure made a snap decision. I hope all is up-front with Mr. Harold. But I guess I can check with Martha Anne to see if everything he tells us is true.

"You have excellent ears, Mrs. Fitzgerald." His eyes twinkle with his smile. "I'm from Cambridge."

Cambridge! A Yankee. We desperately need the money, but will Fitzie overlook such a heinous crime?

Chapter 21

Monday, January 6, 1930

"I'm a graduate of MIT."

I glance from the man who looks so proud he might burst a button to where Fitzie perches tensely on the sofa. Will she kick the fellow out now or let him flounder around a bit?

"MIT?" Fitzie tilts her head slightly. "What is that?"

The Yankee appears incredulous. "Massachusetts Institute of Technology, the finest university in the U.S.A. for a degree in chemistry." Those eyes twinkle again. "I have my Ph.D. in that field."

Aunt Clara joins the conversation. "So we should call you Dr. Harold, would that be correct?"

Mr. or Dr. Harold stares at her, mouth agape, while Fitzie interprets and then peers at him, waiting.

"Well, bless you, madam! Is that American Sign Language?"

Yankee or not, I think I like this man. He didn't assume my aunt was deaf since she's mute. Unless he's a great actor, Fitzie made a good decision, telling him a room is available.

Aunt Clara nods with a smile.

"Then, if I'm going to be living here, I should learn it." He pauses and glances at me. "One should never stop learning."

Fitzie rises. "Well, Dr. Harold, and I shall call you *doctor*, I'm going to put you in the downstairs guest room for the time being. We've reserved it for overnight or weekend guests. Our long-term guests will reside on the second floor. Those rooms afford a bit more privacy, but they aren't quite ready."

"We just finished construction and will be painting and wallpapering tomorrow," I add, looking around for his bag.

Brushing off his immaculate slacks with a delighted smile, Dr. Harold also comes to his feet. "The downstairs guest room sounds fine."

I join Fitzie's side. "Do you have a bag, sir?"

"I left it by the front door." He moves to retrieve it. "Since I plan to stay indefinitely, I'm quite at your disposal for where you choose to deposit me, Mrs. Fitzgerald."

A pretty grin lights her face. "Please call me Fitzie. If you'll follow me? I'll show you the room you'll be in for a few days, and my sister will get you registered."

While they sweep out the door, I follow Aunt Clara to see what she has planned for registration. From the writing desk, she withdraws a small book and shows me where she has written, *Name, former address,* and *signature.* She signs, "I'll collect one week's rent up front."

"You've got it covered. And I like him. He seems to have a sense of humor, which I wouldn't have expected from a chemist." I glance at the door through which he and Fitzie exited. "I'll talk to Martha Anne to see what she knows of him. Maybe later, we'll want to add references to that." I point to the ledger.

"Good idea."

Pearl appears in the parlor doorway. "Would the gentleman like some supper or somethin', Miss Cora?"

"I'll ask, Pearl. Thank you."

In the hallway, Fitzie exits the doctor's room, closing the door behind her, a finger raised to her lips. We walk toward the kitchen. "He's getting settled."

"Do you suppose he's hungry?"

"I asked him. He said just perhaps some tea and cake, if we have any."

I want her thoughts on our first guest. "Do you like him?"

"I do. He's open." She stops in the kitchen doorway and looks at me, searching my eyes. "And I believe I've become a good judge of character over time." She continues into the kitchen. "Excuse me now, dear. I need to take the doctor his cake and tea, make sure he feels a proper welcome."

I need to rethink my decision to eat in the kitchen and not with the guests.

Friday, January 10, 1930

As I dress this morning, my arm still hurts from the allergy shot the doctor gave me yesterday. He said they might not work since the science is still fairly new. I hope they do. According to him, left untreated, a cough can compromise my ability to sing. Absently, I reach beneath my sleeve and rub the swollen area on my arm.

I run down the stairs and slow my steps just before I skid into the dining room. Dr. Harold is seated at Fitzie's right and next to my chair. He and I had a nice, long chat the first night he was here, before he turned in for bed. The man laughs easily, and before I said goodnight, I told Pearl I'd changed my mind about eating with the guests. I hope I'll like any others who come just as well.

"Good morning, everyone." I slide into my seat. As Dr. Harold eyes my attire, a grin lights his eyes. I chuckle. "You forget, sir. I'm still painting or wallpapering your future room."

He sets down his coffee cup. "Ah, yes. And what color is it to be? Purple, perhaps? Or an ostentatious orange? Maybe some little monkeys swinging from jungle branches?"

I laugh. "You'll have to wait to see." I lay my napkin on my lap and reach for the plate of bacon.

"Since I have to wait,"—he nudges the platter closer to me—"I look forward to the surprise." He winks and turns to Fitzie, asking her a question.

I concentrate on eating, though I really want to get upstairs. Sounds of Boone and Jimmy making preparations float through the stairwell. "What time did Boone arrive? I thought we weren't starting until seven."

Aunt Clara signs, "Six-thirty. He said he wants to finish early to have time to sufficiently clean up for your date." She wiggles her eyebrows.

At that, Dr. Harold lays down his fork and picks up his coffee cup. "Do we have a romance here? I like to see young people in love."

It seems our new resident *does* know some sign language. At least, he understands the heart sign. Heat crawls up my neck and into my cheeks.

He chortles. "Ah-ha! I see we do." He sets his cup gently onto its saucer. "When I was young, just an eager eighteen, some fellow students and I went to the World's Fair in New York City. It was there, I met a lovely young lady and fell in love." His eyes glaze with distant memories. "Ahh, the romance of it all. Warm spring evenings. Strolling along the boardwalk." He inclines his head toward me. "The ocean was only a two-block walk from the fairgrounds. Each night, I would pick a bouquet of flowers along our way and present it to her."

Aunt Clara taps Fitzie's arm and signs, "Tell Dr. Harold he could be a writer. He has a poet's soul. I'm surprised he chose chemistry."

Fitzie interprets, and the good man's smile grows. "A wonderful compliment. I suppose I am rather an enigma in my field." He nods at Aunt Clara and raises his forefinger. "However, you would be surprised how much poetry one can find in chemistry."

Amid laughter and looking for poetry in odd places, we all finish breakfast. Dr. Harold heads off to the tannery. Aunt Clara dons her fuchsia beret and moves to a writing desk, Fitzie goes to change into work clothes, and I dash upstairs.

Jimmy and Boone are in Room E with a bucket of pale green paint. I examine the swath Jimmy has on the wall. "Oh, I love this color. It looks like the bottom end of a romaine lettuce leaf. It's easy on the eyes. Now, what can I do?"

Boone lays down his brush and glances at Jimmy, whose back is to us. Boone lowers his head and kisses me. I break it quickly, blushing.

A chuckle rumbles in his throat. He leans close and whispers, "Don't be embarrassed. Jimmy knows all about love. He has a girlfriend."

I duck my head. "I can't help it." Did he say *love*?

He relents and hands me a can and a brush. "Here's the trim color. You can paint around the window, door, and baseboards. I'll get the crown molding."

Fitzie joins us shortly after, and he outfits her as well. She dips her brush in the can of creamy paint and tackles a doorjamb. "At this rate, it will take us a week to finish these rooms."

Boone pauses mid-brushstroke. "Actually, it won't. Wallpaper goes quicker, and I hired some hangers. They are already in Rooms D, C, and B."

My eyes widen. "Can we afford them, Boone?"

"Yes. And the sooner we're done, the sooner you can fill these rooms. Glenice Jo telephoned me last night. There are two men and a couple of ladies at the tannery who are looking for housing."

Fitzie and I share a Charleston leg kick and get to work.

By the end of the day, we have all five rooms papered and painted. Boone and the Hortons have the place clean, and they have gone home. Fitzie calls my aunt up to see them.

"Careful, Clara." She points to Room A's door trim. "Don't touch anything. The paint is still wet in all the rooms. So … what do you think?"

Her smile says it all, but she signs, "Any guest will love this room. It inspires rest."

I haven't seen the wallpapered rooms yet. In Room D, the paper has stripes with lacy *fleur-de-lis* overlays. Room C has a floral print, but it isn't too feminine with its predominant jewel tones.

Aunt Clara applauds this one. "I could live happily in here. It's restful and cheery at the same time."

Room B has an Oriental scene with birds and bonsai cherry-blossom trees plus the standard green pine bonsai. I'd love to try to grow one of those.

"Fitzie, have you ever seen a bonsai tree? I mean in person, not a picture. Do you think they come that way?"

She cups her chin as she studies the paper. "I really don't know. We should look into it. It might be fun. I'll get a book from the library."

Aunt Clara taps my arm and signs. "I'd lay odds Dr. Harold will choose this room."

"Do you think he's partial to bonsai trees?"

My aunt shakes with silent laughter and signs, "No. Because it's closest to the bathroom."

The final Room, A, is painted pale blue. Fitzie links arms with Aunt Clara and me. "Sunday, we will be ready for our guests. Hopefully, those that Glenice Jo told you about haven't found other arrangements. Cora, will you let her know?"

"We're meeting her and her date at the flicks. I'll tell her then." I glance at my wristwatch. "Boone will be back at seven to pick me up. I need to bathe and eat."

In record time, I'm fresh from my bath and hurry through supper. The doorbell rings as I swallow the last bite. Pearl directs Boone to the family parlor. I grab my coat and hat off the newel post, then go join him.

"I'm ready."

By the bookshelf, Boone pauses in his reach and turns. "Swell. Say,"—he turns back to the bookshelf—"do you know where your father's book on Georgia law is?"

How does he know the senator had that particular book? I bite my lip. I want to ask, but I'm not sure I want to know the answer.

"No, I don't. You can ask Fitzie."

He shakes his head and turns away. "No need. I was just curious about a point of law and thought, having been a senator, he might have had a book about it. It's not important." He flashes a wide grin. "Let's go. I've heard good things about this movie."

I dismiss my concern and slip into the coat Boone holds for me. "Me too. I've wanted to see it since it came out last year. In New York, being part of the entertainment industry, I rarely got the chance to see flicks."

The familiar scent of rain is in the air. I hesitate before stepping out onto the porch. "Should I grab an umbrella?"

"Already have one in my truck."

I pat the side of the truck as I get in. "I'm glad we're taking yours. It's comfortable and has character. Have you named her?"

Boone stares at me as though I've lost my marbles. He shakes his head, cranks the engine handle, then hops into the driver's seat. "You're a character."

"What makes you say that? Because I asked if you'd named your truck?"

"Not really, but you're funny. You're easy to talk to and fun to be with."

"And that makes me a character?" I can't help goading him. I like hearing what he likes about me.

He turns left onto Level Creek Road. "I—where is this conversation going?"

"You're nuts." I laugh and slide over next to him on the seat.

His fingers entwine with mine. The last of the tension in me that arose from the senator's library seeps out the cracks around the window, replaced by contentment. A few minutes later, we arrive at the Colonial Theater. While in line for tickets, someone taps my shoulder. I turn around.

It's Martha Anne. I glance at the young man with her. Why, it's Ethan Simms, the tooling artist. So he's her date.

"Hey, you two."

"Hey." Martha Anne takes Ethan's hand. "Boone, this is Ethan Si—"

"We're old friends." Boone reaches for Ethan's hand. "We play baseball together."

Ethan nods. "Yep. Back in school and now, on a men's league. I'm trying to get Boone to join the tannery's team, though."

While the guys talk baseball and buy our tickets, I nudge Martha Anne off to one side. "How did you ever get shy Ethan to talk enough to ask you out?"

She fluffs her hair. "Persistence." She snickers. "And baked goods every day. That finally wore him down."

I can't help laughing. "Oh, before I forget it, on Sunday, we'll be ready for the boarders. Tell them they can come after church to see the rooms, and if they like, they can move in that night. We require a week's rent up front."

The fellas are ready to go in. Martha Anne and I link arms and let them follow us. We select seats three rows back from the screen.

"I'm excited to see a talkie." Martha Anne settles between Ethan and me. "I'll bet you saw plenty in New York."

I take the box of popcorn Boone hands me. "No, I didn't. This will be my first talkie, and I can't wait."

The lights go out, and the film begins to roll. I tilt my head toward Martha Anne. "Did I tell you I met this actress once? She came to see one of our shows."

"Really? That's so exciting."

"Shh." The shushing comes from behind us. We cover our mouths with our hands and, laughing silently, hush as the newsreel begins.

After the movie, the air is cold, and our breath frosts when we leave the theater. We walk down to Bolding's Drug Store, where they have a fountain, and slide into one of the two booths. The menu lists an assortment of pie, ice cream sundaes, malted milks, and ice cream sodas.

Boone nudges me. "What'll you have, Cora?"

"Caramel banana pie." I haven't had it in years, and my mouth waters in anticipation. "And a Co-cola, please."

Boone gets a hot fudge sundae. Martha Anne and Ethan share a banana split. I haven't had so much fun in … well, forever. I feel like I'm fifteen again, only better. In vaudeville, we often went out to eat or have dessert after a show, but it didn't feel like this. There we discussed our acts, what we wanted to change or drop. It was about work. This is about … living. And loving. I glance a Boone, deep in a discussion with Ethan. Martha Anne hangs on every word coming from her beau's mouth.

I'll miss this if I go back to New York.

No, *when* I go back. I have to regain my career. Don't I? Isn't that what I want? I push away my pie half uneaten.

All of a sudden, I'm not so sure anymore.

Chapter 22

Sunday, January 12, 1930

GIGGLING AND CHATTERING LIKE A gaggle of geese, Fitzie, Aunt Clara, Millie, her mama, and I spill into the house after church. Millie's daddy, Mr. Edward, and Boone stay outside to look under the hood of his truck. I slip off my hat on my way into the kitchen to let Pearl know we're home, although we're so loud, I'm sure she hears us.

Her granddaughter, Ruby, is with her and bobs her head. "Hey, Miss Cora." Her shy greeting is so soft, if I didn't know her well, I wouldn't be listening for it.

"Hey, yourself, Ruby. It's nice of you to help out your grandma today." I lay my hat on the table. "There are seven of us. Oops, eight with Dr. Harold. Has he finished moving into Room B yet?" Dr. Harold chose the room Aunt Clara predicted he would.

Pearl wipes her hands on her apron. "Yes'm, he has." She tilts her head toward her granddaughter, who has her back to us, washing a large pot. "Ruby helped him carry his things up."

I lower my voice. "I'll be sure she gets a pay envelope, Pearl. We may need her every day. Three others are coming this afternoon to look at rooms." I grab my hat and cross my fingers over my shoulder as I push through the door.

After dinner, we congregate in the family parlor for a game of charades. Aunt Clara has donned her red beret and sits at the writing desk. How she can ignore all the laughter and concentrate on her work in progress escapes me. It's like the beret renders her deaf.

Miss Caroline and Fitzie move into the lead when Pearl comes to tell me a potential boarder has arrived.

She doesn't enter the room but stands in the doorway. "I showed the gentleman into the guest parlor, Miss Cora."

I nod my thanks and scurry to the parlor. I find a rather dapper gentleman in front of the window, hat clasped in his hands behind his back. His suit fits well but is a little threadbare at the elbows. He turns as I cross the room and extend my hand.

"Good afternoon. I'm Miss Fitzgerald."

By the lines in his face and a few gray hairs at his temples, I judge him to be in his early forties, same as Dr. Harold. He shakes my hand. "James Vaughn."

I gesture to a grouping of chairs. "Will you have a seat?"

"Thank you." He lowers his lanky frame into a wingback chair. "Miss Vance told me you have rooms to rent." His Adam's apple bobs above a clean collar.

I collect my thoughts as I slide into the chair opposite him. "We do. Tell me a bit about yourself."

"I came to Buford a month ago for a job in the shoe factory. My wife is still in Milledgeville, caring for her ailing mama."

He speaks well. "That's nice of her. I'm sorry her mother is ill." I don't want to pry, but I should be aware if his wife will join him here, eventually. "Does she plan to come visit you?"

"Don't rightly know just yet." He's a man of few words.

I fidget with a loose thread on my sleeve. I don't want him to think his wife is unwelcome. "Well, it isn't a problem if she does." I smooth a wrinkle in my skirt. We chat for another five minutes or so, but I don't need any other information, really. Martha Anne's recommendation was high, so I make my decision. "The room is four dollars per week, payable in advance on Sunday evening. If that's agreeable, I'll take you upstairs to see the available rooms."

"Yes ma'am." He reaches in his back pocket and removes a well-worn wallet. He licks his thumb and counts out four singles, then hands them to me.

I fold the money, and since my dress doesn't have any pockets, I slip it under my belt. "Follow me, please."

Upstairs, after viewing the four available rooms, he chooses D, the one with the striped wallpaper. Back downstairs, I have him write his information in the registration book and give him the room key.

"I'll leave you to get settled in. Supper is at six o'clock. You may make use of the parlor anytime."

Back in the family parlor, I close the door, remove the money from my belt, and wave it with a grin. "Boarder number two, a Mr. James Vaughn, has chosen Room D."

Fitzie places her palms together and touches the tips to her lips, gratitude for answered prayer.

Millie's mother, Miss Caroline, claps her hands and rises. "That's wonderful, Cora. You Fitzgeralds have a *bona fide* business now." She crosses her fingers and holds them aloft. "Here's hoping the other rooms fill up today."

"Now, Mama." Millie puts an arm around her mother's shoulders. "You know we need to rely on prayer, not luck."

"Well, of course, I do, sugar. I was merely showing solidarity with Fitzie. Go drag your Daddy from bending Boone's ear. It's time to go home."

After they leave, Boone and I linger for a bit on the porch. He invites me over to the porch swing, and we sit. He gently pushes his foot against the floor, putting the swing in motion. "I'm going to miss seeing you each morning, working with you. Want a part-time job?"

"Ha! You'd lose all your customers. Besides, I think I'm going to have my hands full here. I'm so relieved this is actually happening."

And maybe after a couple of months, I can return to New York and audition for a revue on Broadway. *Please?*

I glance at Boone. His head is back, eyes closed, his lashes resting against his cheeks. If I land a spot in a revue, what about him? Is there a future for us? He hasn't said anything beyond courting me. I've never been courted before, so I can't say for sure, but doesn't courting mean there's intention to marry?

A taxi rolls up the drive, interrupting my musing. The cabbie opens the door and two older ladies exit. Both have gray hair and wear matching dresses but in different colors.

I nudge Boone gently with my elbow. "It's the sisters from the tannery offices."

He raises his head and studies them, a grin slowly pulling his lips. "A couple of cuties."

I swat his hand and rise. One sister waves at me, while the other instructs the driver to wait. I peer closer. Why, they are identical twins. This should be fun.

"Good afternoon. You must be the Sadler sisters." I descend the porch steps and introduce myself. "Please come in, and I'll take you up to see the available rooms. You may choose one—or two, if you prefer."

"We always room together. Always have." The sister in purple seems a straightforward sort.

After an inspection, they choose C, the one with the floral wallpaper. While they examine the closet and the dresser, I search for some small identifier to tell them apart.

"Is it possible to get another chest of drawers?" the sister in purple asks. "It doesn't need to be very large."

I blink at having been caught staring and stammer, "Y-Yes ma'am." Drawing a breath, I motion to the drawers next to the door. "I can have the mate to this one moved from another unoccupied room." I cast my gaze from one sister to the other. "I don't mean to be forward, but which of you is which?"

The sisters giggle. The one in the purple dress says, "I'm Lulamae. My sister is Iris. We have a secret few people are clever enough to figure out. Can you cotton onto it?"

I cross my arms and study them. Their hair is worn in the same style, finger-waved tight against their heads. They each wear a brooch. Lulamae's has tiny lavender flowers. It goes with her purple dress. Iris's is a black-onyx cameo. Her dress is—then it hits me.

"Lulamae, you wear purple. Now, I always think of that color when I think of irises. But Iris isn't wearing her color. There's not a spec of it on her. Is that it?"

Iris claps her hands and laughs. "You're very observant. That's our secret. You won't give us away, will you?"

"I most certainly won't." I'm going to have fun with these two ladies in the house.

Lulamae places her hand on my wrist. "You know, I feel as though I've seen you before. Sister? Doesn't she look familiar?"

Iris crosses the room and stands in front of me. "Yes. She looks like that young woman we saw in Philadelphia. That ventriloquist. Dixie something."

"Dixie Lynn. That's it." Lulamae nods. "You look just like her, dear."

I can't help myself. I throw my voice, making the lamp on the dresser say, "Well, thank you, ladies. I'll be sure to tell Dixie."

Lulamae and Iris squeal in delight. "You *are* her!" Iris says. "Oh my. Wait until I write to Cousin Doris and tell her who our landlady is."

"She'll be pea-green with envy," Lulamae adds. "She always tries to one-up us. Has since we were children. We grew up near each other, you know." She elbows her sister. "I guess we've got her good now."

The squawk of a horn out front startles us. Iris claps a hand to her cheek. "The cabbie. Tell him to bring our bags up, sister. I'll pay Miss Lynn—I mean, Miss Fitzgerald. Oh dear, I hope I don't start calling you by your stage name. If I do, you must forgive me."

My smile stretches. I adore these sisters. Wait until Aunt Clara meets them. I'll bet she casts them as the heroines in a new mystery. While Lulamae tends to the cabbie, Iris pays me for a month.

Downstairs, I record their payment, then ask Boone to help me get the chest of drawers from the Alexander Fitzgerald room and wrangle it up the stairs.

We pause halfway for me to catch my breath. "I can buy another highboy at Drake's, don't you think?"

"As long as you don't need to have an exact match, sure. I'll go with you so we can bring it back right away."

I don't think I will ever get over how accommodating Boone is. The senator would have left me to struggle alone while he smoked cigars with his cronies or glad-handed a campaign donor.

We continue up the stairs and get to the top.

"Cora? Can you come here, please?" Fitzie's voice beckons me from below.

I shrug at Boone. "Duty calls. Can you manage by yourself?"

Boone's grin turns sassy. "When the day comes I can't charm a gray-haired auntie—"

I slap his shoulder and run down the stairs. "Here I am."

Fitzie waits in the foyer with another gentleman. This one appears to be in his late twenties, a lanky, freckle-faced redhead who's all arms and legs.

Mama turns at my approach. "Ah, here's my daughter, Mr. Dobbs. This is Cora. She will show you our remaining rooms."

Once again, I go through the routine of questioning the young man. This one works with Ethan Simms. Finally, I ask, "Mr. Dobbs, are you a tooling artist too?"

He stands taller and grins. "Yes ma'am. And please call me Henry."

After he chooses Room E, he takes his bag up to get unpacked. Poor fellow. His last rooming house burned down. He's been in the hotel for over a month.

In search of Pearl, I enter the kitchen where she's laying a towel over a bowl.

I hitch my thumb over my shoulder. "All but one room is rented. We have the Sadler sisters and three men. That means we are now eight for supper tonight and breakfast in the morning. Can you do that?"

"Yes, Miss Cora, I surely can. I already had my Ruby run to Mr. Bud's house and buy some eggs off him. I've got bread risin' now." She points to the covered bowl. "We have plenty of bacon and grits. But for tomorrow evening, I'll need more groceries."

"I figured as much. That's why we have our guests pay in advance." I retrieve a pad of paper and pencil. Pearl and I decide on the week's menu and the supplies she needs.

Another thought hits me. "What about wash powder? We will have a big load of laundry every Saturday."

"Have that sorted out, too, Miss Cora. We'll send all the linens out to my sister and her daughter. They's takin' in laundry. If'n your guests need their personal things done, too, she be appreciatin' the work."

I nibble on the end of the pencil, calculating the workload if we do it ourselves. An image of Fitzie elbow-deep in sudsy water sends me into a fit of laughter.

Pearl eyes me, then chuckles. "I knows what you's picturin', Miss Cora. Hmm, mmm, mmm. That would surely make a scarecrow chortle."

"We don't need her to do the laundry. Her job is to charm our guests into staying forever. My aunt's job is to captivate them with her literary talent. Yours and mine is to feed them and watch over the house. Your family can provide any other labor we need. Oh, and Ruby?"

Ruby lifts her head from the potatoes she's peeling. "Yes'm, Miss Cora?"

"You have a full-time job, starting now." I pull an envelope from my pocket. "This is for today. Next Saturday, I'll have a full week's wages for you."

Ruby's eyes widen. "I was just helpin' grandma. I wasn't expectin' no pay."

I rest my hand on her shoulder. "The worker deserves their wages."

Pearl nods her head and eyes Ruby. "That's from the Bible, so you thank Miss Cora for mindin' it."

"Yes'm." Ruby shoots me a shy peek. "Thank you, Miss Cora. I'm pleased to work for you."

I smile and glance over the list one more time. "If there's nothing else, I'll go call Venable's and have these groceries delivered, Pearl. I'll leave the money in the jar for you to pay Rocky's deliveryman when he arrives. Do you think the two of you can handle eight people for every meal?"

She tilts her head to one side, looking at me as if I said it never rains on Sugar Hill. "Ruby an' me can handle twice that many by ourselves."

The house quiets down as everyone either takes a nap or reads. Iris Sadler makes use of the guest parlor to pen a letter, "Letting all the relatives know our new address."

Aunt Clara and I settle into the family parlor with books to read. At six o'clock, Pearl rings the newly installed bell by the kitchen door. An unfamiliar thunder pounds on the stairs, startling Aunt Clara and me. Good heavens! Is it a fire?

Chapter 23

Sunday supper, January 12, 1930

AUNT CLARA SHAKES HER HEAD and sends her fingers flying. "Our boarders sound like a hungry herd of hippopotamuses. Or would that be hippopotami? I'm never sure."

Laughing, I follow her to the dining room. "I'm glad it's not a fire. I guess we'll get used to it."

Aunt Clara pauses in the doorway. "One can only hope."

Fitzie enters with a towel-covered platter—yeast rolls, judging by the heavenly aroma—which she sets on the table next to the large, covered soup tureen. She dons her most gracious smile and moves into her place at the head of the table. "Please, find a seat."

After everyone sits, Aunt Clara is in her usual spot at Fitzie's left, so I settle at the foot of the table. My guess is, this will be the way everyone places themselves at each meal.

Fitzie lays her napkin across her lap. "Dr. Harold, will you ask a blessing?"

"Certainly." He bows his head, and the rest of us follow suit. As soon as he says, "Amen," bowls are passed. Pearl has pulled together a hearty chicken and dumpling soup with fresh rolls. I narrow my eyes. She wouldn't have used the rooster, would she? Could I be so lucky?

"Oh, my stars," exclaims Lulamae after taking a taste. "Why, this soup is even better than Papa's cook's." She leans toward Iris. "Don't tell Cousin Doris I said that."

I take a tentative sip. The broth is delicious, completely up to Pearl's standards. I get some of the chicken on my spoon and slip it into my mouth. Tender as can be. So the old bird survives another day. Not that

I *really* want to see him gone. I've kind of grown used to his strutting around the neighborhood, but I sure wouldn't mind if he subdued his crowing the moment he sees the first sliver of sun.

"I suppose I should introduce all of you to my sister." Fitzie gestures toward my aunt, who startles from her soup. Aunt Clara grins and sets down her spoon as Fitzie continues. "This is Clara. She's mute, but she's not deaf, so be careful what you say." Aunt Clara's lips stretch into a wicked grin as Fitzie continues. "She's an authoress and writes delightful mysteries. You never know when *you* might show up in one of her books. Always as a good character, of course."

James stares hard at Aunt Clara. "My wife is an avid reader of mysteries. What's one of your titles?" He plucks another roll from the platter.

Aunt Clara tilts her head to Fitzie, who answers him. "*Once Upon a Clock* came out last year. One of her best sellers is *The Secret of Level Creek.*"

James drops his roll, splashing broth on the napkin he has tucked into his shirt collar. "I've read that. You're Clara Drummond? Well, I'll be. I've read four of your books. My wife and I love them. Wait till I tell her I'm living in the same house as you." He stares at the soggy roll in his soup, shrugs, spoons off a chunk, and tastes it. Seemingly satisfied, he takes another bite.

Lulamae winks at her sister. "It seems we're in a houseful of—"

Oh, please don't. I'm not ready for my identity to be known. Although if they don't follow vaudeville, I'm nobody.

I could have told you that.

"Shush." Iris wags a warning finger at her twin. I mentally aim one at the senator's ghost.

Fitzie steers the conversation back to my aunt. Thankfully, the talk quickly moves to her books. "One warning. If you see her wearing a beret, do not speak to her. She's working."

Mr. James raises a skeptical brow.

Aunt Clara sets down her spoon and signs toward me. "You can tell them I had to develop the ability to concentrate while living in a house with a noisy senator and a vivacious child. Otherwise, I never would have written a single word."

I translate, avoiding adding any personal remarks about the senator—like capricious.

After selecting a roll and laying it on her plate, Iris passes them to her sister. "That is a good skill to have, Miss Drummond. And"—her cheeks turn a delightful pink—"I'm a great fan of yours." She turns her gaze upon Fitzie. "What a wonderful life you must have around these two." Realizing her faux pas, she claps her fingertips over her mouth and sends me an apologetic look.

My hopes to keep my identity—beyond Cora Fitzgerald—secret may not last with the twins, at least the non-purple one. I wink at her to let her know I forgive her. She launches into a story from her and Lulamae's childhood, covering her near-slip.

"Being completely identical, only our parents could tell us apart."

Fitzie returns the platter to the table. "You do appear to be cut from the same cloth as your sister." She peers closely at them. "You have the exact same hairline, and neither of you has a broader face than the other. Not even a freckle's difference."

Iris' laugh is much like Fitzie's in its infectiousness. "Oh, what fun we used to have at school. We played tricks on everyone. To help our teachers, Mama would tie different-colored ribbons on our braids and send a note to our teachers so they would know who wore which color. As soon as we left the house, we'd trade. Then, during recess, we could swap one ribbon, so we each wore both colors."

Even Lulamae's laugh is identical to her sister's. "Actually, the only way our parents could tell us apart was by certain mannerisms. When we were very small, we each sucked our thumbs, but on different hands. But unless we were sleepy, that didn't help much. From birth, our parents put tiny, colored bracelets on us, adding new beads as we grew. Eventually, they no longer needed those. Still, we could even fool them once in a while."

After supper, Aunt Clara, Fitzie, and I retreat to the family parlor. Iris and Lulamae have instigated a game of bridge in the guest parlor.

James and Dr. Harold join them, but Henry begs off. He has a magazine rolled under his arm, and he's going to read one of Aunt Clara's new serialized stories in his room while listening to his radio.

Fitzie chooses to sit in an overstuffed chair, while my aunt joins me on the davenport. We each cozy up in a corner.

I yawn and stretch. "It's been quite a crazy weekend, hasn't it? So, tell me what you think of our boarders." Fitzie gives me her evil eye. "Sorry, guests."

"I think we hit the mother lode. Dr. Harold is a gem. What a wonderful personality he has." Aunt Clara folds her hands in her lap.

Fitzie stretches her legs out in front of her, then crosses her ankles. "I agree. He has an artistic soul. I learned his wife passed away during the second wave of the Spanish flu. Such a shame. I'm surprised he's remained single for over a decade, though. He'd be a wonderful catch for some lucky woman." She dips her chin and looks pointedly at Aunt Clara.

My aunt waves the comment away. "Why would I want to marry anyone? Moreover, why would they want to marry me? I'm disagreeable. I work all the time. And they would have to learn sign language."

"You? Disagreeable?" I take a moment to catch my breath after laughing. "You'd make any man a good wife, Aunt Clara."

Her vehement head-shaking makes her earrings jangle. "I have no intention of ever disrupting my idyllic life. Why, it's just the way I want it to be." Her hands still until she knows she has our full attention. "I have never desired marriage." She smiles at me. "I don't need children, for I have you. And for companionship, my sister." She sits back, crosses her arms. Her demeanor defies any challenge.

I reach over and pat her ankle. "I love you too."

Fitzie's expression is unreadable. I decide not to question her. At least for now, my mama is enjoying freedom from the constraints of marriage to a beast.

Monday, February 3, 1930

With a large basket propped on my hip, I pause in the foyer, taking in the reception desk we set up, using one of Aunt Clara's many writing desks. Miss Amelia was right. We're a real business. We've fallen into a routine that seems to suit us. Aunt Clara keeps the books for Fitzgerald Guest House, although if she's on a deadline, I fill in for her. I act as the housekeeper. There isn't *too* much for me to do. I plan the meals with Pearl, order the food, oversee Ruby's sister, Topaz, and work the garden. Topaz dusts and sweeps daily and changes the bedding once a week. I help with the beds.

Fitzie has taken up baking with Pearl to increase production. "After all," she says, "Pearl's baked goods are well-known," and she says she wants to sell them as her contribution. I keep telling her being the hostess is contribution enough, but she thinks it adds status to Fitzgerald House. The jury is still out on how Pearl feels about Fitzie invading her kitchen, but she puffs with pride when someone comes to the front door to buy a dozen cookies, a loaf of bread, or a few muffins. Then she boasts on the Drummond girls' tenacity.

There is much to boast on, although I avoid doing it. One of Aunt Clara's older books is being serialized in *Ladies' Home Journal.* All of Sugar Hill and beyond talks about her. Just last weekend, Boone and I were in Lawrenceville at a party where one of the guests raved about this mystery she had read. It was one of Aunt Clara's. Boone, bless his heart, asked if she knew that Clara Drummond lives on Sugar Hill and is one of the proprietresses of the Fitzgerald House. That started quite the discussion of the guesthouse, and did we take weekend guests?

On the way home, I had asked him, "What made you tell them about our guesthouse?"

He looked at me as though I had a frog for a hat. "It felt right. And you see how it worked out. You'll have the Alexander Fitzgerald Room booked for weeks. All with locals who want to see Clara Drummond, or Dixie Lynn, or who simply want to sleep in the room where Senator Fitzgerald did."

"He never slept in his office."

"They don't need to know it was an office, Cora. It's smart business to capitalize on your assets. Use what you have to advertise."

"I guess."

"People will always want to rub elbows with famous people. Use that to draw them in, then keep them as customers with your hospitality."

Boone has a good head for business. I didn't tell him I don't mind people coming for Aunt Clara or even Fitzie, but I don't like them gawking at me. People argue that when I'm onstage, hundreds of people stare at me. But it's different. They aren't part of my real life. They can't *touch* me. I'm not even sure I understand it myself. I only know that I get panicky when people find out I'm Dixie Lynn and want to touch me. It's all tied up with the senator, somehow.

A knock on the back door demands my attention. I set the laundry that Pearl's daughter, Sapphire, delivered on the foyer table and go see who it is.

"Afternoon, Miss Martha Anne. Come on in. Miss Cora is—"

"I'm here, Pearl." She lumbers back to the sink and washes her hands as I greet my friend.

The old day dress Martha Anne has on is one she'd never wear to the office. My brows lift. "Why aren't you at work? You didn't lose your job, did you?"

"No. I took off early. Mr. Allen was excited for me and said my mind wasn't on my work, anyway. Look!" She holds out her left hand for me to see. On her ring finger sits a small diamond.

I stare for a moment, then it registers. "Ethan proposed?"

She squeals. "Yes!"

I grab her hands and we twirl around, bumping into Pearl's worktable. She shoos us out of the kitchen.

I pull Martha Anne behind me. "Come on. Let's go into the parlor. I want to hear everything."

Dr. Harold, who just got home, walks past us, an open book in his hands. "Did I hear a barely contained squeal?" When Martha Anne holds out her hand for him to see her ring, a warm smile stretches his lips. "Indeed? Well, congratulations, my dear."

I shouldn't be surprised by his interest—after all, they work at the same place. He continues to the stairs, and we head into the family parlor, where we drop onto the davenport.

Martha Anne flushes with excitement. "He asked me yesterday after church. Oh, Cora, it was so romantic. He told me he's loved me for years but couldn't believe I loved him." She giggles. "Silly man. I said he should have asked me sooner, but he said he was afraid I'd turn him down."

I could use some pointers with Boone. "What gave him the nerve to finally try?"

She blushes and dips her chin. "Because I kept talking to him and finally asked him out." Her nose wrinkles adorably. "Well, I had to do something. And it worked." She grabs my hand. "Can we rent a room from you?"

"I'll definitely hold one for you." I squeeze her fingers. "When is your wedding going to be?"

"We haven't set it, but Ethan told me whenever I wanted is fine with him. I've always pictured a June wedding."

"That doesn't give us a lot of time."

"Mama says it's enough. I'm going to wear a white suit, I think. It's less money than—"

"Oh no, you won't." I give her arm a gentle squeeze. "I've got a dress that will make a perfect wedding gown. It's one I bought from the costume department at the Palace Theatre."

Martha Anne's eyes well with tears. "Oh, how wonderful. But are you sure?"

I smack her knee. "You silly Dilly, I'm absolutely sure. Come on." I pull her up. "I had no idea why I bought it, nor why I brought it home. But now I know. God knew *you* were going to need it."

We run up to the attic. Martha Anne *ooh*s and *ahh*s over the changes there. "What a fun place to sleep. It's like a dormitory." She peeks out one of the dormer windows while I dig through my closet. "You've started a garden?"

"What?" I turn, dress in hand. "Oh yes. With the boarding guests, we need it. I've become quite the farmer, don't you know? Here's the gown."

Martha Anne covers her mouth with her fingertips, her eyes shimmering. Her reaction is everything I could hope for. Made of ivory lace, the top overlays the skirt, stopping just below the hip. The neckline is scooped to the collarbone, and the dress is sleeveless, to be worn with opera-length gloves.

"It's exquisite." Her words come out in an awed whisper.

Deep inside, a twinge of sorrow pricks my heart. The dress struck me as exquisite too. I'd dreamed of the places I'd wear it, but here, now, those visions of Broadway seem very far away. And if I were brave enough to be honest, they're fading faster by the minute.

Chapter 24

I TAP THE FACE OF MY wristwatch as a perfectly brilliant idea unfurls into full bloom. So does a smile. I can't help but grin at Martha Anne.

She narrows her eyes at me. "I know that look. Spill it." And that's what comes of being friends forever—though I'd have told her without her prodding. This idea is simply too good to keep to myself.

"It's five o'clock, and the other Dillies will be home soon. Let's surprise them. You try the dress on, and I'll go call them. You can hide until they're all here."

Martha Anne's grin matches mine. "Let's do it!"

She begins unbuttoning her dress. I run downstairs to the telephone. As soon as I talk to Millie and leave messages for Glenice Jo and Trudie, I search out Fitzie.

She raises her head from a magazine when I enter the family parlor. "Hey, sugar-pie. What's up?"

I sit on the edge of an ottoman. "Guess what?"

Fitzie closes her magazine, giving me her full attention. "You know I'm horrible at guessing. Tell me."

I grin, prolonging the suspense. "Martha Anne is engaged."

Fitzie's eyes widen with her smile. "How exciting! When did Ethan ask her?"

"Yesterday after church. I've called the girls to come over. But here's the really exciting part. It just so happens I bought a dress from the theatre that will make the perfect wedding gown for her. And I brought it home with me. How 'bout them apples?" I jump up and twirl in delight. "She's trying it on now and will give us a fashion show as soon as the others arrive."

Fitzie studies me with one of those mama-looks—the one that sees all the way inside to her offspring's soul. "The dress must make her very happy. I know there isn't a lot of money for fancy weddings. You have a good heart, sugar." She glances at the door. "Do you want to ask the Sadler sisters to join us? They love a good romance, and since they both work at the tannery, I'm sure they'd love to be involved."

"Yes, let's. Did I tell you Martha Anne was going to wear a suit? It's funny, you know." I perch in front of Fitzie again. "I really think God prompted me to buy the dress and then bring it home. And, to tell the truth, I really don't even remember packing it."

Fitzie's smile is enigmatic. "He works in mysterious ways." She lays the magazine on the side table and slides forward in the wingback. "I'm going up to see if the dress needs any altering. You let the Sadler sisters know—they love you girls—and wait for the others. Signal me when they're here. Oh, and did you tell Amelia to come too?"

I rise and link arms with her. "Do you think I'd forget Martha Anne's mama? Millie called her for me." After all, we Dillies became friends because our mamas were best friends.

Miss Lulamae and Miss Iris are thrilled over the news. They scurry into the family parlor to wait for Martha Anne. Today, Miss Iris is wearing a coral-print dress and her signature black-onyx cameo. Her sister is in blue.

Millie arrives with Amelia Vance right behind her. I send Miss Amelia upstairs to join her daughter and my mama, then escort Millie in to meet the twins. My aunt remains hunched over her desk but slides off her tan beret. She hears the commotion, and curiosity gets the best of her.

Millie crosses to my aunt's desk. "Well, what do you think of it, Miss Clara?"

She turns halfway in her chair and signs, "I'm thrilled for Martha Anne. I may even have to include a wedding in this current story. Of course, mine will have to have a murder at the altar. Or on the honeymoon? Hmm." Picking up her pen, she makes some notes.

When Millie laughs, Miss Iris looks confused and turns to her sister. "Nobody translated."

Millie explains. "Growing up around here, all of us learned sign language. It was such fun to be around strangers. They'd see a bunch of little girls making their hands fly faster than lips could move."

That starts me giggling. "Do you remember the time—"

The doorbell rings. Glenice Jo swoops into the parlor. "Where is she?"

I shake my head and point to the settee. "Sit down and wait. She's going to give us a fashion show."

"Why?" Glenice Jo drops onto the davenport.

I start to explain, but Trudie walks in, still in her uniform. "Diner's slow right now," she says by way of explanation. "I have to get back pretty soon for the supper rush."

"Now that all y'all are here, we can begin. Sit tight and I'll signal that we're ready."

In the kitchen, I nod to Pearl, who rings for Martha Anne and our mamas using the bell system Boone installed in the attic for her to alert us when breakfast is on the table.

We don't wait long. When Miss Amelia and Fitzie stand back for her to enter, Martha Anne is a vision of loveliness in ivory satin and lace. The dress fits as though it was made for her. Only the hem will need taking up a little, but the rest is perfect.

Miss Lulamae and Miss Iris clap their hands. The Dillies and I squeal and circle around her.

Millie clasps her hands beneath her chin. "You're so beautiful."

At the same time, the rest of us chime in. "Gorgeous." "Perfection." "Ethan won't be able to take his eyes off you."

Then, my practical side takes over. "What about the veil? She needs a veil." I lift the side of the dress, examining the lace. "It should match this as closely as possible, shouldn't it?"

While they discuss the wedding date and details, I rush into the hall and call Venable's. Doubting he carries a supply of what we need,

I ask, "Can you order lace?"

"I can. I've got a catalog of materials."

"Thanks, Mr. Rocky. Martha Anne and I will come in tomorrow after she gets off work." If we don't find what we want, we can go to one of the department stores.

Back in the parlor, we talk about where the wedding reception will take place. Martha Anne and Ethan want a morning wedding, eleven o'clock, so Miss Amelia thinks the church's fellowship hall is good enough for finger sandwiches and cake.

Fitzie has other ideas. She draws Miss Amelia across the room. "Sugar, we'll host the reception here."

"Oh, we can't—"

Fitzie cuts off her protest. "I won't take no for an answer. Between the parlors, the foyer, and dining room, we have enough space for a hundred guests to move around comfortably."

Miss Amelia looks horrified. "We won't have that many people." Her head twists to her daughter. "Martha Anne, you aren't inviting that many people, are you?"

"Now, Mama, relax. Of course, we aren't. But the Bona Allen family will be invited, so I'm thinking probably around sixty in all." She hugs my mother. "Having the reception here will be splendid. I can't thank you enough, Miss Fitzie."

Mama returns the hug, then urges Miss Amelia to sit. "Don't you worry about anything. We'll handle everything."

Her shoulders relax, her relief evident. "Just nothing very elaborate. Remember the costs. We can't afford much."

Fitzie waves away her concern. "Pearl and her granddaughter can make sandwiches and the wedding cake. Martha Anne, shall we have a hummingbird cake?"

Martha Anne's enthusiastic nodding makes her earbobs bounce. "Oh yes, please."

Fitzie plows on. "Then the menu is done. Finger sandwiches, cake, sweet tea, and coffee."

"Martha Anne?" Trudie links arms with her. "What color flowers do you want? And what kind? My aunt and uncle in Birmingham grow flowers commercially. I can get them for you at the family price."

She squeals. "Ooh, thank you. I love turquoise." No surprise to us, since she wears it the most. "What will go with that?"

"Oh, you should see what my aunt does. She accidentally spilled red food coloring into a glass vase of carnations. She liked the way the water looked, so she left it. A few hours later, the carnations had turned red."

I gasp. "You're kidding! The flowers really turned red?"

Trudie nods. "I'll ask if she can make up some turquoise dye."

Martha Anne is ecstatic. "I've never seen flowers dyed. That will be super spiffy."

"My turn," Glenice Jo says. "Since we wear the same size, you can have my wedding slippers. They can be your something old, unless"— she glances at Miss Amelia—"there's a family piece you'll use."

Miss Amelia shakes her head. "We don't have anything special, and you're sweet to offer your shoes, darling."

"Yes, thank you." Martha Anne kisses Glenice Jo's cheek. "And this dress is my something borrowed. The veil is something new. Glenice Jo's slippers are my something old. Now all I need is something blue."

"The flowers," we all cry out at once.

Our bride blushes. "Oh, right."

Our giggles paint the room in delight.

"Martha Anne, go up and take off the dress for now." I steer her toward the door. "We'll hem it and bring it to you when it's ready. And don't forget to meet me at Venable's tomorrow after you get off work."

Tuesday afternoon, February 4, 1930

Martha Anne and I study the catalog at Venable's General Store. We snipped a small piece of lace from an inside seam to bring with us. Costumes, needing to fit several size actresses, have large seams. We managed to remove a three-inch square. Now, turning page after page, we lay the sample beside each catalogue photo, until finally, we see it.

I stab my finger on the one. "That's it, Martha Anne."

She agrees, picks up the tome with her finger still on our choice, and takes it to the counter. "Mr. Rocky, I need—" She sets the catalog on the counter and turns her gaze to me. "How many yards do we need?"

"You're asking me? I don't know."

"Hold it, ladies. I can help." Mr. Rocky comes around the counter, a measuring tape in his hands, which he gives to me. "Measure from the top of her head to wherever you want it to end."

I take the tape. "Do you want a train, Martha Anne?"

She wrinkles her nose. "I don't think so. That's a bit hoity-toity for me." Her concern over this decision wrinkles her brow.

"I agree. This is a morning wedding, so how about we end it where the top overlays the skirt?"

Martha Anne's worried face relaxes, and her smile reappears. "That's exactly right, Cora. You're so smart." She points out the lace to Mr. Rocky.

After we make sure she can afford it, I check the width of the lace fabric. It's wide enough so we only need one-and-a-half yards. Mr. Rocky notes the amount and promises to order it.

While Martha Anne pays, I peruse the store to see if he has any new seeds in stock. I'd like to expand the garden, and it's almost time to plant a spring crop. I think. I find his copy of the *Farmer's Almanac* sitting on the far end of the counter, and flipping through its pages, I locate the information. Depending on the item, I can plant the seeds indoors as early as next week, then once they sprout, transplant them into the garden in early- to mid-March.

"What are you looking at?" Martha Anne peers over my shoulder.

"Seeds and how to start planting indoors." I let my gaze search for Mr. Rocky. "When will your lace be in?"

"He said about two weeks."

"Let's go, then."

"What about your seeds?"

"I'll call him with my questions."

We're leaving when Alice Farnham enters the store, nearly colliding with us at the door.

Alice turns, an ugly glare on her face. "Watch where you're go—oh, Cora. And Martha Anne. I hear congratulations are in order. I can only imagine what you did to actually hook him." She stares pointedly at Martha Anne's waistline.

My poor friend's eyes grow wide at Alice's inference.

She turns her acidity back on me. "And for you, too, Cora. I hear you've become quite the businesswoman, opening a *boarding* house."

One might think it was a house of ill repute by her emphasis. I smile and ignore her snide remarks. I'm not biting today.

"I hope you're well, Alice. Good day." I put my back to her and leave Venable's, Martha Anne on my heels. Alice's laughter follows us outside.

Thunder peels when we close the door. A storm is brewing, and not just in Martha Anne's countenance.

I grab her hand and pull her forward. "Forget her. Maybe the coming thunderstorm will ground her broom. Go on home."

The storm releases its fury right after I close the front door. Thank goodness, I made it inside first. The sky lights up, and thunder booms almost immediately. A shiver quakes my arms as I slip off my coat and hat, hanging them on the hall tree. Laughter and chatter filter through the door of the front parlor. I'm glad our boarders have become friends. I go in search of Fitzie and Aunt Clara. I want to tell them about my garden plans. They aren't in the family parlor, so I poke my nose in the door of the guest parlor.

Fitzie is in their midst, regaling them with stories from the senator's colorful life. I wave my fingers to let her see I'm home, but I'm not drawn into their fun. Hearing stories about the senator does not amuse me. Besides, the stories fit for guests' ears are mostly fiction, anyway. I go back to the morning room, where I pull out a legal pad and sit, watching the storm and making my list of desired seeds.

Lettuce is number one—that needs to go in next week. Then I want watermelon and tomatoes. The thought of fried green tomatoes makes my mouth water. Next, Pearl asked for cabbage, pole beans, onions, parsnips, sweet potatoes, and turnips. I already have eggplant and squash seeds. That should make a pretty well-rounded garden. Oops. I remember broccoli and add it to the list.

"Miss Cora?"

I look up. "Yes, Pearl?" Her frown concerns me.

"A man from the county wants to see you."

Now, I frown. "Did he say what he wants?"

"No ma'am, jus' to speak with you."

I nod and lay down my pencil. "Where is he?"

"I left him by the front door."

"Good. Thank you." I rise and walk to the foyer.

Standing at the window looking out is a man of small stature. His girth makes up for what his height lacks. He turns at my footsteps.

"Good afternoon. I'm Cora Fitzgerald. May I help you?"

"Yes. I'm Luther Norwood." He withdraws a small notebook from his coat pocket, pulls out a card, and extends it toward me.

I take it. It's official-looking. I raise my gaze to his.

"I'm from the county of Gwinnett. You've opened a business without a license. You are subject to a fine of fifty dollars and an additional five dollars for each day you delay getting one. If you're more than ten days past today, we'll shut you down."

I make a valiant effort to not gasp. Fifty dollars? There goes the very last of my savings. He hands me an envelope, then jots a note in his little book, his glasses sliding down his nose.

"I never knew a license was required to have guests in one's home."

He looks over his glasses without raising his head. "Let's not quibble over semantics, Miss Fitzgerald. Do you or do you not have a sign out front that reads *Fitzgerald Guest House ~ Meals and Lodging*?"

A sign makes me a business? I suppose if I consider it that way, he's right. I swallow nervously. "Yes, I do."

He gives a sharp nod. "You're going to owe back taxes too."

"Back taxes?" Is he crazy? "We just opened up. Our first boarder arrived January sixth, less than a month ago."

His head snaps up from his notebook. "This year?"

Suspicion rises from the pit of my stomach. "Yes." I narrow my eyes. "Did someone telephone your office about me?"

"Yes ma'am. That's how we often find out about people who disobey the laws."

"I didn't disobey anything. I didn't know about it."

"One would think the daughter of a prominent state senator would be aware of the laws of the state."

Does he realize how stupid that sounds? "Sir, for the last several years, since I was sixteen years old to be exact, I have not lived in Georgia. Nor am I a student of the law. This is an honest mistake. One I will rectify tomorrow. And if I'm accused of something, I'd like to know the name of my accuser."

Looking not the least sympathetic, he shakes his head. "I'm sorry. I can't do that."

Chapter 25

I SEARCH THE GUEST PARLOR FOR anything that needs attending to while I await Dr. Harold's return home. He's the smartest man I know and hopefully will shed some wisdom on this dilemma. A book lays abandoned on a side table. There's no bookmark in it, no dog-eared page. I assume it isn't in the process of being read, and I slide it into an empty spot in the bookcase. Nothing else is out of place, so I pace. Finally, a car rumbles up the drive. A black Packard. It's Dr. Harold's.

I barely let him in the door before I take his arm. "Good sir, I'm in need of your advice. Can you spare me a few minutes?"

"Of course, my dear." He closes his umbrella and sets it in the stand. "What seems to be the trouble?"

Compassion shines in his eyes—which is nearly my undoing. My nerves are already so shot, I don't trust myself to talk here. I lead him back to the morning room, where I proceed to tell him about the visit from the county man and his accusations. "I had no idea I needed a license to open the house to boarders. But what really bumfuzzles me is he said I owe back taxes."

Dr. Harold frowns. "How can that be? You only just opened."

I nod emphatically. "My exact response."

He tilts his head to one side and studies me. "What did he say?"

"He didn't. He looked perplexed but said to take it up with the county. I asked him how they found out I was open. Someone tipped them off, he said. That's how they usually find lawbreakers."

"Lawbreaker? You?" A deep shade of red creeps up his neck. "Preposterous!" The word explodes out of his mouth.

I hide a smile. While I didn't mean to raise such ire, his defense is endearing. "Anyway, I'm going in the morning to get the license and pay the fine. What I need is your counsel on is how to find out where this *tip* came from. I want to ask the person why. We can't go on having false allegations fired at us."

He scratches his chin a moment. "Was it in person or a telephone tip?"

"Telephone."

Dr. Harold brightens. "Then here's what I'd do. Ask the operator. I'll be willing to lay odds that she remembers."

"But can she tell me?"

"Better to see if she will. It's easier to ask for forgiveness than permission."

I tap my index finger against my pursed lips. "If that operator was Florence, I have a chance. If it was Blanche, I'm out of luck."

He lifts his fisted hands with their thumbs up. "Here's hoping it was Florence." He starts for the door but turns back. "And what if you don't find out?"

My stomach sours. "Then I have an unknown enemy."

After he goes to his room, I sit and stare out the window. Who dislikes my family enough to lie about us? The only person I *know* who hates me is Alice. But enough to do this? And if so, what can she hope to gain by it? I need some Dilly Club shrewdness.

I go to the telephone, pick it up, and tap the switch hook.

"Operator. How may I direct your call?"

Blanche. "Good morning. The Newcomb residence, please."

"I'll connect you, Cora."

I don't hear the connection with Blanche close, so when Millie answers, I simply ask if she can come over.

"Sure can. Be there in a minute."

Thankfully, she doesn't ask why.

In the kitchen, I pour two glasses of sweet tea, adding ice cubes. "Pearl, when Millie arrives, please send her along to me, would you?"

Pearl nods and I slip into the hall. At the back of the house, the morning room overlooks the expansive backyard. There is a stretch of lawn, behind that is the vegetable garden, and then thick forest. On a day like today, the woods are dark and ominous. Rain pelts the windows. I shouldn't have asked Millie to come out in this.

A few minutes later, she walks in, lending the room her sunny disposition. "Hey, sugar."

My world brightens. "Hey yourself." I point to the cold drink sitting on a side table. "That's for you."

She takes a long swallow and sits in the wicker chair. "So, what's eating you?"

Once again, I explain what the county man said. "While I don't have a beef over the fine for not having a license, I still don't think one should be needed for opening our home to guests. It smacks of politicians' greed. Why, Southern ladies have been doing that since long before the end of the War of Northern Aggression."

Millie throws her legs over the arm of her chair. "I have a great-aunt who turned her home into a boarding house in Savannah after the war. I can ask Daddy, but I don't remember seeing any license when I visited. We sold it after she passed away." She drops her feet to the floor. "I'll have Daddy call the people who own it now and ask about it."

Outside the window, the storm's fury seems to be weakening. "That would be helpful, thank you."

"But let's get back to the *who*. Do you think it's Alice? And do you have any idea why she would do this?"

I shake my head. "I don't. And we don't *know* it was her."

"Granted, but everyone else loves you."

I'm not sure about *everyone*, but I draw a complete blank on adding any other names to the list.

Millie purses her lips. "This calls for a gathering of the Dilly Club. Call the others."

Millie stands in the center of the family parlor. "We asked all y'all here to help our Cora." She lowers herself to the floor and launches into an account of the county man's visit. When she finishes telling the story, Glenice Jo harrumphs.

"It's obviously Alice. She hates all of us, you the most. Unless you follow her around, kissing up to her, you aren't her friend."

Using my finger, I draw circles on the rug, raising its nap. "I think it is most likely her. But *why?* Anyone have an idea?"

Trudie sniffs. "She doesn't need any reason other than she's Alice."

Martha Anne keeps turning her hand, making her engagement ring catch the light. "She's jealous of our friendship. You know, I tried to include Alice back in grade school." Martha Anne raises her eyes, looks at everyone, and shrugs. "She wouldn't have any part of us."

"We don't know for a *fact* that it was Alice." I lean forward, clasping my hands between my knees. "I know y'all want to protect me, but I'm uncomfortable assuming it's her without proof. Even if I had that proof, what would I do with it?" I rise and cross to the fireplace. "If you want the truth, I feel sorry for her. I have all you for friends. Who does Alice have?"

The parlor door opens, and Fitzie enters bearing a tray of cookies, clean glasses, and a pitcher of milk. "Hey, girls, who wants some of Pearl's cinnamon sugar cookies?"

"Better to ask who doesn't," Trudie quips with a chuckle. "I can never get Daddy to bake anything. I love Pearl's cookies."

Glenice Jo takes the pitcher and pours the milk. "Miss Fitzie, what do you think about this license business?"

"It's necessary if the county says it is. However, the fine is another thing. I'm going with Cora tomorrow. Our state senator is scheduled to be in his Buford office."

I startle and shiver. A state senator's office—no matter who he is— is the last place I want to go.

Fitzie picks up the empty tray. "I didn't spend twenty-five years married to the senator for nothing. I'll use it to our advantage." She raises crossed fingers as she leaves, a sign of prayer with a little Southern superstition thrown in.

❦

Wednesday, February 5, 1930

Fitzie and I sit in Senator Culver's outer office. Like my father's was, his is paneled in mahogany, with the requisite cherry-wood desks. Always a display of money and power. I curl my lip while scratching my arm, then lean toward Fitzie. "Just being here gives me hives."

"Hush." She swats my arm lightly, although her lips twitch. "Never tip your hand, sugar. Your father thought Senator Culver was a pushover. That means the man uses common sense and is compassionate. I'll play that angle. Ah—now shush."

The door to the inner office opens. The secretary comes through with Senator Culver following her. She steps behind her desk with a smile. The senator approaches and takes Fitzie's hand when she rises. Like most politicians, he sports a dark-blue suit and waistcoat. His hair is wavy and slightly unruly. I bite my cheek to keep from laughing at the incongruity.

"My dear Mrs. Fitzgerald. How are you holding up?" Fitzie murmurs a polite reply, and he turns to me. "Miss Fitzgerald, I'm glad you're able to be with your mother during her sorrow."

If he only knew. I nod and force a smile. If he knew the effort it's taking not to roll my eyes, he'd present me with a medal. He escorts us into his office. "How may I be of service to you?"

Fitzie waits until he takes his seat. "Thank you for seeing us, Gavin." She takes a breath and blows it out slowly. "I'm … sure you heard Alexander left us with nothing."

Senator Culver tightens his lips and says nothing.

Fitzie presses on. "To support ourselves, we have done what any self-respecting Southern woman would do. We opened our home to guests." She looks down at her lap, then raises her eyes again. It amazes me how she is leading him. He hangs on her every word. "Paying guests."

The man nods. "That would be difficult in the best of times."

He appears sympathetic. But can I trust it's real?

Fitzie clears her throat. "Yes, well, we don't want to take up too much of your valuable time. Here's my problem. Someone contacted the county about us not having a license. Frankly, we didn't know one was necessary. But this person also lied about when we opened. Our first guest moved in on the sixth of January. We are facing fraudulent back taxes and a fine for delayed licensing."

The senator straightens. "Do you have proof of the date?"

I nod. "I brought our register and these." I hand him the registration book, along with receipts for the furniture delivery and those from Boone, chronicling the dates of completed construction.

He dips his head in a firm nod. "This proves your innocence there. I'll have the tax removed. Then, I'll see if I can get leniency on the license fine." He stands. "While you are making your way over to that office, I'll make a phone call." He gestures to the door. "Ladies? It's been a pleasure."

We shake his hand and depart. Before the door closes, he adds, "Be sure to let me know if there is anything else I can assist you with."

The drive to the county offices is a quick one. The Lawrenceville building is nondescript brick with three stories. Inside, we find the directory. I read aloud, "Licensing Bureau, Room 207."

While we ride the elevator to the second floor, I question Fitzie. "Do you think he was sincere?"

"Senator Culver? From what I know of him, he is." The elevator stops, the attendant opens the door, and we step out. Brown-speckled linoleum stretches the length of the hallway. Six identical doors line both sides. Fitzie glances at the number on a door we pass. "He's just a man of few words, so he seems brusque. Ah, it's the next door."

Before she turns the knob, she glances at me, then crosses her fingers and looks heavenward. "Here's hoping that phone call came through."

Inside, we give the clerk our names. He hands us a form. "Please fill this out and bring it back to me." He points behind us. "There is a pen and inkwell at that table you may use."

We take the form, thank him, and go to the table. I glance over my shoulder. He's on his telephone, so I whisper in Fitzie's ear. "He seemed nice."

"Shh. Fill it out and make sure you get the dates right."

I'm done with the form in five minutes. I blow on it to dry the ink. After handing it to the man, he looks over our registration book, then smiles and nods. "Give me a couple of minutes. I'll call you when your license is ready."

Half the butterflies depart my stomach. We wander back to the table to sit and wait. I tilt my head to whisper, "I think we're going to be okay. He wasn't antagonistic. At least, he didn't look at me like I was a lawbreaker." I grimace.

After a few minutes, the fellow comes back. "Mrs. Fitzgerald? Here is your license. That'll be five dollars. The fine is waived." The rest of my butterflies fly away. We pay him and then he presents us with an envelope. "There you go, ladies. You'll have to renew the license annually, so I slipped a form for next year in the envelope for you. Have a pleasant day, and good luck with your guesthouse. Good day."

I hold in the whoop that wants to escape. Once we're in the elevator, I let it go, then clap my hand over my mouth when the attendant grins at me.

I wait until we're outside the building. "I have to say, Senator Culver is an unusual man."

Unless he wants something. The thought stops me. I look at Fitzie. She's relaxed—worry isn't hanging over her. Maybe it's fine.

But like a pooch with a bone, an unsettled feeling gnaws on me.

Chapter 26

Tuesday, February 18, 1930

THE KITCHEN DOOR SWINGS OPEN. Ruby and Pearl enter the dining room, bearing a large platter of fried chicken. Fitzie is exercising her rights as hostess to make our guests' birthdays special. Iris and Lulamae have requested fried chicken. As the platter passes, Iris picks up a wing and examines it.

"This reminds me of a story."

Mr. James looks up from his plate. "A chicken wing?"

Fitzie wags a finger at him. "Careful, good sir." She won't let anything pass that might embarrass someone. "We love Miss Iris' stories, no matter what inspires them." She dips her head to the sweet woman seated to her left. "Please go on, Miss Iris."

She nods, grinning. "Growing up, Lulamae and I were an anomaly in our small town. There was only ever one other set of twins, and they weren't identical." She pauses and selects a second piece of chicken, a fat leg this time. "One year, they separated Lulamae and me. Some hogwash about becoming our own person." She takes a bite of chicken and sighs in delight. "Pearl, this is heavenly."

"Thank you kindly." Pearl dawdles at the sideboard, waiting to hear tonight's story. She always serves the main dish in order to listen. Mealtime has become quite lively at Fitzgerald House.

"Yes, well, one thing my dear sister didn't tell you." Lulamae picks up the story while Iris chews her chicken. "She had trouble learning. We never did find out what it was. But she was terrible taking tests. So if her class had one and mine didn't, we'd trade places, and I would take the test for her."

200

With her forearm on the table, Fitzie leans forward. "How was learning hard for you, Miss Iris?"

"It was reading. The letters would move and trade places with one another."

Everyone's eyes open wide. Is Miss Iris playing a joke on us?

"Nobody ever did believe me. But a few years later, I think it was fourth grade at the first of the year, the teacher was telling all the children her rules. She looked right at me and said, 'And if you don't believe me, just ask Iris.' Well, I told her I never had her as my teacher. My sister Lulamae did."

Lulamae laughs and blots her mouth. "To which the teacher replied, 'You sat in my class when you and she traded places.'"

Iris chuckles. "I guess our teachers weren't as dumb as we thought they were."

Pearl picks up the empty platter, laughter rumbling behind closed lips. "I'll bring in more chicken."

The discussion turns to what could have been the possible cause of Iris' problem. My attention wanders. Glenice Jo and I have a party to plan for Martha Anne. The girls didn't know about bridal showers, but Millie had been to one in Atlanta, and I'd attended two in New York. Of course, Glenice Jo said we *had* to host one for Martha Anne.

As supper winds down, Ruby enters bearing a birthday cake. We all sing to the ladies, and then the guests decide to take their cake and coffee into the parlor for a game of charades. I beg off, having a date with Boone.

"We're going to see *The Iron Mask*."

Aunt Clara startles and signs, "The one with Douglas Fairbanks?"

"Ooh, I love him," Lulamae says. Her ability to pick up sign language impresses me.

"What's so great about Fairbanks that all you ladies always swoon over him?" Henry Dobbs asks.

Dr. Harold laughs. "Why, young Henry, I'd think it obvious. According to the ladies, he's prettier than pumpkin pie at Thanksgiving." Amid our laughter, he rises and picks up his plate and coffee.

I excuse myself and leave them discussing the merits of the actor's looks as they make their way to the guest parlor. Before I leave, I need to balance the books.

It doesn't take too long to finish the task. The account balance looks fairly good, but I'll be happier when we rent the last room. A steady stream of overnight guests keeps the Alexander Fitzgerald Room full every weekend. It was a stroke of brilliance on Aunt Clara's part to advertise in the *Atlanta Constitution*. The senator was a colorful figure in state politics. Curiosity brings many to our door. But I will still be happier when we rent Room E.

I go in search of Fitzie and Aunt Clara and find them in the family parlor, where Aunt Clara is writing while Fitzie mends a pillowcase that young Henry ripped during a nightmare. It seems a giant turtle had him in its mouth. Miss Lulamae is determined to find the meaning behind it. Henry says it's because of a large snapping turtle he tangled with when he was five.

"Fitzie?" I whisper so I don't disturb Aunt Clara.

She smiles, sets down her sewing, and pats the cushion next to her on the settee. "You can speak up. Your aunt is editing."

My shoulders relax and I sit in the chair opposite her. "Good. Last night, Martha Anne told me Ethan's family is giving them the down payment on a small cottage. It's in Buford, on Jackson Street. It's close enough to the tannery so they can walk."

Aunt Clara's fingers fly as she turns and hooks her elbow over the spindle-back chair. "How wonderful for them. I'm sure Martha Anne is thrilled."

I sigh. "She is, but that creates a vacancy for us. We were holding Room E for them."

Fitzie stabs her needle into the pillowcase again. "Have you asked her or Glenice Jo to put the word out at the tannery? People probably assume we're full."

"What about the vacancy sign?" Aunt Clara's hands move with care, reflecting her thoughtful state of mind. "We took that down when you wanted to hold the room."

I forgot the sign. "You're right." I jump up and head for the door. "I'll go put it out again." I pause and glance over my shoulder. "Do either of you have anything to go in the mailbox? I can take it."

Fitzie shakes her head but Aunt Clara nods. "I've got a letter that needs to go out."

Back in the morning room, I pull the sign from the bottom desk drawer. I pick up Auntie's letter and head to the mailbox. The redbud and crabapple trees in the neighbor's field are filled with buds. By next week, they should be blooming, making the walk lovely. Just seeing them makes my throat tickle. I've been on the allergy shots for four months, but I'm not seeing a lot of improvement. I still have a cough, and lately, I notice a little huskiness in my voice. That's not good.

At the mailbox, I hang the vacancy sign beneath the guesthouse placard. We don't get a lot of traffic on the road, but hopefully, someone who needs a room will see it. I hurry back to the house to finish getting ready for my date.

Walking back up the aisle at the theater after the movie, Boone entwines his fingers with mine. "I have always wondered about that story." He looks at me. "Do you really think it was the king's twin brother?"

I shrug one shoulder. "I never thought about it. But can you imagine having to spend your life like that?" I shudder.

We enter the lobby and are moving toward the door when Boone stops abruptly and pulls me back. Alice stands near the door with Walter Teague. Unfortunately, she spies us. Her eyes narrow, then she lifts her chin and leans her head toward Walter, her gaze never leaving us.

"Walter?" Her voice is loud enough to carry across the lobby. "Did you know the Fitzgeralds are running an illegal boarding house? You should be more careful where you send your employees. They could get arrested too."

I stiffen. Every person in the lobby stops and looks at us.

Boone pulls me across the lobby. "That is a bald-faced lie, Alice."

She raises one pencil-thin, sculpted eyebrow. "Says you, but I heard otherwise."

Now I know for sure. Much more easily than the detectives in Aunt Clara's novels, I've found my culprit. "Alice, why are you so intent on hurting us? You know this is a lie. And you never *heard* otherwise. You're the one who telephoned a false accusation to the county."

Walter looks down at Alice and then at me, his face a study of shock and perplexity. "Is that true, Alice?"

"Cora's the liar. She thinks because her father was a senator, she's above the law. I'm a law-abiding citizen. It was my duty to turn her in." Her bold stare is filled with hatred.

Walter's bushy brows pull together. "Cora, if what Alice says is true, I'll have to recommend our workers leave your place."

I straighten my shoulders and look him straight in the eye. "We're licensed. Alice also lied about us not paying our taxes. We opened this year. We don't owe taxes for last year. That accusation is completely false." I square off with Alice. "I want to know why you made them."

She tosses her head. "Ask your boyfriend. He's in bed with Gavin Culver. Maybe—" She levels a nefarious gaze at us. "Maybe they're even like those men we hear stories about."

I gasp.

Boone startles.

Alice turns on her heel and leaves the theater.

Walter shakes his head and sighs. "When Alice first asked me to play a trick on a friend at the Merchant on New Year's Eve, I thought it was innocent fun." He offers a chagrined smile. "I see now, it wasn't." He turns his hat in his hands. "Actually, the moment I saw your reaction to her with Boone, I realized it wasn't. I regret I was part of that." He thrusts out his hand to Boone. "Sorry, old man."

Boone takes Walter's hand, but I can see he's thoroughly shaken. He keeps glancing at me and then just as quickly withdraws his gaze. I don't know what to make of Alice's parting shot—not about Boone being … well … that way. But her reference to Boone being close to Senator Culver rattles me to the core. It has a ring of truth. His *business meeting* comes to mind.

Walter leaves, and we walk to the truck in silence. Boone is lost in his thoughts, and I'm uncomfortable, unable to intrude. The ride back home seems to take forever. When we arrive, I open my door to jump out, but Boone's hand on my arm stops me.

"Cora, you know Alice lies about everything. I hope you don't believe her—" His face turns red.

"Of course, I don't." Not about *that*. "I'm tired, that's all. Confronting her took a lot out of me. I need to go."

His brow creases. "You do know how much I care for you, Cora … don't you?"

Do I? "I think I do."

I slip out of the truck and run into the house. If I'm honest with myself, I don't know how much Boone cares. Not really. And we aren't moving forward in this relationship until I know him better. A lot better.

Wednesday, February 19, 1930
Carrying a box of seedlings, I venture into the garden. It's a mild day. The sunshine is bright, and the temperature is moderate for February. According to the farm report, it's time to put these in the soil. I drop an old cushion to the ground and set the box next to it. I cross the yard to the small, old barn and pick up a hoe and trowel.

All night long, Alice's accusations haunted my dreams. Now, in hopes of finding some clarity, I dig my hoe deep into the garden's soil. Over and over, I turn the dirt and examine it for worms.

"Need worms to make the soil fertile," Pearl's late husband always said. He was our groundskeeper and taught me to garden when I was six or seven. I miss Job. He had the patience of his namesake.

Ask Boone. He's in bed with Gavin Culver.

Clouds skitter across the sky, and I lean on the hoe for a moment, watching them. Another thing Job taught me. To read the sky. When the wind blew and clouds raced, prepare for a coming storm. I look over the seedlings I need to plant and back up again. It's too early for a really bad storm. I flex my shoulders and attack the ground again.

When the soil is turned and furrows lie between small hills, I exchange the hoe for a trowel. Kneeling on the cushion, I dig the holes for the vegetables. Dig, slide cushion, lean, and dig again, setting a plant in each hole. The repetitive, mindless action of planting is where I can think. I'm so confused about Boone. One minute he's—

"Hey, Cora."

Millie's voice rings out from the porch. I glance up and wave.

"Hey. What brings you here?"

She waits until she reaches me. "Do I need a reason?" Squatting next to me, she picks up a seedling, examining it. "Besides, if I help you, you'll get done quicker." She holds out the plant. "What is this?"

I glance at it. "That's a cabbage."

"Huh. How do you know?"

I take it from her and place it in a hole, then cover its roots with soil. "I put the seed package in the box with them. That's the only way I can tell them apart." I point to the other cabbage seedlings. "We'll do all these first." We continue until the rest of the cabbages are in the ground. "I'm glad you came. I need some advice."

"Okay." Millie sits back on her heels, her hand hovering over the seedling box. "Which now?"

"The cauliflower, and see those little stakes? You can mark the rows for me."

She pulls the markers out of the box, reads them, then sticks the cabbage one in the ground at the end of the row. She stabs the cauliflower one into the next row when we finish it.

I move to the last row. "Thanks. These are Brussels sprouts." We continue until the box is empty. "Now, we water."

We take the tools back to the barn and pick up two watering cans, fill them at the pond, and sprinkle the garden. When Millie's is empty, she sits on the grass bordering the vegetable garden.

"So what do you want to talk about?"

My sigh comes all the way from my toes. I flop down next to her and stretch my legs out in front of me. "Boone. I don't know what to make of him, Millie. He confuses me."

She brushes a speck of dirt off her hands. "Tell me what's got you bewildered."

I relay the conversation with Alice and Walter. "Alice's parting comment was that Boone is in bed with Gavin Culver."

Millie gasps.

"While she let the innuendo knife Boone, I think she really meant it figuratively. But you know how I feel about politicians."

Millie nods. "I do—and don't blame you. Your father was a horrible man. I think he was one of those narcissists."

I frown. "What's that?"

"Someone who doesn't or can't love anyone but himself."

"Sounds like him. How did you learn about that?"

Millie unfolds her legs and leans back on her hands. "One of my roommates in Atlanta was going to college to become a psychologist. She told us about some of the different personality disorders and syndromes. When she listed the behaviors of a narcissist, I thought of your father."

"Even so, a syndrome doesn't make it any better. It almost sounds as though I should forgive him for hating me and making my life miserable." I shove the trowel in the box. "I don't want to talk about him, anyway." I crumple the empty seedling tray.

Millie puts her hand on my arm. "Don't be angry." Her eyes plead with me.

I stop my frantic movements. "I'm not angry at you, Millie. I don't know what I am, other than confused." I briefly close my eyes. "The worst part is, I let down my guard and fell in love with Boone."

"Yeah, I know all about that. But Cora?" Millie rises to her knees. "Boone isn't like Lou. Not at all."

"I hope not."

She shakes her head. "I know he isn't. Another thing." She waits until I'm looking her in the eye. "He isn't anything like your father. Besides, it was Alice who made the accusation. Why are you letting her get to you?"

She's right. Boone is nothing like the senator. Why do I let myself worry like that? I need to trust him.

But some voices are harder to turn off than others.

Chapter 27

Saturday, March 1, 1930

I RUN MY HAND OVER THE quilt in Room A, removing the last wrinkle on the bed. "Topaz, I'll empty the wastebasket while you put on the bedspread." She lifts it and deftly flips it in the air, making it fall in near perfection over the bed.

That bed is a neat island in a sea of disarray. I gave up trying to straighten Henry's room after the first few days. "I don't mind the mess," he said that first week. "Reminds me of home."

Pearl pokes her head into the room, her white teeth gleaming from a wide smile. "Miss Cora, there's a woman in the guest parlor. She come 'bout the room."

Thank You.

Then a thought draws my brows down. "Is she young?" That could become a boll weevil in the cotton with Henry being in his early twenties.

Pearl tilts her head and purses her lips, considering. "If'n I has to guess, I'd say she's in her late thirties, maybe forties."

Sweet relief. We need that room rented. "She didn't say where she works, did she?" Another concern hits me. "She doesn't have children, does she?"

"Miss Cora!" Pearl plants her fists on her ample hips. "I don't asks those questions, an' she don't say."

"Of course not. I'm sorry, Pearl. And thank you." She nods and leaves. "Topaz, will you finish up here, please? I'll go interview the lady."

Downstairs, I find a slender woman staring out the window. She's lean to the emaciated side. Her lackluster hair is pulled into a bun at the nape of her neck. Her dress, made from a Gingham Girl Flour sack, appears fairly new. At least, it's not threadbare.

I clear my throat and approach with a smile. "Hello. I'm Cora Fitzgerald, one of the owners here."

She turns and offers a tentative smile. "I'm Katherine Upchurch. Is the room still available?" Her voice is so soft, I can hardly hear her.

"It's not yet rented. Please sit down." I gesture to the davenport. "Tell me about yourself."

She sits in the middle of the settee, perching on its edge like a timid bird. "I managed to get a job at the Bona Allen Shoe Factory. I'm one of the lucky ones." She raises her hand to the back of her neck.

It takes an effort not to frown at the bruise on her forearm in the shape of fingers. I glance at her hand. A thin gold band encircles her ring finger. She's put makeup over the bruise, I'm sure. But it's still visible. "Are you married, Katherine?"

She quickly lowers her hand to her lap. "Yes ma'am. My husband got laid off." She drops her chin. "He hasn't found steady work. We live in Uvalda, and there's no jobs anywhere. He's watching the children. Farming—while I'm here."

I don't mean to be nosy, but I must ask. "How were you able to get a job in the shoe factory, and he wasn't?"

A genuine smile brightens her eyes. "I'm an artist. They needed someone to draw the designs for the toolers. It was divine intervention, seeing that ad in the newspaper."

Her whole countenance changes when she mentions her artistry. The bruise is bothersome but not my business. Her children are, though. I'm not sure how the others would feel about children visiting. "Your art and work sound interesting." I move to the desk for the registry book. "How many children do you have?"

"Two. My Katie, named after me, is eight. Teddy is eleven."

They aren't babies, anyway. But she's younger than Pearl guessed. A hard life and not enough food has aged her beyond her years. I make my decision.

"Katherine?" I hand her the book and a pen. "I'll take you up to see the room. If you decide to take it,"—I hold up the registry book—"I'll have you fill this in. Then, I'll explain all the details and collect your first week's rent. It's four dollars for the room and two meals a day."

"Oh, I'll take it, even if it's a closet. There's nothing else around other than the hotel, and I can't afford that." She pulls three one-dollar bills and two shiny half dollars from a worn-out coin purse and hands them to me. Then she fills in the book while I tell Pearl there will be another guest for supper.

Saturday, March 15, 1930
Only Aunt Clara lingers over her breakfast coffee in the dining room this morning. It's something she often does if she's working out a plot point in her head. All the guests have left for work, and Fitzie is in the morning room, singing. It's just my aunt and me. I slide into my chair, and she raises an eyebrow and her hands.

"Going back to your New York routine?"

I pick up my coffee cup and take it to the sideboard, where a fresh pot is waiting. "No, but Boone and I went to the late movie last night." I pour the coffee and let its aroma help open my eyes.

"Why that one?"

I sit and Pearl brings my breakfast. "Thank you, Pearl. I'm sorry you had to keep it warm for me." She nods. Her smile never reveals if she's displeased or not. "To your question, Boone had a meeting to attend before we could go out."

"What kind of a meeting does a handyman and furniture maker have to go to?" Aunt Clara drains her cup.

"I don't know. I didn't question him." I lay my fork on the plate. "Do you think I should have?"

"Should have what?" Fitzie enters with the newspaper under her arm. She lays it beside me.

"You're finished with it?" She nods and nudges it toward me. "And Auntie wants to know what kind of meeting Boone had that made us have to go to the late movie."

Fitzie glances at the coffeepot, debating, then shakes her head. "It's a good question. Did you ask?"

"No. That's what I was asking Aunt Clara. Should I have?"

"Sugar, Boone is courting you. This is the time to get to know him well. Ask questions." She glances at Aunt Clara. "I'm going to the library. I requested William Faulkner's new novel. It's in and they're holding it for me."

Aunt Clara claps her hands in delight. After Mama leaves, my aunt plops her dark-yellow beret on her head and heads to the writing desk in the family parlor. I need to perform a quick inventory of guest toiletries and ask Pearl for her grocery list. Then I'll study the grocers' advertisements in the newspaper and pour another cup of coffee. I'm still a bit foggy-headed.

I grab a tablet and pen on my way upstairs. In the storage closet, I count the bars of soap. We give each guest one per month. There are only three bars left. I jot *soap* on the list. And *toilet paper*. Running a boarding house takes a little more organization than I originally realized.

I seek out Pearl in the kitchen. "What have you planned for next week's meals? And do we need any laundry powder for our own needs?"

She fishes a piece of folded paper from her pocket. "Here's the list. I needs flour, corn meal, sugar—order the twenty-five pound bag. It's cheaper that way. An' don' let them tell you they don' have one."

I look over her list. "I think I'll check with Mr. Bud about chickens. We should probably start raising our own." I glance up at her. "Have you ever caught and killed one? Can you do all it takes to get it ready to cook?"

Pearl breaks into hearty laughter. "If'n you could see yo' face, Miss Cora." She slaps the table and Ruby chuckles.

"My Auntie Pearl can wring a chicken's neck with a fast twist of her wrist."

The mental image makes me cringe. "I thought we always bought chicken from the grocery, already butchered."

Pearl wipes her eyes. "Not always, honey. In the early days here, hisself wasn't making enough money, and we raised our own. My Job an' me were a good team. He'd catch 'em, an' I'd wring their necks. Together, we'd sit and pluck 'em. But you're right about the cost with so many mouths to feed now. Ruby can help me catch those chickens."

"I'll see if Boone will build the coop for us."

Pearl shakes her head. "No need. My nephews can do that. They's built a lot of chicken coops. Have since they was little. Takes 'em a single day."

I can't help grinning at how far I've come from a vaudeville star. "I think we're about to become chicken farmers. We'll be able to give our guests fresh eggs too."

Pearl points to my list. "You better order six dozen eggs for this week. It'll be a bit o' time before we's ready to gather our own."

I get a fresh cup of coffee and take it and the newspaper to the morning room. I spread the paper and start making notes on the best prices. Allen's grocery has some good sales, but so does Venable's. I'll split my order between them.

After my list is ready, I set the pad aside and read a few news stories. My eyes roam over the pages. I'm about to flip to the next one when the words *boarding house or bordello?* jump out at me.

Buford/Sugar Hill

In an interview, this reporter learned that the late state senator Alexander Fitzgerald's home has been turned into a questionable boarding house.

"Well, you can't be sure," said the anonymous caller, "but having both men and women boarding there? Why, it's indecent. It makes the good folk of this county wonder if it's truly a boarding house, or are they using it for other purposes."

The caller did not want her name used but added, "That actress Dixie Lynn, who we know as Cora Fitzgerald, tried to get a loan from the bank. It's my opinion they didn't lend to her because of this nefarious activity. We all know the morals of actresses."

Alice Farnham again! I jump up. Seething, I run into the guest parlor, where Aunt Clara is writing. "I'm sorry to interrupt you, but this is an emergency." I thrust the page from the newspaper in front of her. "Read this. It's pure slander."

Aunt Clara looks up at me, then takes the paper. Her eyes grow wide as she reads the story, and her face turns red. She slams it to the desk and beckons me to follow her.

"Where are we going?"

Her hands move in angry thrusts. "You're going to make a phone call for me. To the newspaper."

Her stride eats up the floor into the hall. I lift the receiver and ask Blanche for the newspaper, then cover the mouthpiece with one hand. "It's Blanche," I mouth.

"For once, I'm glad it is," Aunt Clara signs. "I hope she listens in and spreads this around."

When the editor picks up, I tell him who I am. "My aunt, Clara Drummond, is with me, and I'm relaying her words. She says, 'Arnold, you've known me and this family for years. I let you carry my serialized stories, which I will pull if you don't print an apology for this claptrap and fire that reporter.'" Aunt Clara folds her arms.

"What are you talking about, Miss Fitzgerald?"

My eyes widen at his lack of knowledge of what is in his paper. "The story on page seven of today's edition. I suggest you read it. Then I suggest you honor my aunt's request for an apology and a retraction."

Paper rustles in the background. I nod at my aunt and mouth, "He's reading."

"What the—excuse me, Miss Fitzgerald. I am profoundly sorry. I did not see this, nor do I know how it got in. When I received the phone call from Miss Farn—oops."

"I already knew who it was. What I don't know is the reason she's determined to destroy my family's reputation."

"Please accept my apologies. We will print a retraction. And an apology."

"Thank you." I hang up. My mouth dries up as tears well in my eyes.

Aunt Clara unfolds her arms and signs, "I think a visit to Alice's father might be in order. This has gone too far. Her slanderous little story could have cost us. It still might. We should threaten to sue."

I grimace. "I don't want to do that."

Her signs are emphatic. "Neither do I, but the threat might take care of it all."

"Let's hold off. Maybe the retraction in the paper will subdue her."

My aunt quirks her mouth. "Don't be too sure."

Fitzie sticks her head in the family parlor door. "Boone sent flowers again."

I raise my eyes from my book. The vase she holds is filled with early spring blossoms. My heart warms at his thoughtfulness. "They're so pretty."

"It looks as though he picked these himself. That boy is a romantic. I'll put these in the foyer since you already have a bouquet in here." She closes the door behind her.

I lay down my pen and lean in to smell the azalea blossoms arranged with small branches from a cherry tree. Boone's attentiveness of late soothes my concerns. Our dates aren't expensive. Walks in the woods, picnics on nice days, and even one evening in the library, quietly reading side by side, and an ice cream soda later. I glance at the door. Fitzie seems to be living vicariously through us. I only hope it doesn't leave her melancholy.

My ledger work finished, it's time to change the beds. I go in search of Topaz. She's in the kitchen, helping her sister and Pearl. "Since you have Topaz busy, I'll change the guests' bedding."

Pearl pauses her stirring in a pot on the stove. "Topaz is almost done, Miss Cora. I'll send her up directly."

"Thank you. I'll start in D, Topaz."

From the second-floor storage room, I pull out crisp white sheets.

In D, I strip Dr. Harold's bed and deposit the laundry outside the door. Once his bed is remade, I glance around the room to see if anything needs straightening or dusting. Topaz is doing a good job of keeping the rooms dust-free. This one is quite neat and tidy, unlike Henry Dobbs' room. Even James Vaughn is neater than Henry, who leaves his clothes all over his room, some hanging out of the dresser drawers. I shake my head and give the bedspread a final smoothing. Last, I run the carpet sweeper over the rug, empty the wastebasket, then move on to Room C.

"Here I am, Miss Cora." Topaz joins me, and the two of us make quick work of the remaining rooms. "Mama will be by in the morning for the guests' laundry and these." She hoists up the cloth bag stuffed with sheets and lugs it downstairs.

I debate whether to straighten Henry's room. My fingers itch to fold his clothes and put them neatly away, but it's not my place. It is my place, however, to empty the wastebasket. I pick it up and take it to the storage room, where a larger one awaits. I'll deposit it all in the incinerator as soon as I dump this one. As I turn the wastebasket over, bright red catches my eye. I lower the small receptacle to the floor, peering inside the larger. It's a flyer of some type. But it's the name that holds me captive.

Boone Robertson.

Is he advertising his handyman work? Maybe that's something we can do. I pick it up, glancing behind me. I feel like a snoop, but clearly, this isn't a personal item. It's been printed. I unfold it.

My heart stops and my blood runs cold.

It's a picture of Senator Gavin Culver shaking hands with Boone. Beneath the photo are the words:

Boone Robertson wants your vote for the Georgia State House.

Chapter 28

Saturday evening, March 15, 1930

"HE'S A LYING DOG. A cad. *Worse* than a cad. He's a skunk!" I wear a path in the parlor rug while Fitzie twists her fingers and shakes her head. Aunt Clara's hands fly so fast I can't begin to understand what she's saying. She's furious with Boone—that much I can make out. Not one of us had any inkling of his duplicity.

"I'm calling the Dillies." I storm out of the parlor and into the hallway, where I telephone Glenice Jo. "Tell the girls to come over here right away."

She doesn't argue or even ask why. I guess she can tell by my voice I'm upset—or does she know something? I narrow my eyes. If she knew and didn't tell me—? I shake my head. No, I can't imagine her betraying me like that.

Back in the parlor, Fitzie pours small glasses of sherry and hands me one. "It will help you calm down."

"I don't want to calm down. I want answers." I stop and take the tiny flute. "But I don't want to cry. If I start, I feel like I'll never stop." I down the sherry in one gulp, set the glass on the coffee table, and drop onto the davenport. "Why, Mama? Why, when I finally give my heart to someone, does something like this have to happen?"

Her eyes well with tears. "For years, I prayed you'd find a good man, sugar. I thought you had." She shakes her head. "I can't understand it either." A tear spills over and trails down her cheek. She mops it with her hankie.

My aunt closes one eye, scrunches her mouth, then picks up a notebook. Her pen flies, and if I'm right, one of her characters will soon either arrest a Boone-like character or knock him off.

Strains of "Weary River" by Rudy Vallee float from the radio, which Fitzie usually has on in the evenings. When he croons, "Fate has been a cheerful giver to most everyone but me," Fitzie blurs before me.

I jump up and switch off the radio. "That's my life exactly, Mama. First, the senator and now, Boone." I drop into a chair and cover my face with my hands. My tears spill unchecked. A moment later, the heat of my anger dries them and propels me to my feet.

"To think, I've forgiven him so many things." I whirl to Fitzie. "New Year's Eve is a good example. Now I know why he had Senator Culver's car to use. Payola. And to think I believed him. It seems Alice isn't the only liar."

Aunt Clara's head lifts from her note-taking, and she turns her gaze to the door. A second later, Glenice Jo comes in, followed by the other Dillies. Upon seeing me, she stops dead. Martha Anne, Millie, and Trudie collide into her back. If things weren't what they are, I'd laugh at them.

Glenice Jo recovers quickly. She slides her gaze from me to Fitzie, then to Aunt Clara, and finally back to me. "What's happened?"

I snort. I really don't care about being ladylike at this moment. "What's happened?" I thrust Boone's flyer at her. "This is what happened." My voice sounds shrill in my ears.

Glenice Jo takes the flyer and opens it. I watch her closely. Her response isn't shock. She grins!

"Yeah, isn't it exciting? He sure has my vote."

She knew? I rub my arms and blink.

Martha Anne claps her hands in jubilation. "I'm so thrilled! Ethan and I are going to work on his campaign."

I stare at my hands, but they don't hold any answers. "You knew this, and you didn't think to tell me?" The reality of the betrayal makes my stomach sour and knees weak. I drop into the chair. Millie's is the only face expressing surprise and concern. She moves to stand behind me, putting her hand on my shoulder.

"Glenice Jo?" Fitzie's voice is soft after my screeching. "What and when did you know?"

"I found out a couple of weeks ago." Glenice Jo bites her lip, seemingly unsure now. "We thought Cora knew. I can't imagine him not telling her. And she knows Boone is a good man. One who truly wants to help the voiceless in our county."

Her eyes plead with me, but I've had a lifetime of seeing politicians up close. I shake my head. "They may start out thinking their motives are pure, but greed and power soon win them over." My voice rises. "They become cheaters, power-brokers, money-grubbing men who look down their noses at everyone. Including their wives." I point to Fitzie. "And daughters." I jump up and pace. "I can't believe you of all people wouldn't tell me." I glance at Martha Anne and Trudie. "Can you understand how betrayed I feel?"

Millie's face turns red. "I know how you feel. Nobody in Atlanta ever told me about Lou." She glances at me. "In their defense, they thought I knew."

Martha Anne's head nods so hard she's in danger of rattling her brains. "Honey, I honestly thought he'd talked to you about it. I really did."

I believe her but I can't believe— "And you honestly thought I'd be okay with it? Do any of you even *remember* my childhood?"

She cringes. "I guess I thought Boone being who he is would rise above those memories. I wouldn't hurt you for the world, Cora. Please believe me."

"I don't want to. I want to stay mad at all of you. Except Millie." I reach over my shoulder and squeeze her hand.

Tears spill down Trudie's cheeks. Martha Anne's expression is one of real chagrin. Glenice Jo's eyes shine with unshed tears. These girls are my Dillies—friends since early childhood. They didn't betray me. They've made a mistake, but I know they love me. And I love them. And I don't like making them cry.

"But I can't—stay mad at you. The real focus is Boone. What hurts so badly is he never gave me a hint he wanted to run for office." Letting go of Millie's hand, I rise and stand next to Fitzie. "He's heard me mention how the senator neglected Mama." I lay my hand on her shoulder, wishing I could have protected her. "I told him the man was a womanizer—how he'd leave a paramour's house and then parade Mama in front of photographers as though he was the perfect husband. He made me sick."

I wrap my arms tight around my middle. "All y'all saw my bruises. Every one of them from *his* hands. Did you know that he tried to rape me when I was five?"

They gasp. I allow that to settle in for a moment, then gesture to Aunt Clara. "Thank God she caught him. Aunt Clara stopped him by threatening to tell the world if he ever touched me again."

By the time I close my mouth, I'm shaking. My friends are in shock, and it makes my heart weep.

Anger is an exhausting emotion. I drop onto the davenport next to Mama. My stomach roils like it wants to spew its contents. I take a few deep breaths and force my emotions to calm. A memory of the times these good friends surrounded and protected me dissolves my anger at them.

"I'm sorry I misdirected my outrage at all y'all. I guess when we hurt the most, we lash out at those closest to us. Forgive me for that."

Glenice Jo sits cautiously next to me. "It's okay to be mad at us. It's just that we were so sure he'd told you."

Martha Anne wrings her hands. "When he campaigned at the tannery, he said something about you. I don't remember what, but it made me assume you knew."

I share a glance with Fitzie. "You see? He's exactly like the senator. Appearance and assumption trump truth. Well, Mr. Robertson is out of my life. I never want to hear his name again. I never want to even see his face again. He's killed my love with this." My head believes my words, but my heart is shattering.

Tears sprout in everyone's eyes. Mama and Aunt Clara weep openly, mourning for me. I'm the only one who remains dry-eyed. I can't let myself cry. If I do—

The door opens, and Pearl enters. She glances at all of us drowning in tears. "Uh, Miss Cora?"

"Yes, Pearl? What is it?"

"Mr. Boone is at the door."

Chapter 29

Saturday, April 19, 1930

BOONE FINALLY GOT IT THROUGH his voter-driven cranium that I won't see him. Poor Pearl had to be the one to tell him. Every time, after that first day that she sent him away from our front door, she'd walk back to the kitchen, shaking her head and mumbling about stubbornness. Instead, he now sends letters that I return unopened. I've given Pearl instructions to refuse all flowers as well.

I do what I can to stay busy and not think about him. Along with the garden, the new chicken coop the Horton brothers built gives me something to occupy my mind. The hens we bought are happy and laying eggs.

I just wish my heart would fall in line with my brain. If it weren't so melodramatic, I'd hold a funeral with my friends and family in attendance. Then, we could properly mourn my murdered love and be done with it.

I bend and rip out another of the tenacious weeds that invade the garden. The tedium of the task numbs my mind a bit. I focus on how well the vegetables are growing. And why not? I've had lots of time to give them all the attention they need. I'm looking forward to harvesting, although that will be a while yet. The Brussels sprouts aren't even teensy buds on their stalks yet. The cabbages are small too. It's going to be longer than I thought for these to be ready.

I'm planting watermelon seeds plus several more produce varieties we started in the kitchen. By summer, we'll have fresh vegetables on our table. All our guests have taken an interest in the garden. Today, several of them help, and Mr. James picked up the mule and plow Mr.

Bud offered. I need them to increase the size of our small field if it's going to feed a dozen people.

Even the Sadler sisters and Katherine want to help.

"It's the least we can do, isn't it, Iris? The meals we get at Fitzgerald House are better than anywhere we've ever boarded," Miss Lulamae says. Even Katherine nods with a shy smile.

Although she helped me gather eggs this morning, I haven't gotten much of Katherine's story yet. I can't help but wonder about her, leaving her children with her husband. Is he good to them? Surely, he must be, or she wouldn't leave them with him. These times are hard for everyone, and I give her credit for being willing to put food on their table. We're so blessed to have the tannery here. It keeps folks employed in the county.

Mr. James pulls off his hat and wipes his forehead with his sleeve. "With this rising humidity, I believe we might be in for some rain later tonight. That'll be good for the garden." He plops his hat back on his head and clicks his tongue. "Gid' up, mule."

At the end of the final tomato row, Katherine bends next to me and slips a seedling into the soil. I slide a chicken-wire cage over it. "That's it for this row." I glance at the number of boxes behind me. There's only a few left. "My goodness, I planned to work all day, but with everyone helping, we only have the sweet potatoes, peas, and the watermelon left."

"The twins are in a race to see who gets their rows done first." Katherine's soft chuckle surprises me. It's the first time I've heard it. She steps into the next furrow and drops a rooted sweet potato slip into the ground, then straightens and stretches. "I got a letter from home this morning." She glances around us, then quickly lowers her eyes. "I have a confession to make. It's been eating at me since I got here."

I stop and face her in alarm. "What's wrong?" I hope I can help her. I really like Katherine.

"I told you a falsehood. My children are with my parents, not my husband." Her mouth pulls down and her eyes harden. "The last time he beat me, he also took a swing at my kids. I hit him over the head with a frying pan, grabbed the children, and skedaddled." Her gaze seeks mine.

If she's looking for judgement, she won't find it here, at least not from me. My jaw tightens and I lift my chin. "I'm glad you didn't stick around for another beating."

She stares at me for a moment, then visibly relaxes and exhales. "Thank you." She picks up her box and continues to plant, but the floodgates are open. "He drank all the time. At first, I thought it was because he had trouble finding a job, but even when he gets work, he continues to drink. He spends most all his wages on liquor while the children and I go hungry. Then he lost that job too. That began a cycle. If I said anything, he beat me."

"I'm glad you found us. Has he tried to take the children or find you?"

"My parents won't allow him near them, and they sure won't tell him where I am."

I stand and shade my eyes against the sun. "How did you really get your job up here?"

She smiles. "Daddy knows another tooler's daddy. As soon as he told us about the opening, I hustled up here. I do need to tell you …" She pauses and bites her lip. "In a few months, my parents are going to move up here. They managed to sell their house. When they get here, I'll move in with them."

Naturally, I understand, but that will leave a room empty. Still, we found her, and I'm sure we'll find someone else. I just hope they're as nice as Katherine. "That will be swell for you. I hope we'll get to see you once in a while, though. I'd love to meet your children. And your parents."

"I'd like that." She bends to her work and we continue in silence. I guess she's said all she has to say.

I straighten and stretch the kinks out of my back. Dr. Harold crosses the lawn with a bundle of stakes under one arm and a roll of twine in his hand. When he reaches me, he sets those on the ground and takes over poking the holes for me to drop in the seeds. He's the kind of man daddies should be.

With the stick, he points to the stakes and twine. "I brought those for the peas. When we finish here, young Henry will be along to help me."

It's been a fun day. We've worked hard, to be sure, but the work is filled with laughter, getting sprayed with the garden hose, and eating sandwiches and drinking sweet tea in the shade.

Fitzie and Aunt Clara join us for the impromptu picnic. They inspect our work and declare it perfect. Fitzie directs a question to no one in particular. "I hope you planted radishes. I do love them so."

Dr. Harold tucks her hand through his elbow and strolls with her to see the "salad rows," as he calls them. She laughs at something he says, and the tilt of her head is quite coquettish.

Hmm, this is something I hadn't noticed before. Dr. Harold is a good man, though. If she wants to … an ache fills my heart.

Aunt Clara nudges me. She hands me a ham sandwich, then signs, "It's too early to be sure."

I don't begrudge Fitzie finding love, if she does. But right now, it's not easy for me. I finish my sandwich and go back to work. We don't have a lot left to do. Mr. James takes the mule and plow back to Mr. Bud, while I make sure all the plants have some water. The sky doesn't have the look nor the air the feel of the promised rain.

Empty promises. Irony. The epithets of my life.

Miss Iris turns off the water. "This has been a wonderful day. I hope you allow us to help more often. I miss not being able to garden."

We take the last of the tools back to the barn. If we do much more gardening, the building will need some work. There's a board on one side that needs replacing, as its bottom has rotted and the nails have given way. Leaning the hoe against the other side, I make a note to ask Pearl about Jimmy fixing it.

"Before we left home to work up here, we had a lovely garden at Daddy's." Miss Iris hands me a trowel. "Would you allow me to buy some flower seeds to plant at the edges of the field?"

I lay the tools in their box on the dilapidated potting bench.

"Certainly, and thank you. That would be lovely." I close the door, and we walk across the yard.

Mr. James, young Henry, and Dr. Harold are playing catch on the lawn. The baseball gets past Henry and rolls to my feet. Once, back in high school, a baseball went out of bounds and landed at my feet. I can hear the crowd cheering, smell the hot dogs. Then Boone—

I pick up the ball and throw it back to the men.

Miss Iris glances at me, then over her shoulder at the barn. "Tell me about your barn. Why is it so small?"

I swallow the bitter gall rising in my throat. The senator fancied himself a gentleman farmer. She doesn't need to know that. "We only had a small tractor, one pony, and a few tools."

"What happened to the tractor and the pony?"

I steel my heart against yet another haunting memory. "They both died."

Sheer will does nothing to raise my spirits in a hot bath. My spirits aren't paying attention, and tonight is Martha Anne's bridal shower. She deserves a happier hostess. Fitzie and Aunt Clara have spent weeks embroidering two sets of sheets and pillowcases for her. Millie and I went together and bought a lovely peignoir set in pale pink satin. I don't begrudge my sweet friend any of her special moments, it's just that … I only pray nobody mentions Boone tonight. *Please?*

When my skin looks like a raisin, I climb out of the tub. With the party being held here, at least playing hostess will keep a smile painted on my face. No matter how much my heart cries, I won't allow my feelings to ruin Martha Anne's night.

In my robe, I go upstairs to dress, trying to picture the luxury of having a bathroom on the third floor, just for Fitzie, Aunt Clara, and me. After a quick perusal of my closet, I pull out a yellow and apricot gown and slide it over my head. A festive scarf wrapped around my head in a turban and fastened with a feathered brooch makes me resemble a fruit salad. With no time to change, I shrug one shoulder at my reflection and go down to the kitchen to check on the refreshments. Pearl stands at the worktable, spreading icing on the cake.

"Please thank Jimmy and George again for the chicken coop. The hens have settled in nicely."

"I will, Miss Cora."

I reach over her shoulder and snitch a strawberry before she can smack my hand. "Ooh, these are good. Where did you find them?"

"Miz Allen sent them down for Miss Martha Anne."

"That was swell of her. She must know Martha Anne's partial to them. Is there anything you need me to do?"

"No, you go an' try to have fun."

I don't know if I can do what she asks.

In the parlor, I make sure everything for the games is ready. Notepads and pencils have been laid on the coffee table by Aunt Clara. A bowl of flowers sits on a sideboard, where we will put the cake. I turn the bowl a bit to the left and move one of the pink peonies to balance the arrangement.

The doorbell rings. I plaster on a bright smile.

Wiggling her hips as she slides onto the settee, Glenice Jo scootches me over. "Consequences was fun. I don't think I've ever seen Martha Anne blush so much."

I offer an appropriate chuckle. "You didn't let—"

"I saw Boone yesterday."

I stiffen at the mention of his name. "I don't want to hear it."

Glenice Jo sighs. "You need to hear, Cora. You should see him. He looks as though he lost his best friend."

"He's good at making you see what he wants you to. But it's not reality." And my trusting friend is blind to it. "He's proved he's just like the senator."

"He's not—"

I put my hand up to stop her. "No. Not another word."

She sighs again and sips her coffee.

I set my empty cup on the coffee table. "Look, I'm sorry, okay? Today is for Martha Anne. Let's not ruin it."

A grimace is my only answer. It'll do. Glenice Jo will eventually understand that part of my life is over. Dead and buried.

Millie claps her hands for our attention. "It's time for Martha Anne to open her gifts." Millie takes each package and hands it to our bride while Trudie records the giver and the gift for thank you notes.

Even I laugh when Martha Anne nearly weeps in delight over the cast-iron skillet from her mama. "It's *yours!* Already seasoned with years of love." Her expression turns to one of horror. "What did Daddy say?"

"I haven't told him." When Fitzie gasps, Amelia laughs and waves away her reaction. "I still have my mama's skillet." She winks at the other mamas. "And my granny's. Our family passes down skillets like some do jewelry."

My fingers go to my grandmother's amethyst necklace resting on my collarbone. I share a soft smile with Fitzie. She knows I wouldn't have the tiniest notion of how to use a skillet … other than for a weapon.

Martha Anne continues to open her gifts, gushing over each. When she sets the last one aside, Pearl carries in the cake. It's one of those new red velvet ones, and the novelty delights everyone.

While they get their slices, I gather up the wrapping paper, folding each carefully for Martha Anne to save.

The bridal shower can't be over too soon for me. My heart grows heavier with each minute, and I'm drowning in the tears it sheds.

Chapter 30

"CORA, SUGAR-PIE? WHERE ARE YOU?" Fitzie's voice calls from the front hall.

"In the morning room." Beside me, Aunt Clara taps her foot, waiting for me to finish reading the pages of her last chapter. My eyes fly over the final paragraph. "It's wonderful. Your best, I think."

Her brows remain knitted together. "You're sure? The denouement isn't contrived?"

I'm surprised she thinks so. "Absolutely not. It's clear to me why she killed him."

Her hands fly. "And the jury's decision? Is it satisfying?"

"Completely. Why are you so nervous about this book?"

"It's a new publisher. A bigger house, and I don't want to start off on the wrong note." She tucks the papers under her arm, then kisses the top of my head. "Thank you. I trust your judgment."

Fitzie pushes the door open and glances at her sister. "Ah, did Cora agree with me?"

Aunt Clara nods, her cheeks turning pink. "I don't mean to doubt you, Sister, but you think even my worst writing is wonderful. I taught Cora to be a discerning critic. It's what I need." She adds a smile to remove any sting.

Fitzie laughs. "You *are* wonderful. Even *Three Little Whispers* was a great story. It's that critic's fault if he didn't understand it. The reading public loved it."

Aunt Clara's orange beret is back on, her eyes fixed to the manuscript as she leaves the room. I return my attention to the accounts book open on the desk.

Fitzie still faces the now-closed door through which Aunt Clara exited. "Are the actors and actresses you work with as lacking in self-confidence as Clara?"

A wave of melancholy crests over me. "Most artistic people are, especially when they make a living from their creativity."

I miss my friends in vaudeville. I need to get a copy of *Variety* so I can keep up with them. It's about all I will have left of that life soon. The doctor isn't optimistic about a professional singing career for me. I'm still hopeful but try not to allow my aspirations to get too high.

Fitzie pulls a chair close to the desk and sits. "Sugar-pie, I'm worried about you. I can tell you're depressed. And I know why."

I hold back a sigh. "It's something I will simply have to get over. I guess it's still too new."

She raises one skeptical eyebrow in an expression I think all mamas practice in front of the mirror. "It's been four weeks. Normally, you pop back from disappointment and hurt. I think your heart is more entwined with his than you realize."

As sure as lava rises in a volcano, I'm about to erupt. I take a couple of breaths to calm myself. It doesn't work. "He lied to me." The words burst from my mouth.

She shakes her head. "He didn't lie."

"Not telling me is just the same, Mama." I jump up and pace. "I don't know how you or the Dillies can expect me to forgive that and then go on loving him as if nothing happened. I can't." I turn to face the window.

She rises and crosses the room, her footsteps barely audible. Her hand falls softly on my shoulder. "I don't want you to let what the senator did to you or me ruin the rest of your life, sugar. That lets him win." Just as softly, she moves her hand to my cheek and searches my eyes before turning to leave. Her footsteps stop at the door. "Cora." She waits for me to look at her.

I peer over my shoulder.

"I know your heart is broken. But the part that still lives loves him."

She closes the door. I stare out the window, seeing nothing. How can I forgive Boone? The trust is gone. Why didn't he tell me? It's life-altering to change his career from furniture-making to politics. When a man courts a woman, shouldn't he ask for her opinion? How could he think I wouldn't care?

My father neglected us. Then when he was home, he showed nothing but displeasure at being around us—except when he had need of parading his "little family" in front of the press.

Boone is dead wrong if he thinks my opinion doesn't matter. And I don't feel as though I'm able to forgive him. It would be like forgiving everything the senator ever did.

Thursday, May 8, 1930
Doc Abernethy tilts my chin upward, points a small light down my throat, and inserts a horrible probe thing. "Without causing you great discomfort, I can't be one hundred percent sure. However, your symptoms tell me you have lesions on your vocal cords." He withdraws the strange-looking probe with the mirror on it. "There may well be nodules, as well."

My heart sinks faster than the Titanic. I swallow, relieved that thing is out of my throat. "What does that mean?"

With his foot, he hooks a rolling stool and pulls it over to him and sits in front of me. "I'm afraid, my dear, it means you won't be singing professionally." He pats my knee.

First, I lose the man I love, and now I'm losing my career? It's too much. I can't give up that easily. "Is there nothing I can do?"

"Short of surgery, not really. Oh, with many weeks of rest and no talking, you can get rid of the huskiness, but the moment you begin the rigors of professional signing, you'll be hoarse or have laryngitis by the end of the first day."

Weeks without talking? The doctor and the office blur. I close my eyes. First Boone and now my career. I take a shaky breath.

Doc pats my knee again. "Are you going to be all right, my dear?"

"I've got some getting used to the idea to do, but yes, I'll be okay." I guess. It's not as though I had a career as a singer and lost it. Besides, I've turned into a pretty decent farmer. And I know sign language. What more can a girl want?

I burst into tears.

Thursday evening, May 8, 1930

I haven't told anyone about Dr. Abernethy's diagnosis yet. There is barely a month left before Martha Anne's wedding. For everyone's sake, I hide my emotion and put on a cheerful face. They all seem to believe I'm over Boone, and although they're clearly sorry, their relief is also evident. They don't need the added worry about my voice.

I only wish my cheerful act would work on me. Inside, I'm drowning in tears. The senator has won, and I'm turning into a bitter old maid.

I look up from my plate. Miss Iris and Miss Lulamae somehow manage not to be bitter. Did they love and lose? What is their story? One of them—I check her brooch, purple—Miss Lulamae—catches me watching her. She tilts her head in question. Abashed, I smile and quickly look away. Voicing my thoughts would be rude.

Miss Iris' gaze bounces between her sister and me. As if sensing my quandary, she clears her throat and nudges Miss Lulamae.

"Sister, do you remember the time we had our big chance to shine?" She sweeps her gaze around the table. "We were fifteen, and for our church's Christmas cantata, we were to lead the choir from the vestibule to the choir loft. During the processional, we were to play a version of 'O Come, All Ye Faithful' on our instruments. We were excited, and our parents were so very proud."

Miss Lulamae chuckles. "Unfortunately, I remember it all too well. I was responsible for the alto on my clarinet. You played the melody on your cornet. We practiced until it was flawless and fully memorized."

Miss Iris' eyes sparkle with humor. "The big moment arrived, and we began our grand march. We played beautifully together for several measures until—"

"Until Iris froze and forgot her part. Did I mention her part was the *melody*? Let me just tell you a clarinet tooting an alto harmony sounds absolutely nothing like the melody. With our parents' blessing, we both gave up the instruments right after that."

Their laughter eases my embarrassment but doesn't answer my questions. After supper, I go out on the front porch for some time alone. Keeping up a cheerful front is exhausting. I lower onto the porch swing and with one foot, gently rock. The action soothes.

The front door opens, and Miss Lulamae pokes her head out. "May I join you?"

I can't deny her, though it takes a momentous effort to paste on a smile. "Please." I move over a bit.

She takes her place and leans her head back. "What is it you want to know, child?"

I startle. Is she really that good at reading people? "How can you tell I want to know something?"

"Ha! I've lived my entire life watching people look at me the way you did. As if you're trying to find out what it's like to be a twin. Or why I'm an old maid?"

Caught. Heat rises in my cheeks.

She laughs. "I thought so. Of course, I'm not really so brilliant. The absence of a certain young man around here gives a good clue. And then your valiant-but-failing effort to show us you don't care is another. Am I right?"

Unbidden tears blur the early evening. I nod, not trusting my voice. My also-failing voice.

She pats my hand. "A heart that's been broken for love is probably the deepest hurt of all, lesser only to the loss of a child. I was around your age, twenty and four. Back then, most girls married at sixteen. Neither my sister nor I were raving beauties, by any stretch of anyone's imagination." She chuckles. "We had lots of friends but no suitors. Papa didn't have money for dowries. Unfortunately, I fell in love with a young man who was not a gentleman." She glances sidelong at me with a sorrowful smile. "I'm ashamed to say he stole from me what a bride saves for her husband."

The shock of her words leaves me without any. We rock in silence for a moment.

"Six months later, he married a wealthy girl. I never told our parents. Iris knew, of course, and kept my secret. By God's grace, I wasn't pregnant, but I'd lost something precious. I knew I couldn't deceive a potential bridegroom, so I stayed an old maid. Iris made a covenant to never marry and remain single with me."

Whoa. That's a tremendous sacrifice. Perhaps some types of love are stronger than we suppose. Yet I think of Aunt Clara, who never married either. "And you were never bitter?"

"It was as much my fault as his."

Aghast, I stare at her. "That's crazy."

"Not as crazy as you might think. I let myself be persuaded by his good looks instead of his character. Anyway, I knew to avoid bitterness, I had to forgive him."

There's that word again. "How do you forgive when you're the victim? When you don't feel like forgiving?"

Voices from within the house draw closer. She rises and pulls me up with her. We walk to the far corner of the porch, away from the door.

"Cora, my dear, forgiving is a choice, not a feeling. You can forgive the person and still hate what they did. My wise old granny once told me, 'If you continue to live with unforgiveness, it's like swallowing poison and waiting for the other person to die.' Don't drink that cup, child." She pats my cheek and goes inside.

Heaven help me, I don't want to be bitter. I don't like being sick at heart. I don't like having a broken soul. But Boone lied to me. How can that be repaired? How could I ever trust what he tells me?

Chapter 31

Friday, May 16, 1930

WITH ONLY THREE WEEKS LEFT before Martha Anne's wedding, Fitzie, Aunt Cora, and I need to shop for our gowns. Martha Anne's family can't afford to buy them for the bridesmaids, so she opted for us purchasing what we want, but all in the same color. She chose turquoise. Thankfully, it looks good on all of us.

Fitzie and I link arms with Aunt Clara as we stroll up Peachtree Street. Downtown Atlanta is worlds away from Buford and Sugar Hill. Streetcars run down the middle of the road every few minutes. Multistoried brick and stone buildings grace every square foot along the boulevard. Each store window rivals the last for the most eye-catching display of merchandise.

"This is such a treat, Clara. We haven't shopped for new dresses in forever. And we haven't come to Atlanta in more than two years."

Since Aunt Clara's arms are captive at the moment, she merely turns her palms up in a giving motion and smiles.

With my elbow, I squeeze her arm. "Well, thank you for sharing your royalty check with us." That evokes a huge grin from her. Her new book is doing extremely well.

I haven't been paying much attention to the buildings we pass, and when we turn the corner, I stop. "Davison's? I haven't been here since I was what—fifteen?" A lifetime ago.

Fitzie leans forward and grasps the door handle. "Are you ready for some fun?"

She pulls it open and we step inside, where we're plunged into a heavenly scented world. They must perfume the air with toilet water.

The light from six gigantic crystal chandeliers makes everything sparkle. It's a fairy world.

I raise my eyebrows at Fitzie in delight. I'd forgotten how much fun shopping is with her. She throws back her head and laughs. "Come on. Let's wander through the costume jewelry on our way to the dress department."

The newspapers say the country is in a depression—the Great Depression, they're calling it. But looking around Davison's, it seems to me not *everyone* is pinching pennies.

I have to wonder if the senator's greed led to his losses. Whatever the cause, it has left us in a precarious place for a while. Pearl says God blessed me with the saving idea of the boarding house. I know she's right.

Have I thanked You? My heart warms with gratitude.

Everything in the costume jewelry counter glitters like real gems. The saleladies must polish them each day. Aunt Clara's gaze sweeps across a selection, then she picks up a pair of earrings. They are large faux-aquamarines set in narrow silver ropes.

Fitzie holds up the card bearing the earrings against Aunt Clara's ear. "Stunning. These would go so well with your peacock gown. Why don't you get them?"

Peering in the mirror, my aunt selects another pair, similar but a little smaller. She places their card by her other ear. Back and forth, she turns her head while she makes up her mind. The patient saleslady smiles behind the counter.

Finally, my aunt lays down the large earrings and stretches out her hand holding the smaller ones.

The clerk takes them. "Will that be all?" She glances at me. "Anything for you?"

I shake my head. "I need to choose a dress first."

She rings up Aunt Clara's earrings and hands her the package. We move through the departments, past the shoes, where I have to physically drag Fitzie away—she has more shoes than anyone I know—and come to the dresses. We bypass the daytime wear and go straight to evening.

I spy a color I like a few racks away. "Y'all find what you want to try on, and we'll meet at the dressing rooms."

I slide hangers on the racks, feeling the fabrics beneath my fingers. I prefer soft, silky ones to linens. When my hand lingers too long on a red gown, I give myself a mental shake. I'm here for turquoise. A moment later, my gaze halts on a green dress with bits of gold in the pattern.

The color of Boone's eyes.

My heart drops, and with it, my joy in the day. Why does he have to intrude in my fun? My motions become jerky as I flip through the dresses, looking for anything turquoise. Finding one, I yank it off the rack without bothering to check its style and lay it over my arm.

Why can't my brain forget him? Banish him from all thought. Forget his eyes.

I select two more gowns and join Fitzie and Aunt Clara at the entrance to the dressing rooms. The saleslady ushers us into a carpeted and mirrored sanctuary, hanging our choices inside individual rooms.

Fitzie pokes her head out her door. "You go first, Cora. Let us see when you're ready."

Since my aunt is making a sacrifice paying for these, I'm determined to have fun, even if it hurts. I slide the first gown over my head. The soft silk falls cool against my skin. The dress clings to my waist and hips. I like these new styles, after all the formless tubes we wore in the last decade.

Both Fitzie and Aunt Clara love it. I slip on the next. What was I thinking? The neckline plunges almost to my navel. Blushing, I peel it off. "Y'all are not seeing that one."

"Why not?" Fitzie's voice filters through the door.

"Ha! It's indecent."

"Why did you pick it, then?" Amusement tiptoes around her words.

Why, indeed? "Let's just say I wasn't thinking."

The next gown isn't right either. Guess I'll take the first one. As I step out of my dressing room with the hanger in hand, I turn over the tag. Oh my! It's not cheap at $11.95. I cringe and hand it to Aunt Clara for her decision. She waves away my concern.

"Darling girl, people are staying home and reading. As long as they like my books, we'll be all right." She hands my gown to the clerk with a smile, then shoos her out.

Fitzie is next. I sit on the padded bench and wait. After a minute or two, she exits and stands before me in a cloud of chiffon the colors of a sunset. Layers of pink blend into coral then red with a touch of gold, and finally, a hint of turquoise. My jaw drops. This is my mother?

"It's exquisite, Mama. You'll outshine the bride."

Her brow crinkles. "Oh dear, do you think so?"

Yes, that's my mother. Always thinking of others. "Don't worry about it. You're the grand hostess of the reception. And it's perfect. Martha Anne will love it too. I can hear her squealing over it."

Aunt Clara joins us wearing a caftan that looks like she found it in Africa. The center is red and gold, but the sides are a geometric pattern of black, gold, and two different blues.

"Where did you find that?"

She grins and her hands move with fluidity. "Over at the edge of the dress section. A sign above them said 'imports.' You know me, I had to see what those were." She glances in the mirror. "I don't care if anyone likes it or if I shock them all. I'm taking it."

Fitzie throws one arm around Aunt Clara's shoulders. "Not many women can wear caftans well. You look divine in it. Best of all, it appears comfortable."

She's right. "It's *you*, Aunt Clara. Exotic."

Fitzie peers at her wristwatch. "It's almost noon. Let's have dinner at the Biltmore."

Aunt Clara settles the bill, and we stop back at the jewelry counter for Fitzie. She finds earrings that have all the colors in her gown. I'll lend her Granny Drummond's amethyst necklace to go with it. I'll wear pearls I already have.

We leave our packages with the customer service desk and walk to the Biltmore. The weather is beautiful, and there are so many store windows to inspect, the nearly two miles seems short.

The Biltmore, large and impressive, was built just four years ago according to Fitzie. The lobby is cavernous and a little cold with all its marble. Fitzie doesn't stop to ask directions to the dining room, so I assume she's been here before. Indeed, she leads us directly to an arched doorway, where a tuxedoed maître d' greets us.

"Ah, Mrs. Fitzgerald, how good to see you again. And Miss Drummond. How delightful to have you back. I got your new book last week and I'm thoroughly devouring it. Had I known you'd be in, I'd have brought it for an autograph." He reaches beneath his podium and whips out a card. "Would you oblige me?"

My gracious aunt gives him the autograph. When he slips it in his pocket with a satisfied smile, he spies me. His eyes widen. "Miss Lynn?"

Oh, this man could be a maître d' at the finest restaurants in New York. He knows his customers, but how does he know me? I smile and give a small nod of my head.

"I saw you in Philadelphia while visiting my sister. Your talent is legendary." He grabs a stack of menus. "Follow me, ladies. So you'll have some privacy, I'll place you at a discreet table overlooking the gardens."

He leads us into the opulent dining room. Several crystal chandeliers as large as the ones in Davison's hang above us. The room is lined with arches and ornate columns. Where those lead, I have no idea. A few diners wave or smile at us as we pass. One or two whisper behind their hands.

I wait until the maître d' leaves us. "You sure couldn't come here on a clandestine dinner meeting. Is he that way with everyone?"

Fitzie shrugs. "I have no idea. He knows me because of the senator. Clara has her own fame, as do you, sugar."

Mine will be short-lived. I'm still holding back from telling them the result of my last doctor's appointment.

We order and I do my best to enjoy the Waldorf salad. After tea and a shared slice of cake, we leave. Back to Davison's for our packages, then on to the car. The drive home takes close to ninety minutes. In

Buford, we pull up to the stop sign near town.

Fitzie leans forward from the back seat. "Cora, turn and park over there, please." She points past my shoulder to a spot in front of the drugstore. "I need to pick up my vitamins."

I drive up to the curb. Next to me, Aunt Clara is asleep, so we leave her in the car. Near the drugstore's entrance, a crowd gathers on the corner.

My curiosity piques. I slip my clutch bag under my arm. "You go on in. I want to see what's up."

Fitzie disappears through the door, and I wander down the block. As I draw close, a familiar voice rings out. "A vote for Boone Robertson means a voice for *you* in our statehouse."

I do an about-face but not fast enough. He spots me. I can't run in high heels, but I scurry back to the car. Just before I grab the door handle, he reaches me.

"Cora, please. I want to talk to you."

"We have nothing to talk about." I yank open the door.

"Aw, come on. Please?"

Aunt Clara wakes up, and her eyes widen when they take in Boone. Her gaze leaves him and rests on me.

"Hey, Boone, get back there." A man rushes over. "You're not finished with your speech."

"Hang on, Zeke. I'll be right there." He tosses his words over his shoulder, but his gaze never leaves me. "Cora? I want to—"

I close the door. "Go back to your public, Boone. They're interested in what you have to say. I've heard it all before."

He stands for a moment, watching me roll up the window. Zeke calls him again. He turns halfway and takes a step but hesitates. Puppy-dog eyes stare back at me. I turn my head.

Aunt Clara signs, "He's leaving, but the boy sure seems downhearted."

I shake my head. "Whenever there was an audience, the senator used that same expression when he was leaving to join his political pals." I can't allow myself to believe it.

This hurts worse than the news about my throat. How can a heart break over and over and keep on beating?

Friday, June 6, 1930

I hurry through supper. The rehearsal for Martha Anne and Ethan's wedding is at seven o'clock. Laying across my bed is a dress with small bunches of lavender and pink posies printed on a navy background. It's an in-between frock—not a day dress and not evening wear. Perfect for the rehearsal. After slipping it over my head, I smooth the collar so it lays flat.

Back downstairs, I drop my handbag on the foyer table and listen for a moment, trying to distinguish Fitzie's voice from the guests' chatter. By the boisterous hubbub in the parlor, I take a chance and peek inside. Sure enough, she and Aunt Clara are with the boarders, playing charades. It looks as though Fitzie and Dr. Harold are a team. She's sitting in a club chair, and he's perched on the arm, looking at the piece of paper she's holding.

Fitzie glances up when I enter. "Are you off? You look lovely."

I run my fingers along my belt. "Thanks, but this evening isn't about me. We're rehearsing for Martha Anne's wedding tomorrow. I'll be home around nine o'clock, I think. Trudie is picking me up."

Fitzie waggles her fingers, her attention already drawn back to the game.

A horn honks out front. I peek through the window, then grab my handbag. I hop into the passenger seat of her Model T and run my gaze over Trudie with a smile. "New dress? That color of yellow is fabulous on you."

A halfhearted smile curves her mouth. "Thanks." She shifts into gear, and we head down the driveway. The recent rain makes it a little slick. "I hope we don't get stuck." Her knuckles are white on the steering wheel.

It didn't rain *that* much. "Trudie, is something wrong?"

She keeps her eyes straight ahead. "Wrong? No, nothing. I'm just tired, worried a little about Daddy being on his own tonight."

I don't get it. The supper rush is over. I won't push it, but something has her uncomfortable. The ride is quiet, which is so unlike Trudie. "Is everything okay at the diner?"

"Sure. No problems at all."

I give up on conversation. After a few more silent minutes, she turns into the church parking lot but doesn't stop. Oddly, she drives around to the back of the building.

I'm starting to get a bad feeling.

We come in a back door and walk down a long hallway to the narthex, where we enter the sanctuary. Several of the others are already sitting in the pews down front. The minister, Brother Ken, is in a discussion with Ethan and Martha Anne. They all look up when we walk toward them. Martha Anne glances at Ethan, and a small frown mars her brow.

Something is decidedly strange. A side door opens, and a man steps through, his back to us as he closes the door behind him. My heart jolts at the sight of those familiar broad shoulders.

It's Boone.

Chapter 32

Friday, June 6, 1930

I STARE AT TRUDIE, MY JAW slack. "How could you?"

I turn and stalk up the aisle, hurrying to the restroom in the narthex. Once again, they've betrayed me. No more maybes, I'm going back to New York. With the boarding house full, Fitzie and Aunt Clara will be fine. I can't sing but if I have to, I'll wash dishes. Work in a dime store. Anything to get away from Sugar Hill and Boone Robertson. I stare at myself in the mirror. My face is red and my eyes—

The door opens and Glenice Jo storms in, followed by Millie and Trudie.

I turn on Trudie. "You knew! You knew he'd be here, and you didn't tell me."

She cringes, but Glenice Jo doesn't give her a chance to reply. She grasps me by the shoulders. "Act like you got some raising. This isn't about you."

My very words to Fitzie slap me in the face.

"You're so caught up in what you think Boone did to you." Glenice Jo glares. "You're forgetting about Martha Anne and Ethan. Boone is Ethan's friend and a groomsman. You're not going to ruin this wedding. I won't let you. You're going to put on a pint of Dilly dignity and go back out there. This wedding *is* going on, and you're in it."

My knees go weak. "She doesn't expect—?"

Glenice Jo knows how my mind works. "No. Boone is my counterpart. She wouldn't do that to you."

Millie takes my hand. "She had an argument with Ethan over this, Cora. A real fight. I was afraid she'd call off the wedding."

Millie blurs before me, and I bite my lip. If Martha Anne was that upset, I can't let her down.

I look at my friends. "Help me."

Glenice Jo slaps her hand against the sink. "Don't you dare play helpless with me, Cora. You're strong and you can do it for Martha Anne. She's out there crying because she loves you and knows this hurt you." The hard line of her jaw softens. "We all know it hurt you. There's no question about that. The real question is, what are you going to do?"

Never have I seen Glenice Jo so angry. And never have I let my friends down so badly. I have to go through with it—no matter how much my heart is breaking. I square my shoulders and open the door. "Just don't expect me to speak to him."

Glenice Jo is right behind me. "Don't worry. I'll handle that."

We gather at the front of the church, the tension so thick you'd have to melt it before you could spoon it over ice cream. Brother Ken explains what we're to do and when. I try to school my eyes. They want to wander to Boone, but when they do, he's always watching me.

I focus hard on Brother Ken like a nearsighted nanny and force myself to pay attention. He sends us up the aisle to the foyer, where we wait for his signal. As maid of honor, I go last, just before Martha Anne and her daddy. Thankfully, the best man is Ethan's brother. I vaguely remember him from school.

We go through the routine twice, then Brother Ken tells us we've got it and he'll see us all tomorrow. It's over, at least for now. I allow my gaze to flit through the church. Boone is nowhere to be seen. I never saw him leave. No doubt something to do with his campaign or his political pals.

Martha Anne walks over to me. "Can you forgive us?"

Do any of them have the smallest niggling of how difficult this is? It's the hardest thing I've ever done. "Of course I can. It's natural for Ethan to want his friends alongside him when he takes his vows." I hold out my arms to her.

She falls into my hug. "Cora, I'd never do anything willingly to hurt you."

Maybe not, but she has. All of my friends have. Like Boone, they didn't trust me enough to tell me. I'll get through tomorrow, somehow. But come Sunday, I'm on my way back to New York.

Saturday, June 7, 1930

All night, I toss and turn as sleep evades me. Over and over, I see Boone entering the church backward. Somehow, it seems appropriate, but I don't know why. Then Glenice Jo's anger and Martha Anne's pleading eyes add to the haints surrounding me. Will I never be free of hauntings?

The worst part of all this is for a few weeks, rage over Boone's betrayal kept me going. But eventually, anger fades. And it leaves my heart bare. Broken and exposed. Tears seep out the corners of my eyes, wetting my pillow.

By the time the rooster crows, my heart is battered and sore. Today is going to take every ounce of my strength to make it through. I can hardly force myself out of bed. I lay there in a sleep-deprived stupor.

At least I don't have hours to stew. The wedding starts at eleven, and with the reception at noon, it will all be over by two o'clock. If I can hang on that long. I can. I will. For Martha Anne.

We're supposed to be at the church by ten am. Finally, at eight o'clock, I force my feet to the floor and stand. After a bath, I don my robe until it's time to leave. Tying its belt, I descend the stairs, dropping into my chair at the table. Pearl hands me a cup of coffee, setting a carafe next to me.

"Looks like you need that." She peers closely at me, then sets a plate of cheese grits in front of me. "I'm praying for you, little girl."

I lift my chin and look up at her, then lay my head against her arm. "Thank you. I'll miss you when I go back."

Last night, I told Fitzie, Aunt Clara, and Pearl that I had to go back to New York. Even if I have no more dreams to strive for on Broadway, I have to leave Sugar Hill.

Pearl's eyes fill. She snuffles as she retreats to the kitchen.

She'll be back and will protest if I don't eat, so I force down most of her love offering. But this morning, my stomach tries to rebel. Only force of will keeps the grits from spewing out.

After two cups of coffee, I go back upstairs to change. I slide the gown Aunt Clara bought for me over my head. It's lovely, but I've lost weight and it hangs on me, instead of clinging to my now-non-existent curves.

Way back when, Trudie and I had the right idea, but she's the only one who remains strong enough to not fall in love.

Once again, Trudie picks me up so I can leave the car for Fitzie and Aunt Clara. We talk quietly of banalities on the way over to the church—the perfect weather, how pretty the wildflowers are.

Finally, Trudie reaches over and squeezes my hand. "Hang in there, sugar. It'll be over soon."

Not soon enough.

She returns her hand to the steering wheel. "I'm going to miss you so much when you go back up north. More than when we were sixteen."

"I'll miss you too. If you ever get tired of slinging hash, come visit me." I haven't told the others I won't be here after tonight. Only Trudie. She doesn't cry as easily as the other Dillies. It's one trait we share—or shared. Lately, my tears are close to the surface.

"What are you going to do there, Cora? You told me what the doctor said about your voice." She puts her arm out the window to signal for a turn. "I've seen you try to wait tables."

I chuckle, which is most likely her intention. It's hollow, but she grins, accepting it. Oncoming cars keep us from turning.

"Yesterday, I made a couple of phone calls, and there are smaller theatres that still have vaudeville shows. Fortunately, they're thrilled to book Dixie Lynn." I stare out the window. "I'll do what I can—work at ski lodges and bar mitzvahs."

She glances at me. "Do you think you'll ever come back?" The final car goes by and she completes the turn.

I can't imagine never coming home again, especially after the changes in the house finally exorcised the senator's ghost. "Someday. When I can finally think about Boone without my heart tearing apart."

At the church, we find Martha Anne in the classroom that brides use nearest the narthex.

I raise my eyebrows, trying to look bright-eyed. I hug Martha Anne, who hasn't donned her dress yet. "Are you nervous?"

She squeezes me. "As a long-tailed cat in a room full of rocking chairs."

"There's no need. You'll be the most radiant bride in Sugar Hill history." I kiss her cheek now since I haven't put on my lipstick yet. "Be blessed."

We help Martha Anne into her gown. I'm letting her keep it. I won't ever wear it, but that's another secret I don't tell her right now. I allow her to think she'll return it to me when she gets back from her honeymoon. Fitzie will inform Miss Amelia to put it in a garment bag to save for Martha Anne's future daughters.

Glenice Jo hands me the bridal veil, her gaze piercing. I smile and give a conspiratorial wink to reassure her that come the devil or penny-size hail, I won't let them down. But the desire to flee grows stronger as the clock hands climb closer to eleven.

Then, the door opens. Martha Anne's mama and daddy come in. Miss Amelia's hankie is already twisted and wet. Mr. Noah views his daughter and has to clear his throat.

We move into the narthex and wait for the music to start. Martha Anne whispers with her daddy. A moment later, Boone arrives for Miss Amelia. My heart thumps and my breath comes rapidly. His eyes briefly meet mine. For that second, I see the man I fell in love with and he blurs.

Please, God, no. That's not who he really is.

He blinks, then swallows, and taking Miss Amelia's hand through his arm, he escorts her up the aisle to her seat.

See how easy it was for him? He's over you. If he ever was in love.

The Dillies are next. Then, finally, it's me, Martha Anne, and her daddy.

I turn to my dear friend. "Are you ready, Dilly-girl?"

Martha Anne's grin is anticipatory and she glows. "I'm ready. Love you, Dilly-girl. And Cora?" She lays her hand on my shoulder until my eyes meet hers. "Thank you. I know how hard this is for you."

I shake my head. "I'd walk on hot coals for you."

The music changes. I start down the aisle. It looms long ahead of me, and all I see is Boone at the end. I swallow. How many times did I envision my own wedding with him waiting for me? I feel dizzy and lightheaded. My steps falter. Can I do this?

Trudie shifts her bouquet, catching my attention. I lock my gaze on her. I *will* do this. One more step. One at a time until I'm there. I take my place in front of Millie and turn, signaling the organist.

The wedding march begins, and Martha Anne floats down the aisle on her daddy's arm. My sweet friend is a woman now, beginning her married life.

I feel outside of myself and left behind. This is even harder than I imagined. When the time comes, I take Martha Anne's bouquet. I straighten her veil when she turns. Brother Ken talks and blesses. They repeat their vows. He prays. And then, mercifully, it's over. We follow Martha Anne and Ethan back to the narthex.

My smile remains frozen in place during the photos. The photographer takes forever getting each shot, posing us where he wants. I try to keep my gaze on Fitzie and Aunt Clara, who sit waiting for me, but my attention is on Boone even if my eyes are not.

Ethan says something to him and Boone smiles.

What did you expect? He was never in love with you.

Chapter 33

When we arrive home, a few wedding guests are already there, with Dr. Harold and the Sadler twins acting as host and hostesses for us. Fitzie and Aunt Clara circulate around us as we form the receiving line. I slip into my stage personae, enabling me to smile graciously and nod but avoid too many comments. Several pairs of eyes stray from me to Boone and back, their expression questioning. I pretend I don't notice.

Finally, we're able to mingle, and I immediately escape into the kitchen. "Pearl, what can I do to help?"

"Nothin', Miss Cora. We's got—" Seeing my pleading eyes, she shakes her head, sets down the bowl she's stirring, and takes both my hands in hers. "Miss Cora, you cain't disappear on your guests. Be tough. You know, God never promised an easy life."

"But does it have to be *so* hard?"

"Trials birth compassion for others, little girl. We grows from 'em, an' one day, you'll look back and see the Lord's fingerprints on your life."

She releases my hands and turns me around by the shoulders. "Now go."

"I love you, Pearl." As I push through the door, I hear her whispered words, breathed like a prayer.

"And I loves you like my own."

There are wedding guests in every downstairs room. I head to the guest parlor, hoping to find one of our boarders. Dr. Harold is there and relief washes over me ... until I see who he is entertaining.

Alice Farnham.

Her folks are friends with the Allens, which likely explains why she's here. It wouldn't be proper to leave them out. Still, the shell around me will crack if I get in a confrontation with Alice. I quickly leave before she sees me.

Spotting Martha Anne, I cross to her and squeeze her hand, then go in search for something to occupy me so I can avoid conversation. The foyer table is laden with gifts. Inspecting each box for the giver's name should take a few minutes. Then, I can look over the guest book. Make sure everyone is signed in.

A few minutes later, Ethan's brother claps his hands to gain attention. Pearl and her granddaughters enter with the wedding cake. She outdid herself on it. Topaz created frosting flowers all over its top. They take it to the dining room, and everyone follows Ethan and Martha Anne.

His brother toasts the bride and groom. The cake is cut and passed out. Finally, a half hour later, Martha Anne and the Dillies are in the Alexander Fitzgerald bedroom. We didn't rent it this weekend so Martha Anne could use it. She thought to use my bedroom in the attic, but I couldn't have her see my packed bags.

She lovingly runs her hand down the skirt of her wedding dress. "I'll always be grateful for you letting me borrow this, Cora. It's a dream gown."

I smile and keep my secret. "You're welcome, Dilly-girl. Now get into your going-away suit. Your husband is waiting."

Her eyes grow large and she blushes. "Husband. That sounds so grown up."

Her giggle doesn't, though, and we all laugh with her. Ten minutes later, we're on the front porch, throwing rice at them as they run to Ethan's car. The groomsmen have tied strings of tin cans to the bumper underneath the *Just Married* sign, so everyone will notice them. We stand waving, and then they disappear down the driveway. I'm close to the end of my strength. Tears are near the surface.

Alice shoulders her way past me, smirking. "That will never be you."

Oh great. Now she's channeling the senator. I draw myself up to my fullest height, smile graciously, turn away—

And run smack into Boone.

"Oh!" I step back. "Excuse me."

Hopeful eyes stare into my mine. His mouth opens, and he reaches out his hand.

Mine tremble. I shove them behind my back. "I'm sorry, I'm needed in the kitchen." Heart pounding, I dash past him, fleeing to safety.

"Cora!" Footsteps pound after me.

I barge through the kitchen door, panting. When he doesn't follow, half of me is grateful.

Pearl eyes me but doesn't try to send me out this time. I plunge my hands into the sink and start washing dishes. My tears drop into the water. I want to go to sleep and when I wake up, discover it was a bad dream, and I'm back on a vaudeville stage, still the darling of audiences.

Fitzie pushes through the kitchen door. "I thought I'd find you here. I ambushed Boone after I saw you flee." She slides her arm around my shoulder. "Everyone is gone, sugar-pie."

I dry my hands. "Thank you for waylaying him. What did you say?"

She eyes me for a moment. "I asked him to help me carry a large wedding gift to Ethan's car."

Was that all? I'm not so sure, but she isn't forthcoming at the moment. "Well, thank you." I fold the towel and lay it on the counter. "Mama? Will you come with Aunt Clara when she takes me to the station tonight?"

"Of course, darling. I'll give you a proper send-off. And I promise not to cry." Tears fill her eyes. "Oh dear." We chuckle at our shaky emotions. I'll miss her more than ever before.

"I'm going to change, then spend a little time in the garden."

Fitzie waves me off, and I leave her and Pearl quietly talking. Upstairs, I hang my dress in Aunt Clara's closet. I won't be taking it with me. I slip into wide-legged trousers. If I shock people, I don't care. They're comfortable for traveling, and I'm done with conforming to expectations. I take a final look around me, memorizing each corner of our hideaway. I'll miss this attic bedroom. More, I'll miss Mama's whispers in the night.

On my way through the kitchen, I grab a basket and Pearl's shears, then wander through the garden. More tomatoes are ready to harvest. I've enjoyed Pearl's fried green tomatoes, so I pick a few green ones along with several plump, red, ripe ones. I won't be here to eat these, but Mama will. She's always been partial to tomatoes. And fried okra. I bend and harvest several nice pods.

When the basket is full of the garden's fresh offerings, I take them to Pearl. I'm at sixes and sevens and don't know what to do with myself until it's time to leave.

"Come talk to me, Cora." Dr. Harold's voice harkens from the guest parlor.

That man is beyond canny. I poke my head through the doorway. "How did you know I was out there?"

He simply smiles and pats the davenport next to him. "Come sit." I settle next to him, and he lays a hand on my arm. "Are you all ready to go?"

"I am." That's all I can say around the lump that forms in my throat.

"I've grown exceedingly fond of you. Are you sure there isn't any way we can talk you into staying?"

I turn my head and let my gaze meet his. "If I don't go, I feel as though I'll drown. But—" Dr. Harold somehow exacts complete honesty from me. "I truly don't know if I'll survive up there."

He nods slowly and considers his words. "We never really leave sorrow behind. It's not something you can outrun. You can keep your mind busy, and eventually, you grow somewhat immune to it, but it's always there." He takes my hand between his. "You choose whether to unpack it or leave it alone on a shelf in your heart."

"Is that what you did with your wife's memory?"

He sighs and his eyes glaze. "For a long time, every night I'd pull out her memory. I missed her more than words can say. But"—he peers at me over his reading glasses—"eventually, I didn't open the past as often. And it didn't hurt anymore. I could remember something from our lives together with affection but not sorrow."

"You're a wise man, Dr. Harold. I hope I can do that." I lay my head on his shoulder for a moment.

He pats my cheek. "I know you can, Cora. I—"

A scream splits the air.

"Fitzie!"

Dr. Harold and I jump up, and I run to the foyer. "Fitzie? Where are you?" Aunt Clara meets me there. Pearl is hot on her heels.

"Help. Cora, help me!" Her cry rends the night air out front.

"Mama!"

I fly out the door. Fitzie lies crumpled at the bottom of the porch steps. One leg is beneath her, and her arm looks funny.

"Pearl, call the doctor!" I squat next to Mama. "What happened?"

Her eyes close. "It's so stupid. I was … going to take a little … walk to the … graveyard. I haven't been in … weeks. Something, a shape coming toward me … distracted me, and I … missed a step. Ohh." She groans. "I think … I'm going to … be sick."

I help her roll slightly to her side so she doesn't choke. "Someone, get me a towel, please."

A moment later, one appears, held by Dr. Harold. "Thank you."

Pearl nudges me aside. "I'll clean my Miss Fitzie." She gently wipes Mama's mouth. At the end of the walkway, that blasted rooster crows and struts toward us. Pearl jumps up and, flapping the towel, chases it away. "You scat, you orn'ry fowl, or you're gonna end up as soup."

The rooster skedaddles.

Fitzie laughs, then winces. Dr. Harold kneels next to Mama. "Fitzie, Dr. Abernethy's been called. He said he'll be here in a few minutes. I want to lay a blanket beneath you if we can do it without hurting you. That way, when he gets here, we can move you inside."

Mama looks into his eyes and nods. She trusts him completely. He takes the blanket Pearl hands to him. How does she always know what we need? He tucks it next to her. We manage to tilt her and roll her enough to get it beneath her. She only winces and bites her lip once.

While we get her on the blanket, Dr. Harold performs a visual examination. "Fitzie, I don't see any skin broken, so I'm not sure if you have compound fractures or not. We're going to leave you until—ah, I see a car coming up the drive." He nudges me.

I hurry down the steps to greet Doc Abernethy as he climbs out of his car. He bumps his head, mussing his thick, silver hair. I explain the accident, and he grabs his bag.

"Fitzie?" Doc kneels beside her. "The day didn't have enough drama with a wedding that you needed to add more?"

She harrumphs, and it relieves some of the tension. "Are all y'all gonna leave me out here or take me in?"

Doc lays a hand on her shoulder. "Let me examine you first and stabilize your arm and leg. After that, we'll move you."

His gentle examination only makes Fitzie moan a couple of times. "You've fractured both your arm and your ankle, but they appear to be clean breaks. I won't be sure until I get you x-rayed. I'm going to give you a pain injection. Then I'll splint them. Once that's done, I'll take you to the hospital."

Fitzie shakes her head. "Oh no. No hospital. I can't go."

"Mama, Doc needs to have you x-rayed. What if it isn't so simple?"

Her eyes meet mine. "What about—?"

I shake my head. Doc sticks the needle in her arm. "Forget about it. I'm not going anywhere." Not yet. I can't leave while Fitzie's hurt. "There's time enough for that later. Right now, my concern is you."

We wait a few minutes, but soon, Mama's eyes flutter shut. Exhaustion and the pain medication do their work. Doc gently straightens her leg and splints her ankle. Then he does the same for her arm.

An ambulance rumbles up the driveway. Doc explains he called for it before he came. They load Mama in, and Aunt Clara and I follow Doc in our car to Grady Hospital in Atlanta.

When we arrive, nurses bustle and patients shuffle in the hallways. Aunt Clara and I both wrinkle our noses at the antiseptic smell. I fill out the paperwork while Doc takes Fitzie to be x-rayed.

Dr. Abernethy finds us in the waiting room an hour later. "I'm keeping her overnight. I want to be sure she doesn't go into shock."

Aunt Clara startles and grabs my hand. My heart drops. "Do you think she might? Is that bad?"

He takes Aunt Clara's and my hand. "If she does, she'll be here to get immediate help. The nurses will call me, give her oxygen, and make sure she's stabilized. You can come back tomorrow around noon and take her home. I've put plaster casts on her. No weight on that ankle and keep a sling on her arm."

I glance at Aunt Clara. "How long will she be immobile?"

"About six to eight weeks." Doc lets go of our hands. He reaches in his pocket and withdraws a paper, which he shows me. "These are some care instructions for sponge baths. I'll stop by every day to check on her."

Aunt Clara is pale. This has frightened her. I pull her close. "It's going to be all right. We can have her bed moved into the morning room. It's next to Pearl's bathroom and at the back of the house."

Auntie signs, "I'll sleep there, too, in case she needs me."

Doc nods his approval, then adds, "She'll be bedridden for a few weeks but later can move about with crutches. But no stairs."

We go into her room to say goodnight. It's after nine o'clock, and nurses are still coming in and out, readying her for the night. Fitzie is pale, and I've never seen Aunt Clara so nervous. She's patted Mama's good leg on and off for the past ten minutes. I gently pull her hand away.

"Cora?" Mama lays her unfettered hand on my arm. "Are you okay?" Her speech is a little slurred due to the pain medications.

I nod as I bend over and kiss her. "I'm fine, Mama. And I'm not going anywhere. When you're all well, we'll talk about what I'm going to do."

Chapter 34

Friday, August 1, 1930

I'M GRATEFUL DOC ABERNETHY MAKES a house call to remove the cast on Fitzie's arm. Moving her is such an ordeal, and she's taken longer than expected to heal. He poises a small handsaw over her cast. "Don't be nervous. I've yet to cut off an arm while removing one of these."

She doesn't miss a beat. "If you wouldn't mind, I'd prefer not to be the first. Is my ankle getting out of jail too?"

Doc shakes his head. "Not yet, but I'm leaving a pair of crutches for you. But be careful and no stairs. We don't want you falling down again and breaking something else."

After he leaves, I settle Fitzie in the family parlor with Aunt Clara.

"I'm going shopping with Martha Anne and Millie. Do you want me to pick up anything for you while I'm out?"

Fitzie taps her jaw with her finger, thinking. "I could use a bottle of Watkins Mulsified shampoo. Make sure it's the coconut oil. Now that my arm is free, I can stand at the sink and shampoo my own hair."

"I'll swing by the store before we head home. Aunt Clara? Do you need anything?"

She raises stained fingers. "Yes, please, a bottle of India ink."

"Okay, I can get both at the drugstore. I'll see you in a couple of hours."

I crank the car engine, and after it catches, I climb into the driver's seat and back out of the garage. First stop is Millie's. I honk the horn and she runs out the door.

"Morning, Millie-billie."

She eyes me. "You're in a good mood."

She's right. It's been eight weeks since the wedding, and the last few days have proved a turning point of sorts for me. "I'm anxious to see Martha Anne's house now that she's got it decorated and has the new settee."

We drive over to Buford and pull up in front of their bungalow. The small Craftsman house is white with dark-gray shutters on its tall windows. The covered veranda, painted the same gray, runs the short width of the home and has two rocking chairs on one side of the front door and a porch swing on the other end.

We hop out and run up to the door. Martha Anne opens it at the first knock. "I'm so glad you're here." She pulls us inside, and, with a sweeping gesture, shows us her parlor. "Taa-daa."

With soft green walls and dark wood trim, it's cozy and inviting. The floral-print davenport adds a feminine touch in the rather masculine room. An overstuffed, dark-green chair I guess to be Ethan's sits across the room. A radio resides next to it.

Martha Anne giggles. "I know there isn't room to swing a cat in here, but it's cozy and we love it."

I lay my handbag on a shelf by the door. "I do too. It's perfect."

Millie chimes in, "Me, three."

Martha Anne shows us the bedroom. I can see her and Ethan's artistic influence on the small space. The house can't be much larger than our attic, but it's so cute. I adore it.

"It's perfect for a young couple." I glance over my shoulder at her. "Are we ready to go?"

"Well …" Martha Anne draws out the word. "I do have one more room I want to show you."

Indulgently, we follow her. When she opens the door, the room is tiny. A bassinet stands in one corner.

I snap my head to her. "What?"

"The doctor called with the test results." Martha Anne squeals. "The rabbit died."

My jaw slackens. "You mean—?"

"Yes! I'm expecting." Her eyes shine with unshed tears of happiness.

We screech and hug, then we jump up and down.

"Stop!" Millie tries to subdue us. "Martha Anne shouldn't be jumping."

The object of our joy just laughs. "It's fine. Doc Abernethy says I can do anything I normally do, although I'm not supposed to lift anything over five pounds—not that Ethan will let me, anyway."

I've never seen my friend this happy or so in love. A small part of me grows melancholy. I shake it off. No more. "Come on, let's go shopping. We have a baby gift to buy. Oh, Martha Anne,"—I link arms with both my friends—"what fun we're going to have spoiling your baby. Wait ... do you realize this is our first baby Dilly? You've *got* to have a girl."

We leave the car at Martha Anne's since she lives so close to downtown Buford. Window shopping is a favorite pastime. When we reach Allen's Department Store, we head straight to the infants' section. There, we examine all the clothing, blankets, diapers, and more.

"Why, they've got everything a baby could ever need." I run my fingers over a satin-trimmed blanket. "Why have we never noticed this department before?"

Millie smirks. "Why would we? None of us were expecting."

I shrug, acquiescing to her insight. "Without knowing if it's a boy or a girl, I'm choosing this soft, green blanket." I pick it up. "Wait, do you think the baby will get its tiny fingers tangled in the tatting around the edge?"

Martha Anne shakes her head. "No, and I love it."

"And I'll paint pictures of baby animals for the nursery." Millie points to a display of framed prints.

After I pay for the blanket, we head back toward the drugstore. I pick up Fitzie's shampoo and Aunt Clara's ink. Martha Anne has a salad ready for our dinner at her house, so we leave the drugstore.

Out on the street, Glenice Jo hurries toward us. Why isn't she at work? I glance at my wristwatch. Ah, it's noon.

Martha Anne waves. "I invited her to join us."

When she reaches us, she grasps my elbow, tugging me. "Come

with me. You've got to hear this."

She half drags me toward the tannery office. Martha Anne and Millie follow excitedly. I scowl over my shoulder. "What's up?"

Glenice Jo doesn't say a word. All I hear are birds singing in the trees. Wait, a voice rises above the birdsong. We round the corner, and she stops.

On the steps of the tannery office, Boone has the audience enthralled.

"The voiceless in this county need a champion."

My heart splits right down the carefully built-up scars. I turn away. "I don't know what your intention was, but—oh, never mind." I try to push forward, away from the crowd, but the Dillies block me.

Glenice Jo glares. "Listen!"

"What most people don't know is my parents died when I was barely six."

Wide-eyed, I stare at Glenice Jo. "He never told me that."

She smiles and nods encouragement. I quit trying to leave and grow still. In my heart, I hear a voice, but it isn't the senator.

Turn around.

I turn halfway.

"I was put in an orphanage and, a few weeks later, onto one of the orphan trains."

Look at him.

I pivot to face him.

Boone waves away a fly buzzing him. "A couple on a farm in Missouri took me. Being big for my age, I was worked hard. I had to sleep in the barn, never the house."

Are you hearing him?

I take a step closer.

His words are spoken softly, sincere, not didactic for the sake of impressing—like the senator.

Because they come from his heart.

"When I turned ten, I ran away. I lived by my wits, running errands for pennies and stealing food."

My heart aches for the little boy he once was.

"Somehow I ended up in Buford. I was just twelve. Amos Calhoun found me behind his shop and coaxed my story from me. Most of you know the rest. He took me in, made me go to school, and when I graduated, he apprenticed me. Friends, I've seen the underbelly of society with its corruption and cronyism. I believe I can be an honest voice in Georgia's statehouse."

I soften toward him. I believe he will too. Somehow, I feel the broken places in my heart healing. I mouth "thank you" to Glenice Jo, then turn to head to Martha Anne's.

"I want to thank all of you for your support, but today I'm withdrawing my bid for office."

I stop. What? I turn back and find his eyes on mine. My heart quickens.

"There's someone I love and have wounded. I have to try to win her back."

A low rumble swells across the crowd. Here and there, people shout for Boone to reconsider. He ignores them and weaves his way toward me, never once looking back.

I can't move. My friends are behind me, gently pushing me forward. When Boone reaches me, he takes my hands.

His words are soft, for me alone. "Cora, I love you. I want to prove myself to you. Prove you can trust me. I promise I will never leave you out of a decision ever again." He searches my eyes. "Will you give me a second chance?"

"I never knew any of this. I had no idea you suffered so. Why didn't you tell me?"

"I'm not good at sharing feelings, Cora." He blinks and swallows. "But I promise, I'll try."

"I always want to know how you feel about things." Now, I have to ask the one question that scares me spitless. My whole future lies in his answer. "Why are you running for office?"

His hold on my hands tightens. "The orphan train." He drops my hands and scrubs his through his hair. "I tried to tell people how I was nothing more than a slave on that farm. I know how Pearl's family and others felt. Nobody sees you. Nobody hears you. Nobody cares." He takes my hands again. "The futility of my situation is why I ran away. And I swore if I ever got to where I could be a voice for people, I would."

"But why didn't you tell me?"

"I started to a few times. I even tried to write it once. I never mailed that letter." Sorrow pulls his features down. "It was misguided of me, but I knew how much your father's neglect hurt you, and how his abuse damaged you. I wanted to put it off as long as possible to protect you from the anguish you might feel—since there was no guarantee I'd win. And if I didn't, you'd have gone through all the horrible emotions for nothing." His gaze pierces all the way to my soul. "If I won, I planned to show you how different I am than your father, Cora. I want you by my side always—to work *with* me."

This is the man I fell in love with and the one I want to spend my life with. Every wound the senator inflicted on me disappears like pollen in a windstorm. Forgetting where we are, I throw my arms around his neck. "I love you."

His arms wrap around me. "Will you marry me?" His eyes are so hopeful. I want to tease him but can't. Besides, Fitzie was right. I never stopped loving him. I lick my lips, searching for moisture.

"Yes!"

He dips his head and kisses me.

A few people snicker, then more, and finally, the whole crowd laughs.

Laughter is contagious. I giggle and break away. I glance over my shoulder, then gaze back into his eyes.

"I think the good people of Buford will have my skin if I don't let you try to be that voice for them."

Epilogue

BOONE TAKES MY HAND AND guides me toward the door that has been nailed shut for eleven months. From the inside, the windows are covered, so I haven't been able to see through them. A little like our relationship was at first.

This past year, Boone has proven himself to me every day. The sweet man tells me everything, asks my opinion about all of it. I learned a valuable lesson. While Asa was good to him, without parents to show Boone how to share his feelings, he never understood he needed to. Once he did, though, he hasn't stopped.

Love for him overflows my heart, all its scars healed. A very wise woman once told me our trials birth compassion. Boone's make him the perfect public servant. Mine made me stop and see the voiceless. He won his election, and now, I help him in his work. Best of all, the senator no longer haunts me.

Behind this door is Boone's surprise for me. Our cottage, separate but attached to the main house.

A few days after he started the build, he came to me with the strangest look on his face. "You've got to come see this, Cora. You won't believe it." He led me to the back wall of the morning room at the rear of the house where he's placing the addition. He pointed to a board. "Look behind that."

I pulled the loose board toward me. It snapped off and behind it, inside the wall, was a metal box. "What is it?"

Boone grinned. "If my hunch is right, it's the money the senator hid."

We took it to Fitzie. Boone was right. Inside was five thousand dollars. Fitzie gave it to us for our cottage and her future grandchildren's education. She was satisfied knowing she'd "been right all along and flummoxed the old goat."

She doesn't need it. Fitzgerald House is full, and if *my* hunch is right, she and Dr. Harold will tie the knot in the next year or so.

Right now, Boone stands beside me, about to reveal our home. "Keep your eyes closed until I tell you." His voice betrays his excitement.

I cover my eyes with one hand and cling to his with the other. "Don't let me trip."

His lips touch my cheek. "I won't."

I hear the latch click. "Okay, open your eyes, my love."

I'm standing in a parlor, cozy but not too small. "Oh, Boone! We have our own fireplace." I throw my arms around his neck. "I love it."

"In here is our bedroom." He guides me through the doorway. "I made our furniture too."

I take in the spacious room and run my hand over the bed's footboard. It's as smooth as Martha Anne and Ethan's baby Helen's bottom.

"It's perfect." I blush, imagining us in this bed.

He chuckles. "There's not a kitchen, since we don't need it. But we do have our own bathroom."

"You've thought of everything. And you finished it right on time."

Saturday, September 12, 1931
Mama and Aunt Clara adjust my veil and give me a final teary-eyed hug. Ethan steps up and escorts them both to their seats.

Dr. Harold pulls my hand through his arm. "Are you happy, my dear?"

I nod, not trusting my voice. I swallow and try again. "Thank you for giving me away. You've become very special to me." More than special. I truly hope he and Fitzie get married. I love him as a father. Even more, he'll be the perfect grandfather to our future children.

Then, the music changes. My Dilly-girls walk before me. They loved me when I was unlovable. They withstood my anger, seeing what I couldn't in Boone when my sight was blinded by the senator. I'm so grateful to them. They're the best friends a girl could ever have.

There will soon be more weddings in our future, but this one is mine. I step into the doorway. Dr. Harold nods to me. It's time.

At the end of the aisle, Boone waits for me, his eyes glued to mine. His Adam's apple bobs as he swallows.

For a brief second, I raise my gaze to heaven.

Thank You.

The music swells, and I walk toward my future, more in love than I could ever imagine.

The End

Author's Note

SUGAR HILL WAS A MILITIA district before it incorporated as a city in 1939. Its early history is closely tied to Buford's and remains so. The two cities still share the zip code to this day.

However, detailed Sugar Hill history was not chronicled in print until it incorporated. This left me dependent on oral history. Unfortunately, finding people who were old enough to remember events and locations in 1929 was difficult. Most have either passed away, have dementia or Alzheimer's, or are too old or of ill health to be interviewed.

I gleaned what I could from Buford's history and talking to descendants of the city founders. There are instances where I've taken literary license. Venable's General Store didn't open until 1930, but I wanted to give Cora past knowledge of Rocky Venable, since it was the closest to where her house was placed.

Because of the Allen family, Buford became widely known for its leather production and earned the nickname "The Leather City." The Bona Allen Tannery became the city's largest industry despite setbacks from several fires. Business thrived during the 1930s, likely as a result of the Great Depression forcing farmers to choose horses over expensive tractors, thereby increasing the demand for saddles, collars, bridles, and other leather products.

The saddles were available through the Sears mail-order catalog, and many Hollywood actors used saddles made by the Bona Allen Company, including cowboy actors Gene Autry, the cast of *Bonanza, and* Roy Rogers, who used a Bona Allen saddle on his horse, Trigger.

Today, a statue of Roy Rogers and a Bona Allen saddle-maker saddling Trigger is located in downtown Buford. In 2003, Tannery Row became home to the Tannery Row Artist Colony, which houses galleries and studios for artists.

HUMMINGBIRD CAKE

INGREDIENTS

2 C chopped pecans

3 C all-purpose flour (spoon & leveled)

1 tsp baking soda

1 ½ tsp ground cinnamon

½ tsp allspice

½ tsp salt

2 C mashed banana (4 ripe bananas, spotty and brown)

1 - 8 oz can crushed pineapple *slightly* drained

3 large eggs, at room temperature

2/3 C vegetable, canola, or melted coconut oil

1 C packed brown sugar

¾ C granulated sugar

2 tsp pure vanilla extract

Cream Cheese Frosting

16 oz block cream cheese, softened to room temp

3/4 C unsalted butter, softened to room temp

5 C confectioners' sugar

1 Tbsp. milk

2 tsp pure vanilla extract

1/8 tsp salt, or more to taste

Instructions

Preheat the oven to 300°F. Spread pecans onto a lined baking pan. Toast for 8 minutes. Remove from the oven. Turn oven up to 350°F, then grease and lightly flour three 9-inch cake pans.

Whisk the flour, baking soda, cinnamon, allspice, and salt together in a large bowl.

Whisk rest of ingredients in a medium bowl. Pour wet ingredients ʿredients and whisk until completely combined. Fold in 1 toasted pecans. (Save the rest for garnish.)

Spread batter evenly between the 3 prepared cake pans. Bake for 26-29 minutes or until a toothpick inserted in the center comes out clean. Rotate pans halfway through baking.

Remove cakes from the oven and allow to cool completely in the pans set on a wire rack. Once completely cooled, remove cakes from pan, and using a serrated knife, level the tops off so they're flat.

Make the frosting: In a large bowl, beat cream cheese and butter together on high speed until smooth and creamy. Add confectioners' sugar, vanilla, milk, and salt. Beat on low speed for 30 seconds, then switch to high speed and beat for 2 minutes. Taste. Add more salt if needed.

Assemble and frost. Garnish with leftover toasted pecans. Refrigerate for at least 30 minutes before slicing.